PRAISE FOR
SUSAN
MALLERY

"Susan Mallery is warmth and wit personified.
Always a fabulous read."
—*New York Times* bestselling author Christina Dodd

"Ms. Mallery's unique writing style shines via
vivid characters, layered disharmony and plenty of spice."
—*Romantic Times Magazine*

"Susan Mallery writes a powerfully emotional western.
Memorable characters spring from the pages
to capture your heart..."
—*Affaire de Coeur*

"Great story! A powerful beginning to a saga...I loved it!"
—*Rendezvous* on *Wild West Wife*

"Susan Mallery's deft characterization
and sweetly sensual Americana romance
is one of the 'feel good' books of the season."
—*Romantic Times Magazine* on *Justin's Bride*

Susan Mallery's first book was published in January 1992, and she quickly became a reader favorite. Her books consistently appear on the Waldenbooks bestseller list, the *Ingram* list and the *USA Today* bestseller list. She has been nominated for many awards, including the Colorado Romance Writers Award of Excellence, the Holt Medallion, several *Romantic Times Magazine* awards and the prestigious RITA Award given by Romance Writers of America.

Susan makes her home in the Pacific Northwest with her handsome prince of a husband and her two incredibly cute but not very bright cats.

MONTANA MAVERICKS

SUSAN MALLERY

WILD WEST WIFE

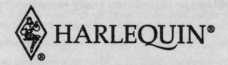

HARLEQUIN®

TORONTO • NEW YORK • LONDON
AMSTERDAM • PARIS • SYDNEY • HAMBURG
STOCKHOLM • ATHENS • TOKYO • MILAN • MADRID
PRAGUE • WARSAW • BUDAPEST • AUCKLAND

Special thanks and acknowledgment are given
to Susan Mallery for her contribution to the
MONTANA MAVERICKS series.

ISBN 0-373-83486-1

WILD WEST WIFE

Dear Reader,

As a longtime fan of the MONTANA MAVERICKS series, I was especially honored to be asked to write this "prequel" explaining the beginnings of the fictional town of Whitehorn. While the legend of Caleb Kincaid and Ruth Whitefeather will be explored in the upcoming *Montana Mavericks: Big Sky Grooms*, set near the turn of the century, *Wild West Wife* takes place twenty years before that, when Whitehorn was a small town with a big problem.

There's something almost magical about writing about the Old West. I adore old Western movies and television shows, and bringing that era to life is both a challenge and a privilege. The two main characters in my book represent the very best of that time. Jesse Kincaid is both honorable and stubborn. Vowing to right a wrong, he won't let anyone or anything stand in his way. Of course, then he meets Haley Winthrop, who redefines the word determined. They seem to want completely different things—until time and a stirring of the heart shows them that they have more in common than they each realized.

I hope you'll enjoy your visit to Whitehorn. I know I was very sad when the book ended. I didn't want to say goodbye to these two wonderful characters.

Susan Mallery

To Tracy Farrell, senior editor at Harlequin Historicals,
for allowing me to participate in this project.
Every now and then I get the urge to visit the Old West,
and Tracy always graciously welcomes me back.

Chapter One

Montana, 1879

Jesse Kincaid might not have sold his soul to the devil, but he'd come as close to it as a man could and still expect to head north upon his passing.

Despite the faint sound of hoofbeats in the distance, he allowed himself to be distracted by the quiet beauty of the late afternoon. Winter had finally left Montana and the lush growth of spring promised a long and warm summer. The calving season had gone well...at least that's what he'd been told. He couldn't speak from firsthand experience. The herd he and his father had built over the past ten years had been scattered when the ranch had been attacked and his father murdered. Nothing was left but a partially burned house, a legion of memories and the promise he'd made to exact revenge on those responsible.

Because of that, because of the vow he'd sworn on a cold, rainy night the previous October, he now stood by the rutted path that passed for a road and prepared to defy all that his parents had taught him. Because of that, he risked his very soul, raising his rifle as the weekly stage came into view.

He had a momentary second thought. He'd played pranks

as a child—just as all boys did. But he'd been raised with good values and a strong sense of right and wrong. Doing the wrong thing for the right reason didn't set well with him.

"You don't have a choice," he muttered aloud, knowing that while the end didn't justify the means, sometimes justice had to be helped along.

Six powerful horses pulled the large stagecoach. The conveyance swayed, the leather straps under the carriage doing little to absorb the bumps of the road. They were too far away for him to be able to see in the window and identify the passengers, but he knew she was there. He'd received a wire two days before saying she'd made the connection and would be arriving in Whitehorn today. Stoner might be expecting her, but Jesse was determined to make sure she didn't arrive. At least not right away.

He fitted the butt of the rifle against his shoulder and took careful aim. One well-placed shot would break the axle he'd weakened earlier and bring the carriage to a stop without too much risk. The trick was to time it so they didn't tip. While he might be prepared to kidnap an innocent woman and hold her hostage, he didn't want anyone's death on his hands.

The path leveled out just before a sharp turn. The horses slowed in anticipation of the bend and Jesse pulled the trigger.

The single gunshot spooked the horses. Two of them reared up and pawed at the air. The driver held tightly on the reins and yelled at them to calm down. Seconds later there was a loud *crack* as the weight of the carriage split the axle and the rear of the stagecoach sank to the ground.

The left rear wheel splintered, then the right rear came loose and rolled away. The instant deadweight jerked the horses in their harnesses and the animals stopped. Several frightened cries filled the afternoon, startling birds into flight.

Jesse walked toward the stagecoach. He'd lowered his

rifle, but he was alert and prepared to use it if pushed. Pray God no one decided to play hero and make that necessary. As Jesse stepped out of the bushes, Charlie, the driver, spotted him. The older man looked shaken, but otherwise unhurt.

Bushy gray eyebrows drew together. "That you, Jesse?" Charlie asked. "You hear that? We was shot. Damnation, I want to know who the hell is shooting at the stage. We ain't got no money on this run. Folks know that. Supplies and passengers. Next week is the payroll. Damnation, I hate it when people can't keep the schedule straight."

He glanced around uneasily, then climbed down, moving awkwardly on the tilting stage. "You see anything? You get a look at the good-for-nothing who done this?"

"Stop right there," Jesse said quietly.

Charlie ignored him. "It just don't make sense to me. Why this run? We ain't got nothing important. Shoot. Now we all gotta walk to town. You know how far that is?"

"About four miles," Jesse said. He'd already figured that out. He'd been careful when he'd picked the spot to attack the stage. He wanted them close enough to town that they could walk in and tell everyone what happened, but not so close that he wouldn't have time for a clean escape.

Charlie pulled off his worn hat and wiped his bald head. "And we was running early, too."

"Charlie," Jesse said, raising his rifle to his shoulder. "I need you to let your passengers out."

Charlie's watery brown eyes widened as he noticed the gun for the first time. "Jesse? What's going on?"

"I've got some business with one of your passengers. That's all. Just do what I tell you, Charlie. I don't want to hurt anyone."

The stage door rattled from the inside. "Sir!" a man called. "We seem to be trapped. Sir? I say, stage driver? Can you hear me?"

Charlie rolled his eyes. "Damn fool prissy Easterners. Got a load of 'em. Not a one has a lick of sense 'cept for

Miz Winthrop. She even figured out I've got a name, if you can believe that.''

Jesse bit back a curse of impatience. So much for his life of crime. He couldn't get Charlie to pay attention to him. He took aim at the left front wheel and put a shot cleanly through one of the spokes.

Charlie jumped. "Damnation, Jesse, what's going on? You could've just asked me to stop the stage. You don't have to keep shootin' it. There ain't gonna be enough left for kindling.''

"Put your hands behind your back.''

"What?'' The old man stared at him. "Jesse? You mean you're doing this? You're gonna hold me up?''

"Yes, Charlie. I don't have a choice.'' He moved next to the other man and drew out the length of rope he'd strung through his belt loops. It took only a couple of minutes to secure Charlie's hands behind his back. Gently, he led him to the stage. "Have a seat,'' he said and helped him sit down.

Confusion darkened Charlie's gaze. "Jesse, I've known you for years. Since you were just a boy. This ain't like you, son.''

"I know.'' He shrugged, then added, "I'm sorry.'' As if the feeble words would make a difference.

"Would someone please tell me what is going on out there?'' the cultured male voice demanded. "I say, stage driver, we are quite thoroughly trapped in this conveyance. While we are unhurt, the ladies are most uncomfortable. We can't see any Indians, but perhaps a small bribe would be enough—''

Jesse jerked open the stage door, effectively cutting off the man's tedious commentary. The unexpected action sent the male passenger sprawling facedown into the dirt. Jesse barely spared him a glance. Instead he stared intently into the darkness of the stage, searching the passengers for the one he sought.

Three terrified women stared back from the floor of the

stage where they lay in a pile of skirts and petticoats. The best dressed of the three was obviously the wife of the complainer. Her pinched expression and pale, bejeweled hands spoke of her unfamiliarity with hard work. The second passenger looked like Jesse's grandmother, and he had a jolt of conscience at the thought that the unexpected stop might have injured her.

"Ma'am?" he said, trying to sound as unthreatening as possible. "Are you hurt?"

Gray corkscrew curls covered her forehead and danced across her weathered skin as she slowly shook her head. "Mr. Prichard said we were likely to be attacked by Indians, but you don't look like an Indian to me. This is an attack, isn't it?"

She sounded nearly excited by the prospect.

"Yes, ma'am, it is, but I'm not going to hurt you."

The wealthy woman clutched her hand to her flat bosom and moaned. "He means to ravish us. Surely that is a fate worse than death."

Jesse glanced at her husband, still sprawled in the dirt, and figured if her alternative was bedding down with him, then yes, it probably was. Then he wondered what the woman thought he was going to do. There were, after all, three of them and only one of him. Surely she couldn't expect him to ravish them all on his own. He enjoyed his time with the ladies, but he had his limits.

The thoughts were nearly enough to distract him. Nearly. But even as he decided he wasn't going to reply to the question of ravishing, he turned his attention to the third woman…and the reason he'd had to hold up the stage in the first place.

He hadn't realized he'd created a picture of Haley Winthrop in his mind until he was surprised by her appearance and realized his picture was wrong. She was young, but he'd expected that. Wide green eyes, filled with as much curiosity as fear, seemed to dominate her face. Freckles and a faint tan told him that she frequently went without a proper bonnet. She sat on the floor of the off-balance stage and held the older woman protectively in her arms. She didn't look big enough or strong enough to hold off a half-grown boy, but there was a set of determination in the angle of her chin. Maybe she was tougher than she looked. He hoped so, for her sake.

"Miss Winthrop," he said politely. "I'd like you to come with me."

The wealthy woman moaned. "He's going to ravish us all. Harold? Harold, you must save me."

Harold stirred on the ground. "Yes, my love. Unhand those women, sir."

Jesse thought about pointing out the fact that he hadn't gotten to the point where he was actually touching one of them so there was no unhanding to be done. Instead, trying to ignore the bad feeling at the base of his spine, he turned and found Harold holding a small derringer aimed at his heart.

"It's very effective," the other man said. "And I'm not afraid to use it."

"Me, either," Jesse told him and slipped a cartridge into the rifle. "Want to see who's still standing after a shooting competition?" he asked calmly as he took a sight on Harold's skinny chest. "At this distance you'd be real hard to miss."

"Jesse, what in tarnation are you thinking?" Charlie demanded. "You can't kill him, even if he deserves it."

Jesse knew that and he didn't appreciate the reminder. While Harold was busy trying to figure out if he could get out of this situation without getting shot, Jesse decided to settle the matter for both of them. Without warning, he kicked hard, hitting the other man's wrist. The derringer went spinning and Harold yelped like a dog.

"You broke it," he managed, cradling his injured wrist in his good hand. "I heard a bone snap. Good Lord, what kind of creature are you?"

"A desperate one." Jesse returned his attention to Haley

Winthrop. "Miss, I'd rather not have to hurt anyone else. If you'll please come with me."

The woman stared at him. Her curiosity had long since faded, leaving behind only fear. Color fled her cheeks. The paleness reminded him of another woman who had always been afraid. He pushed away those memories. They would accomplish nothing. He had to do whatever he could to see justice done. If that meant kidnapping an innocent woman, he would do it. *Was* doing it.

In the quiet of the afternoon, he heard the faint call of the birds that had returned to their tree branches. The warmth of the day had bled away, leaving the air chilly. The nightly freezes continued and would do so for a few more weeks. The passengers would need the remaining daylight to get to Whitehorn before nightfall. They didn't have a lot of time to waste.

He reached past the rich woman and grabbed Haley's arm. His action obviously startled her. He nearly had her to her feet before she started to resist. She squirmed and braced her legs against the floor of the stage.

"I won't," she cried. "No! I won't leave with you. Let me go. You don't know what you're doing. My fiancé will hear about this, I swear he will."

"I'm counting on it," Jesse muttered.

The grandmother turned on him suddenly and landed a quick kick against his knee. Her feeble strength barely registered, but Harold's wife decided an attack was a good idea and wrapped her arms around his waist.

"I've got him, Harold. Shoot him. Shoot him now."

"I don't have my gun anymore," her husband lamented, still making soft moaning noises. "I swear he broke my wrist, Lydia. I may never be the same."

"No great loss," Jesse said under his breath. He ignored the older woman, and Lydia's enthusiastic attack, and focused his attention on Haley. She squirmed, but he didn't release her arm.

"I don't want to hurt you," he told her.

"Of course not," she snapped. "Kidnapping is a colorful way of welcoming strangers to town. Forgive me for not wanting to participate in your well-planned entertainment, sir. Obviously I don't travel enough to appreciate the experience."

This was getting him nowhere. He was trying to pull her up and keep from bruising her. While he might not appreciate her sarcasm, he recognized the truth in her words. There was no way to kidnap a woman and maintain the illusions of being a gentleman.

He tightened his hold on her and jerked her once, hard. She gasped as he pulled her upright. Before she could gain her balance, he dragged her out of the carriage and onto the road. Then, quickly, he bent at the waist, bumped his left shoulder against her midsection and straightened. Her legs kicked out at him and her hands pummeled his back, but he simply wrapped his arm around her thighs to hold her bottom half still. He ignored the top half.

"You can't do this," she screeched as she hung over his shoulder like a sack of flour. "I refuse to allow this."

"No one's asking your permission. Charlie, which bag is hers?"

"Don't tell him!" Haley demanded.

Charlie's mouth dropped open. "Jesse, do you know who she is?"

"Yeah, I do." That was the point of the kidnapping. He kicked at the tapestry carpetbags that had spilled out with Harold. "Which one?"

The grandmother pointed to a plain, worn, brown bag. The handle straps had long since broken and had been replaced by a couple of pieces of rope. A long rip down the center had been repaired with small, neat stitches of black thread. Either Stoner had sent money for the ticket and nothing else, or his mail-order bride didn't waste funds unnecessarily.

Jesse grabbed the bag and whistled. His horse stepped out of the wooded grove on the side of the rutted road.

He'd tied the second gelding to his saddle and that animal walked alongside his mount.

"I won't go with you," Haley said, her voice more muffled as her struggling settled her harder against his shoulder. He figured she was having some trouble drawing in enough air. If she kept up her squirming, she was going to pass out. Of course that would make her easier to handle.

"You don't have a choice," he said and glanced at the stage. Harold still sat on the ground, holding his injured wrist. Lydia had moved to her husband's side, but Jesse wasn't sure if she was offering comfort or seeking protection. The grandmother watched him warily, but he figured she wasn't likely to best him with a surprise attack.

He slipped the rifle into the holster on his mount, then moved to the second horse and hoisted Haley across the saddle. Before she could regain her composure enough to scramble off the other side, he had pulled a rope from the open saddlebag and secured her feet together.

"It's a long way down," he told her as he walked around the horse and reached for her hands.

She jerked them away and tried to glare up at him. Green eyes flashed fire. "You are evil and disgusting and you will be punished."

"Yes, ma'am. I'm sure you're right. But first they have to catch me and I mean to make sure that doesn't happen."

He grabbed her wrists and tied them, then he squatted in front of her. "If you struggle too much, you'll slip off the saddle. Now hitting the ground is going to hurt like hell. You might even break something. But your real worry is the horse. You spook him and he'll rear. There's no telling where those hooves of his are going to hit. If they land on you, well, horses have killed people before."

"If you were so concerned about my safety, you wouldn't be taking me in the first place."

Jesse fingered the brim of his hat. "You know, you might have a point there." He stood up and surveyed the broken stage, then the passengers. "You've got a couple hours until sunset, so I suggest you get headed for White-horn." He nodded west. "It's that way. Charlie?" He looked at the old man. "When you tell Stoner I kidnapped his mail-order bride, I need you to give him a message for me. Tell him all I want is to talk. He can name the time and the place and I'll be there. I'll send someone to contact him to get that information."

"He's gonna kill you," Charlie said.

"I'm sure he'll try," Jesse agreed. After all, Stoner had already murdered Jesse's father, not to mention several other ranchers in the area. What was one more death on his conscience?

"But if he wants his chance, he's going to have to meet with me," Jesse told the stage driver.

"Jesse, you're making a big mistake," Charlie said. "It's not too late. Leave the girl with me. No one has to know what happened today."

Haley let out a squeal of disagreement. "Of course people have to know. This man is dangerous and he should be locked up. My fiancé will see to that. Mr. Stoner will come after me and make you pay for what you've done."

"I hope you're right," Jesse said as he swung into his saddle. "It's getting late, Charlie. You'd best get these folks to town. I don't think they'd take kindly to spending the night on the side of the road."

With that he reached down and grabbed the other horse's reins, then urged his gelding into a walk and headed into the screen of trees. Within a couple of minutes, the stage and its passengers were lost from view. In less than five minutes, the sounds of their complaining had faded, to be replaced with the familiar chirps, trills and rustles of the forest.

He spared a glance for his captive and tried to ignore the flicker of concern when he saw that she'd stopped struggling.

"Miss Winthrop?" he asked.

"What?" The word came out on a gasp of air.

Now that he had her attention, he felt foolish. Was he supposed to ask if she was all right? Of course she wasn't. Her arms and shoulders would be aching from their unnatural position. The saddle would dig into her belly and ribs until she wasn't sure if she was going to faint or throw up.

"If you promise not to try to escape, I would be willing to let you ride astride in the saddle."

"Fine. I won't try to escape."

That was too easy. "I don't think I believe you."

"You should, Mr. Jesse whatever-your-last-name-is. When I give my word, I mean it. So if I tell you I won't try to escape now, I won't. But I will try eventually and I'll succeed. And when I do, I'll find my fiancé and bring him back so he can shoot you for the dog you are."

Quiet venom gave her voice strength. Jesse felt the first grudging flicker of respect. He drew his horse to a halt and stepped down from the saddle. "You and Stoner didn't correspond much before he brought you out here to marry you."

It wasn't a question, but she answered it all the same. "No, we didn't. He sent me a letter stating what he was looking for in a wife, and I responded. Then he sent me a ticket."

"Wouldn't it have made sense to get to know the man a little before agreeing to marry him?" he asked as he approached her.

"I know all I need to."

He untied her feet and stepped back in case she tried to kick him. But she didn't. Maybe she *was* a woman who kept her word.

"Lucas Stoner is a kind, honorable man," she went on. As he walked around the front of her horse and reached for her bound hands, she raised her head and glared at him. "Decent. He would never do anything like this."

"You're right," Jesse agreed, thinking that Stoner wouldn't have bothered with kidnapping an innocent woman. He would have shot her dead on the spot, if he thought it would make his point.

He pulled the rope free of her wrists. She started to wiggle. "Don't," he told her. "You'll fall."

He grabbed her around her waist and lifted her off the saddle, then found himself in the uncomfortable position of having to turn her in his arms so she could stand. In the process, his hand slid against her right breast.

She went rigid at the contact and jumped back as soon as she gained her balance. Both arms came up to cross protectively over her chest. Jesse felt himself falter, not sure if he should apologize or pretend the moment never happened. Despite the tingling in his hand and the impression of soft, yielding curves burned into his brain, he decided on the latter.

"Can you ride astride?" he asked.

She watched him warily for a heartbeat or two, then shook her head. "I've never been on a horse before. But it doesn't look difficult." The implication being if he could do it, anyone else could be equally successful.

For the first time in months, Jesse felt like smiling. "You're right. It doesn't look difficult." He laced his fingers together to form a step and bent down. "Grab hold of the saddle," he instructed. "Put your left foot in my hands and I'll raise you up high enough. You just swing your other leg over the horse's back and sit down. Couldn't be easier."

Haley's expression hardened. "Why don't I trust you?"

He shrugged. "Because you're smart. Don't trust me, but do as I say. We need to get going and if you don't cooperate, I'll throw you back over the saddle and tie you up again. It's your choice."

The twist of her mouth told him that she didn't care for her limited options, but she did as he requested. She braced her left foot against his hand and reached for the saddle.

"Are you ready?" he asked.

She nodded.

He lifted gently. But not gently enough. With a muffled shriek, Haley soared over the horse's back and landed hard on the other side of the animal. Jesse ducked under the gelding's head to make sure she was all right. She sat in the dirt, her skirt up around her knees, her mouth twisted in anger and pain.

"You did that on purpose," she said accusingly.

He raised his hands in surrender. "I didn't. Maybe it's just a little harder than it looks."

Anger turned to disgust as she looked away from him. For the second time that day, Jesse found himself thinking about smiling.

"Don't you dare laugh at me," she commanded, as if she could read his mind.

Of course her words made the amusement rise up in his throat.

"It's not funny!"

"Yeah, it is."

He could almost feel her reluctance as she grudgingly rose to her knees and rubbed her rear. "All right. Maybe I underestimated the skills required to ride a horse. But I want to try again. I would rather fall a dozen times than be tied up over the saddle. Agreed?"

He met her steady gaze. He'd come up with the plan of kidnapping Stoner's mail-order bride because he'd run out of other ways to see justice done. Once he'd made up his mind, he hadn't allowed himself to think about the woman, or what the kidnapping might mean to her. He certainly hadn't expected to admire her spirit.

Jesse held out his hand to her and she took it. When he pulled her to her feet, she winced and shifted her weight as if trying to ease the pain from her fall. He didn't know a damn thing about Haley Winthrop and he didn't want to. But one point was perfectly clear. No woman deserved to end up with a man like Lucas Stoner, and the hell of it was, if Stoner gave him the information he wanted, he, Jesse, would turn her over to her fiancé without a second thought.

Chapter Two

Three tries later Haley found herself sitting on top of a
very tall horse. The hard saddle was uncomfortable, but it
was a lot better to be upright on it than thrown across it.
She shifted uneasily and tried not to let her fear show. At
least her skirt was full enough that the fabric fluttered down
to cover most of her legs. She didn't allow herself to think
about exposed ankles and feet, which were a lot easier to
ignore than the fact that a strange man had just kidnapped
her.

"You gonna be able to hang on?" Jesse asked.

She nodded firmly. She might be his prisoner, but she
wasn't going to cower like a dog. If necessary, she could
survive on pride and grit. She'd done it before.

Without warning, his horse started walking. As Jesse was
holding on to her mount's reins, she found herself moving
forward, too. The odd swaying, rocking motion nearly
caused her to slide off the saddle. She made a quick grab
for the leather and clutched it tightly with both hands. Instinctively, she clung with her leg muscles. Every part of
her tensed.

After a few minutes of the steady pace, she was able to
loosen her grip a tiny bit. They were in a wooded area with
trees so thick, the branches were practically a roof. It was
still early enough in the year that not all of them had leaves,

and she could look up and see patches of sky. In a few weeks the leaves would be so thick it would stay dim and cool, even during the hottest part of summer.

Below them the ground was hard, with a few patches of snow in the shaded areas. Dead leaves covered everything. She inhaled deeply, absorbing the unfamiliar smells of damp earth, the trees themselves, plants, leaves and the sweat of the horses. So different, she thought, half exhilarated, half terrified. She was used to the city. Those smells and sounds were familiar. Not pleasant, but known. Out here, she wasn't sure what to expect.

Several strands of hair had worked loose from her tight bun and she raised one hand to push them off her face. The steady walking gait was getting easier to move with and she found herself relaxing a little more. Her heartbeat finally slowed, making her realize how hard it had been thundering and for how long. Ever since the sharp gunshot had cut through the rhythmic sounds of the stage rolling over the rough path and the carriage had crashed to the ground. One minute she'd been speeding toward her happy destiny and now...

She stared at the man in front of her. He wore a dark coat that barely came to his hips. The combination of thick fabric and broad shoulders made him look huge and forbidding. His hat was pulled low, and even if he'd been facing her, she would have had trouble seeing his eyes.

She looked away, preferring the view of the trees and plants to watching him. She didn't want to think about what had happened or about the fact that she wouldn't get to Whitehorn tonight. If she allowed herself to dwell on that, she would become even more afraid. Then she would shake and possibly even cry. And what use were tears? In all her twenty-one years, crying had never once accomplished anything.

But it was hard not to think about what was happening. She'd come so far, with such high hopes. After years of barely surviving in Chicago, she'd finally had a chance to be happy, only to have it snatched out of her grasp. If this…this…*villain* hadn't stolen her away from the stagecoach, she would be meeting her beloved at this very moment.

Haley closed her eyes and pictured what it would be like. She touched the white collar of her green dress, the collar she'd carefully preserved throughout the difficult journey. The clean collar she'd put on only a few hours before at their last stop before Whitehorn. She raised her hand higher, to the intricately arranged hair she'd spent an hour on that morning, working in the dark, trying not to wake the two other women in the shabby room. She'd so wanted to make a good impression on Lucas Stoner.

She opened her eyes and smiled. Even his name was perfect. Lucas Stoner. He sounded strong. And tall. While their correspondence had been brief, with him simply responding to her letter of interest with a stagecoach ticket and a few lines of instructions, she'd studied his words and his handwriting until she felt certain she knew the man. Lucas Stoner was good and honorable, kind yet firm. He was the sort of man others respected. She wasn't sure what he looked like, except perhaps for his height, of which she was very confident. But his appearance didn't matter to her. She'd seen too many handsome men who beat their wives and children, or stole, or even killed. What she cared about was on the inside of the man and she knew Lucas Stoner was the incarnation of all pure virtues.

To think that if she'd been allowed to continue on her journey at this very moment she might be meeting him for the first time. She'd pictured the moment a thousand times. The way he would tilt his hat, then take her hand and help her down from the stage. The shy smile they would share, the polite and awkward conversation about which they would both laugh later.

But instead of beginning her new life, she was stuck on the back of a hideously uncomfortable horse, in the wilderness, facing Lord knew what.

"You're quiet," her captor said.

She looked at him, but he hadn't bothered to turn around. "Yes," she answered.

"Just making sure you're still there."

"You're holding on to my horse's reins. Where would I go?"

He did glance at her then. A long steady appraisal over his shoulder. Dark eyes met her own. "You could have slipped down and run off."

"You would have heard me. Besides, I gave you my word."

His firm mouth twisted slightly. "It's going to take me a while to trust your word."

"I hope we're not together long enough for you to form an opinion of my honesty."

"You're a plucky little thing, aren't you?"

Plucky? She raised her chin. "I'm not afraid of you, if that's what you're asking. I'm not afraid of anyone."

He faced front again. "Must be nice to live that way. Fear can chew a man up inside. Like I said. Plucky. That's good. You're going to need that to survive out here. The land is hard on folks. Especially women."

She glanced around at the tall trees and the endless sky beyond. Ever since they'd left Chicago, she'd been eager to see what the great West of the country had to offer. The sheer size overwhelmed her. Until she'd answered Lucas's ad for a bride and had decided to accept his proposal, her entire world had consisted of twelve square blocks in a poor part of the city. She rarely ventured past those familiar streets.

What she'd seen on her journey had excited her. There was so much life, so much land. Different places, and people. She couldn't remember all the wonderful sights and she'd barely been able to sleep for the excitement of trying to relive all that she'd seen during the day. Everything was bigger and the colors were brighter. Winter in Chicago was shades of gray. The sky, the snow, the dirt, even the people.

"I don't believe it's harder out here for women than it was in the city," she said.

"Women die there?" he asked.

"Yes."

"Then maybe it's just different."

She didn't want to think about death. Especially not now when a stranger had kidnapped her. She wanted to think about Lucas and how he would surely come rescue her.

A faint rustle caught her attention and she saw something flash through the trees. It might have been a deer, but she wasn't sure. She opened her mouth to address the man, then snapped it shut. Was polite conversation appropriate under the circumstances? She didn't think so.

"What should I call you?" she asked. "The stage driver called you Jesse. Is that what you prefer?"

"It doesn't much matter. I'm Jesse Kincaid. Make do with what you'd like."

Calling him by his first name was a little informal, but the man had stolen her away, so using *Mr. Kincaid* was just too strange. As she mulled over the dilemma, she noticed it was getting darker. The sun had disappeared from the visible bits of sky and the shadows lengthened perceptibly. A shiver rippled through her. Unfortunately, it wasn't just from cold.

What would happen when they stopped for the night? What would he do to her? She'd heard stories, too many of them. Stories of women at the mercy of strange men.

"We'll have to make camp soon," Jesse said.

She jumped, wondering how he'd known what she was thinking. Her unexpected action made her horse step to the side suddenly. She shrieked and grabbed the saddle with both hands.

Jesse reined in his mount and reached for her. He gripped her upper arm, steadying her. "It's all right," he said. "I've got you."

Which shouldn't have reassured her, as he was the reason she was frightened in the first place, but it did.

When her horse was calm again, he released her. "There's a stream a little up ahead," he said. "We'll stop there for the night. I'm going to have to ask you to promise not to run away."

She glared at him. "Why should I do that? I don't want to be with you. I want to be in town with my fiancé."

"If you don't give me your word, I'll have to tie you up. It will make your evening very uncomfortable."

She thought about how he'd so casually lifted her onto his shoulder, then flung her across the horse. Anger filled her. She knew it was only there to camouflage the fear, but she didn't care.

"No! I won't do this," she told him. She wanted to be in town. She wanted to be with Lucas. Finally she had a chance at being happy, at living in a safe place and belonging, and no one was going to take that away from her.

She snatched at her reins. In the process of steadying her, Jesse had released his grip on them. He grabbed for her, but she was faster. She slapped her horse's neck. The animal bolted forward, the force of the movement nearly tossing her from the saddle. But she clung on to the leather and gripped the reins tightly.

"Dammit, Haley, you'll get yourself killed."

She ignored him, just as she ignored the sound of hoof-beats behind her. The brush and trees grew close together here. There were branches all around her. They plucked at her clothing and pulled at her hair. The musty odor of the forest was thicker, too, seeping up from the ground and filling the air with a heady aroma that, under different circumstances, might have been pleasant.

Her horse moved faster. She didn't know where they were or where she might find Whitehorn, but right now all that mattered was getting away. Later, she would figure out how to find Lucas. For now, there was only escape.

"Haley, look out! Pull back on the reins."

Jesse's frantic words made her look up ahead. Tree branches jutted out on the path, forming a thick, impenetrable barrier. The horse would probably be able to duck underneath them, but they would hit her in the center of her chest.

She screamed low in her throat as she began to saw on the reins. Her horse didn't slow. If anything, the animal went faster. The branches seemed to rush forward. She screamed louder and tried to sit up. Behind her, the sound of hoofbeats got louder but she knew Jesse wasn't going to reach her in time.

At the last possible second, her horse dug in and stopped. She felt powerful muscles bunch with the effort and then found herself sailing through the air. Twigs and new leaves clawed at her arms and face, then the ground rushed up to meet her.

She landed on a patch of snow. The impact knocked the breath from her body, leaving her stunned, aching and unable to breathe. She tried to sit up, tried to inhale, anything to relieve the hideous pressure in her chest. At last she drew in a shaky mouthful of air, then another.

Every part of her hurt. Her back, her arms and legs, her shoulders, even her hair. The cold, damp snow soaked her dress, but she didn't have the strength to move. She just wanted to lie here until Lucas found her and took her to town.

But the man looming over her wasn't her fiancé. He was big and as cold and unyielding as the ground beneath her. Without saying a word, he crouched beside her and began touching her.

Haley was too stunned from the fall to protest. Her eyes burned and she fought tears as large, male hands moved over her arms, then her legs. She flinched against the invasion, wondering why she'd been spared attack for so many years in the city, only to find herself at some man's mercy out here.

She told herself to fight him, to scratch and kick until she drove him off. But there was nothing left inside. The failed escape attempt had used up her last reserves.

"Nothing feels broken," he said, sitting back on his heels. "Can you stand?"

She blinked several times. "Wh-what?"

"I asked if you can stand up. Are you hurt?"

She rolled until she was kneeling, then slowly pushed herself to her feet. Once there, she staggered a step or two until she regained her balance. Straightening her shoulders, she stared at her captor. "I'm not hurt."

"Good. Hold out your hands."

When the meaning of his words sank in, she thought about running. But where was there to go? If she hadn't been able to escape on horseback, she wouldn't make it on foot. There would be another chance tomorrow, she told herself as she brought her arms up and held them stiffly in front of her.

As he wrapped a length of rope around her wrists, she studied his lean face. The stubble darkening his jaw, the set of his firm mouth. "You'll be punished for this," she said defiantly. "You'll be caught and punished."

He finished his task, then shrugged. "You're probably right. But it will be worth it."

Daisy Newcastle lifted the cover off the china serving dish and smiled. "More soup, Lucas?"

The tall man sitting across from her at the small table shook his head and tossed his napkin on the table. "I don't know how you do it, Daisy. I've paid three dollars for a meal like this in the city and never tasted anything so delicious." He leaned forward and cupped her chin. "You're a treasure."

The feel of his fingers against her skin made her want to shiver, but instead she smiled winningly and lowered her gaze as if embarrassed by the compliment. "You're so sweet to me," she said. "I don't deserve you."

He squeezed once, then released her. The light from the lamps around the room caught his profile. As she stared at the left side of his face, she acknowledged that Lucas

Stoner was a handsome man, with strong features and thick, dark hair. But when he heard a noise outside and turned toward it, she saw the other side. A thin scar cut down his right cheek, the line marring the flesh from his cheekbone to the corner of his mouth. The two sides of his face were much like the man himself. Viewed one way, he was handsome, successful and charming. But the other side of him, the scarred side, was ruthless and forbidding. He was a cruel man for whom life held no meaning, save perhaps his own. She played a dangerous game, teasing a lethal opponent. Yet she didn't have a choice. She would risk everything for the man she'd once loved. She couldn't bring him back from the grave, but she could try to make his murderer pay.

That thought was as close as she came to allowing herself to think about Michael Kincaid, Jesse's father. About his senseless murder and the destruction of his ranch. She dropped her hands to her lap and clutched her fingers tightly together in an effort to control the rage and helplessness that swept through her. It had been nearly six months, but the pain lingered. In some ways it wasn't as fresh as when she'd first learned the news, but she'd loved him too much to let him go easily.

So for Michael, and for Jesse, too, she invited Lucas Stoner to her small house and into her bed in the hope of learning enough to get him arrested. For justice's sake she played the whore and made him believe he was all she'd ever wanted.

Sometimes when she wondered how she could stand it another minute, she reminded herself she wanted to see Stoner in prison, then she wanted to watch him hang. With any luck his death would be slow and painful. At least that was what she prayed for each and every night.

"Did I smell pie?" he asked and raised the left corner of his mouth in a mocking imitation of a smile.

"Yes. I know it's your favorite dessert and I couldn't help myself."

He leaned forward and pressed his mouth to hers. The feel of his hot lips and the scent of his body made her stomach turn. She forced herself to stay completely still until he'd straightened back in his seat.

"Thank you," he murmured.

"Anything for you." She rose to her feet and began clearing the table. As always, she refused to think about what would happen in the next few hours...what always happened. The idle chatter about his day and how brilliant he was. How he sipped coffee from the delicate cups that had been brought to this country by her English grandmother. The way he would set the cup on the table in front of the sofa, place his hands on his thighs and leer at her.

"I think it's time, Daisy dear," he always said, then waited for her to lead the way to her bedroom.

She hated it all. Especially his calling her "Daisy dear." But at least he was quick. Sometimes he didn't bother undressing all the way. He simply unbuttoned his trousers and thrust himself inside of her. Sometimes, if she ignored the burning pain and telltale wetness he left behind, she could convince herself nothing had really happened.

As she took a step toward the kitchen, someone knocked on her front door. Daisy frowned and glanced at the grandfather clock in the hallway. It was already dark and after seven. Who would be calling at this time of evening... especially when Stoner left his carriage carelessly in front of her house for everyone in town to see?

She set the dishes back on the table and brushed her hands against her skirt. "I'll just get that," she said.

"Perhaps I'll come with you." Stoner pushed back his chair and stood.

Daisy crossed to the door and pulled it open. An older man stood on her small porch, his hat in his hand. He looked familiar, but she couldn't put a name to his face. Stoner moved close behind her and supplied the information.

"Charlie, what are you doing here?" he asked.

"Mr. Stoner, I've brung you a message."

Daisy frowned at the man, realizing he drove the stage. "Were you expecting a package?" she asked, glancing at Stoner over her shoulder.

"In a manner of speaking," he answered. "What message? Was there a problem?"

Charlie turned his hat in his hands, spinning it faster and faster. He swallowed twice and a muscle twitched in his cheek. "Mr. Stoner, we had us some trouble with the stage."

"Would you like to come in?" she asked Charlie.

"That won't be necessary," Stoner said, never looking away from the driver. "What happened?"

"There was a holdup."

"I didn't have any packages or money on the stage."

"I know that. But you did have…" Charlie trailed off and glanced pointedly at Daisy. "You know."

"My mail-order bride. Yes, I *do* know. Go on."

Charlie began speaking, but Daisy wasn't paying attention. So the woman had arrived. There was nothing to be done about her, of course. The poor innocent had answered an ad from a man looking for a wife. No doubt she thought she was marrying someone kind and ordinary. Not a monster. Not Lucas Stoner.

"Jesse Kincaid took her off, bold as you please. Right in front of all of us."

That got Daisy's attention. "What did you say?"

Charlie's head bobbed several times. "That's right, ma'am. Jesse kidnapped Mr. Stoner's bride. Said he would bring her back when Stoner agreed to talk with him." He shrugged. "So that's what I come to tell you."

Daisy didn't want to look, but she forced herself to turn slowly and raise her gaze to Stoner's face. The cold, ugly hatred there made her shrink back against the door frame.

There were several moments of silence. All Daisy heard was the sound of the hat brim brushing against Charlie's callused fingers and the faint ticking from the clock in the hall.

"Thank you for bringing me that information," Stoner said at last. "I'll take care of it."

Charlie bobbed his head again. "Yes, sir, Mr. Stoner. I just wanted to be the one to tell you. When he took her off, she wasn't hurt or anything."

"Thank you," Stoner repeated, drew Daisy inside the house and firmly shut the door.

Daisy tried to gather her composure. She had to figure out how to act. She hadn't known about Jesse's plans, so her surprise about that had been genuine enough. The fool boy was trying to get himself killed, she thought grimly, then pushed the thought away. There was no time to deal with Jesse's folly right now. First she had to handle Stoner. She was supposed to be his loving mistress, and as such, news about a mail-order bride should bother her. Stoner had no way of knowing she'd overheard him talking to the wire operator when he had sent the money for the woman's ticket.

"Lucas?" she asked, as he led the way back into the dining room. "I don't understand."

He motioned for her to take her seat. She hesitated, then did as he requested. She rested her hands flat on the table and opened her eyes wide. For a couple of heartbeats, she allowed herself to remember the pain of watching Michael Kincaid hanged for a crime he didn't commit. As always, the memory of the senseless death brought tears to her eyes. She blinked as if trying to hide them.

"A b-bride," she said, deliberately stumbling over the word.

"I know, Daisy dear. This is a shock."

"More than a shock. I thought—" She shook her head and turned away. "Lucas..."

He took the chair next to her and grasped both her hands in his. "I don't have a choice. Look at me."

She drew in a deep breath for courage and did. His faked concern made her supper rise in her throat.

"You know about my ambitions," he said.

She nodded. "You're going to be governor."

"And more." He smiled as if she were a bright student and had provided the correct answer. "That requires the right kind of connections and the right wife."

Daisy hung her head. "I have no connections, nor am I a young, blushing bride."

"You are a beautiful woman and I have no intention of ending our relationship."

She sucked in a breath, then turned her mouth up into a smile. Pray God he didn't notice the lie. "Really? But I don't understand."

"She will be a convenience, nothing more. I specifically wanted an orphan. She has no family to appear and refute whatever I may say about her past. But she will be little more than a decoration to appease the world. You will still warm my bed at night." He leaned close and kissed her. "Often."

Her pity for the faceless young woman vanished. She, Daisy, was still going to have to allow Stoner to have his way with her. At least for now. Which was fine with her. She still wanted Stoner dead.

"But she's been kidnapped. What are you going to do?"

His expression hardened again. "I will take care of Jesse Kincaid myself."

Just like you took care of his father, Daisy thought angrily.

"He can't be allowed to go around kidnapping innocent women," Stoner continued. "I will think of something suitable."

Daisy realized she had to warn Jesse. On the heels of that concern came the knowledge that he'd known by kidnapping Stoner's bride-to-be he would be tangling directly with his enemy. Perhaps that was what he wanted—a way to flush Stoner into the open. He had a plan. Of that she was sure. The best thing she could do to help was to stay close to their mutual enemy and learn all she could. Eventually Lucas Stoner would make a mistake. They only needed one. Then she would be standing right in front to watch the man hang.

Chapter Three

They made camp in a small clearing beside a rushing stream. Haley leaned against a thick tree, trying not to think about where she was or why she was there. The pretending to be strong and brave only worked for a short period of time. Sometimes, the fear won anyway.

A shiver rippled through her. Her dress was soaked from where she'd fallen in the snow, but she didn't have anything else to change into. The small carpetbag Jesse had brought with them contained a nightgown, stockings, her brush and comb, some hairpins and two spare petticoats. Her other dresses were in her trunk, still tied to the stage.

The snap of a twig caught her attention and she turned toward the sound. Jesse moved back into the clearing. His arms were full of tree branches, which he placed on the ground. Next he gathered small twigs and some leaves. He pulled a tin of matches from one of his saddlebags, then lit one and touched the flame to the kindling. The fire caught instantly.

"If you stand close to the heat, your clothes will dry," he said without turning around.

Haley glared at his back. She didn't want to give him the satisfaction of responding to his suggestion. But another shiver rippled through her and she knew she was risking a serious chill if she didn't get warm soon. So she approached

the growing fire and turned so her damp skirts were closest
to the flames. She was careful to keep her gaze from meeting Jesse's. As it got darker and the sounds of the night
surrounded them, it was more and more difficult to forget
she was alone with this man. What was he going to do to
her?

Don't think about that, she ordered herself. *Think about
Lucas.* So she tried to picture his face, his eyes, his warm
smile. She got lost in a daydream of how he would tell her
he'd been so worried about her. She would tell him about
her adventure and he would gently take her hand and offer
comfort. They would—

Something settled on her shoulders. She let out a scream
and tried to jump. Strong hands held her in place.

"Just until you stop shaking like a wet calf," Jesse said,
smoothing a coat over her. "I have a spare. I figured a city
girl wouldn't know how to dress for Montana nights."

She wanted to throw his gift back in his face, but she
could feel the weight of the fabric and the warmth lingering
from his body and all she wanted to do was snuggle into
the soft sheepskin lining. Despite her annoyance at the im-
plied insult, she knew he was right. She didn't have a warm
coat.

"I—" She clamped her lips shut. She was *not* going to
thank him. He didn't deserve it.

He also didn't seem to expect it. He moved away and
began setting up the camp. He filled a coffeepot with water
and put it on a flat rock he rolled into the fire. Next came
cans of beans and some hard, flat chunks of bread. He
heated the beans in their can, then used a bent fork to push
them onto two plates.

Somewhere in the process, he removed his hat. Haley
didn't notice the exact moment he did so, but suddenly he
wasn't wearing it. As he crouched by the fire, the light
illuminated his features. Stubble darkened his jaw, making
him look forbidding. Dark eyes and a straight mouth gave
nothing away. She didn't know what he was thinking and

she decided she didn't want to know. When he stood up, she realized he was much taller than she. The top of her head barely came to his chin. He'd already proved he could physically overpower her without a moment's pause.

The fear returned and with it a sensation of helplessness. She glanced around, but there was no one to help her and nowhere to run. The vast star-filled sky seemed to mock her. In the middle of the wilderness, what did the fate of one unknown woman matter to anyone?

The woman had gotten real quiet.

Jesse told himself it was a good thing, that her silence was better than her threats, but to tell the truth, he'd spent a lot of the past two years in his own company and he'd gotten tired of the quiet. But he couldn't think of anything to say. And if the little glances she kept throwing at him were anything to go by, she was terrified. Despite the large fire and his coat, she kept shivering. He knew her dress was wet from where she'd fallen in the snow, but there wasn't anything he could do about that. It was unlikely she had a spare in her small carpetbag and he didn't have one with him, either. She was just going to have to shiver until she dried out.

But he could try to reassure her fears. Somehow.

He searched his brain, wondering what he could say that would bring her a measure of comfort. He felt another of those darting glances. She'd cleaned her plate and set it on the ground beside her. From here he couldn't see if she'd finished her coffee or not so he reached for the pot, rose to his feet and headed toward her.

She sat in a half crouch across from him. As he approached, she stiffened, then slowly stood up. He'd untied the ropes around her wrists so she could eat. She'd pushed her arms through the coat sleeves. The garment hung down to her thighs, making her look small and childlike.

"More coffee?" he asked, holding up the pot.

She dropped her cup to the ground as her hands curled into fists. "Stop it," she said softly. "Just stop it."

He paused in midstep. "What are you talking about?"

"This." She made a motion that took in him, the camp and the horses. "All of it." She cleared her throat and her voice got stronger. "I'm not afraid. You can do whatever you have to and I won't be afraid. But don't make me wait and wonder. Just get it over with. Whatever you're going to do to me, I can bear it. I just can't stand the waiting!"

Jesse took a step back and stared at her. The firelight illuminated half her face. Her green eyes had darkened to the color of shadow while her skin seemed to glow. But it was her mouth that caught and held his attention. Her lower lip quivered. He didn't know if she was terrified or just close to tears and he didn't want to know. Dammit all to hell, he hadn't wanted to do this from the start. If there'd been another way to make Stoner listen to him...

But there hadn't been, he reminded himself. The past six months had proved that. Stoner was too smart to make a mistake and Jesse had no choice but to force his hand.

"I'm not going to hurt you," he said.

She made a sound that was half laugh, half strangled sob. "Yes, I've heard the men always say that right before they ravish the woman. That it won't hurt. That she'll like it." Her chin raised slightly in a gesture of defiance. "I don't care because I won't be afraid of you. So ravish me or kill me, but just do it *now*."

Her words sank in slowly. Jesse felt an unfamiliar heat on his cheeks, then realized he was blushing. "I'm not going to do that," he said quickly and returned to the fire. After putting the coffeepot back on the rock, he shoved his hands into his pockets.

"Kill me or r-ravish me?"

"I'm not going to hurt you at all. You've got this all wrong."

"Forgive me for misunderstanding the kidnapping. Perhaps you merely meant to show me this beautiful countryside. Of course. How silly of me. Allow me to admire the beauty of the night sky. There are so many stars out. It's lovely. You *are* a thoughtful host.''

He had to admire her guts. She was still visibly shaking with cold and fear, yet she spit at him like a barn cat facing down a coyote. She had about as much chance of winning this encounter, too, but by God she wasn't going to let her fear best her. He had the brief thought that life would have been easier for Claire if she had had a little of Haley Winthrop's spirit. But Claire couldn't help what she'd been and he knew better than to speak or think ill of the dead.

He pointed to the log he'd rolled over for her to sit on. "I'm not going to hurt you," he repeated. "You might as well make yourself comfortable." He sat on the ground on his oilcloth and stared at the flames. She didn't move.

"I didn't want to kidnap you," he said, figuring he owed her some explanation for what had happened.

"So you made a mistake. How unfortunate...for all of us."

Her frosty words almost made him want to smile. Almost. "I have a ranch, or rather I had one with my father. It's a few miles from here. A great piece of land with plenty of room for grazing cattle and there's lots of water."

"How lovely for you." She was just as sarcastic as ever, but he noticed she'd lowered herself onto the log and was leaning toward the fire.

"A couple of years ago I headed south to bring up a herd of longhorns from Texas. We wanted to breed them with the stock we already had and build up our cattle." He paused, remembering the plans he and his dad had made. The dreams they'd had for success as ranchers. There were opportunities available to men willing to work hard. He remembered his mother and Claire. The land wasn't as forgiving when it came to women.

"Did you?" she asked. "Did you bring the herd north?"

"Yeah. Nearly two thousand head of cattle. But when I got back, the ranch was gone."

That caught her attention. She straightened in her seat and stared at him. ''What do you mean, gone? The land is still there, isn't it?''

''Oh, yeah, the land is there, but the cattle had been scattered and the house was mostly burned. My father was dead.''

He stared into the fire and remembered that time. Those days—the shock of seeing the half-burned house. The silence broken only by a few birds flying overhead.

''What happened?'' she asked.

''He was murdered. Falsely accused of helping renegades who have been attacking local ranches.'' Rage welled up inside him; the familiar heat had kept him alive through the long, cold winter. ''I know my father as well as I know myself. He was a decent man who never broke the law. He wouldn't have helped any renegades. I asked around in town and found out there had been a quick arrest and a quicker trial. He was hanged in two days. It happened about four months after I left for Texas, so by the time I got back with the herd, people had mostly forgotten.''

He heard Haley catch her breath. ''I'm sorry for your family,'' she said. ''But what does this have to do with me?''

''I know who's responsible. Lucas Stoner is behind my father's death and he's responsible for the other attacks on the ranches around here. So far I haven't been able to prove it, but you're going to help me change all that.''

Haley sprang to her feet. ''No! I won't listen to this and I'm certainly not going to help you. How dare you imply that Mr. Stoner is anything but a good and kind man? He's honest and hardworking. While I appreciate and sympathize with the death of your father, that does not give you the right to kidnap an innocent woman and hold her against her will.''

Jesse shook his head. ''You've never met Stoner.''

''So?''

''How can you claim to know what kind of man he is?''

That pointed chin came up a notch again. "I have read his letter. I know the man."

"Lady, I think living in the city has addled your brain. You don't know this man, and trust me, you don't want to know him. If anything, you should be grateful I kidnapped you."

"Grateful? Why, you are nothing but a lying dog. Lucas Stoner is a gentleman and you have no right to even speak his name. You are a criminal, a liar and I'm not sure what else."

Jesse was too stunned to protest. She was comparing him to Stoner and Stoner was coming out the winner? "You got all this from one letter?"

She nodded, her green eyes flashing fire. "My fiancé is a wonderful man and I'm lucky to be engaged to him."

Haley was grateful for the argument. Not only did talking about Lucas make her feel less alone, but the anger gave her strength. She wasn't sure if she believed Jesse's claim that he didn't want to hurt her. She hoped he wasn't lying, but she had no way of knowing for sure.

"Must have been a hell of a letter," Jesse muttered as he turned back to the fire and poured himself more coffee.

Haley knew if the truth were told, it hadn't been much of a letter. Just a few lines of Lucas telling what he wanted in a wife. She had replied with a long detailed description of herself, her character and her life in Chicago. His answer had been the stage ticket west.

So she wasn't completely sure of Lucas's character, but she had been able to interpret several qualities from both what he wrote and what his words probably meant. And when the little voice in her head asked why, if Lucas was so wonderful, did he have to advertise for a wife, she reminded the voice, and herself, that there weren't many women in the West. Besides, her entire future depended on the character of Lucas Stoner. She couldn't bear the thought that he was anything less than perfect.

"It's getting late," Jesse said. "If you want to wash up,

go on down to the stream to take care of your business. We need to turn in soon.''

His words reminded her of the pressure low in her belly and the fact that she hadn't had a moment's privacy since he'd kidnapped her. While she was surprised he was willing to trust her on her own, she wasn't about to question the fact and hurried in the direction of the running water.

Once by the bank, she found a clump of trees and carefully lifted her skirts. It was dark and she worried about what kinds of creatures might be lurking in the shadows. Still the outdoors was cleaner smelling than any privy in the city.

When she'd finished, she made her way to the stream and quickly washed her face and hands. The water was like ice, but so clean and sweet tasting, she had to drink several handfuls before reluctantly turning back to the camp.

It would be easy enough to run away, she thought. She could simply disappear into the darkness.

A bird hooted from the high branches above her head and something rustled in the leaves next to her. She jumped. Her choices were the enemy in the form of Jesse Kincaid, or the unknown of the forest. For now the man was less frightening.

But as she got closer to the camp, her step slowed and she wondered if she would be better off taking her chances with the creatures of the night.

To distract herself, she thought about what he'd told her about his family and the death of his father. She didn't know anything about her own family. She'd been delivered to the orphanage when she was only a few weeks old and no one had ever come looking for her in all her twenty-one years. She had often wondered what it would be like to have people related by blood, people who cared where she went and what she did with herself. That was one of the reasons she was so looking forward to getting married. Lucas was going to care about her. In time, he would love her and she would finally belong. He was…

He was *not* responsible for the death of Jesse's father. She knew that for sure. He couldn't be. There had to be a mistake.

Before she could figure it all out, she found herself entering the camp. The first thing she saw was two bedrolls stretched out on opposite sides of the fire. Relief filled her, chasing away the chill and the last of the fear. Jesse had meant what he said. He wasn't going to ravish her.

When she hesitated, he pointed to the one closest to her. She walked to it, then sank down on the thick blankets. "How did you know I'd come back?" she asked.

"You didn't have a choice. You're a city girl and you wouldn't survive half a day in these woods, let alone half the night."

She thought about the unfamiliar smells, sights and sounds and knew that he was right. As long as he kept his word and didn't try to take her, she would be fine. In a few days she would be in town and this would all be just a bad dream.

He tossed the rest of his coffee into the bushes, then stretched out on his bedroll. "I'm not going to tie your hands," he said. "If you try to escape in the night, I'll probably hear you and drag you back. Then I will tie your hands, and your feet, too. You won't like it."

"I'm not going to try to escape." At least not tonight, she thought. Maybe tomorrow, when it was bright and she was rested.

"If I don't hear you, you're going to be on your own out there," he said as if she hadn't spoken. "There are a lot of hungry critters who would like to have someone just like you for supper."

"You don't scare me," she told him.

"I'm not trying to scare you, I'm telling you the truth."

She raised herself on one elbow and looked at him. "It doesn't matter if you try or not, I'm tough. I've been on my own since I was twelve. Some backwoods criminal isn't about to make me do anything I don't want to do, so don't even try.''

He raised himself on one elbow, too. "You don't say."

"I do say."

He lifted his eyebrows, then smiled. "Good."

She'd expected several reactions, but not a smile. Not from him. Not after what they'd been through.

Her first thought was that he was surprisingly handsome, in a rugged kind of way. The second was that he looked kind when he smiled, and he made her want to smile back. Which was ridiculous because the man had kidnapped her. So she stretched out on the bedroll and pulled the blankets over her. The wool smelled of horse and hay and the outdoors. She inhaled the scent and thought it was very nice. Clean and safe smelling.

Logs snapped on the fire. In the distance, something howled a mournful cry. An answering yip filled the night. When there was silence again, Haley turned on her side, toward the fire.

"Jesse?"

"Yes?"

"Tell me about Lucas Stoner."

He was quiet for so long, she thought he wasn't going to answer. Then he said, "I thought you knew everything about the man."

"I know some things. What he told me in his letter and what I figured out for myself. But there's a lot I don't know."

"You know he killed my father."

She sighed. "I don't believe that. There has to be some mistake."

"There's no mistake." Jesse's voice was bitter.

"I don't want to talk about that."

"I don't blame you. I don't imagine any bride wants to hear that her fiancé is a murderer."

"Never mind," she said and closed her eyes.

She heard Jesse draw in a deep breath. "I can't tell you

about him without telling you what I know he did, but if you ask me something specific, I can probably answer that.''

"Is he handsome?" Haley wasn't sure where that question came from. She'd never thought of Lucas as being good-looking or not. In her mind, he simply existed. But now that she'd asked, she found she wanted to know.

"I'm a man, Haley. How would I know?"

He had a point. "Is he ugly?"

"I don't think so. He has a scar on his face, though. That might bother you."

"A scar? What does it look like?"

"It's a thin, pale line on the right side of his face, from his cheekbone to about an inch from the corner of his mouth. And before you ask, I don't know how he got it."

Haley drew her knees to her chest and thought about the scar. He must mind having it. Anyone would. In a way it made Lucas a tragic figure, which made him more approachable. The scar wouldn't matter to her. She would find him just as easy to love. She would tell him after they were married. After all, she'd worked with a doctor for several years and she was completely used to seeing things more unpleasant than a scar.

She felt herself start to relax and she pulled the blankets up over her shoulders. Tomorrow Lucas would come find her, she was sure of it. They would get married and she would begin her new life.

Chapter Four

It was still dark under the trees when Jesse woke up. He could see the first fingers of light filtering through the branches as he rolled onto his back and got his bearings. Slowly he turned his head toward the fire, then rose on one elbow. Haley was still there, curled up on her side, the blankets pulled to her chin. So she hadn't tried to run. He was pleased, but a little surprised. She was tough and he admired that. He suspected her fighting spirit would cause her to try to escape again. He could only hope that he would be able to catch her. Being tough wasn't going to be enough to keep her alive out here in a wilderness that didn't show anyone mercy.

He continued to study her. Sometime in the night her light brown hair had come loose from its pins. Soft-looking strands spread out on the pile of clothing that was a make-shift pillow. She was, he acknowledged, very pretty. Claire had been pretty, but in a more traditional sense. He supposed at one time his mother had been beautiful, before the hardships of ranch life had leached the color from her face and hair. This wilderness was hard on women, which was why it would be better for everyone if Haley just turned around and returned to Chicago. At least she would be safer there.

Still, he knew better than to tell her his opinion on the

subject. She was about as stubborn as she was tough. He
had to admire that, even though he knew it was going to
make the situation more difficult for him. Despite everything, despite her sharp tongue and her misplaced faith in
her fiancé, he liked her. A useless piece of information, he
thought, sitting up and reaching for the coffeepot. Haley
wasn't for him, and even if she was, he wasn't going to
get involved with a woman ever again. He refused to be
responsible for another woman's death.

He walked to the stream and washed his face, then filled
the coffeepot. Six months of living under a real roof at the
Baxter ranch had softened him some. He'd spent more than
a year on the trail before that and he knew it wouldn't take
long for him to get used to being outdoors again. Of course
he wasn't going to be out here all that long. Just as soon
as Stoner agreed to talk to him, he could let Haley go and
get on with his quest for justice.

As he stirred the cold fire and added more kindling, he
heard a faint sound. He half turned as Haley's eyes fluttered
open. She drew her eyebrows together as she glanced
around. Her gaze settled on him. Fear followed confusion,
then she remembered and stiffened slightly. With a reaction
that he knew was involuntary, she reached for the buttons
of her green dress, checking them as if to make sure they
hadn't been disturbed. At the same time, her other hand
reached down to smooth her skirt. Then she blushed.

Jesse looked away, fighting embarrassment of his own.
He'd told the woman he wasn't interested in ravishing her.
Why didn't she believe him? But he knew the answer to
that question. He was a stranger to her. A man who had
taken her away against her will and was holding her captive. Why should she believe anything he said?

"The coffee will take a few minutes," he said, his voice
gruff. "You should go clean up. We'll be moving out right
after breakfast."

She scrambled to her feet and walked briskly toward the
stream. When she was gone, Jesse collected their blankets

and rolled them up. He gathered the saddlebags together and as he set them next to the blankets, he felt something hard inside one of them. Without wanting to, he opened the flap and reached inside.

The brooch was wrapped in a piece of soft cotton. He squatted down and flipped open the edges of the cloth, until the beautiful piece of jewelry winked up at him. A pink cameo edged in gold. The carved face showed a beautiful woman in three-quarter profile.

His father had given the piece to his mother before he, Jesse, had been born. He remembered her wearing it nearly every day. She used to laugh and finger it, saying it was too fine for daily wear, but too beautiful to be left in a box. It was, she'd often said, a legacy of the love she and his father shared. When Jesse fell in love, she would give it to him to give to his bride.

So when Claire had arrived, she'd been given the Kincaid cameo brooch and she'd worn it at the base of her throat. His mother had been pleased by how the jewelry suited Claire. Then Claire had died and his mother had taken the brooch back. Jesse had ceased to believe that it was given as a legacy of love. He doubted the pin was cursed—it just didn't have enough power to ward off the inevitable. Or maybe love wasn't strong enough. Or maybe it was something else entirely. For while Michael Kincaid had loved his wife desperately, he, Jesse, had never come close to loving Claire. It was an ugly truth and one he didn't want to face. But today he couldn't ignore it. He hadn't loved her and she'd known. Perhaps that had been the real reason she had died.

Haley crouched in front of the stream and shivered as her hands dipped into the frigid water. This morning there was still ice on the muddy banks. It crackled as she shifted her weight. But she didn't mind the cold water or the chill of the early morning. Instead she had to hold in a laugh of pure pleasure.

Everything was so clean. The scent of the air and the earth, the taste of the water, the ground, the sky, all of it. Clean, new and alive. She splashed water on her face, and caught her breath at the coldness. Then she drank several handfuls of the sweet liquid. A few drops ran down her chin and soaked the collar of her dress, but she didn't mind. Montana was more wonderful than she had allowed herself to believe. It was big and beautiful and, no matter what, she was never going back.

She rose to her feet and, arms open wide, she spun in a circle. Her loose hair hung down her back. She shook her head, enjoying the feel of the thick strands moving against her. The rising sun touched her face, warming her skin. As she stretched, she felt stiff and a little sore. Probably from her horseback riding yesterday. She rubbed her rear and wrinkled her nose at the thought of getting back on the horse again. But it was unlikely Jesse would have another way for her to travel. At least being on the horse was much better than being trapped in the swaying stagecoach. The first two days of the journey her stomach had been queasy and she'd been afraid she was never going to feel better.

A familiar and tempting smell caught her attention. She sniffed, inhaling the scent of coffee. Her stomach rumbled. She turned and headed back toward the camp, her nose leading her when she nearly lost the narrow trail.

As she broke through the brush surrounding their small clearing, she saw Jesse squatting on the ground, staring at something in his hand. She approached him and when he didn't turn away, she bent down and studied what he held.

It was a woman's brooch. Gold with a carved cameo in the center. The gold caught the rising sunlight and seemed to wink at her. "It's lovely," she breathed. "Is it yours?"

He looked at her. It was the first time she'd seen his face in daylight. Yesterday, when he'd kidnapped her, he'd been wearing a hat pulled low over his forehead. Last night he'd taken the hat off, but it had already grown dark and she'd only seen him by firelight. Now she stared at him in the full brightness of day.

He had regular features, with a straight nose and dark eyes. His hair was a little shaggy, thick and straight, with a few strands falling over his forehead. Stubble shadowed his cheeks and jaw, outlining his firm mouth. A mouth that looked as if it never smiled, yet he had last night...hadn't he?

He didn't want to answer her question. She could tell by his silence and the way he carefully wrapped the pin in its piece of cotton and placed it in his saddlebag. Had it belonged to someone in his family? An old sweetheart? It wasn't her business, she reminded herself.

She turned to the fire and grabbed their coffee cups. The brew was nearly ready.

"It belonged to my mother," he said, startling her.

She spun toward him. "Really? It's very lovely."

He shrugged. "My father gave it to her when they were married."

"Your mother died?" she asked.

"About three years ago."

She heard the pain in his voice. "At least you can remember her," she said. "And you have the brooch."

"I know." But she could tell by his shuttered expression that he didn't think it was much.

If only he knew how precious the remembering could be. There had been so many times when she'd lain awake at night and desperately wanted to remember something... anything. But she'd been an infant when she'd been left at the orphanage and there weren't any memories to be had. She'd contented herself with making up stories about a family that didn't really exist.

The coffee sputtered. She bent low to the fire and grabbed her skirt, then used it to protect her hand from the heat of the pot as she poured them both a cup.

"You've been around open fires before," Jesse commented, coming up behind her and taking the cup she offered.

"I've been around every kind of fire and cookstove you can imagine," she said. "Big black monsters in restaurant kitchens and tiny flames in shacks on the edge of the neighborhood."

He frowned and sat on the log by the fire. She settled next to him. He produced a couple of hard biscuits and some dried beef. "Why so many places?"

"I worked for a doctor," she said, taking the food. It wasn't what she would have requested, but she was hungry and there didn't seem to be much choice. She'd long ago learned to eat when food was around because it might not always be available. "I assisted him as he cared for patients, so I went with him to their homes or where they worked."

Jesse looked surprised. "You had a job?"

"Of course. How do you think I took care of myself?"

"Didn't you live with your family?"

"I'm an orphan."

"I'm sorry," he said. "I didn't know."

"There was no reason for you to."

He glanced at the saddlebag containing the brooch. "Do you remember your family at all?"

She shook her head. "I was left at the orphanage when I was first born. I like to think I have many brothers and sisters and they just lost track of me, but I know that's not true."

"How did you get from the orphanage to working for a doctor?"

She took a sip of coffee, not sure if she should answer the question. She didn't much like talking about her past. Dr. Redding had often said life had not treated her well, but she didn't think it had been any more unkind to her than to most people.

"The orphanage kept us until we were twelve, then we were sent out to work."

His gaze narrowed. "At twelve?"

She nodded. "We could stay after that, but we had to pay room and board. That's what I did. I found a job cleaning. Scrubbing floors, that kind of thing." She made light of that time, not wanting to dwell on what it had been like. She didn't want to remember her cracked and bleeding hands, so raw from the hot water and lye soap. She didn't want to relive the pain in her back from the endless scrubbing. It was, she'd found out, only slightly better than working in a laundry, where she'd only lasted three days before deciding it would be easier to simply starve to death.

"One of my friends worked for Dr. Redding," she went on. "When a position became available in his office, she recommended me. I cleaned there, but it was easier than what I'd done before. Then one day, one of the nurses was ill and I accompanied him as he visited patients. I found I liked it a lot more than cleaning and he said I had a talent for helping the sick."

"How old were you?" Jesse asked.

"Nearly fifteen. After a few months I was earning enough to leave the orphanage. I rented a room in a nice house. It was in the attic, but still it was mine."

She could remember how proud she'd been the first night she'd slept in that narrow bed. In the morning the room had been freezing and she'd bumped her head on the sloping ceiling, but none of that had mattered. She'd found a place that was hers. And she'd done it all by herself.

Jesse continued to study her. She wondered if she'd missed a smudge of dirt on her face and tried to casually wipe her cheeks.

"That's not what I imagined," he said at last. "You've been through some difficult times."

She shrugged. "I suppose. It's all I know."

"Do you miss Chicago?"

She thought about the tiny room that was so hot in the summer and so very cold in the winter. She thought about the sick and the dying, the stench of the open sewers, the fear of being attacked when she walked home late after tending an ill patient. In the past four years only three men had invited her out for an evening and she hadn't liked any of them. There were, she knew, lots of young men in the city, but she didn't know how to meet them. While a few friends had offered to introduce her to brothers and cousins, she always felt shy and silly and she'd refused. So she remained alone.

"No," she said softly. "I don't miss it. I wanted something different than I had there. I know how to work hard and I'm not afraid. Mr. Stoner and I can build a good life together here."

She thought about her fiancé and wondered if he was already out looking for her. It would have been difficult to get men together in the darkness, but she was sure that first thing this morning, they would begin the search. Perhaps they'd already started. Her heart quickened. At this moment, he could be on horseback, retracing the journey she'd taken with Jesse. Perhaps in a few short hours, she would be with him.

A quick movement caught her attention. Jesse stood up, his body stiff with tension. She knew it was because she'd mentioned Lucas. Well, none of this was her fault. Jesse was the one who had kidnapped her and if he didn't want her talking about Lucas, he could take her to town and let her go.

"How long do you intend to keep me prisoner?" she asked.

"For as long as it takes."

"You want money? Is that it?"

He turned his cool gaze on her. "No. Not money. Information. A confession."

Frustration filled her. "Why do you insist on blaming him for what happened to your family? I'm sure he wasn't—"

He cut her off with an angry flick of his hand. "Lady, you don't know what you're talking about. You have one letter from a stranger and nothing more. You've never met the man, nor have you spoken to anyone who knows him. If you want to believe he's the archangel Gabriel, that's your business, but I don't want to hear about it anymore. As far as I'm concerned, Lucas Stoner is a murdering son of a bitch and I want to see him hang.''

She opened her mouth, then closed it. This wasn't the time to reason with him. Later, when he'd calmed down, she could try to explain the situation to him. Or maybe it was better if they avoided the topic altogether.

''You are entitled to your opinion,'' she said stiffly and took a bite of the dried meat.

''Thank you,'' he said sarcastically. ''Now if you'll hurry up your breakfast, we have a lot of ground to cover today. I want your word that you won't try to escape.''

She'd forgotten about her plans until he mentioned them. In the daylight, the forest didn't look so frightening. Maybe she could find the road, then make her way to town. Wouldn't Lucas be proud of her for getting away all on her own!

''Don't even think about it,'' Jesse told her. ''If you don't give me your word, I'm going to tie your hands. If you remember from yesterday, it's not a very comfortable way to travel.''

She popped the last bit of beef into her mouth and turned her back on him. Although she hadn't promised, he seemed to take her actions as agreement because he didn't bother with the rope. Which was fine with her. There was no way she was going to just accept her fate. She had a life she needed to get on with and Jesse Kincaid wasn't going to stand in her way. At the first opportunity that presented itself, she was going to run.

Chapter Five

Haley couldn't remember ever having been this thirsty, hot, tired and sore. She stayed in the saddle by sheer will alone, simply because she knew it would hurt too much if she allowed herself to fall to the ground. Not that she was sure she could feel a whole lot more pain. Her thighs felt as if they'd been stretched two inches too long. Her rear was one giant bruise. The sun beat down unmercifully and she could feel her face burning. If only she had a bonnet. Or a glass of water. If only she was still in the carriage. A queasy stomach was simple compared to this.

To make matters worse, Jesse didn't seem to notice. He rode a few feet ahead, sitting comfortable in his saddle as if he'd been riding since before he could walk. He probably had been, she thought grimly, tugging at her suddenly too-tight collar and wishing a few clouds would appear in the brilliant blue sky. From time to time she heard a faint noise that sounded suspiciously like whistling. As if this were a great adventure to him. As if her suffering meant nothing.

If she were standing on solid ground instead of undulating on this poor excuse for transportation, she would stomp her foot and tell him exactly what she thought of him.

Then she heard the most perfect sound. At first she was afraid she was imagining it. The soft rush of water over rocks. A stream? Her mouth watered at the thought and she rubbed her cracked, dry lips.

"Is there a stream up ahead?" she asked.

"Yeah." He glanced at her over his shoulder. "I thought we could take a break there."

"I'd like that." Gratitude filled her and she nearly smiled at him before she remembered it was his fault she was suffering in the first place. If he hadn't come along, she would be in Whitehorn by now, possibly entertaining Lucas before the wedding. Or she might actually *be* getting married at this very minute. Her new, perfect life would be starting. But instead, she was stuck in the wilderness, dying of thirst and slowly roasting alive in the afternoon sun.

She would never have guessed it got hot in Montana in the spring. Last night the temperature had dipped below freezing, but today was just like summer. Under other circumstances, she might have enjoyed the unexpected warmth. Under other circumstances, she might have been willing to make polite conversation and be an agreeable companion. But right now all she wanted was to get off the horse and have something to drink.

Five minutes later, she reined in her mount and slowly slipped to the ground. There was an awful moment when she wasn't sure her legs were going to support her. Everything shook. Her thighs, her knees, her insides.

Jesse dismounted and grabbed her horse's reins. "You might want to walk around for a bit," he said. "That'll ease the stiffness."

"I doubt it," she told him, not bothering to look at him.

She made her way to the stream and crouched down by the flowing water. It was as icy as the one they'd camped by last night and she nearly laughed her delight. Again the taste was almost sweet. In some ways she felt as if she'd never really tasted water before. This clear, nearly sparkling liquid was nothing like what she'd grown up drinking. There was no odd color or odor, no taste of the barrel. The closest she'd come had been rainwater and that was a rare treat.

When she'd sipped her fill, she straightened and walked around on the bank. Moving did help, although she wasn't going to admit that.

Jesse walked down to the edge of the bank and broke a branch off a sapling. She'd noticed him doing things like that before. He'd taken a length of ruffle from one of the petticoats in her carpetbag and cut it up into small pieces, one of which he lodged in the broken branch.

"What are you doing?" she asked.

"Leaving a trail."

She glanced across the stream to the other side. It was thick with trees, but she thought she saw a narrow path. "Are we going that way?"

"No."

She frowned. "Then why…" Her mouth hung open for a moment, then she snapped it shut. She thought about all the times he'd stopped to break branches or leave bits of cloth. He usually did it when they changed direction or stopped. But the broken branches and pieces of petticoat didn't lead to them. Jesse was using them to send her rescuers in a different direction.

"You're tricking them," she said, as the anger returned. This time she was standing on the ground, so she placed her hands on her hips and stomped her right foot hard. "You're sending them away from where we're going."

"That's right," he said as easily as if he were agreeing to the day of the week. "I want them close, but I'm not ready for them to find us."

"Find me, you mean." Frustration boiled as her anger flared. "You want to keep me as long as you can."

Dark steady eyes studied her. "I want to keep you as long as necessary, Haley. I'm not doing this because I want to. I'm doing it because it's the only way to get Stoner to talk to me. When he gives me the information I need, I'll let you go."

"But I want to go now!"

"I'm sorry. I can't do that."

He sounded sincere, but that wasn't good enough. She looked around for a rock or a branch. Something with which to threaten him and convince him to let her go. She could feel her promise of happiness disappearing with every passing minute. She'd already waited so long. She wanted to meet Lucas. She wanted to be with him.

Jesse finished tucking the length of torn fabric in the tree branch and crossed to her. "Haley, I know this is difficult for you. I'll turn you over to Stoner as soon as I can. I promise."

"I'm not interested in your promises. You're nothing but a criminal. You've kidnapped an innocent woman, kept her in the woods and Lord knows what else you have planned."

A dull flush climbed his cheeks. He pushed his hat back on his head. "We've been over that one already. You know I'm not going to hurt you."

She did know, but she wasn't about to admit it to him. "I hate this," she said, turning away from him. "I want to go to town. Just let me go."

"I can't."

"You won't."

"You're right. I won't."

She stalked over to her horse and waited until Jesse joined her. When he made a step by lacing his fingers together, she wanted to scream in frustration. Why was this happening to her? How dare he treat her like this?

Then she was settling onto the saddle. Every part of her body clenched in protest. She did not want to spend one more hour on this horse.

"I'm going to get a quick drink of water," Jesse said, turning toward the stream. "I'll be right back."

She watched him walk away, hating him and the circumstances that had brought her here. If only she could convince him to—

Her gaze settled on him as he crouched at the water's

edge. She glanced in the other direction and saw his horse
waiting patiently. This was her chance, she thought suddenly. She could escape and get to town on her own.

She urged her horse close to his, then slapped his mount
on the rump. The animal jumped and started to move away.
Haley didn't bother waiting to see if it kept going. Instead
she collected her reins and kicked her horse hard. The gelding leapt forward. Unlike her first flight yesterday, this time
she was prepared for the momentum. She crouched low and
hung on, keeping control of the reins. A frustrated cry rose
up behind her, but she didn't bother turning. This time she
was going to do it. This time she was going to get away.

The countryside flashed by quickly. Haley steered her
horse down to the edge of the stream where there was
plenty of room for it to run. The wind whipped her hair
out behind her and cooled her heated body. The fear and
pain faded, replaced by exhilaration. She liked feeling free.
At last she was taking matters into her own hands.

Up ahead the bank narrowed. She tugged on the reins,
urging the horse into the forest. The thick trees forced her
to slow the animal. She didn't want a repeat of the previous
day, when low-lying branches had blocked the path. After
a few minutes, she drew her mount to a stop and listened
for the sound of someone following. But there wasn't anything except the call of a few birds and the thundering of
her heart. She'd done it!

Over the next hour or so, Haley let the horse pick its
way through the thick grove of trees. She had a general
idea of where she was heading because she'd started keeping track of the sun's slow descent. They were trotting now,
a bone-crushing pace that made her want to audibly whimper with each step. But they were also moving toward
Whitehorn. Perhaps by sundown she would have made it.

She kicked the horse into a faster pace. The animal
obliged and soon they were racing along. She laughed at
the pleasure of it. Once again she heard the rushing sound
of water, but it was too soon to stop.

The horse slowed, but she kicked it again, wanting it to keep running. She needed more distance between herself and Jesse. The animal slowed a second time. She leaned forward and kicked harder. Then she saw it.

This particular stream had been flowing hard and fast enough to cut a gully through the forest. It was about eight feet deep and three feet wide, with steep muddy banks. There was no way for them to walk down and judging from the bunching of the horse's muscles, her mount planned to jump the distance.

Haley screamed, but it was too late to stop. She bent as low as she could and wrapped her arms around the horse's neck. Even as the animal leapt out into nothingness, she felt herself being lifted and flying. Fear exploded into her, a heartbeat before she hit the ground. There was a moment of silence, then the world spun once and disappeared into blackness.

Daisy opened the door to the land office and stepped inside. She heard voices, but didn't worry about interrupting. If Stoner didn't want anyone listening, he would have turned the lock. She walked to the counter and placed her covered basket on top, then looked at the two men standing next to Stoner's large desk.

Stoner glanced up, saw her and smiled. She returned the greeting, knowing her pleasant expression would mask the hatred in her heart.

"I'll just be a minute, my dear," he told her.

She nodded and turned to glance out the front window, as if the conversation in progress held no interest for her. But in truth she strained to hear every word Stoner told Vernon Lindsay, Whitehorn's excuse for a sheriff.

"I want him found," Stoner said. "Do whatever you have to as far as Kincaid is concerned. In fact, I would consider it excellent news if he was killed while you were trying to arrest him."

"I can't just shoot him if he doesn't put up a fight."

"I doubt Jesse Kincaid will come quietly, Lindsay. But if you don't have the stomach to do it yourself, I'll take care of it later. The point is, I don't want the girl hurt. I haven't decided what I'm going to do with her."

"I've got men out looking for them now," Lindsay said. "But he spent two years on the trail and I'm sure he's learned a trick or two. It might be a while."

"I'm aware of your limitations," Stoner said. "If he's not found in the next couple of days, I'll decide what I want to do."

"I heard all he wants is to talk with you, Mr. Stoner. He's not asking for ransom."

There was a pause and Daisy wondered how the sheriff would pay for the insolence of offering a suggestion. The man was saved by the land office door opening again and three large, burly men walking in.

Daisy forced herself to smile politely at the unwashed, hulking brutes. They were Stoner's cousins and the trio he sent out to clean up anything he might consider untidy. They had fingered Jesse's father, Michael, as the man supplying guns to the mysterious renegades who had begun to plague the neighboring ranches.

"Miss Daisy," they said as one and tipped their dusty hats to her.

She nodded.

Stoner glanced up. "I want to talk to you," he said. "Lindsay, let me know if you hear anything."

"Yes, Mr. Stoner."

Lindsay waited for the three larger men to make their way past the counter before he headed for the door. Daisy watched to make sure Stoner took his cousins out back for some privacy before she stepped toward Lindsay and touched his arm.

"Do you really have men out looking for Jesse?" she asked.

Lindsay turned to look at her. She could smell the alcohol on his breath and seeping from his body. His skin was a shade somewhere between white and gray, and his blue irises were surrounded by yellow instead of white.

"They're looking," he said. "But Jesse's not going to be easy to find."

"You can't let them bring him in," she said, her voice low but heated. "Stoner has been looking for an excuse to kill Jesse and this is all he needs. If you arrest Jesse Kincaid, he'll be dead in less than two days. You know that."

Lindsay brushed his too-long blond hair from his forehead. His hands were shaking. "I'm doing what I have to."

Daisy leaned closer and lowered her voice. "Jesse hasn't done anything wrong and you know it. He's trying to clear his father's name. If you don't want to help him, then at least have the decency to stay out of his way."

Lindsay started for the door.

Daisy went after him. "You won't help, will you?"

"I can't."

She shook her head. "Bought and paid for by Stoner. What kind of man are you?"

Lindsay straightened. The drink might have defeated him for the moment, but he wasn't completely vanquished. "I know what I am, madam. And I'm not the only one Stoner bought and paid for."

She shouldn't have been surprised and yet she was. His words shocked her, sending color to her cheeks. It took all her pride to keep from ducking her head in shame. Whitehorn was a small town. No doubt everyone knew about her affair with Michael Kincaid and how she now allowed Lucas Stoner into her bed.

"I understand that I'm little more than a whore," she said stiffly. "But at least I'm doing all I can to see that the Kincaid family is vindicated. What are you doing?"

Lindsay reached out toward her, then dropped his hand back to his side. "I'm sorry, Mrs. Newcastle. I shouldn't have said that."

"Don't bother, Lindsay. We're both sorry excuses for decent folks. We fight our demons in different ways. But know this. While I understand you have a job to do, I won't let you or anyone hurt Jesse. If you do, I'll kill you myself.''

Lindsay reached for the door, then paused. He turned his watery gaze on her and nodded. "You know," he said at last, "that would be a true act of kindness and I would thank you for it.''

Jesse cursed loudly. His horse flicked its ears as if trying to understand what he was saying.

"Dammit all to hell," he muttered again. "Where is she?''

Bad enough that she'd caught him not paying attention. He'd known she was angry, frustrated and sore; he should have realized that she would try to escape. He couldn't even comfort himself with the fact that she'd broken her word. When he thought about it, she never promised anything that morning. He'd just taken her silence as assent.

He'd been married long enough to know that wasn't true. Women were stubborn creatures. Haley was tougher than most and one determined lady. He should have seen this coming and been prepared. Instead he'd been caught like a doe trapped in a mud bank.

He swore again, even though it didn't accomplish anything. She'd come this way and judging from the stripped branches and stirred earth, she'd been traveling quickly. He glanced around at the trees and the close branches, wondering why she'd gone from a trot to a full-out gallop. She and her horse had been making good time. She was even heading toward Whitehorn…sort of.

Jesse glanced up toward the sky. The sun would set within the hour. She would be safe on her horse, but eventually she'd have to stop and once she was on foot, she was in danger.

A faint rustling caught his attention. He reined in his mount and listened. Then he grinned. She was right up ahead, making enough noise to alert a deaf man. He had to give her credit for making it this far. She was one scrappy woman.

His horse moved forward. Jesse headed for the sound but before he could break through the trees, Haley's horse nosed its way out first.

Jesse stared at the riderless horse. Something cold and tight squeezed in his chest. Haley hadn't made it this far. Somewhere, somehow, she'd been thrown. He wanted to think she'd dismounted to get a drink of water, but his gut told him otherwise. She would have kept on going for as long as she could. All she wanted was to get to town and find Stoner. Nothing would have stopped her from that.

He tried to convince himself she'd been rescued by the men undoubtedly following them, but he knew better. Even if they had a carriage for her to ride in, they would have taken her horse with them. So she'd been thrown and was out there now wandering around alone. Unless she'd been injured.

The pressure in his chest increased. He told himself his concern was because he needed Haley healthy so he could use her to bargain with Stoner. He didn't really care about her. Except he knew he did care, at least a little. Despite everything, he didn't want her injured…or worse.

He got down from his horse and began to study the ground. The trail he'd been following was still clear and fresh. She'd been on her horse when the animal had come this way earlier. He could tell by the depth of the hoofprint in the soft ground. The gelding had been carrying a rider. So all he had to do was continue to follow the trail. Eventually he would find Haley.

At least that was what he told himself as he swung back in the saddle and headed west. Every few minutes he glanced up at the darkening sky. Tonight the temperature would again drop below freezing. Without a fire, Haley would die. If the wolves and bears didn't get her first. If she didn't fall and break something, or if she hadn't already.

He urged his horse on faster, studying the ground with an intensity that made his head throb. It was, he told himself, because he needed his prisoner alive and well, and for no other reason at all.

Chapter Six

Haley clung to the side of a tree. The world had finally stopped spinning. She wasn't sure how long she'd been unconscious, or if she really had blacked out at all. She couldn't think straight. If the pain of being on a horse was difficult, the pain of falling twice in two days was many times worse. Knowing she had only herself to blame for her present circumstances didn't make them any easier to bear.

She drew in a deep breath. The action didn't hurt as much as it had just a few minutes ago. She leaned heavily against the rough, scratchy bark because it was too much effort to stand on her own. She'd been walking for what felt like hours. Stumbling really, calling for her horse, for Jesse, for Lucas. At this point she would be happy to see savage Indians. It was cold and getting dark. Soon the sun would set completely. Then what was she going to do? She didn't have any food, or the means to start a fire. How was she going to survive?

The questions made her head ache more. Weariness settled on her like a damp cloak, sucking out the last of her reserves. She sank to her knees and fought against the urge to cry. She would not give in to tears, she told herself. She was strong and tough and she would make it through this.

"Jesse," she called out, knowing in her heart that he

was her only hope. "Jesse, where are you? I'm over here. Jesse?"

Had he given up? Was he even bothering to look for her? Maybe he'd decided she was too much trouble and that he would find another way to get what he wanted. Maybe—

"Stop it!" she said aloud. "You're trying to scare yourself. Just stop it! Of course he's looking for me. He needs me to bargain with Lucas. And if nothing else, Jesse isn't the kind of man who would leave me out here alone."

An odd opinion to have about her kidnapper, but she believed it and that belief comforted her.

She shifted on her knees, trying to find a less painful position. The ground was chilly and the cold seeped in through her skirt and petticoats. A shiver rippled through her. It was going to get worse, she knew. There were many poor in Chicago and she'd seen what happened to them when they slept outside in the winter. The lucky ones only lost fingers and toes. Those not so lucky died.

Something rustled in the brush to her left. She looked toward the sound. "Jesse?"

There was a soft yipping in reply. An animal!

"Oh, God." She leapt to her feet and stood with her back to the tree. "Get out of here," she screamed. "Shoo, run away. Leave me alone!"

The creature rustled again. Haley glanced around and saw a good-sized rock a few feet away. She picked it up and heaved it into the bushes. The animal yipped again, then the rustling stopped.

"It's gone," she told herself, as she wrapped her arms around her chest. "It's gone and I'm fine."

She was fine. She was going to be fine. What was the alternative?

Slowly, even as it got darker and colder, some of the fear left her. Perhaps it was because she would rather be afraid out here than afraid in the city. To die in the wilderness wasn't as terrifying as being attacked in the street, or burned alive in a dark, windowless room.

So she huddled by her tree and occasionally called out Jesse's name. The pain in her head subsided to a manageable throbbing. He would come for her, she told herself again and again. He wouldn't leave her out here.

But as time passed, she grew less certain. And the realization that she was going to die out here, all alone, made the tears come. She crouched with her back up against the tree, brushing the drops away as they fell. The cold crept up her skirt and made her shiver. Her teeth chattered. She tried to think about being warm, about a blazing fire, but that only made her discomfort worse.

She shouldn't have run away. She should have stayed put and found another way to—

A gunshot cut through the night. Haley jumped and pressed her hand over her mouth to hold in a scream, not knowing what the sound meant. Had the men who must surely be looking for them found Jesse? Was he dead? Maybe it was Indians, or outlaws or someone frightening and she would be better off staying quietly here by the tree. Maybe she should—

Another sound drifted to her on the chilly breeze of the night. The faint whisper of her name. And then she knew. Jesse had fired his gun to let her know where he was. He was looking for her and couldn't find her, so he wanted her to find him.

She took off in the direction of the shot and his voice. She screamed for him. "Jesse! Jesse, I'm over here."

He called back an answer. She raced through the trees and the brush, ignoring the branches that caught at her clothes and scratched her face and hands.

She stumbled over a tree root, fell to her knees, then righted herself and kept running. Her chest ached from lack of air, her legs were heavy, but she pushed on.

"Haley? Are you all right?"

"Yes," she called back and broke through a few waist-high bushes. Jesse stood in a clearing, the two horses behind him. In the darkness, she couldn't make out his features, but she recognized the size and strength of him.

"Jesse."

He turned toward her. "Dammit, Haley, what were you thinking? You could have been killed."

She recognized his anger as concern and once again she fought the tears. "I'm fine," she murmured, barely able to form the words.

He strode over to her, put the rifle on the ground and grabbed her forearms. "Are you hurt? What happened?"

Before she could answer, he pulled her roughly against him.

She went willingly because she had no thought to protest. He was warm and she felt so very cold. Strong arms came around her and despite his strength, his embrace quickly gentled. She leaned against him, absorbing his heat. He rubbed her back.

"Running off was damn stupid," he said. "You could have died."

"I know." She buried her face in his shoulder. "But I had to try."

"Don't do it again."

"I won't." She could smell the pleasant scent of his body. As she snuggled closer, she tried to remember if she'd ever been this near a man. She didn't think she had, and felt a pang of loss. It felt nice to be hugged. Especially by Jesse.

"You could have died."

She raised her head and found him staring at her. In the darkness, she could barely make out his eyes boring into hers. She thought she read concern there, but she wasn't sure.

His mouth twisted. "We'd better get camp set up and a fire started." He shifted until his arm was around her, then he led her toward the horses. "Did you fall off the saddle? Are you hurt?"

"No. My horse jumped over a stream and I couldn't stay on. When I hit the ground, everything went black. I've been wandering around for a while, waiting for you to find me."

He grabbed the coat draped over her saddle and wrapped it around her. "Sit down," he said, pointing to a fallen tree. "I'll get the fire started, then we'll eat."

As he worked, she huddled inside the sheepskin coat. Gradually the shivers faded. By the time he got the coffee brewing, she was nearly thawed, although her feet felt as if they would be frozen forever.

"Did I get close to town?" she asked as he opened a can of beans. "I know I was heading west. At least I thought I was."

He dumped the beans onto two tin plates and set them close to the fire. The light illuminated his features and she saw the corner of his mouth turn up in a smile. "You were heading due west, but Whitehorn is a little north of here. If you'd kept in that direction for a while you would have eventually run into an outpost."

Well, that was something. At least she wasn't completely lost. "How far is the outpost?"

"About fifty miles."

The hint of a smile turned into a grin. She opened her mouth, then snapped it shut. "Fifty miles? I wouldn't have made it."

"I know." He looked very pleased with himself.

"You think you can tell me what to do just because you're the only one who knows where we are and where we're going."

"Don't you forget it, either," he said.

Without wanting to, she smiled in return. She'd made her escape, which at least salvaged her pride, and now she was safely back in camp. Perhaps it was better this way. She believed that Jesse wouldn't hurt her, so for now she could be patient. Eventually she would get to Whitehorn and be with Lucas.

The thought of her fiancé brought a familiar gladness to

her heart. How lucky she was. Lucas Stoner was everything a woman could want in a husband. Tall, kind, gentle, loving. She continued to recite the familiar list, and as always the words brought her a measure of comfort. But the thought of marrying Lucas also made her feel slightly wistful, and for the life of her, she wasn't sure why.

Haley kept her word and didn't try to run away again. Probably she hurt too much, Jesse thought as he reined in his gelding and waited for her to catch up. It was their third day on the trail and she was barely keeping pace with him.

As her horse tramped along next to his, Jesse glanced over at her. She'd given up trying to keep her hair in a tidy bun at the base of her neck. Instead, she wore it in a long braid that hung down her back. The sun had left freckles on her nose and cheekbones and fatigue had left shadows under her eyes. None of the scratches she'd gotten wandering in the forest had become infected although a few red marks still marred her otherwise smooth skin.

She looked at him and rubbed her left cheek. "Do I have dirt on my face?"

He shook his head. "You look tired."

"I am. The ground is hard and I'm not used to sleeping outside." She glanced at the sky, then at the trees around them. "Although I think I could get to like it around here. Maybe a little bit more if I could actually sleep under a roof."

"Soon," he promised and wondered if he was telling the truth. "Go on with your story."

She thought for a moment, then nodded. "As I was saying, this poor woman was about to give birth to what later turned out to be twins and her husband kept swaying on his feet. The doctor told him to leave, but he'd promised her to be with her through the birthing. It was her first time and she was so afraid. Anyway, sure enough, his eyes rolled back in his head and he dropped to the floor like a stone. The whole house shook."

She chuckled at the memory. "He was a large man, too. Tough. Worked in the railroad yard. The doctor was so surprised, he went over to the man to see if he was all right. Which left me to deal with the mother. Of course the twins decided they were ready to be born, so there I was, juggling slippery babies and one excited mother while the father was out cold through the whole thing."

"Was he all right?"

"Sure. He had a bump on the back of his head, but otherwise he was fine. And very proud. Two beautiful baby boys had come into the world." She grinned. "I told the mother that next time she should tell her husband to stay outside the room, where he belonged."

Jesse urged his horse forward and hers followed suit. "Didn't that frighten you?"

"What?"

"Delivering babies by yourself?"

"The first time it did. But I've done it many times since. When the doctor is busy with something else, I take care of whatever comes up. My nursing is good experience. I've heard there aren't a lot of doctors around here, and it can be a long trip to town. I'll be helpful to Lucas."

Jesse didn't want to think about her with Stoner because he didn't want to think of any woman cursed with that fate. Especially not Haley. She was bright and funny, and she deserved more. She had spirit and an inner strength he respected.

"Your face is all scrunched up," she said. "What are you thinking?"

"That you're very different from my wife."

"Your wife?" Haley's eyes widened. "You're married?"

He shook his head. "I'm a widower. Claire died about four years ago. She was…" His voice trailed off. For the first time since he'd lost her, he found himself willing to talk about her. Maybe it was because he knew he wasn't going to be with Haley very long. Or maybe it was because

Haley was in a similar situation and he wanted to warn her of the pitfalls.

"Claire was the youngest daughter of my mother's second cousin. She was from the South—a small town near Atlanta, Georgia. She wanted to get married and I needed a wife, so our family arranged the match."

Haley tilted her head as she studied him. "So you had a mail-order bride, too."

"Yes." He shrugged.

"What happened?"

A simple enough question. What had happened? "We weren't well suited to each other and she wasn't prepared for the life here."

Not suited didn't begin to tell the truth. Claire had been as delicate and fragile as a soap bubble. All pale skin and slender build, she'd never worked a day before in her life. The reality of ranch life had frightened her and she'd spent much of her time wandering through the rooms of the house, as if looking for a part of herself.

"She didn't like Montana?" Haley asked.

"Not really. She thought it was too cold and the ranch was too isolated."

He wasn't willing to say more, or tell Haley how his wife had actually died. He didn't want to think about that day, or any of the days before. He didn't want to picture Claire in his mind. She always wore white and that was how he remembered her. A slender, wisp of a woman in a pale gown, as if she'd already turned into a ghost.

"You must miss her very much."

He had regrets but little else. "No, I don't miss her at all. That's the tragedy of Claire's death. Once she was gone, I rarely thought of her." He glanced at the sky. "We're going to be stopping early today."

"Really?" She sighed. "I'm glad. I'm still sore from riding. I just want to take a nice walk around and stretch."

She was still talking as she slid off her horse. Jesse didn't want to do it, but he had no choice. She'd already proved she was more than capable of running off.

While she was occupied with her horse, he walked up behind her. In one quick movement, he captured her wrists and quickly secured them.

"What do you think you're doing?" she demanded, tugging at the bindings. "You're tying me up. You can't do that. I don't understand. You haven't tied me up in a couple of days. I'm not going to run away. Jesse, why are you doing this?"

He swept her into his arms and set her on the ground. She started kicking, but he quickly subdued her, then tied her ankles.

Green eyes spit fire. "Jesse Kincaid, I demand an explanation. I have obeyed your every order."

"You ran away," he reminded her, his voice calm. "Twice."

"I know, but—"

Her words were silenced by the bandanna he slipped into her mouth. He secured the ends behind her head. She worked at the material, trying to spit it out, but it didn't budge. Shrieks of outrage cut through the afternoon, but they weren't as loud as her screaming and Jesse knew it was the best he could do.

"I have to go talk to a friend of mine," he said, crouching in front of her, careful to stay out of reach of her bound but kicking feet. "I won't be gone long, but I need to make sure you'll be here when I get back." He motioned to the ties at her wrists and ankles. "I'm really sorry, Haley."

Muffled sounds exploded from her. Obviously she wasn't impressed by his apology. He stood up.

"You'll be safe enough here. I'll be back before sundown."

She shrieked. This time he thought he made out what she was saying. *What if you don't come back?*

She had a point. Bound and gagged, she was as vulner-

able as a newborn. It was a risk they were both going to
have to take.

"I'll be back," he promised. "You'll see."

He secured her horse to a tree, then got on his mount
and headed out. Her muffled screams of protest faded
quickly.

Less than an hour later, he'd reached the meeting place.
A few minutes after that Bart Baxter rode up on his black
gelding.

Bart grinned. "I don't have to ask if you got her," he
said. "Everyone's talking about it. You made a real impression on a couple from back east. They've been talking
up a storm about how you held up the stage and attacked
poor innocent passengers."

Jesse grimaced. "The man pulled a gun on me."

"I saw it, Jesse. It wasn't much of a gun."

"Agreed, but he was less than a couple feet from me.
Even a fool like that wouldn't have missed."

"Did you have to go and break his wrist?"

"I just kicked him. How was I to know he was delicate
as an eggshell?"

Bart's grin broadened. "To hear him tell it, he wrestled
you to the ground like a bear, but ultimately you got the
better of him." He'd raised his voice slightly so it sounded
cultured and easternlike.

"Great," Jesse muttered and pulled his hat lower over
his forehead. "Lindsay got men out looking for me?"

"Some. I asked around and so far they haven't found
your trail."

"A blind man could see it," Jesse said, wondering how
on earth they'd missed the very obvious clues he'd left. He
looked at his friend. "Anything from Stoner?"

Bart shook his head. "Nothing. I got him word that I
was the one he should come see and I was real obvious
when I was in town today, but he didn't talk to me. You
want me to go to him directly?"

"No. You're in this too deep already. I don't want to

give Lindsay an excuse to arrest you. So far there's just a rumor that you're involved.'' He frowned. ''I wish you'd change your mind about helping me. I don't want anything to happen to you. Christine would kill me.''

''My wife understands and wants to help, too. Don't worry. Lindsay isn't going to do anything to me. You're the one in danger here.''

Maybe, Jesse thought. But so far the plan wasn't working. Stoner was supposed to be frantic over the loss of his bride and willing to talk. Or at least pretend he was.

''Stoner hasn't said anything about Haley?'' he asked.

''Not that I heard.''

''You think he's going to want her back?''

Bart grimaced. ''He paid for the ticket. You can bet he's going to want to get his money's worth. He'll want her. I think he's trying to wait you out. He's probably hoping you'll get nervous and make a mistake.''

Maybe he already had, Jesse thought grimly. Maybe the kidnapping hadn't been a good idea, although it was too late to change that now.

Bart shifted in his saddle. ''How's it going? Is she giving you a lot of trouble?''

''Not if you don't count her trying to escape twice in two days.''

''But you caught her.''

''Both times.''

''Where is she now?''

Jesse flinched. ''I left her tied up by her horse. Gagged her, too.''

Bart whistled softly. ''You're gonna have a hell of a reception when you get back.''

''Yeah.'' If he knew Haley, she would spend the entire night telling him exactly what she thought of him. No doubt she'd want to take after him with the frying pan. The thought made him smile. Then he remembered her future and the smile faded.

''She doesn't know what she's getting into,'' he told his

friend. "With Stoner. She's got some strange idea that he's a virtuous man."

Bart shrugged. "She's going to be surprised by her bridegroom then," he said, dismissing Haley's fate. He unfastened a sack from his saddle and handed it to Jesse. "Here's some food for you. Christine is convinced you're going to starve to death while out in the forest."

Jesse took the cloth bag. "You could remind her I survived two years on the trail without her to feed me. Besides, Haley can cook."

"Christine doesn't put much store in city women." Bart shifted on his saddle. "I'll head back to town tomorrow or the next day, then I'll come find you. Same place in three days?"

"Sure." Jesse didn't want to be so quick to leave Haley to Stoner, but he didn't have a choice. He was determined to clear his family name, at any cost. She'd come out west to marry Stoner of her own will. She wasn't his business or his problem.

"How are the cattle doing?" he asked.

"We're starting roundup soon. I'll be branding your cattle along with mine."

"Make sure you use the right brand."

Bart grinned. "I'll keep an eye on my boys, although they're a loyal crew and they just might let one or two slip."

"I owe you that at least," Jesse said seriously. "I appreciate you taking in my herd. When this problem with Stoner is solved, you and I are going to settle up."

Bart brushed off the offer with a wave. "You and your father looked out for me when I was a greenhorn, Jesse, and I haven't forgotten that."

"We'll talk later," Jesse said and glanced up at the sky. The sun was starting to set. "I have to get back and so do you."

They shook hands and said their goodbyes. Jesse kicked

his horse into a fast trot and headed back the way he'd come. He didn't want to leave Haley alone any longer than he had to—even though his friend was right and he was going to get a hell of a reception when he returned.

Chapter Seven

Haley was angry enough to wish she could tie Jesse Kincaid to a railroad track and watch a train run him over. She banged the spoon against the side of the pot and refused to be distracted by the enticing smells coming from dinner. The fact that he'd returned as he'd promised, and had brought something delicious for them to eat was all well and good, but it didn't make up for what he'd done to her.

"How long you going to stay mad?" he asked.

When she turned to glare at him, he shifted his weight from foot to foot. Good. She hoped she made him uneasy and uncomfortable and that he felt guilty about what he'd done.

"For a lot longer than this," she told him curtly. "How could you do that to me?"

"We've been over this, Haley. I didn't have a choice."

"Of course you did. You could have just left me behind. I told you I wouldn't run away."

He shrugged. "I had to be sure you'd still be here when I got back."

"What if some wild animal had found me? I would have been defenseless. Or what if something had happened to you? I would have been trapped out here to slowly freeze to death. Or what if Indians or renegades had found me?"

"Don't you think you're taking this too much to heart?"

She rose to her full height and planted her hands on her hips. "Let's tie you up for the afternoon and leave you and we'll see how much you take the situation to heart."

"I wasn't going to let anything happen to you."

She exhaled in frustration. "You weren't here to make sure it *didn't* happen."

"I'm not going to apologize for what I did. You're my prisoner. I know you didn't like being tied up, but it's over now. Is the stew ready?"

She glared at him. "You're not going to distract me, Jesse. You had no right to leave me like that and you know it."

She watched his face. A muscle tightened in his jaw, but other than that, there was no hint as to what he was thinking.

"I know these woods," he said at last. "You were safe. I wouldn't have left you otherwise."

She wanted to believe him. For a while Jesse had actually seemed concerned about her welfare, but then he'd tied her up and abandoned her. Dying in the wilderness was one thing, but being left bound like an animal was quite another.

"I didn't know I was safe." Her words were supposed to come out angry and defiant, but instead they sounded frightened and small. "I didn't even know if you were coming back."

He took a step toward her, then paused. The sun had nearly set, so the only real light came from the fire. With the blackness of the forest behind him, he seemed to fade into the shadows, a large, potentially dangerous man of whom she should have been terrified. But she wasn't. Jesse was all that stood between her and the unknown lurking beyond the edges of the camp.

"I'm sorry," he said at last, surprising her and possibly himself with the sentiment.

She dropped her hands to her sides and shrugged. "I just got scared and there was nothing I could do."

"I understand. You're pretty tough most of the time, but being left like that would frighten anyone."

"I know you didn't want me running away, but I would have given you my word. When I ran off yesterday, I hadn't promised."

"I know."

"I don't lie."

His dark eyes searched her gaze. She didn't look away. He nodded. "I know that, too."

"Promise me you won't leave me tied up again."

"I don't know if I can."

She stomped her foot. "Jesse, I won't put up with that. I swear I'll fight you and—" She pressed her lips together, trying to figure out exactly what she would be doing. "Well, I'll think of something."

He grinned. "I'm sure you will."

For the second time, his smile took her breath away. Haley found herself wanting to see him smile again and again. She wanted to hear him laugh, and laugh with him. The desire confused her. Jesse wasn't anything to her. She was engaged to another man, practically married. She shouldn't be noticing anything about Jesse. And yet...

She gave him a quick smile in return and went back to the simmering stew. It was just the circumstances, she told herself. The fact that they'd been traveling together. It led to a familiarity that was unusual. She should be grateful he was a relatively pleasant traveling companion. If he'd been a cruel man, the past few days would have been unbearable. When she was safely with Lucas, she would forget about this time and Jesse's smiles. She would forget the sound of his voice and how he was handsome, in a rugged sort of way. Lucas would—

She nearly dropped the spoon. How could she have forgotten?

"Did you have word from Mr. Stoner?" she asked.

Jesse had moved close to the fire and was in the process of pouring himself a cup of coffee. "I didn't go into town,

Haley. I met someone a couple miles from here. So no, I didn't see Stoner or talk to him.''

"But he's worried about me, isn't he? He's going to do what you want so you'll return me? Isn't he? I am his fiancée and I know that's important to him. It would be important to any man.''

She realized she was nervous and talking about nothing so she forced herself to be quiet. Jesse took a sip of coffee.

"Stoner knows you're out here with me," he said slowly, as if choosing his words with care. "He was ready to give me what I wanted, but I changed the terms of the deal.''

She stood up and stared at him. "What?''

Jesse took another sip of coffee. "I demanded a ransom. A hundred dollars.''

"A hundred dollars," she whispered, echoing his words. "It's too much money. Who has that much money?''

"Lucas Stoner, for one," Jesse said grimly. "It'll take him a couple of days to get it, so I've given him that extra time. Don't worry, Haley. He'll come through.''

She glanced at him. "I thought you only wanted information.''

"I changed my mind.''

Haley's head spun. A hundred dollars. She couldn't imagine that much money existing in the world. It had to, of course, but were people really that rich?

"Do you think he'll pay?" she asked.

He nodded. "Stoner is definitely going to pay.''

She should have been comforted by the words, but she had the feeling they were talking about different things. A voice deep inside whispered that something wasn't right, but she couldn't figure out what. Maybe Jesse really needed the money. If he'd lost his family and his ranch, he might be in financial trouble. She would offer to help, but she didn't have anything of her own. Everything that was important to her in the world was in a trunk in the stage. Hopefully someone remembered to take her things to Whitehorn. Once there, Lucas would look after them. At least he would if he thought about it. Men didn't always remember the details.

She stirred the stew one last time, then poured it onto their plates. She wanted to question Jesse further, but didn't think he would give her any more answers. In the end, she wasn't sure it even mattered. As long as she got to Whitehorn and married Lucas, everything would be fine.

Daisy picked up two bars of soap and put them in her basket. She'd put off shopping as long as she could, but eventually she'd had to come to the mercantile. Even though it was the middle of the afternoon and there weren't many people in the store, she felt as if the entire world was staring at her.

Telling herself to keep her chin high didn't help much, especially when women who had once been her friends now looked the other way when they saw her. She knew what they were saying, what *she* would say if she were in their position. Under the circumstances, she couldn't even blame them. Whitehorn was a thriving community with all the social rules that went with any town. Some of the rules were more relaxed than in actual cities, but boundaries could only be stretched so far. Then they snapped back in place. She could feel the pressure of those bands on her back. Soon they would release and she would be left standing on the outside, looking in. If she wasn't already.

But she had her pride, if nothing else, she told herself. And her money was just as good as everyone else's, so she got pleasant service from the clerk at the counter.

She walked to the end of the aisle. She'd already bought flour and sugar. Maybe some more tea, she thought, moving down to the rows of tins. Something exotic would lift her spirits. Recently, life had taught her to take simple pleasures where she could find them.

At the far end of the mercantile, by the bolts of fabric, women gathered around the newly arrived pattern books.

A few months ago Daisy would have joined them. She would have discussed the latest styles in bonnets and skirts, fingered lacy trims and fretted over buttons. Now, although she longed to hear their familiar conversations, she didn't dare intrude. A few of the ladies would be polite and speak to her. One or two would casually turn away as if they hadn't seen her, but some would deliberately cut her. Most days that wouldn't bother her, but today, for some reason, she wasn't feeling especially strong. So she didn't risk joining them. Instead she started for the counter.

As she approached the clerk, the front door opened. The small bell suspended from the ceiling tinkled. Daisy turned to look at the new customer and her heart rose into her throat. Dr. Leland Prescott swept into the store with the easy confidence of a man comfortable with himself and his position in the world.

Her first thought was to run, but she had nowhere to go. She clutched her basket tighter, knowing it was just a matter of time until his gaze found and settled on her. She told herself she would smile, nod and then pretend he wasn't there. She told herself that her nerves came from shame and nothing else. They had to. They couldn't mean what she feared they meant. Not after all this time.

She was nearly at the counter when he noticed her. His very handsome face broke into a smile. He swept off his hat and nodded. ''Mrs. Newcastle, what a pleasant surprise.''

''Dr. Prescott.''

His hair was the color of gold, his eyes an intriguing combination of colors that would usually be called hazel. He was tall, broad and at least two years younger than she was. A well-educated man who had settled in Whitehorn because he'd always wanted to live in open spaces. At least that was what he told her about himself. He was the local doctor, known for his skill and his compassion. There were rumors that he'd lost a wife in childbirth many years before. Single women or married women with single daughters flocked around him. He was kind, charming and, with the exception of Jesse Kincaid, by far the best catch for fifty miles.

"You're looking particularly lovely today," Leland Prescott said, never taking his gaze from her face.

Daisy knew for a fact that her beige dress did not flatter her complexion. She hadn't been sleeping well and there were dark circles under her eyes. She was willing to admit her hair probably looked nice because she'd been blessed with thick curls that adapted easily to several styles, but she suspected it wouldn't matter what her hair looked like, or possibly if she even had hair at all. For reasons she neither understood nor could explain, Leland was interested in her.

"Thank you, Dr. Prescott."

"You're welcome. Are you finished your shopping or may I accompany you through the store? I'd be happy to carry your basket."

He made a move as if to take it from her, but she clutched it tightly to her chest. "I was about to leave."

His generous mouth straightened with obvious disappointment. "Had I known you were here, I would have arrived sooner so I could have spent more time with you."

"I—" She faltered, not sure what to say to him. Instead of searching longer, she glanced at the clerk. "Billy, have they loaded the flour into my buggy?"

The clerk nodded. "Yes, ma'am. And the sugar, too. Did you want me to take out a sack of coffee?"

Even though she didn't need it, she nodded, simply to get the boy out of earshot.

"I haven't seen much of you lately," Leland said. "You've been keeping busy?"

The flush of embarrassment was as quick as it was intense. Her cheeks felt as if they were on fire. How could he ask that? He had to know what she was doing with Stoner. Everyone knew.

"Dr. Prescott, I—"

He took a step closer until they were only a few inches apart. Before she could stop him, he'd taken the basket from her hands and set it on the counter.

"I've been a patient man, Daisy," he said quietly. "I know that you loved Michael Kincaid, and while he was alive I respected that. After his death, I gave you time to mourn. It's been more than six months. I want to know if you're ready to let him go."

She squeezed her eyes shut. She could feel the interested stares from the women in the back of the store and she didn't want to look at them. Yes, she and Leland would be the subject of many speculative conversations this night.

She knew some women went their entire lives without being blessed by love. She'd been more fortunate than most. Her late husband had wooed and won her when they were both just eighteen. After his premature death, she'd thought she would always be alone. Then she'd met Michael Kincaid. Michael had also loved and lost, and together they'd comforted each other. While her feelings had grown stronger, his had not. He'd been willing to visit her bed, but he hadn't wanted to marry again. She'd tried to understand and the town of Whitehorn had turned a blind eye.

Then Leland had moved here. He'd taken to Daisy right away. His gentle courtship had confused her. Her heart was supposed to belong to Michael and yet she'd been tempted by what Leland offered. Including the propriety of marriage. Then Michael had been murdered. Leland had been a friend and she'd allowed him into her life, perhaps into her heart. Her feelings had changed toward him, but before she could figure out what that meant, she'd decided to help Jesse in his quest to clear the family name. She'd deliberately set out to seduce Lucas Stoner.

Now she was little more than a whore. If Leland hadn't figured that out yet, he soon would. And then he wouldn't want her anymore.

She wanted to curl up in a ball and hide forever. She

wanted to tell Leland what she was doing and why, and ask him to understand, to forgive and to wait. How unlikely, she thought. Men did not understand when women they cared about took other men into their beds. A man like Leland had his choice of women. He'd been more than generous when he'd claimed to understand her relationship with Michael, but he was too good and too noble to forgive a second and much larger transgression.

"I am still tied to Michael in ways I can't explain," she said.

He leaned closer. She could smell the faint fragrance of his body and it made her yearn for him. "Daisy, I have feelings for you, but I won't wait forever."

She looked at the floor. "I know. I don't want you to wait. I want you to—"

The bell above the door chimed again. She glanced up and froze as Stoner walked into the mercantile. He spotted her at once and gave her that lazy, proprietary smile.

"Hello, Daisy," he said, moving around Leland and pressing a kiss to her cheek. "I thought I'd seen you come in here. Prescott." He nodded at the other man.

She felt Leland's gaze on her, felt his unasked questions, but there was little she could say.

Billy walked in from the back. "Everything's loaded, Mrs. Newcastle," the boy said and took her basket. "I'll add this to your account."

"No," Lucas said, loud enough to be heard by everyone in the store. "Put it on mine."

The blush returned, hotter and brighter than before. Daisy couldn't think of a single thing to say. Protesting would only make it worse.

Billy frowned in confusion. "Are you sure, Mr. Stoner?"

"Very sure. It's the least I can do, Daisy. Don't you agree?"

She didn't answer, couldn't answer. The tightness in her throat would not allow her to speak. Instead she nodded once, then keeping her chin high, she headed for the door.

Someone moved past her. She glanced to her left and saw Leland there, carefully holding open the door. Questions darkened his eyes. Questions and something that looked like disappointment. Behind her, in the far corner of the store, she heard the whispered conversations. Only one word carried to her.

Whore.

She raised her chin a little higher and stiffened her spine. She might be a whore, but she still had her pride. In the end, that and the knowledge she was doing all she could to see Stoner hang were going to have to be enough.

"The snow piles up higher than the doorways sometimes," Haley said. "People freeze to death. Lots of places burn down because people don't have heat so they start fires in their rooms."

Jesse reined his horse in to let her catch up. "I didn't know it got that cold in Chicago."

She looked at him and raised her eyebrows. "I would bet my winters are as cold as yours. And as hard. Just because it's the city doesn't mean it's any easier."

"I thought it would be." He shrugged. "I've never lived in the city."

"I don't think you'd like it." She studied him. "I can't picture you working in a factory or driving a carriage in town. I think you're much happier out here."

"You're right." He wondered if he was that easy to figure out or if Haley had put some thought into her comment. They'd been talking enough that she could know him.

Over the past three days, they'd settled into a routine. They rode through the wilderness, stopping every couple of hours to water the horses and stretch. Every morning Haley promised not to run away and he promised not to tie her up. Sometimes they went hours without talking, but most of the time they discussed their different worlds, their lives and their pasts. The only subject they avoided was the future. Jesse knew she didn't want to hear about his plans

to bring Stoner to justice and he didn't want her going on
about how wonderful the man was.

Haley raised her face to the sun. "I'm getting freckles,
aren't I?"

He looked at her pretty face and nodded. "On your nose
and cheeks."

She sighed. "I always did freckle easily and I was never
very good about wearing a bonnet. I don't suppose it matters as much out here, though." Then she began telling him
another amusing story from her work with Dr. Redding.

She was nothing like Claire. He was constantly amazed
at the differences between the two women. Claire had been
afraid of everything, unused to hard work and timid about
telling him what she wanted. Haley seemed to revel in each
new experience. She did more than her share when they set
up camp and his ears were still smarting from the verbal
lashing she'd given him when he'd left her tied up so he
could go talk to Bart. He hadn't thought he could enjoy a
woman's company for any length of time, but he was enjoying hers. He liked her. If only he hadn't lied to her.

Jesse glanced around to check where they were, then
turned them a little east. He hadn't planned on lying, but
when she'd asked him if Stoner had been concerned about
her, he hadn't felt he had a choice. How was he supposed
to tell her that the man she considered perfect in every way
had done little or nothing to get her back? He knew Stoner
was playing a waiting game, but Haley wouldn't believe
that. For reasons he didn't understand, Jesse didn't want
her hurt more than was necessary.

So he'd invented a lie, telling her he'd asked for a ransom. Eventually she would find out the truth, but until then
she could continue to believe Stoner was the handsome
hero she longed for.

Haley drew in a deep breath. "I love how it smells out
here."

"You keep saying that. It's not so special. Have you ever
smelled a barn?"

She looked at him and grinned. "Have you ever smelled an open sewer in the summer? No, Jesse, you're going to have to take my word on this one. Montana smells much better than Chicago."

"If you say so."

He reined in his mount and swung to the ground. Once there, he broke off a couple of branches and secured a small strip of cloth on a bent twig.

"Are there really men after us?" Haley asked.

"Yeah. Lindsay—he's the sheriff—has a half dozen or so looking for us." Although in Jesse's opinion they were doing a damn poor job of tracking them. He couldn't figure out if Lindsay's men were incompetent or they'd been told not to look too hard. Despite being bought and paid for by Stoner, it was possible Lindsay was having an attack of conscience.

He glanced up at the sky. It was nearly time. "We're going to be stopping soon," he said. "There's a good place to make camp up ahead."

She, too, looked at the sky, then at him. He suspected she knew they were stopping early but didn't say anything about it. "Was your ranch near here?" she asked instead.

Jesse mounted his horse and turned it due east. "About fifteen miles north of here."

"Was it big?"

"Yes. We had nearly three thousand cattle, plus the two thousand I was bringing north from Texas. My father wanted to have the largest ranch in Montana."

"Where are your cattle now?" she asked.

"Most of them are scattered around on different ranches. They'll be safe there. When I get all this settled, I can round them up and begin rebuilding the herd. A friend of mine has my Texas cattle at his place."

"So you'll go back to the ranch?"

"It's my home."

"Is there anything left?"

He shrugged. "The barns were untouched. About half

the house burned down, but there are a few walls and a bit of roof. It could be rebuilt. Everything inside is gone. Either stolen or burned or destroyed.''

She brushed a strand of hair off her face and met his gaze. ''At least you have a home that you can rebuild. I've never had that. Oh, I've rented rooms and I suppose in a way they were mine, but it's not the same. You belong somewhere, Jesse. You have a past and you're going to have a future.''

He'd been bemoaning his fate, but she reminded him that he did still have something worth keeping. ''You're right.''

''You also have the brooch that belonged to your mother. Did the renegades leave that behind?''

''No. The men who killed my family stole it. One of them gave it to a saloon girl in town and a friend of mine saw her wearing it.'' He remembered his shock when Daisy had sent him the note telling him where he could find the family treasure. The girl had been willing to part with it—for a price.

''So you know who one of the men is?'' she asked.

''Orin Stoner.''

Haley started visibly. ''What are you saying?''

''That Orin Stoner gave my mother's cameo pin to a saloon girl.''

''Is he Lucas's brother?''

''No, a cousin. There are three cousins. They've been hanging around town for a while now. About as long as the renegades.''

Haley bit her lower lip. ''I'm sure there's a reasonable explanation.''

''No doubt,'' Jesse agreed grimly, knowing exactly what it was. The cousins worked for Stoner, doing whatever he told them to do. Including murder. But knowing and proving weren't the same thing.

They came to another small stream. Jesse reined in his horse. ''We'll make camp here tonight.''

''But it's early,'' Haley said as she slid off her horse.

"I have to go meet someone."

She whirled around and faced him. "Oh, no. Jesse, you're not going to tie me up again. You promised."

He had just that morning. Right after she'd promised not to run away.

"Haley, I can't just leave you here."

"Why not? I'll be fine. I'll start the fire and supper. I know how. I've been helping and it's not that hard." She tucked her hands behind her back. Green eyes pleaded with him. "Jesse, you can't leave me tied up again. You can't."

She was right; he couldn't. Dammit all to hell. "I know I'm going to regret this." He unhooked his saddlebags and tossed them to her. "The matches are inside. You sure you can start the fire?"

She nodded vigorously. "I swear I can. You'll see. I'll even make biscuits. There's plenty of time."

"You won't run," he said, stating a fact rather than asking a question.

She smiled. "Where am I going to go? It's been more than five days and for all I know we're a hundred miles from town. I'll be right here. Just make sure you come back before sundown."

"I will," he said, and headed back into the forest.

He felt odd about leaving her. As he tried to figure out why, he realized it wasn't so much that he was worried about her running off, or even her safety. It was that he was going to miss her while he was gone.

Chapter Eight

Haley watched Jesse ride away. She stayed perfectly still, half expecting him to change his mind and come back to tie her up. Instead he disappeared down the narrow trail. Eventually the sound of his horse faded into the distance and all she heard was the call of the birds and the rustle of a breeze through the budding leaves.

She glanced around the small clearing that would be their home for the night. Tall trees surrounded the area. There were broken branches and logs on the ground. The sun was still high in the sky and she figured it was at least three hours until dark. Plenty of time for Jesse to meet his friend and return, and plenty of time for her to get them settled.

She knew he had flour in his supplies. She could make biscuits for dinner instead of just hardtack and dried beef. But the first thing she had to do was build a fire.

She cleared an area about a yard square, then began collecting wood. They'd been fortunate in that there hadn't been much rain recently and the wood was dry. When she had enough big pieces, she searched for kindling, then went to the saddlebags for matches.

She opened the flap and stuck her hand inside. An assortment of items filled the leather bag. As she grabbed the metal cylinder containing the matches, her fingers brushed against a hard knot of cotton. Without realizing it, she let go of the matches and pulled out the clump of cloth instead.

It was, she thought as she unwrapped the layers of fabric, Jesse's mother's brooch. She held her hand toward the sun and watched as the light glinted off the shiny gold. The piece of jewelry was stunning. Bright and beautiful—a gift any woman would treasure.

She sat on a log and studied the pin. What appealed to her wasn't the loveliness of the cameo as much its history. She stroked the woman's carved face and felt its warmth. What had Jesse's mother thought as she'd pinned this to her dress each morning? Had she been happy with the constant reminder of her husband's love? What had Claire said the first time Jesse showed her the brooch and told her that when she married him, she would carry on the tradition and wear it?

Something stirred inside her. A longing and a need to belong. She'd spent her entire life wanting to be a part of something larger than herself. Often she'd visited families with Dr. Redding. She'd seen how they gathered around one another when one lay sick or dying. She'd heard the laughter of unaware children, the words of sadness from the adults, the prayers for relief and healing. She'd seen husbands and wives embrace, parents in joyful tears over a turn for the better of a sick child. She understood that families existed, but she'd never been a part of one. It was a dream of hers, that she would have a husband and then children. That she would hold them and love them and in time create a family that was good and whole.

She might never have an heirloom like this herself, but there was always the possibility of starting a tradition of her own. In the meantime, it was nice to know Jesse had this from his mother. And from his wife, although Haley didn't really want to think about her. It made her feel odd inside. Sort of irritated, as if someone had been playing a piano very loud and off-key.

She pushed the thought away and found herself wonder-

ing about Lucas Stoner. Had his cousins really stolen the
cameo from Jesse's ranch? It couldn't be true. Lucas
wouldn't be a part of anything like that. She was sure of
it. There had to be another explanation. Yet how had the
other woman—the saloon girl, Jesse had called her—gotten
the pin?

There wasn't, she told herself, any way for her to figure
out these answers on her own. She was going to have to
wait and talk to Lucas in person.

Slowly she rewrapped the brooch in the cotton and
tucked it in the saddlebag. Then she removed the matches
and started the fire. When it was burning, she went through
their supplies and decided she could use the lone can of
peaches to make a cobbler in one of the tin plates. The
sides were nearly high enough and they had almost all the
right ingredients. It might not taste perfect, but after what
they'd been eating, it would be a pleasant change. Besides,
she would like to surprise Jesse when he got back.

She smiled, imagining the look of pleasure on his face.
The way his mouth would turn up in a smile and the crin-
kling at the corners of his eyes. Maybe she wouldn't tell
him right away. Maybe she would pretend they were back
to hardtack and beans and not let him know that—

She paused in the act of opening the tin. What was she
doing? Why was she concerned about what Jesse Kincaid
might or might not like for supper? The man had kidnapped
her. She should hate Jesse, or at least be plotting ways to
escape. Instead, here she was, planning on making him dessert.

Nothing made sense. Although Jesse had kidnapped her,
he had his reasons. She might not agree with them, but she
understood them. He'd gone out of his way to be kind to
her. He'd never deliberately frightened her or been cruel.
So maybe it wasn't so terrible that she didn't hate him.
Maybe it was all right for them to be friends.

She dumped the peaches into the pan, then spooned on

the flour mixture. She used the second plate to form a pro-
tective cover and slipped the container toward the fire.

Was Lucas worried about her? she wondered. Did he
think about her and hope she was all right? She wished
there was a way to let him know that she was fine and still
looking forward to meeting him. Yet even as she thought
the words, she realized that while she was anxious, a part
of her wasn't in so big a hurry anymore. He was, after all,
a stranger.

She'd tried to imagine what he would be like, even as a
small voice inside whispered instead she'd been imagining
what she *wanted* him to be like. Would he be kind and
noble and have all the virtues she'd assumed? Would he
care about her? She tried to tell herself that people could
grow to love each other. But Jesse had admitted he'd never
loved his wife.

Haley pulled her knees to her chest and wrapped her
arms around her legs. She didn't want that to be true for
her. She'd lived her entire life without love. She wanted
something different for her future. She wanted love and
affection and respect. She wanted to care about someone
and have that person care about her. Would Lucas Stoner?

Thinking about all of this was only making her nervous,
so she went about setting up the rest of camp. After filling
the pot, she started coffee, then looked through the remaining supplies and planned dinner. When the cobbler was
golden brown, she pulled it out of the heat and set it on a
rock to cool. All the while, she kept her eye on the sun's
descent and listened for the sound of Jesse's horse.

But no hoofbeats disturbed the silence of the forest. As
the sky darkened, she wondered where Jesse was and when
he would return to her. Concern grew into worry and she
didn't know why. So what if he didn't come back? She
would survive. She had supplies and a horse and eventually
someone would find her or she would make her way to
town. There was nothing to be frightened of.

Even so, she started at every sound and found herself

praying for Jesse's safe and swift return. To her surprise she realized her concern wasn't as much about her own safety as his.

Jesse paced by the large rock that marked their meeting place. A quick look at the sun reminded him that Bart wasn't late; he, Jesse, was early. He told himself it was because he was anxious to hear the news. He wanted to know that Stoner was ready to deal—that this nightmare was about to end. Yet some twisting in his gut made him admit there was more at stake here than just the fate of his family's name and his ranch.

He heard a sound and turned toward the trail leading south. Bart broke out into the clearing and waved a welcome. Jesse grinned at the large sack tied to the back of his friend's saddle.

"I see Christine is still afraid we're going to starve," he called as Bart approached.

Bart pushed back his hat and nodded. "You know how she gets, always worrying about everyone. She isn't feeling well enough to cook, but there are plenty of supplies. I figured either you or the woman can put something together."

"Her name is Haley."

Bart looked at him for a moment, then dismounted and handed him the bag. "Haley," he repeated. "All right. She can cook, can't she?"

Jesse nodded, wondering why he'd bothered pointing out her name. It wasn't important right now. But he hadn't been able to help himself.

Bart leaned against the rock and folded his arms over his chest. "You're not going to like this."

Jesse secured the bag to the back of his saddle and turned to face his friend. "You've heard from Stoner." It wasn't a question.

"Yeah. He rode out to the ranch yesterday and said to give you a message. He said that Haley's been out here with you too long. He's not interested in taking soiled property from the likes of a Kincaid, and if you want her so much you can keep her.''

Stunning cold swept through him. Stoner didn't want her? He swore under his breath. If Stoner didn't want her then there was no bargaining for her release. He'd kidnapped her for nothing.

He stiffened. ''Did he actually say he wasn't interested in soiled goods?''

''Those were his exact words. I was kind of surprised. After all, he should know that nothing was going to happen. That wasn't the point of this.''

Jesse swore again. ''That doesn't matter. Why the hell didn't I think of that? By keeping Haley out with me all those nights, I've compromised her reputation. I suppose everyone in town knows about this?''

''About the kidnapping?''

Jesse nodded.

His friend raised his eyebrows. ''You made sure everyone on the stage knew who you were and what you wanted. People talk, you know that. Of course it's been a source of gossip. What did you think would happen?''

''I didn't think. Not about what this would mean to Haley.'' When he'd concocted this plan, Stoner's bride was just some nameless, faceless woman and he'd never given her reputation a thought. But now, it was different. Now Haley would suffer the consequences. How was he going to tell her the truth? Not only did her beloved fiancé not want her, but she'd been branded a fallen woman.

''You kidnapped her to get to Stoner,'' Bart reminded him. ''Why does she matter now?''

He couldn't explain what had happened to change things, but something had. At first he wouldn't have cared one way or the other, but now Haley's feelings were important.

''You're going to let her go, aren't you?'' Bart asked. ''There's no point in keeping her.''

"I can't just drop her off in town. She'll be humiliated by Stoner's decision and rejected by the town."

"So send her back to wherever she came from. If you don't have the money for a ticket—"

Jesse cut him off with a shake of his head. This wasn't about money. He had plenty. Between the sale of some of his father's stock and a few heads of the Texas longhorns he'd brought north, he had cash. No, the problem was Haley didn't want to go back to Chicago. She'd hated it there, and she'd already admitted to wanting to make a new life for herself here.

"I can't send her back," he said.

He paced to his horse and back. Now what? The plan to force Stoner to talk had fallen apart. He was stuck with Haley and some of her problems were his responsibility. Dammit all, he didn't want to disappoint her and tell her that Stoner wasn't interested anymore. She'd built up such a perfect picture of the man that telling her the truth would break her heart.

"Jesse, you're worrying about the wrong thing," Bart told him. "That woman—Haley—is the least of your troubles. There's more to the message from Stoner."

"What is it?"

Bart drew in a deep breath. "He said to tell you if you still wanted to talk, he was willing to have a conversation. As long as you came into town and met him there."

"I see."

"It's a trap."

"I know." He was tempted, but not stupid. He wouldn't be meeting Stoner on his own territory. Not when Stoner had already killed his father, along with buying the sheriff. "I want him to pay, but I've been patient this long. I'm not going to risk it all now."

But in the end, he might be forced to meet Stoner on his terms. Maybe he could make it work, if he planned well enough. "I've got a lot to think about," he said. "Are Lindsay's men still out looking for us?"

Bart shrugged. "I haven't heard, but I would guess so. Stoner might not want the woman back, but he still wants you strung up. Kidnapping is a serious crime, even out here. So be careful."

"I will." He took off his hat and slapped it against his thigh. Now what?

Bart read his mind. "What are you going to do?"

"I don't know. I've got to come up with another plan for Stoner. In the meantime, I've got Haley to worry about. I can't send her back to Chicago and I can't take her to town."

"Bring her to the ranch."

Jesse stared at his friend. "Your ranch?"

"Sure. Christine's still sick a lot and I'm sure she would welcome the company. It's too quiet there for her. I worry some." His eyes darkened with concern. "At least she'd have someone to talk to during the day while I'm out with the herds. Stoner wouldn't have to know. Besides, I'm guessing you're getting tired of sleeping out in the cold. So far we've had good weather, but you know it's going to rain eventually."

Bart was right. They'd been lucky, but that luck could break at any time. Then they would be cold, wet and miserable.

The ranch was a good idea. Haley would be safe and he could have some time to figure out the next step. There had to be a way to catch Stoner. The man had to make a mistake eventually.

"Thanks," he told his friend. "I'd like to bring Haley to the ranch. It'll probably be in a couple of days. I want to leave a few more false trails for Lindsay's men to follow, so they don't know we're heading to your place."

"I'll tell Christine," Bart said, moving to his horse and swinging up into the saddle. "We'll have the guest room waiting."

The two men said their goodbyes and Jesse headed back to camp. As he rode he wondered what he was going to tell Haley. His gut told him she wouldn't believe the truth, even if he tried to explain it to her. In her mind, Stoner was too noble not to want to marry his bride, regardless of what had happened to her.

Eventually she would have to know and then she was going to be furious. But in time she would thank him. Better to be alone than to be married to a lying, murdering son of a bitch like Lucas Stoner.

Jesse returned to camp shortly after sundown. He saw the fire flickering up ahead and smelled the tempting aroma of something sweet. Apparently, Haley had already started dinner with the sparse ingredients on hand. But he had no doubt she'd be pleased to see the supplies Christine had provided.

As he rode into camp, Haley stepped out of the shadows. "You said you'd be back before sunset. What was I supposed to think?" she asked, her voice low and angry. "What if something had happened to you? I don't like being left here alone and having no way of knowing if you're going to return or not."

Something unfamiliar flared in his chest. Gratitude maybe? Warmth fanned by her concern for him? How long had it been since anyone gave a damn about his comings and goings? He'd been on his own for several years. Ever since he'd left Whitehorn for Texas. It felt surprisingly good to be fretted over.

"I'm sorry you were worried about me," he said as he dismounted. "There's a bright moon tonight, so it was easy to find my way to camp."

"That's not the point." Her green eyes snapped with fire. "I've been here all afternoon, by myself, in the middle of the wilderness. It's not right to leave me like this. Even though I'm not tied up, I have no way to protect myself. I don't even know where town is."

She went on and he found himself fighting a smile. Most women would be in tears, but not Haley. She was tanning his hide with her scolding words. He knew it was wrong to like that she'd been worried and that he had no business admiring her spirit, but there it was. In the past days, she'd become more than just a means to an end. She'd become important.

Before he could figure out a way to explain that last thought, she said, "It's just good manners, Jesse. I wish you could be more like Mr. Stoner."

That stopped him cold. He stared at her. "What did you say?"

"I said Mr. Stoner would never do something like this. Under the circumstances, you've treated me very well and I appreciate that, but it was wrong to kidnap me. If you were a true gentleman, like Mr. Stoner, you would understand that."

The irony of the situation nearly overshadowed his outrage. Here he was trying to think of ways to keep her from knowing her fiancé no longer wanted anything to do with her, while she was comparing him to the man and finding him wanting.

"I guess you're right," he said and led his horse to a patch of grass. "Stoner is so damn noble and kind. Understanding, virtuous and just about perfect. I could learn a lot from him."

"Exactly," Haley said, trailing after him and beaming. "Not that you haven't done your best."

He nearly told her the truth. Just to let her know what her precious Mr. Stoner was really like. But when he glanced at her pretty face, he found he couldn't do it. He couldn't be the one to steal the light from her eyes.

"So what happened?" she asked. "Did he agree to your terms?"

He had thought about this all the way back to camp and he still hadn't come up with a way to spare her. Yet he had to.

"I—" He thought for a minute, then continued. "He

agreed to the hundred dollars, but I decided to raise the price.''

Disappointment made her shoulders droop and her mouth twist. ''Jesse, why? I don't understand. Why are you doing this?''

Because Stoner is a bastard and it's for your own good. But he didn't say that. Instead he shrugged and slipped the saddle off his horse.

He didn't like lying to her but he didn't have another choice. In the meantime, he had to keep her away from town. The last thing she needed was to know that her reputation was all but lost. She was right about one thing, though. He wasn't a gentleman. If he was, he would consider fixing her reputation by marrying her.

Marriage. He shook his head. He'd sworn he would never do that again. Not even to save Haley. She was tough, but this country demanded too much from women. In the end he would make her understand and she would be grateful he was letting her go. She might not want to return to Chicago, but there were other cities. He could help her get started somewhere. They would have to talk about it. Just not right now.

''Jesse?'' She touched his arm. ''Are you angry at me? Is this why you're keeping me from Mr. Stoner?''

''No, Haley. It's not about that.''

It was because she had a dream and he respected that. He'd been without one for so long, he couldn't bear to see hers destroyed.

''Then what?'' she asked.

''I can't explain it. But don't worry. Stoner is going to get the rest of the money. It will take a few days, but not that long.'' The lie tasted bitter, but it bought him time.

''I see.'' But the shadows in her eyes told him she didn't see at all.

''We can't keep going around in circles,'' he told her. ''I'm going to take you to a friend's ranch. You'll be safe there and it will be a lot more comfortable than the trail.''

"Will I still be your prisoner?"

He nodded. "They're good people. They'll treat you well. As long as you don't run off, you can move around freely."

She dropped her hand to her side. "When will we get there?"

"A couple of days."

"I still don't understand," she told him. "I wish..." Her voice trailed off.

"You wish what?" he prompted, then knew it had been a mistake.

She looked him square in the face. "I wish you were more like Mr. Stoner."

The hell of it was, she probably really did. He tried to think of an answer, but he couldn't, so he turned on his heel and walked away.

Chapter Nine

It took her a few hours to figure out Jesse wasn't talking to her. At first Haley had assumed he just hadn't slept well and was tired. After all, every time she woke up the previous night, she'd glanced over and seen Jesse sitting by the fire and sipping coffee. This morning, they'd broken camp without much more than a muttered "Good morning."

She shifted in her saddle and wondered if she should bother saying anything. Maybe he wasn't just tired, maybe he was angry. Which was fine with her, because she was angry, too. Just thinking about what he'd done yesterday made her get all hot and furious. How dare he raise the price on her ransom? And why? That was what really annoyed her. She couldn't figure out a reason.

Did Jesse need money that badly? She squinted against the glare. The morning had dawned cold and gray, but now there was just enough sun to hurt her eyes when she looked up at the sky. She stared at his straight back as he rode a few feet in front of her. He'd gone to a lot of trouble to kidnap her, so he had to be concerned about something. Was Lucas rich?

She shook her head. While she didn't doubt that Lucas was well off, could someone who ran the local land office really be rich? Besides, if Jesse had wanted money that badly, he would have robbed the stage while he was kidnapping her. Or robbed it next week when it would be carrying the payroll that Charlie, the driver, had talked about.

"Are you really taking me to a ranch?" she asked.

Jesse was silent for a long time, then he nodded. "Yes. In a couple of days. You'll like it there."

"I'd rather go to town."

"I'm sure you would, but I can't take you there right now."

Frustration bubbled inside of her. "But why not? Jesse, you have to let me go. It's time. If it's about the money, I'm sure Mr. Stoner will pay you. He's an honorable man. He's—"

She paused as Jesse stiffened visibly on his horse. Quickly, she tried to remember exactly what she'd just said. One word in particular had bothered him. Honorable.

Of course. Jesse believed that Lucas was responsible for the death of his father. While Haley knew there was some kind of explanation for everything that had happened, Jesse was reacting out of pain and a desire for revenge.

Before she could figure out what else to say, Jesse spoke up. "Just give me a little more time," he said, without turning around. "The ranch will be easier for you than riding all day. After a short while, Lucas will come through with the money and you'll be free to go."

"Are you sure I won't be locked up when we get there? I'd rather stay out here than be confined to a single room."

He did look at her then. Probably for the first time that morning. He reined in his horse and turned it so they were facing each other.

Shadows darkened the skin under his eyes. His mouth was an unyielding line. Despite his straight posture, he looked weary, as if he'd been fighting a battle for too long and had lost hope for a victory. She shivered slightly and pulled her coat tighter around her body. Overhead the clouds thickened, completely blocking out the sun.

"I'm not taking you to prison," he said, his voice low and flat. "The Baxters are friends of mine and they'll treat you like a guest. You don't have to worry about being locked up and forgotten. I promise."

She searched his face, then spoke. "All right. I believe you." She had to. Jesse had never broken his word to her. She wanted to say more, to explain that she understood a little of what he was feeling, but she suspected he wouldn't appreciate her concern.

He turned his horse again and continued through the forest. As the morning stretched on, the light began to fade as storm clouds rushed in. Haley could smell the promise of rain. At least it wasn't cold enough to snow.

Time passed. She huddled in her coat and wished they would stop and build a fire. Maybe in a shelter of some thick branches. Once it started raining, they weren't going to have much luck staying warm. She would like to spend at least a few hours nice and toasty before she had to shiver through the storm.

Just thinking about the fire made her smile. She could almost smell the burning wood, the—

She opened her eyes wide and glanced around. "Do you smell that?" she asked.

"Yeah." Jesse sounded grim. "Smoke. If it's what I think it is, we're already too late."

"For what?" she asked.

Instead of answering, he kicked his horse into a trot, then a canter. As her mount followed, she was forced to cling to the saddle with both hands. She kept hold of the reins, but they were loose and slapped against the animal's neck.

Trees seemed to rush past as they raced through the forest. The cold air burned her cheeks and eyes. Twice she nearly lost her balance and slipped from the saddle. She shrieked and righted herself. Jesse never slowed.

After what seemed like days but was probably only a half hour or so, they crested a rise and reined in their horses. Haley stared down at the shallow valley below. The land was lush and green with hundreds of head of cattle grazing. At the far right edge of the valley stood what was left of a house.

Even as she watched, flames burst through the roof. Slowly, as if guided by an invisible hand, the structure shuddered, then fell in on itself. Smoke rose toward the gray heavens.

"What happened?" she asked, too stunned to believe what she was seeing.

"Renegades," Jesse said flatly. "Dammit, I knew we'd be too late. Come on. Let's see if anyone is left alive."

At his words, she shifted her gaze from the house to the land around the structure. Her stomach lurched when she saw several shapes lying on the ground. None of them moved.

Haley kicked her horse and followed Jesse down into the valley. Inside her head, she made a list of what supplies they had and what she wished they had. If the people were burned... She didn't want to think about that. Burns were the worst. There was so much pain and so few ways to keep the wounds from getting infected.

She glanced around and spotted a well. At least there was water. They would need bandages, maybe splints. The latter would be easy. They could use timbers from the still-burning house.

Jesse had barely started to dismount when Haley slid out of her saddle and hurried toward the bodies. There were five in all. What looked like a family with two young sons, and an older man.

"One of the ranch hands," Jesse said, kneeling down next to him. He touched the man's face and his neck, then peeled back his coat and stared at the bullet wound in the center of his chest. "He's dead."

Haley nodded and went to the two boys. Both had been shot in the back. While she was used to death and the grisly destruction of accidents, her stomach lurched at the sight of two murdered children. Who could do something like this?

She crouched next to the youngest. He looked barely seven or eight. "What threat were they?" she asked quietly as tears formed in her eyes. She brushed them away impatiently.

"They weren't a threat," Jesse told her. "They were a lesson. Their parents obviously didn't listen."

A faint moan caught her attention. Haley turned toward the sound and saw the woman stirring slightly. She'd been shot, too. A gaping wound in her chest pumped blood with each beat of her heart. Jesse checked the father and at Haley's questioning look, he shook his head. The man was dead, too.

With a competence learned through years of helping Dr. Redding, Haley ripped a length of cloth from the woman's petticoat and folded it into a square. She applied pressure to the woman's chest, knowing she was doing too little, too late. Death was inevitable, but she had to try something.

Haley brushed hair from the woman's face and sent up a prayer that it would be quick. Tears continued to fill her eyes and she remembered Dr. Redding telling her that she was too softhearted for her work. The good doctor had been right.

The woman moaned softly. "My babies," she gasped. "Are they all right? Did the men hurt them?"

"They're fine," Haley soothed, speaking the lie without a second thought. To her mind, the dying shouldn't be allowed to worry about things they couldn't control. "They're with your neighbors and will be perfectly safe."

The last part of her statement was correct at least, she thought. The boys were safe in the arms of angels. She believed the Lord took care of children who died before their time.

"Do you need anything?" Jesse asked Haley. "Whiskey or blankets?"

He looked worried and uncomfortable. "Both," Haley

told him, although she suspected the woman would be gone before he returned with the supplies. At least collecting the items would give him something to do.

She checked the cloth and found it was soaked with blood. The woman's breathing grew more shallow. It wouldn't be long now.

She shifted so she was kneeling on the cold ground and gently stroked the woman's cheek. "It's all right," she murmured. "I'm here. It's time to let go. Your boys are safe and your husband is waiting for you. Don't you want to see him again?"

Unexpectedly, the woman opened her eyes and stared at Haley. Her face was gray and her lips trembled as she tried to speak. "He's a good man, but stubborn. I told him to let them take the ranch. As long as we have each other, we can always start over. But he wanted to fight." Her eyes closed slowly.

"Hush. Don't think about that now. It's done. It's done." She took the woman's hand in her own and squeezed. The pressure was returned, albeit faintly.

"I do love him," she whispered, her lips barely moving. "I loved him from the time I was a girl." Her mouth turned up slightly. "Handsomest boy in the county. Those kisses of his always did have a strange power over me." She stiffened. "I can almost see him. Hank? Is that you?"

Her breath caught, then she laughed softly. "Foolish man, I do love you so."

And then she was gone. The hand in Haley's went slack, the breathing ceased, as did the flow of blood. The heart and soul of the woman disappeared, leaving behind only the body.

Haley bowed her head and prayed as she did each time someone she'd tended died. At least this one hadn't suffered and she'd had someone waiting for her on the other side.

"I brought the—" Jesse paused, then crouched next to Haley. "I'm too late, aren't I?"

She nodded. "At least it was an easy passing." She looked at him. His eyes reflected her own pain and confusion. "I don't understand. Who would shoot a woman and her children?"

"You don't want to know."

If this was more about Lucas, he was right...she didn't want to know. But this wasn't the time to argue.

"Now what?" she asked.

He set several blankets on the ground next to her. A bottle of whiskey nestled in the folds. He stood up and shrugged. "Now I dig the graves."

As he turned and walked toward the still-standing barn, the first drops of rain began to fall.

It was dark by the time they took shelter for the night. Two of the cowhands had ridden in to investigate the gunshots they'd heard. They'd helped Jesse with the graves, then had ridden into town to report the murders to the sheriff.

Haley glanced around the small cave and wished they could have stayed at the ranch in the barn. But Jesse had said they couldn't risk Sheriff Lindsay coming out to investigate. They would be safer away from the valley.

So they'd ridden through the rain and now she was cold down to her bones. Freezing water dripped from the soaked clothing. Her fingers were stiff, her feet ached and she felt as if her teeth would never stop chattering.

"You all right?" Jesse asked as he gathered a few dry pieces of wood to start their fire. "You're awfully quiet."

"I'm awfully cold," she managed through numb lips. "I don't think I'll ever be warm again."

"Hold on, Haley. I'll get this going and you can sit right next to the flames. They'll warm you up quick enough."

"Maybe." Although she had her doubts. Besides, much of her chill came from the inside. As often as she tried to force the images from her mind, they kept returning. If she closed her eyes she could see those dead children and hear the last few breaths from the dying woman. The senseless murders made her angry and very sad.

The sound and flare of a match cut through the dark silence of the cave. The kindling caught immediately and Jesse carefully fed larger pieces of wood. When the blaze was burning steadily, he searched their small shelter and returned with an armful of fuel. There was more right outside and he ducked into the rain to collect enough to last them the night.

Haley moved close to the fire and held out her hands. She could feel the heat but it wasn't going to be enough. Her clothes were soaked, as was her hair. A shiver shook her.

"You're going to freeze to death," Jesse told her when he returned and dumped the extra wood by the entrance to the cave.

Despite the fire, it was dark inside, darker than it had been in the forest. As Jesse moved toward her, his shadow danced behind him on the rocky walls. He seemed to loom larger in this confined space—a dangerous man who had kidnapped her and kept her his prisoner.

She told herself she was just being fanciful. This was Jesse. She knew him and she trusted him. But something inside of her shuddered at his approach.

He drew off her coat and fingered the sleeve of her dress. "You're soaked clear through," he said.

She nodded. For reasons she couldn't explain it was difficult to talk. Her throat had closed up and she couldn't seem to get enough air into her body.

"I brought the blankets from the ranch," he said, motioning to the pile of saddles and saddlebags against the far wall. "You'll never get warm while you're wearing that dress. Go ahead and take it off, then you can wrap yourself in a blanket. Your dress won't dry in the night, but at least you won't catch a chill."

She stared blankly, sure she couldn't have heard him correctly. Take off her *dress?*

He shifted uneasily and swore. "Dammit, Haley. After all the time we've been together, I'd like to think you trust me. If I wanted to force myself on you, I would have already done it."

His words made her flush. "I know. It's just..." She gestured helplessly. Didn't he understand? She'd never undressed in front of a man before. "I'll be better this way," she said, motioning to her dripping gown.

"No, you won't." He crossed to their pile of belongings and pulled out a blanket, then he turned his back to her. Holding one corner in his left hand, he fished around with his right until he had the thing stretched out behind him, like a screen. "Take off your dress now."

The tone of his voice warned her he was rapidly losing patience. She didn't want to push him to the point where he threatened to do it himself. While he'd been right about her trusting him, she wasn't ready to carry things that far.

"All right," she agreed and reached for the first button on her bodice.

The thick green wool was stiff, cold and wet, making it nearly impossible for her to work quickly. When she'd unfastened the buttons, she pulled up the skirt and released her four petticoats and let them fall in a heap. Next, she struggled to get her arms out of the sleeves.

"You need any help?" he asked, still with his back to her.

"No," she said quickly. "I'm nearly finished."

She tugged on the left sleeve and finally got it pulled down, then she shoved the dress onto the dirt floor of the cave. As the rapidly cooling night air hit her bare arms and shoulders, she jumped. She hadn't thought it was possible to be even colder, but she was. Stepping over the pile of wet clothing, she reached for the blanket and wrapped it around herself, then shifted closer to the fire.

"All done?" Jesse asked, without turning toward her.

"Yes. Thank you."

She heard him moving, but didn't have the courage to

face him. At least one part of her was warm, she thought as embarrassment flamed her cheeks. She felt naked and exposed. Telling herself the blanket more than covered her wasn't enough to keep her from feeling awkward. What exactly did one say to a man while one was waiting for one's clothing to dry?

A flash of white caught her eye. She turned and saw Jesse spreading her dress out over a rock. When he reached for one of her petticoats, she gasped and tried to snatch it from him.

"Stay where you are," he told her, his voice gentle. "You're still shivering and I don't want you getting sick."

"But you can't—" She motioned to her petticoats. He was a *man*. He couldn't touch her private things.

"It's all right, Haley. I was married, remember? They're just petticoats."

"I see." Mortification stiffened her spine and she turned to face the fire. She forced herself to think about getting warm and ignore the images in her head...the ones of Jesse's strong hands on her undergarments.

Despite her best efforts, the thoughts would not fade. Another shiver rippled through her, but this one wasn't from the cold. At least it didn't feel the same. Something tightened in her stomach. Her reaction frightened and confused her and, to distract herself, she said the first thing that came to mind.

"What happened at the ranch?"

Jesse joined her by the fire. He spread out oilcloth and several blankets and gestured for her to sit down. He sat next to her. "Same thing that always happens. The renegades showed up without warning. There was a brief battle, which the renegades won, as usual. If the rancher gives up his land without any more trouble, he can take his family and leave. If he fights for what's his, everyone dies."

"I don't understand," she said, pulling the blanket tightly around her shoulders. "They just take the land? No one has stopped them?"

"We've tried. Lindsay, the sheriff, has tried, though I don't think he's putting much back into finding them. It's not in his best interest."

"What does that mean?"

Jesse's dark eyes focused inward. "He's been bought and paid for by your fiancé."

She didn't like the sound of that. "Nonsense. The town pays the sheriff's salary."

"Some of it. Stoner makes up the difference, and a little more. He's got a vested interest in Lindsay's activities."

Haley didn't want to believe that. She wanted to refute what Jesse was saying, but he was starting to make her doubt herself. Worse, he was starting to make her doubt Lucas, and that was the one thing she didn't want to do. Lucas was her future—her hope for what she'd always wanted. She'd left everything familiar on the basis of who and what she imagined him to be. If he wasn't wonderful, where would that leave her?

She pulled her knees close to her chest and hugged her legs. "Jesse, I'd really like to hear about all that's been happening around here. Could you tell me about it from the beginning?"

He looked at her. "You're not going to like it."

"Maybe you could leave out the accusations. You know, toward Mr. Stoner."

He pulled off his hat and slapped it against his thigh in a gesture of frustration. "Dammit, Haley, why do you have to be so stubborn? You're a smart woman. Why won't you see the truth? Why is it so important that Lucas Stoner be a saint?"

"I don't want him to be a saint," she answered with a shrug. "I just want him to be a good man. I want…" She hesitated, suddenly feeling foolish about her dreams.

Jesse touched her upper arm. His heat warmed her, even through the blanket. "What do you want?"

"You promise you won't laugh?"

He set his hat on the blanket next to him and shook his head. "You have my word on that."

His word. She could trust that—and him. "I want—" She drew in a deep breath. "I want to belong. I want to have a man who cares about me. I want a good life. Nothing fancy—I don't need to be rich. I'm willing to work hard to make a success of things. I want happy, healthy children and a home of my own. I want memories and friends and roots for my family." She bit her lower lip. "This probably seems silly to you."

He stared into the fire. "I think I understand what you're saying. But Stoner isn't the only man around. Why him?"

"He's the only one who wants to marry me."

"There will be others."

"I don't think so." She wondered how much more she should risk confessing. "I'm twenty-one. That's practically an old maid. There haven't been many men in my life." Actually there hadn't been any, but he didn't need to know that. This was embarrassing enough without confessing that truth.

"I really liked working with Dr. Redding, but I never met anyone suitable. The hours were long and I didn't have a family or connections to introduce me to anyone so..." Her voice trailed off again.

"So being a mail-order bride seemed like the way to make your dreams come true."

She looked at him, but he didn't seem to be teasing her. His expression was serious. In the firelight, his stubble-darkened face seemed cast from stone. As if he were a beautiful statue left here by an unknown artist.

"Yes," she said. "I thought I could find everything I'd ever wanted in Montana." She shivered again and hugged the blanket close.

Jesse rose to his feet and walked to the saddlebags by the cave wall. "I think we could both use a drink. It'll warm us from the inside."

"Spirits?" she asked as he pulled a small flask from one of the leather bags. "I don't drink spirits."

"Normally, I don't either, but I think tonight's an exception." He unscrewed the cap and handed her the container. "Take a sip," he told her. "Not a big one or you'll choke."

She took a small mouthful and nearly spit it out. Instantly her tongue and gums began to burn. She swallowed quickly and the fire roared down her throat.

"What is that?" she asked, her voice raspy, her eyes filling with tears.

"Whiskey." He took a mouthful, then settled next to her again.

They were silent for a while. Jesse offered her another drink, but she refused. He took a couple more swallows, then screwed on the cap and stared into the fire.

The heat seeped inside her. The shivers were farther apart now and she could feel tingling in her toes. Maybe she wasn't going to freeze to death after all.

A question hovered on her tongue for a couple of heartbeats, then she forced it out. "Would you please tell me about the raids, Jesse?"

He answered without turning his attention from the flames. "They started a few months after I left for Texas. According to my friend Bart, the first couple happened within days of each other. Ranch families killed, houses burned down, stock scattered."

"Does anyone know why they attacked?"

He shook his head. "Bart and I have marked all the raids on a map. Some of the places have water rights, some have mineral rights, but most of them are just open land, with nothing special about them. It doesn't make sense. If I knew why, I could go to Lindsay and force him to act."

She appreciated that he was keeping Lucas out of his story. "Is the land valuable?"

He shrugged. "I suppose it could be, but there's so much of it." He half turned toward her and grabbed a thin stick from the fire. After smoothing the fine dirt by their blanket, he drew a large square, then began making circles at various points.

"Here's Whitehorn," he said, pointing to the largest circle. "My ranch is here. Some of the others are here and here." He pointed to more circles. "The latest raid happened today." He drew another circle.

Haley shifted to her knees and leaned over the drawing. The circles formed a rough line just west of Whitehorn. The line ran north and south.

"We've thought about the railroad," Jesse said. "If the ranches ran east and west, we'd know that's it."

"Why does that matter?" Haley asked. "Why can't the railroad run north and south?"

"There isn't anything south of here. No big cities, no industry. It's all either east or west."

She looked at him. "Texas is south of here. Isn't that where you went to get your cattle? Maybe someone wants to do the same thing, but with the railroad."

Jesse stared at her, his expression startled. Then he started to laugh. The amused sound filled the cave and Haley found herself smiling back.

"What's so funny?" she asked.

He dropped the stick, leaned forward and squeezed her upper arms. "That it's so simple. I don't know why Bart and I didn't think of that ourselves. You're right. There could be a railroad coming north. Out west everything seems to run east and west, but it doesn't have to."

His humor faded. "It all fits. The raids, the timing of it. Just as ranches are growing out here and there's a need for more cattle. We also need railroads to take those cattle to market. Stoner has all the deeds, he knows who owns what. After all, he runs the land office." He stopped talking and his expression turned grim. "I'll bet the son of a bitch is one of the investors. He's going to get rich off of all of us."

Haley shrugged away from him. She hated the way he

talked about Lucas. Jesse didn't understand her dreams
were all she had. Lucas Stoner was her only hope. She
desperately needed him to be all things good. After all,
she'd committed herself to marry a stranger. If he wasn't
a decent man she would be trapped for the rest of her life.
"Jesse, don't. Stop blaming Mr. Stoner. Maybe he doesn't
have anything to do with this. I'm sure there's a reasonable
explanation for everything that's been happening."

Jesse glared at her. "I'm damn tired of hearing about
your precious Mr. Stoner. The man's a murderer."

"No, he's not. He's good and kind and—"

"I don't want to hear about him," he said, interrupting
her.

"I'm not going to stop talking about him, so you'd better
get used to listening to me."

"I'll make you stop."

He didn't scare her. Jesse might talk tough, but he would
never hurt her. "I'm not afraid of you."

He grabbed her arms again and pulled her close to him.
"Then you should be."

Before she could figure out what he was going to do and
how best to protest, he bent his head slightly and pressed
his mouth to hers.

Chapter Ten

Jesse never meant to kiss her. All he'd wanted was to find some way to shut Haley up. Between learning Stoner wouldn't negotiate for her release and stumbling on the burned-out ranch, he was frustrated and starting to feel as if he was fighting a battle he couldn't win. Worse, without meaning to, he'd destroyed Haley's dream of happiness.

He thought if he frightened her, she would at last be silent. Or at least keep her opinions of her bridegroom to herself. What he hadn't expected was a gut-wrenching reaction to holding her in his arms.

She was so damn soft. He knew that women were softer than men. Brief experiences with paid ladies had taught him the fundamentals of what went on between a husband and a wife. But those times had been quick and, except for the physical release, unsatisfying. With Claire he'd felt awkward and brutish, too large, too fumbling, too uncivilized for her delicate sensibilities. She'd been a wisp of a woman, all bony angles and rigid countenance.

But Haley was soft. Her upper arms yielded to the bite of his fingers, so he gentled his hold. Somehow, without him even being sure what exactly had happened, he found himself brushing her lips with his. He'd never kissed a woman in anger and he knew it was wrong to do so now. Yet even as he tried to pull back he realized the anger had faded, washed away by a wave of desire that left him hard and trembling.

He wanted her. The certainty pounded in his head with the same intensity as the pressure that throbbed between his legs. Even as he acknowledged he could never have her and that doing this was wrong—even as he gathered his strength to pull away and end what should never have started—she put her hands on his chest.

It was an unconscious gesture at best. He knew that just as he knew the fastest draw would win a gunfight. But it didn't matter. The sensation of those small, trusting hands on his body was more than he could resist. He'd already kidnapped the woman and ruined her reputation in town. Kissing her now couldn't make things worse.

He tilted his head so he could move his mouth slowly against hers. Her lips parted slightly as she gave a little gasp. He felt her shudder, as if she were profoundly affected by what they were doing…by what *he* was doing to her. He moved his hands up to her shoulders and was shocked to feel warm skin next to the still-damp fine cotton of her chemise. The edges of the blanket had slipped down. To where, he wasn't sure and he forced himself to keep his eyes closed so he wouldn't be tempted to look and see how much of her sweet flesh had been exposed.

As he slipped his fingers up her delicate neck, she shivered. He didn't know if it was from the coolness of the night, or from his touch. He found himself wanting it to be the latter. He wanted her to feel the same intense longing he did. He wanted her body to burn with need, to swell and change, to prepare itself for him. Even though he could never take her.

He cupped her face in his hands and swept his thumbs across her cheeks. He broke the kiss and looked at her face. She was flushed and several strands of hair had pulled loose from her braid. In the blanket that hung precariously on her shoulders, with her mouth slightly parted and her breathing as quick and labored as his, she looked beautiful and intensely feminine. A deep hunger inside him called out to her.

As if responding, her fingers curled into his shirt and her eyes slowly opened. Her pupils were so large, he could barely see any hint of green around the blackness. The corners of her mouth turned up slightly.

"I've never been kissed before," she said, her voice soft, the flush on her cheeks deepening. "It's very nice."

Her words stunned him. Never kissed? Haley was a beautiful woman. Were all the men in Chicago blind or just stupid?

Then he realized he was fiercely glad. He wanted to be the first man to kiss her. He wanted to be the first man to do many things, but he wouldn't dishonor her more. It was enough Stoner had said her reputation was in tatters. Ruined in the eyes of a town was one thing, ruined in fact was another.

But she tempted him, with her sweet-smelling skin and her full mouth. Tempted him until he had no choice but to lean close and kiss her again.

Her breath caught in her throat and her lips parted. He found he didn't have the strength to refuse that invitation, however unintentional. He swept his tongue across her lower lip. She gasped and sagged toward him. He continued to hold her face in his hands, turning her slightly to allow him to slip inside and taste the beguiling essence that was Haley.

She was warm, her smooth teeth contrasting with the suppleness of the inside of her lower lip and the waiting temptation beyond. At first she didn't respond. Her body stiffened and the fingers digging into his chest froze as if the entire practice was too shocking to consider.

Then he found and stroked the tip of her tongue. She inhaled audibly. With a small, tentative movement in return, she kissed him back. Fire shot through him, as if he'd been consumed by the flames. His muscles clenched, his blood roared in his ears. Even as he told himself to show restraint, he moved his hands down her shoulders to her back and hauled her against him.

If she'd resisted, he would have stopped. If she'd given a faint whimper of protest or had even stiffened slightly, he would have released her and apologized. Instead Haley melted into him. Her body was as supple and yielding as a bouquet of spring wildflowers. She folded against him, her arms coming around his waist, her legs nestling against his.

With only the blanket to cover her, without the layers of petticoat and her skirt between them, he could feel the slender length of her thighs, the tapering of her calves, the trembling that rippled through her. She was small, but not slight. He felt muscles beneath her skin. While she was completely feminine in every way, there was a strength about her. A promise of health and vitality that Claire had never possessed.

And then her mouth parted wider and he could think of nothing but kissing her. Of the feel of her welcoming wetness, of the sensations that filled him, of the need. He ran his hands up and down her back, then lower, resting his palms on the curve of her hips. She shifted slightly, encouraging. He knew she didn't know what she was asking, sensed she had no idea of the potential danger of the situation.

He wanted her. He wanted her more than he'd ever wanted a woman before in his life. He tried to tell himself it was just that he'd been without for so long, but he knew it was more. The desire filling him wasn't all about release—it was specifically about Haley. It was about how she felt in his arms and how much he would miss her when she was gone from his life.

He pulled back, breaking the kiss. She sagged against him, resting her face in the crook of his neck. He could feel her hot breath against his neck. Her breasts brushed against his chest in a teasing rhythm that matched her breathing and would very quickly make him vibrate with longing. He toyed with the end of her braid, then began finger-combing the loose strands of hair.

"I didn't know kissing could be like that," she whispered.

He kissed the top of her head. "If you'd known, you would have let some man kiss you before, right?"

She laughed softly. "I think that just might be true."

He didn't have the heart to tell her it wasn't usually like this. Kissing could be very nice, but it wasn't always spectacular. That was the word he would use to describe kissing Haley. Spectacular. And maybe a little frightening. He didn't want his time with her to mean anything to either of them. As soon as he figured out what to do with her, he was going to send her on her way. She wasn't part of his plan. He wasn't interested in getting married again and Haley's dream was to marry, to establish roots and raise a family. They had nothing in common.

Even as he told himself he was being sensible, he found himself touching a finger to her chin, urging her to look at him. When she did, he found himself kissing her again, even though he knew it was foolish and reckless.

But when she kissed him back, all thoughts of being sensible faded. There was only the feel of her body in his arms, her mouth on his, her tongue stroking and tasting, invading his mouth and leaving him intensely hard with desire.

Somehow, as he shifted to hold her tighter, her blanket loosened, then fell to her waist. Even as he told himself not to look, he found himself gazing at her, at the bare arms and the pale ribbon that held her chemise together above the swell of her breasts. And though he knew it was a mistake and wrong and not anything a gentleman should do, he slowly moved his hand up her left arm, then across her shoulder, then down to the ribbon. He traced a line at the place where tiny ruffles met soft skin. She shivered.

She surged against him, as if urging him onward. It was a completely unselfconscious action from an innocent. He had no business listening to her silent, but completely clear request. If he was any kind of decent man he would—

He moved his hand lower and gently cupped her breast. She stopped kissing, stopped moving and, judging from the silence, even stopped breathing.

He kept his fingers still, letting her grow accustomed to his touch, all the while savoring the feel of her curves against his fingers. She fit him perfectly, filling his palm. Not too large, not too small. He brought his thumb and forefinger together over the tiny bead that was her taut nipple. As he gently squeezed the tight flesh, she whimpered low in her throat, then deepened their kiss. Her arms wrapped around his neck and she pressed into him, surging toward him, seeking more.

He could take her now—here in the cave, with the fire in front of them and the storm at their backs. She would let him. Then he would have done what Stoner had accused him of. He would have ruined her.

Haley found herself caught up in a whirlpool of sensations. She didn't know what part of her body to think about first. There was the delicious taste and feel of Jesse's lips against hers, his tongue stroking—almost *dancing* with—hers. His hand on her breast made her heart flutter and her legs feel all heavy and achy. Low in her belly an odd pressure built. She wasn't sure what that meant, but she liked it. She liked everything he was doing with her. She wanted it never to stop.

But it did. Reluctantly, or so it seemed to her, he pulled back. He gave her a smile that looked more pained than amused and drew up the blanket she hadn't known had fallen.

"We don't want you getting sick," he said, although his voice sounded odd. Strained and tight, as if he were in pain.

"I'm fine," she said, knowing it was too brazen to ask him to kiss her again, but wanting to, nonetheless.

Jesse solved her dilemma by standing up and walking

over to the saddlebags. "You rest there. I'll see about supper."

He moved to the side of the cave. Haley stared after him, confused by his manner. Was Jesse angry with her? She didn't think so. There was no reason. He'd kissed her and she'd liked it. Wasn't that better than her not liking it?

She frowned and wondered if it was because of how they'd started kissing. She'd been talking about Lucas and Jesse had gotten angry. He'd grabbed her to make her stop talking. Perhaps he'd meant to frighten her. If so, he should have tried something much less nice than kissing. He was right—if she'd known it was so lovely, she would have let one of the men she'd known kiss her instead of resisting so hard.

She thought about the few men of her acquaintance and decided that maybe she wouldn't have wanted them holding her so intimately. She couldn't imagine wanting to press herself against them the way she'd pressed against Jesse. And the thought of their tongues in her mouth made her shudder, but in a completely different way than she had just a few minutes before. Obviously she wasn't interested in kissing just anyone. But it had been glorious with Jesse.

She exhaled softly. If kissing Jesse had been that nice, imagine what it would be like with Lucas. Her heart thudded a little faster in her chest. He would be even more handsome than Jesse...well, maybe not *more* handsome, but *as* handsome.

But for once she couldn't bring her imaginary bridegroom into focus. The image in her mind had slipped out of reach and she couldn't grab onto it at all. When she tried to think about being with Lucas, all she saw was Jesse.

Clutching the blanket tightly around her, she got up to help with supper. They worked in silence, moving easily around each other, having grown familiar with the routine of their preparations. Haley felt warm inside, as if she'd been told a wonderful secret that no one else knew. She found herself smiling for no reason and wanting to be close to Jesse. When she reached past him for the coffee and brushed her arm against his, he jumped.

"Sorry," she said quickly, wondering what was wrong.

"My fault," he muttered and took a step away. "Look, we're going to be heading out early tomorrow. At first light."

"All right."

He shoved his hands into his pockets and stared over her left shoulder. "I'm taking you to the ranch."

She poured herself some coffee and set the pot back on the flat rock near the fire. Some of the glow in her belly faded. "I thought you said it would take a couple of days for us to get there. That you didn't want to go directly to the ranch in case we were being followed."

He shrugged. "The rain will wash away our tracks anyway. There's no point in staying out here any longer than we have to. It will be better for you at the ranch. You'll be safer."

From what? she wanted to ask, but didn't. Jesse had kept her safe while they were in the forest. Despite the promise of a roof over her head and no more sleeping on the ground, she found she wasn't that excited about going to the ranch. She would rather have stayed out here with him, although she couldn't quite figure out why.

The storm passed in the night and they awoke to clear skies without a hint of clouds. By the time they'd broken camp and started for the ranch, the sun had crested the trees and was warming the morning. Whatever had caused Jesse's mood the previous evening, he was fine when he woke up, telling stories about the Baxters and their ranch.

"So you've known them a long time," Haley said, wondering why she was suddenly nervous about meeting this couple. From everything Jesse had said, they were nice people.

"Since Bart first came to Montana. He'd promised Christine's father he wouldn't bring her out west until he had a proper house for her. The way the cattle were keeping him busy, it was going to be three or four years before he got the building finished. So my father and I rounded up some neighbors. We got the house up in a few days and Bart left to bring his bride to Whitehorn.''

Haley had to hold in a sigh. That sounded so romantic. She wondered what it would be like for someone to care about her that much. To love her. It was what she'd always wanted. Someone to belong to, to care about, to love and be loved in return. Sometimes she wondered if she expected too much from life. Perhaps it was enough that she'd survived. But she hated to think there couldn't be more.

"How long has Christine been in Montana?''

"Two years. She's a sweet lady. You'll like her.'' He reined in his horse and looked at her. "She's feeling poorly, so maybe you can help her.''

"Is she sick?''

Jesse shifted on the saddle. "Not exactly. She's expecting a baby in a couple of months.''

Haley urged her horse forward. "Is she having troubles?''

"No, but it's her first and Bart says she's nervous about having the baby.''

Haley nodded. She'd seen many frightened first-time mothers. So much was unfamiliar. "I'll be happy to talk with her and take care of her when she's not feeling well,'' she said. "If she'll want me to.''

"I'm sure Christine will appreciate having a woman to talk to. Ranch life can be lonely.''

"I know, but...'' Her voice trailed off. She looked at Jesse. He hadn't put on his hat yet and his dark hair gleamed in the sunlight. "Don't they know the truth about me?''

"What truth?''

"That I'm your prisoner. That you kidnapped me. Why would a woman like Christine want to have anything to do with me?''

He frowned. "You're not exactly my prisoner, Haley."

"Of course I am. I didn't ask you to take me away from the stage."

"I know, but it's not what you're thinking."

"I'm not sure what I'm thinking. I'm very confused about this. Are they going to keep me locked up?"

"Of course not. They're my friends."

And she was his prisoner. Or didn't that matter?

"You'll be free to move around as you would like," he said stiffly. "Don't try and make your way to town. If you run away, you will be locked up. Just be patient, Haley. A few more days and everything will be settled."

She wanted to believe him, but it wasn't that simple anymore. Her feelings about marrying Lucas were undergoing a subtle change. She wasn't sure if it was the realization that she was about to pledge her life to someone she'd never met, or if Jesse's constant insistence that Lucas was a scoundrel had finally affected her. Either way, she wasn't as anxious to meet her fiancé as she had been just a couple of days ago. Still, she'd promised to marry him and he'd sent a ticket to bring her west. They were betrothed and nothing could change that.

She tried to make herself feel better by thinking about how wonderful her life was going to be when she and Lucas were together. But the daydreaming didn't work its usual magic. So instead she studied the countryside, noticing the new grass sprouting up in the sunny patches of the forest and the new leaves budding on the trees.

Time passed too quickly for her and by midafternoon their horses trotted down a rise toward a ranch house. Some of the wood was more weatherworn than the rest, indicating there had been a couple of additions to the original structure. Haley noticed a front porch that looked new. Earth had been turned on the southwest side, probably for a vegetable garden. She wondered what it would be like to plant, then harvest fresh vegetables and maybe even fruit. To put it up with her own hands, then use it to feed her family through the winter. She would like to learn how to do that and wondered if there was someone in town willing to teach her.

As they rode closer, she saw a man come toward the house from the barn, then the front door opened and a woman stepped outside. Haley's stomach tightened. The nerves were unexpected and she wanted to tell Jesse she couldn't do this. She would rather be alone with him in the forest, sleeping outside, risking rain and even snow, than face these people.

But Jesse didn't give her a chance to protest, and all too quickly they were slowing in front of the house, where the man had joined his wife.

Bart and Christine Baxter were a handsome couple. He was tall, with dark hair and a beard. His wife was petite, a couple of inches shorter than Haley. Slender, although her belly was full. Thick auburn hair had been piled on top of her head. Her face was elfin but pretty and her smile welcoming.

Haley slid off her horse awkwardly, not sure what to say to these people. Jesse grabbed her hand and pulled her to the porch.

"Bart, Christine, this is Haley Winthrop. Haley, Mr. and Mrs. Baxter."

Christine came down the steps and pulled Haley into a hug. "Don't be silly, Jesse. We're not going to be formal." She released Haley, only to smile brightly and squeeze her hand. "You must call me Christine, and I'll call you Haley. Welcome to our ranch."

Christine looked her over thoroughly. "Oh, my, you have been on the trail for a while, haven't you? I would imagine you're aching for a bath and some clean clothes. No one thought to get your trunk from town, I'm sure." She glanced at her husband, then at Jesse, and raised her eyebrows.

The two men shuffled under her stare but didn't respond. "I thought not," she said. "Men. Whatever are we to do with them? Come along, dear. I have a few things that should fit you. They might be a tad short, but otherwise, I suspect they'll do fine.''

Haley found herself being ushered into the house. She was torn, instantly liking the friendly woman, but not wanting to be separated from Jesse.

She glanced over her shoulder. He gave her a reassuring wink. ''We'll see you at dinner.''

Before she could answer, Christine pulled her inside and firmly closed the door. ''I told Bart you'd want your things, but he forgot to get your trunk when he was in town. I swear, I'm surprised he manages to remember to come home for supper every night. Now, let's look at you. Oh, child, you are exhausted. I can see it in your eyes. Let's get you to your room. I can have hot water ready in no time at all. Then you can take a nice bath.''

She walked as she spoke, leading Haley through the house. ''It's not much, but I like it. We've added on. When I first arrived, there were only three rooms. Not exactly the house Bart had promised my father he'd build for me, but I was so in love with him, I didn't mind. We've been very happy here.''

She pointed to her left where three sofas grouped around a fireplace. ''The parlor that we rarely use. If Bart and I are alone, we're usually sitting at the table in the kitchen, which is through there.'' She motioned to her right.

Haley saw a dining room and beyond that an open doorway that led to the kitchen.

''The bedrooms are through here. There are three. One is for us, another is being prepared for the baby.'' She rested her hand on her full belly. ''The other is the guest room. I think you'll be comfortable there. Compared to sleeping outside, it's going to be like staying at an expensive hotel.''

''Better,'' Haley managed, feeling awkward as her hostess led her down a short hall. The house was very nice, but she wasn't comfortable. Why was Christine treating her like a guest?

They came to the guest room. A large four-poster bed took up most of the room. There was a small dresser and a rug. A window overlooked a pasture behind the house. Haley glanced around in confusion. Her gaze settled on the door. There was no lock.

"I don't understand," she blurted out. "I thought—" She bit her lower lip, not sure what to say.

"Haley?" Christine said, her voice kind. "What's wrong?"

"I'm Jesse's prisoner," she blurted out. "Didn't he tell you? He kidnapped me from the stage."

The other woman's kind expression didn't change. "I know. It's all right. You're not a prisoner here. You're our guest, for as long as you would like to stay." Christine smiled. "You don't know how much I'm looking forward to having another woman to chat with. Bart is wonderful and I adore him, but it's just not the same. So don't be angry if I talk your ear off."

Haley didn't understand what was going on. Why was she being treated this way? Why wasn't Jesse taking her to town? But when Christine repeated her offer of a hot bath, Haley was too tempted to refuse. As her hostess went to the kitchen to see about heating water, Haley crossed to the window and looked out at the ranch. She wasn't sure where Whitehorn was, but it shouldn't be too difficult for her to find out. There weren't any guards, or too many people around. She would be able to escape and make her way to town.

Not today. She was tired and she really wanted a bath. Maybe tomorrow. When she was rested. She would find Lucas and get started on her new life once and for all.

Chapter Eleven

Jesse pushed away his empty plate and smiled at Christine. "We ate pretty well, considering we were outside for more than a week, but this is the best meal I've ever had."

Christine laughed and shook her head. "I'll take the compliment, even though I know you wouldn't say it if you hadn't been forced to eat beans nearly every night."

"He's right," Haley added. "Everything is delicious." She smiled shyly at their hostess.

"All these kind words will go to my head." Christine picked up the silver bowl still half-full of biscuits. "You've only had three, Jesse. Are you sure that's enough?"

He knew she was teasing him and he didn't mind a bit. Christine was a fine cook and he'd been enjoying the Baxters' hospitality for several months. She knew he had a soft spot for her biscuits.

"If you insist," he said, taking two more from the serving dish.

Bart snagged a couple for himself and reached for the bowl of butter. Conversation continued to flow easily around the table as Jesse's friends caught him up on the local gossip he'd missed while he and Haley were on the trail.

Soft lamplight cast shadows on the dining room walls, as candles illuminated the table. He'd thought they would be eating in the kitchen, but Christine had wanted to use the dining room on Haley's first night at the ranch.

Jesse turned toward Haley and saw her looking at him. He gave her a quick wink. He wasn't sure if it was the lighting in the room, or the dress she wore or how she'd fixed her hair, but she looked even more beautiful than she'd been on the trail. Light brown curls danced across her forehead. She'd gathered the rest of her hair up on top of her head in an intricate style that left her neck bare. Her borrowed dress was gray and trimmed in bits of green ribbon that matched the color of her eyes. Tiny sleeves accentuated slender, pale arms and nearly bare shoulders.

As he remembered what it was like to touch those shoulders, to taste her full mouth and feel her press herself against him, the normally delicious biscuits turned tasteless in his mouth. He found himself wanting to be anywhere but here…as long as he was alone with Haley. He wanted to take her in his arms and repeat what they'd done the previous evening. His body ached for her; his hands burned to stroke her smooth, warm skin.

He shook off the thoughts, reminding himself he'd had no right to kiss her and certainly had no business wanting more. She wasn't for him. A long time ago he'd decided to cut himself off from any possibility of marriage. Nothing had happened to change his mind.

Bart finished his biscuits and took a sip of coffee. "One of my boys was in town today," he said as he put his cup down. "There was another raid."

Jesse nodded. "Yesterday. Haley and I saw what happened. The house was still on fire when we got there, so I figure we were about an hour too late."

Bart leaned forward. "Don't go blaming yourself for that, Jesse. You know if you'd arrived while the raiders were still there, they would have killed you as easily as they've killed everyone else."

Jesse grimaced. Bad enough that the rancher and his wife

had been shot, but there was no reason for two innocent kids to die, too.

He pushed his plate farther to one side. "Haley and I talked about what the renegades are doing and she pointed out what you and I have been missing all along."

Using forks and knifes, he outlined an area on the table-cloth, then tore up a biscuit so the crumbs could represent different ranches.

"We assumed if there was a railroad involved, it would have to run east and west," he continued. "What Haley reminded me is there are plenty of cattle in Texas and ranchers are starting to bring them north. Why couldn't the railroads be considering a north-south line?"

"Well, I'll be damned," Bart muttered and looked at Haley. "Good thinking, young lady. We should have seen it. Makes sense." He smoothed a hand over his beard. "Of course Stoner has to be one of the investors."

"That's what I thought, too."

"He runs the land office, so he has access to all the records. Easy enough to reclaim the land when folks are run off it, or murdered." Bart's voice filled with anger.

Christine put a soothing hand on his arm. "Honey, you're doing the best you can."

"It's not enough," Bart muttered.

Jesse found himself watching Haley, wondering what she was thinking about his friend's opinion of her fiancé. At Bart's words, she stiffened in her chair, but didn't say any-thing. Various emotions chased across her face. Disbelief, outrage, resignation. He suspected the latter meant that while she didn't accept his or Bart's opinion of Stoner, she knew she couldn't change their minds about the man.

A wave of frustration swept through him. He wanted to lean forward and demand that she tell him what she saw in a man she'd never met. Stoner was a murdering bastard who thought of no one but himself. He was—

Jesse shook his head. He was getting all worked up for nothing. Haley had never met Stoner. She didn't know the first thing about him. She'd imagined her fiancé to be the man she wanted him to be because she had a dream she desperately wanted to come true. None of it was real.

Not that it mattered, he told himself. He wasn't jealous of her feelings for Stoner. He didn't care about Haley one way or the other.

The lie sat heavily on his conscience and he amended it. He cared some about Haley, because she was his responsibility. But caring and maybe a little wanting didn't mean he'd changed his opinion on having a woman in his life.

Conversation drifted away from the raids. Haley was asking questions about Whitehorn. He liked listening to her talk. She had strong feelings on most things and while he didn't always agree with what she said, he respected her.

He glanced around the table, glad to be with friends, relieved that Haley was safe. Even if he would rather have been out in the forest with her. He missed being alone with her. Not just because he wanted to kiss her again, but because he'd come to like their conversations in the evening. He liked hearing about her plans for the future and about her past. She told interesting stories about the city and seemed fascinated by his tales of ranching life and living on the trail for over a year.

"My, yes, I'd be happy to teach you to put up vegetables," Christine was saying. "It's not difficult, although it takes a lot of time. Usually I—" She gasped and jumped slightly in her chair. Then she flushed and laughed uneasily. "Sorry." She touched her rounded belly. "The baby." She shrugged. "What was I saying? Oh, the canning. I can show you if you'd like."

Haley responded, but Jesse wasn't listening. He stared at Christine's stomach and thought about the new life growing there. A baby. He'd always wanted children, had assumed he would have them. Although Claire had been delicate and unhappy, he'd hoped motherhood would help her adjust. But there had been no children, and then she'd died.

There were those who had told him the best way to recover from his loss was to marry again. He hadn't been able to admit he wasn't mourning because he'd loved Claire—he hadn't. But her death, followed by his mother's unexpected passing, had taught him that loving anyone was too great a risk.

Bart leaned forward, resting his arms on the table. "You still think Stoner's cousins are behind the raids?" he asked.

Jesse nodded. "Who else could it be? They'll do whatever Stoner tells them."

"But we have no proof. We have to catch them in the act or Lindsay won't believe us. If there's absolute proof, he'll have to arrest Stoner, despite what he owes the man. Or are we hoping for an unlikely miracle with that one?" He swore under his breath. "I wish to hell that Stoner didn't have the sheriff in his back pocket."

The women had stopped talking and were listening to what Bart was saying. Out of the corner of his eye Jesse saw Haley stiffen at his friend's comment, but she remained silent.

Bart slapped his hand on the table. "We'll make up a map tonight and fill in all the ranches in the area. If we're right about the railroad coming north, there should only be a half dozen places left in the way. We can stake them out or somehow figure out how to prevent another raid."

"Agreed."

Bart leaned back in his chair. "We're going to get him, Jesse. I swear to you, we're going to get him."

Jesse nodded. He knew Bart blamed himself for Michael Kincaid's murder. Bart had been gone during the arrest, mock trial and hanging. He believed that if he'd been in Whitehorn, he could have prevented the tragedy.

Jesse wasn't so sure. Stoner was determined and wouldn't let anyone get in his way. If Bart had been around to protest, he might have found himself hanged as well.

At least they had a plan, and some information. For the first time since his return from Texas, he felt a flicker of hope. Stoner had been lucky for a long time, but it looked as if his luck was about to run out.

When they'd finished with dessert, Haley rose to her feet and helped Christine clear the table. She followed the other woman into the kitchen and set the dishes on the counter next to the sink. Then she glanced over her shoulder to make sure the men were busy talking to each other.

She leaned close to her hostess and offered a reassuring smile. "I couldn't help but notice that you jumped when the baby kicked," she said. "If you don't want to talk about it, I'll understand, but I wondered if everything is going well with your pregnancy?"

Christine set her plates next to Haley's and clutched the counter. "Am I that simple to read?" she asked.

Haley heard the strain in the other woman's voice and instantly began studying her. Christine's color was good, her breathing steady. There were no telltale signs of illness, no obvious bloating, no hint of blue around her mouth or fingertips.

"I..." Christine shook her head. "I'm fine. At least according to Dr. Prescott, who has been so very patient with me." She raised her hands and covered her face. "It's not that I don't want this baby," she said fiercely. "I do. It's just that I'm so frightened."

Haley moved close to her and placed an arm around her shoulders. "I understand. This is your first baby, isn't it?"

Christine nodded. "I never had any brothers or sisters and I've never been around children very much. I don't know anything I'm supposed to do or feel." She dropped her hands to her sides. "I'm getting bigger and bigger, my back hurts, and I don't know if I'm going to be able to stand the pain when the baby is born. Bart tries to understand, but he doesn't and I'm just—" She stopped talking as her eyes filled with tears.

"I cry all the t-time," she said, her voice breaking. "I feel so stupid."

"You're not stupid, you're just going through a lot of changes." Haley squeezed her tight. "You're going to love having a baby, I promise. They were the best part of growing up in an orphanage."

Christine sniffed. "You're an orphan?"

Haley nodded.

"So you didn't have any brothers or sisters, either."

"Actually, I had dozens. There were many children there. But I liked the babies best of all. I liked how they smelled and felt when I held them, and you're going to like it, too."

"Oh, I wish I could be sure."

"I'm sure." An auburn strand had escaped from Christine's neat bun. Haley tucked it behind her ear. "When I was in Chicago, I worked for a doctor. I've delivered lots of babies. You're going to be fine."

Christine looked relieved. "You think so? I've talked to Dr. Prescott about this, but I'm not sure he understands. He tries and everything, but…" Her voice trailed off.

"He's a man," Haley said. "Lots of women talked to me because they didn't think they could talk to Dr. Redding. They didn't like it when the midwife wasn't available and they had to have him come." She grinned. "Of course he didn't much like being their second choice."

Christine gave her a shaky smile in return. "I hadn't thought of that."

"If it makes you feel any better, I'd be happy to stay with you when it's your time."

Christine stared at her. "But you hardly know me."

"That doesn't matter. You're going to teach me how to can vegetables."

"That's hardly the same thing. Canning is easy."

"So is having a baby. At least for me. You'll be the one doing all the work. I'll just stay with you so you have someone to talk to."

Some of the tension faded from Christine's face. "I'd

like that.'' She touched her belly. ''The baby isn't due for another couple of months.''

''I thought as much. That will be fine. I'll be married by then and you can send word to me in town. I'll explain everything to Lucas and I know he'll understand. He's the kind of man who would like me to help others.''

Christine stared at her. ''Lucas Stoner?''

There was something odd about Christine's voice. Haley hoped she wasn't going to start on some long story about Lucas being responsible for Jesse's father's death.

But Christine didn't say anything about Lucas. Instead she squeezed Haley's hand. ''You're very sweet. Thank you. I do feel better knowing you're going to be with me.''

''My pleasure.'' Haley picked up the coffeepot and headed for the dining room.

She had, she realized, made a friend. Warmth filled her chest. She'd been lonely for a long time and it was nice to finally start belonging.

As she entered the dining room, Jesse looked up and saw her. He smiled. His mouth turned up and the corners of his eyes crinkled. She found herself smiling in return. The warm glow in her chest became a fire. She didn't understand it, but she also didn't want anything to change. Despite everything, this past week had been one of the nicest in her life. Even though she had a fiancé and a future waiting for her in Whitehorn, she found herself wishing they could go on like this forever.

Chapter Twelve

When Jesse woke up the bunkhouse was empty and the sun had already cleared the horizon. He rolled over and glanced around, wondering how he'd managed to sleep through the noise the cowboys inevitably made when they got up in the morning.

When he'd first returned from Texas with his herd of longhorns, only to find his father dead and the ranch house ruined, the Baxters had invited him to stay with them. He'd refused their offer of the guest room and had instead claimed a bed in the bunkhouse. Most of the time he took his meals with the men, and when he wasn't investigating Stoner and his father's death, he worked both his and Bart's cattle.

As he pulled on jeans and boots, he realized he'd long since missed breakfast, but Christine would have coffee up at the house. He cleaned up at the sink just inside the back door, then made his way up the path. He knocked once before entering.

Christine stood at the stove and raised her eyebrows when she saw him. "Don't tell me you're just now getting up. It's nearly noon."

A quick glance at the clock on the wall told him that it was barely after seven, but that was still late by ranch standards. "I guess I was tired. Your mattresses are a lot softer than the ground. Is Haley up yet?"

"Haley's been up and helping me with breakfast and chores since before dawn," Christine said, her voice teasing. "You're just a lazy good-for-nothing."

He snagged a cup from the open cupboard, then poured some coffee. Christine finished stirring soup in a large pot and walked around him to the counter, where she dumped dough onto the already floured surface and began kneading.

"There are some biscuits in that bowl there." She nodded toward a cloth-covered container on the kitchen table.

He crossed to it and fished out a biscuit, then took a bite. "Where's Haley?" he asked when he'd swallowed the mouthful.

"Out collecting eggs." Christine gave him a quick smile. "She wants to learn everything about ranch life, so I gave her a list of chores to pick from. She wanted to do that one, if you can believe it. Said something about never having collected eggs before." Her smile faded. "I suppose they don't have many chickens in the city, but I can't imagine what that must be like. Do you realize there are people who *pay* for eggs? It's shameful."

He finished the first biscuit and took a second. "In the city there are folks who have to pay for everything."

"I'm from Ohio, and there were plenty of towns, but nothing that large. At least I grew up on a farm so the ranch wasn't all that different. But for Haley." She shook her head. "I figure she'll get tired of collecting eggs in a couple of days, but for now I'm grateful for the help."

He eyed her swollen belly while trying not to be obvious about it. "How are you feeling?"

"What's Bart been telling you?"

"Nothing."

She stared at him. "I know my husband's concerned about me. You're his best friend. So?"

Jesse sighed. He should have kept his mouth shut. "He's wondering if you'd be better off staying with friends. Just until the baby's born. So you wouldn't be alone all the time.''

He half expected her to get angry and take a piece out of his hide. Instead Christine nodded slightly and sniffed. ''That's so like Bart, and the reason I married him. He's a good man. Caring and worried about me.''

To Jesse's horror, a tear slipped out of the corner of her eye and rolled down her cheek. Her hands were buried in dough so she wiped her face on her left shoulder and sighed. ''Don't mind me, Jesse. I've been weepy ever since the baby started. Bart's mentioned that to me, too. When you get things settled with Haley, I just might do that. I know I'd miss him, but I would feel better not being alone. Of course if I stay here, Haley has said she'll be with me and that will help.''

She continued her work, her strong hands sinking into the dough. He waited, but there weren't any more tears. He released a nervous sigh. If Christine, who was normally calm and strong, was this easily upset while she was with child, he hated to think what would have happened to Claire if she'd ever been pregnant. Under the circumstances, it seemed unlikely his late wife would have survived the experience.

''Jesse, I have a question about Haley,'' Christine said.

He noticed she wasn't looking at him as she spoke, which he didn't like. ''What?''

''Why does she think Lucas Stoner is a saint?''

He pulled out a chair and sat down. He had figured when the two women went off together in the kitchen they were going to talk about Christine's baby. Haley had experience with that sort of thing and she would do a good job calming the other woman. Looked as though they'd had time to discuss other things, too.

''Haven't you told her the truth?'' she continued, turning toward him, her hazel eyes wide with confusion. ''You must have talked about him.''

''Some.''

"That doesn't tell me anything. She actually stood here in my kitchen and told me she would be happy to be with me when it was my time. That Mr. Stoner wouldn't mind because he was the kind of man who would enjoy her helping others."

"Haley has some peculiar ideas about her fiancé."

"I understand that. What I want to know is why. The man is a lying, cheating murderer, who isn't fit to live."

"You don't have to convince me," Jesse reminded her.

"Haley deserves to know the truth."

He took a sip of coffee. "I know that, Christine. You think I like hearing what she says about the man?"

"Then why haven't you explained things to her?"

"I tried. When I first kidnapped her, I told her about Stoner and my father, about the raids and everything." He shrugged. "She's a stubborn woman, a little like you in that respect."

"I'll take that as a compliment. Go on."

"There's not much else to tell. She didn't want to hear anything bad about him. She has her own ideas about Stoner and they are that he's damn near perfect. I know someone has to let her know the truth, but I can't be the one to do it."

"Why ever not?"

"Because her dreams about Stoner are all she has." He didn't know how to explain the situation to Christine without betraying Haley's secrets. For reasons he couldn't explain, he felt that all they'd talked about in the forest was between the two of them and it wouldn't be right to share it with anyone else. Even his best friend's wife.

"She's been through some tough times," he said at last. "She's an orphan, with no one to look out for her. She thinks marrying Stoner is going to change that."

"What happens when she finds out the truth?" Christine asked. "These lies aren't going to help her then."

"I know. It's just that I don't want to take her dreams away from her."

"She can always get new dreams, Jesse. The loss of a dream won't kill her, but marrying Stoner might. Have you thought of that?"

"I don't want to hurt her."

Auburn eyebrows, a few shades lighter than her hair, raised slightly. Jesse felt himself stiffen. He could read Christine's thoughts as easily as if she'd spoken them aloud.

"I'm *not* falling for her," he said loudly. "Don't get any ideas about that. You know how I feel about women on the ranch."

"I'm not dead and I've lived on a ranch for more than two years," she pointed out mildly, her voice calm and a marked contrast to his. "In fact I'm thriving."

Jesse pressed his lips together and didn't answer.

"She's very different from Claire."

That much was true. He would be hard-pressed to find two women more opposite than Haley and Claire. "She's in love with Stoner."

"She's made up a dream about a man she's never met. There's a difference."

"None of it matters. I'm not interested."

"I see." Christine returned her attention to the dough. "Too bad. Haley seems very special. It would be a shame to let her get away."

"I agree," Jesse said, clutching his coffee cup. "But she's not mine to keep."

"You're crazy," Bart told him as Jesse finished hitching up the wagon.

"Maybe, but I've got to talk to Lindsay."

His friend put his hands on his hips. "You're going to have a hell of a time proving Stoner's guilt if you're in jail."

"Lindsay's not going to arrest me."

"How can you be sure?"

Jesse couldn't, but he wasn't going to tell his friend that.

He was feeling restless and the only thing he could think about was telling Lindsay about their ideas for the railroad. The man had once been a decent sheriff. There had to be a spark of honor left in him. If Jesse could just convince him to investigate Stoner, they might have a chance.

"I'll see Lindsay, get Haley's trunk from the stage office and be back before supper. Nothing is going to happen." Jesse climbed into the wagon and picked up the reins.

Bart snorted in disgust and moved out of the way. "If you get arrested, I'm not breaking you out of jail."

"Deal," Jesse said and grinned. "I'll be fine. Don't worry."

"Be careful," Bart warned as Jesse headed out. "Stay away from Stoner."

"I will," Jesse called back over his shoulder.

That was one piece of advice he *was* willing to take. As much as he wanted to confront his enemy, he knew the danger inherent in that action. Talking to Lindsay was as much risk as he was willing to take right now. Soon, he promised himself. Justice had been a long time coming, but soon it would arrive and Stoner would get what he deserved.

A couple hours later he drove slowly into town. Several people stopped to stare at him. He smiled politely and tipped his hat. No doubt word had spread about him holding up the stage. He was pleased that no one seemed afraid of him. Folks around here had known him for years. Most of them knew of his struggle to clear his father's name and many had offered quiet support. Unfortunately, few had the conviction or backbone to stand up to Stoner directly.

He went to the stage office first and collected Haley's trunk. The man behind the counter made him sign for the luggage, which he did, then he loaded it in the back and tied it down. As he drove past the land office, he was careful to avert his gaze.

Luck was with him. Lindsay was not only in his office,

but was sober, too. As the front door opened, the sheriff turned to look at him.

Lindsay's eyes were red and there was a yellowish cast to his skin. The man looked ill, but his expression was alert. He leaned back in his chair and placed his hands flat on his desk.

"You come to turn yourself in?" Lindsay asked. "I wouldn't have expected that, Jesse."

"You know that's not why I'm here."

Lindsay raised his eyebrows. "Then I think I'm insulted. I'm the sheriff in town and this is my office. You've been charged with kidnapping. Right now several men are out looking for you."

Jesse walked forward and leaned down, bracing his arms against the top of the desk. "I don't care about that. I want to talk about Stoner."

"You've got nothing to say that I want to hear."

Jesse ignored the familiar feeling of frustration. "It's the railroad, Lindsay. He's running people off their ranches because the railroad is coming through. I'll bet half my herd that he's one of the investors, too."

"That's crazy. There's already a line not that far from here. They wouldn't bring in another one so close."

"Not heading east," Jesse said. "South."

Lindsay's bloodshot eyes widened. "Never."

Jesse nodded. "From Texas. You know it's possible. Remember those longhorns I brought up myself. Folks around here are real interested in having some for themselves. There's beef to get to market. Towns are growing all over. Think about it."

Lindsay was quiet for a while. "So what if it's true? That's not against the law."

Jesse slammed his hands on the desk and straightened. "Dammit, listen to me. Everything Stoner is doing is against the law. He's murdering innocent—"

"Stop right there." Lindsay stood and glared. "I don't want to hear any of this."

"You didn't use to be a gun for hire," Jesse said. "There was a time you were a good, honest man. My father always respected you. Probably right up to the time you arrested him on charges you knew weren't true."

Lindsay flushed. "That's enough, Kincaid."

Jesse ignored him. "How do you sleep at night? Or don't you? Is that why you have to drink? So you can't remember my father's face when you hanged him? How many others haunt you, Lindsay? How many faces of the dead come back to remind you of what you've done?"

"Stop it!" Lindsay ordered. "Stop it and get out. If you don't, I'm going to arrest you."

Jesse fought against the anger. Giving in to it would accomplish nothing. "Interesting that you haven't already. But you know the truth, don't you? You don't want me caught because you're hoping I can bring Stoner down." He took a step toward the man who had once been a friend of his father's. "Help me. Help us."

Lindsay looked away. "No."

"Why?"

The drunk smiled, but there was no humor in his expression. "I like living too much."

"Then why are you trying to drown yourself in a bottle?"

"I'm doing what I have to do, just like you, Jesse. We're not that different."

"Yes, we are. I'm doing what's right. You're doing what's easy."

Lindsay sat down and leaned heavily against the back of the chair. "It's not that easy. Get out, Jesse. Get out and don't give me a reason to lock you up. Or shoot you. Neither of us would like that."

As Jesse watched, Lindsay reached into a bottom drawer and pulled out a bottle of whiskey. He took a long swallow, then slowly wiped his mouth with the back of his hand. A shudder rippled through him and he seemed to shrink into himself. In a matter of moments, he looked like an old man near death. Disgusted, Jesse turned on his heel and stalked from the office.

Once outside, he didn't know what to do. A peculiar restlessness took hold of him. Going back to the ranch was the safest route, he reminded himself. Anything else risked too much.

Even though the advice was sound, he found himself walking quickly down the boardwalk, heading to the office near the end of town. As the one-story building came in sight, his step quickened until he was nearly running. Maybe he was a fool. Bart would sure tell him that. Maybe he was risking it all, but he didn't feel he had any choice in the matter.

He crossed the street, then stepped over the boardwalk in one long stride and flung open the door. The wood crashed against the wall.

Beyond the chest-high counter was a large desk. The papers had been pushed to one side to make room for a white tablecloth and two place settings. Both occupants turned to stare at him.

Involuntarily, his gaze settled on the woman. He recognized Daisy Newcastle. Heat flared on his face. He wasn't sure if his embarrassment was for her or himself. He knew what she was doing and why. He hoped she didn't know how uncomfortable he was around her, how difficult it was to know she had once shared his father's bed and now she slept with their enemy.

He was, of course, a hypocrite. While he didn't approve of what she was doing, he used the information she gave him, even as he spent as little time as possible around her. He wasn't proud of his attitude. He wondered if his aversion to her was guilt because the elder Kincaid had used her and let her bear the consequences of their well-known affair. Perhaps he was destined to carry on the family shame of treating this woman badly.

In his defense he reminded himself that if his father had

married Daisy, the woman would be dead now. Dead at the hands of Stoner's cousins.

He shook his head. Nothing about the situation was simple.

Daisy stared at him blankly, as if she barely knew who he was. As if they hadn't had several secret meetings to discuss their plans. But he recognized her actions as a way to keep Stoner off the track. He let his gaze slip over her as if she were insignificant, then settled his attention on his enemy.

As always, Stoner was perfectly groomed, wearing an expensive suit designed to emphasize his size and strength. He'd seated himself so his scarred profile faced away from the door. Those who judged others on appearance would claim that Lucas Stoner was a successful gentleman. To Jesse, who saw beyond the facade of well-made clothes and trim haircut, there was only evil personified.

Stoner touched a napkin to his mouth, then placed the cloth on the table. "If you've come about the Winthrop girl, I've no interest in soiled leavings of the Kincaid family." He placed his hand over Daisy's and smiled. "With one notable exception."

Color stained Daisy's cheeks, but she didn't say anything. Jesse felt his hands curling into fists and he forced them to relax. While he wanted to rip the man apart, right now he had to be calm.

"I'm not here about Haley," Jesse said.

Stoner looked surprised. "Haley, is it? So you're on familiar terms with her. I would expect you to have to force her, but I had hoped that she would put up a token resistance. Obviously I misjudged her gravely. Perhaps the kidnapping was for the best, then."

Stoner's dark gaze met his. In that heartbeat Jesse realized he wouldn't be turning Haley over to this man. He couldn't do that to someone he hated, let alone a woman he'd come to admire. No matter what, even if Stoner confessed everything, he would protect Haley from this fate.

The realization gave him strength, but did little to combat the anger pulsing through him. He sucked in a breath to defuse it. "We know about the railroad," he said quietly. "Soon everyone will know what you've done and why. There's not much time left for you, Stoner."

The other man leaned back in his chair as if he weren't the least bit concerned, but Jesse would have sworn that he saw a muscle twitch in his jaw. Or maybe that was just wishful thinking.

"You've always got a scheme," Stoner said. "Why can't you accept the truth? Your father was a traitor and when he was caught, he received what he deserved."

The anger grew inside and Jesse struggled to control it. He wouldn't do anyone any good if he was in jail. He had to stay free to investigate Stoner—and to keep Haley safe. "You murdered an innocent man and I'm going to prove it," Jesse said. "You might want to start watching your back."

Stoner leaned forward. "Is that a threat?"

"No. It's a promise."

"I could have you arrested for kidnapping my bride."

"A woman you no longer want? Go ahead and try. You might think you've bought and paid for this town, but there are still a few people who own their own souls."

"How intriguing. I must look into that."

Jesse ignored him and walked to the door. "It's just a matter of time. Your luck is going to run out and I'm going to be standing right at the front of the crowd to watch you hang."

Chapter Thirteen

Haley paced restlessly through the parlor. Every few minutes she glanced out the front window, hoping to catch a glimpse of Jesse returning from his unexpected trip to town.

At lunch, when Christine had told her he had gone to Whitehorn, she'd been surprised. Not only that he was risking the visit, but also that he hadn't told her he was leaving. On the trail, neither of them had been able to go away without the other knowing. Even though it shouldn't matter, she felt funny that he had left without saying anything to her. He should have... She shrugged, not sure what Jesse should have done.

She pressed a hand against her nervous stomach, and wondered what caused the fluttering inside. Was it concern that Jesse might be captured and arrested? Was it worry about whether or not he would talk to Lucas Stoner about her release? Was it anticipation about the possibility of finally meeting her bridegroom? Whatever the reason, she wished he would hurry back and answer her questions.

"Jesse," she whispered, liking that the sound of his name had the ability to calm her.

A flash of movement caught her eye and she hurried to the window. But it was only one of the cowboys riding back to the ranch. Christine had told her Jesse had taken a wagon into town so he could bring back her trunk. That was so like him—thinking of her and her comfort.

"Are you waiting for Jesse?"

The sound of the voice made her jump. Haley spun and saw Christine standing in the entrance to the parlor. She smiled at her hostess. "Yes, I am. I know it's silly. He might not be back until later, but I'm anxious for news."

Christine glanced out the window. "We all are. I hope nothing happens to Jesse." She paused as if she were going to say more, then she pressed her lips together.

Haley knew they were worried about the same thing—about the sheriff arresting Jesse. "I'm sure he thought it was safe," she said, trying to convince herself along with Christine.

"He's been wrong before," the other woman said, then she shook her head. "But he can be a stubborn man. Bart tried to talk him out of it, but he wouldn't listen. We can only hope Sheriff Lindsay doesn't want to risk stirring up the town."

The churning in her stomach increased. "I'm sorry to be the cause of trouble."

Christine moved close and rested her hand on Haley's shoulder. "You're not responsible for any of this. You came to Whitehorn in good faith, expecting a happy bridegroom, not a kidnapping. Jesse's the one who should be apologizing, not you. When all this is over, I'm sure he will."

"He doesn't have to," Haley said, thinking that if she had to be kidnapped by someone, she would rather it be Jesse than anyone else she could think of.

Christine looked at her for a moment as if trying to read her thoughts. Then the other woman rubbed her lower back and sighed. "Everything hurts today and I didn't sleep much, so I'm going to lie down for a while. At least until it's time to prepare supper. Will you be all right on your own?"

"Yes, thank you. In fact, why don't you let me start supper? I'm a pretty good cook."

"That would be lovely." Christine gave her a brief hug, then left the parlor.

Haley's gaze followed the other woman until she disappeared around the corner. She recognized the whisper of envy drifting through her. Envy for the other woman's happiness, her husband and her expected baby. All the things Haley had wanted for herself.

Soon, she told herself. If Jesse had seen Lucas in town, then soon she would be a bride. She would leave the ranch, go to Whitehorn and start her new life.

She paused expectantly, waiting for the usual flood of anticipation, but nothing happened. She tried to picture Lucas, but again she couldn't imagine any man. Except Jesse. Maybe that was the problem. She'd spent too much time in Jesse's company. She liked him, enjoyed being around him and appreciated his kindness. He was handsome, caring and his kisses made her feel—

"Don't think about that," she said aloud. She was going to marry Lucas Stoner. She should *not* be reliving Jesse's wonderful kisses. Even if they were the guilty secret that she thought about every night before she fell asleep. Even if she longed to have him kiss her again.

She sank onto the sofa facing the window and covered her face with her hands. If only Jesse had never kidnapped her, then she would be married right now. She wouldn't have met Jesse and he wouldn't have kissed her so she wouldn't have to be thinking about how much she was going to miss him when she moved to town. She wouldn't worry about being disloyal and confused. If only Jesse wasn't so convinced that Lucas Stoner was responsible for his father's death. If only she could be sure Lucas was the perfect man she envisioned him to be. If only she could believe that she could trust him as much as she trusted Jesse.

Haley dropped her hands to her lap and straightened.

That was what all this was about, she realized. She trusted Jesse. He'd taken care of her, looked out for her. To the best of her knowledge, he'd never lied to her. So why was he lying about Lucas?

Worse, what was going to happen to her if he wasn't lying? What if he was telling the truth?

The voice in her head had whispered the possibility from the first moment Jesse had told her his opinion of Lucas Stoner. She desperately wanted Jesse to be wrong—otherwise she would have lost her dream. But what if he wasn't? What if Stoner was everything Jesse said? She couldn't marry a murderer. She couldn't marry the man who had killed Jesse's father and destroyed his ranch.

She rose to her feet and crossed back to the window. From here she could see the barn and the pastures beyond. It was another beautiful spring day, with a bright blue sky and a few puffy, white clouds. The trees had burst into a dozen shades of green and flowers had sprung up everywhere. Had Jesse's ranch been like this?

She remembered the burned-out buildings and the dead family they'd discovered a few days before. Without closing her eyes she could see the destruction, feel the woman's concern for her children and her pain at dying so young. Had the same thing happened on Jesse's ranch?

"Lucas Stoner is a fine gentleman," she whispered frantically. "A good man. Kind, successful, loving." But the familiar words didn't work their usual magic and instead of feeling relieved, she felt unsettled and worried.

"Tell me what to do, Jesse. Tell me what's right. Is Lucas Stoner really horrible or are you wrong about him? What is—"

She saw something out of the corner of her eye and glanced up. A wagon came round the bend, following the narrow track that led to the ranch house. As she recognized the driver, her heart began to pound hard in her chest and it was all she could do to keep from clapping her hands together with pleasure. Jesse had returned. The sheriff hadn't put him in jail after all.

She hurried to the rear of the house, then stepped out into the bright afternoon. The tension fled her stomach, leaving behind only a slight tingling. The same sort of tingling she'd felt when he'd first kissed her. The same sensation she experienced each night when she thought about him kissing her and holding her.

Her step quickened and she reached the barn just as Jesse drew the horse to a stop. He glanced down at her, but didn't say anything. There was something wrong—she knew by the tightness of his expression.

"What happened?" she asked.

"Nothing." He stepped down and brushed past her. "I got your trunk from the stage office." He walked to the rear of the wagon and lifted out the large, heavy trunk and set it on the ground. "I don't think anyone has opened it, so all your things should be fine."

She barely gave the battered case a glance. "I don't care about that. Are you all right?"

His dark gaze refused to meet hers. "I'm here, aren't I? Lindsay didn't throw me in jail. Don't worry."

He stepped past her. She reached out and took hold of his arm. Under her hand she felt the shifting of his muscles, coiled strength that made her feel safe. "Jesse?"

At last he looked at her. Something shadowed and ugly moved through his eyes and then was gone. She stared into the impassive face of a stranger. Despite their time together, she felt as if she didn't really know this man. What had happened to him? What was he hiding from her?

"Did you see Mr. Stoner?"

His mouth straightened. "Yes, I saw your Mr. Stoner." His voice was low and angry. "What a fine man you've chosen, Haley. Too bad you can't be with him just yet."

"You're not letting me go." It wasn't a question.

He answered anyway. "No, I'm not letting you go. Not

now. Maybe never. Maybe I'll just keep you here as my prisoner. Stoner can rot in hell waiting for you.''

She felt a tension in him, the way his muscles hardened as if he were preparing to do battle. Perhaps he should have frightened her, but he didn't. She knew with a certainty she couldn't explain that Jesse wasn't ever going to turn her over to Stoner. She couldn't have told how she'd come to believe that, but she did.

Haley dropped her hand to her side and braced herself for the heartache. There was none. She probed her heart and only found confusion. There were circumstances and forces at work she didn't understand. For one brief moment she allowed herself to fantasize that Jesse wanted to keep her for himself. That the kisses they'd shared meant as much to him as they had to her. Then she firmly squashed that hope. Jesse saw her as a means to an end, nothing more.

He led the horse into the barn and she followed. While he unhitched the horse and began to rub it down, she watched him, wondering what had happened to upset him. What had he and Stoner said to each other? There were several bales of hay in the corner. She sat on one and rested her elbows on her knees. The smells were pleasant—horses, hay, grain, hints of fresh air and spring flowers.

''Was your ranch like this?'' she asked without thinking. As soon as the words left her lips, she hunched slightly, half-expecting him to yell at her.

Instead he continued to brush the horse with steady strokes. He was silent for several minutes, then at last he spoke. ''The ranch house was bigger. Two stories, with a porch that wrapped all the way around. About the same number of acres of land, but we had more water.''

''Is the land still yours?''

He nodded. ''Stoner tried to claim it, but I came back in time.''

''When all this is…'' She hesitated, not sure how to describe the situation. "When everything is settled, will you move back?"

"It's my home. I don't have anywhere else to go. I'll probably tear down what's left of the ranch house and build something else. The cattle have been left to fend for themselves, so I'll need to round up the herd and check brands." He shrugged. "My father and I had talked about starting a breeding program. That's why I went to Texas to bring up the longhorns. They're survivors, but the meat's stringy. We wanted to breed them with the cattle we have, trying to get the best from both of them."

"You're still going to do that, aren't you?"

"I suppose. Bart has my Texas cattle on his land. When I'm ready, I'll take them over to my place." He shook his head. "That seems a long way off right now."

"It's not," she told him. "You've got the information about the railroad. Soon you'll have solved the mystery and be able to get on with your life."

"We *think* we know about the railroad. We could be wrong."

"Then you'll figure out what else it could be. You've come so far, Jesse. You have to make it." She pictured herds of cattle grazing on endless acres of Jesse's ranch land. "You won't be able to do all the work yourself," she said. "You'll have to hire some men."

"A couple dozen at least. That won't be hard. Cowboys are coming through Whitehorn all the time."

"Too bad you don't have a couple of sons to help."

She'd spoken without thinking. He looked at her, his expression still unreadable. She remembered too late that his wife had died. Was it in childbirth?

"There weren't any children, were there?" she asked tentatively.

He dropped the brushes to the ground and led the horse into a stall. When he returned, he collected the grooming tools and placed them in a box, then settled on a bale of hay a few feet from hers.

"No children," he said, the two words clipped.

"It's not too late. You could still—"

"I have no interest in getting married again."

"But—"

He sprang to his feet and glared down at her. "You don't understand, Haley. This isn't the city. The winters are long and cruel. The wind sounds like someone is screaming and it can last for days. In the summer, the sun beats down hot enough to drop a horse. Big ranches mean living miles from neighbors. The life is isolated and there's plenty of hard work for everyone. Too much work."

She straightened and pressed her hands against her thighs. "You think I don't know about hard work? At least out here it's just the wind screaming. In the building where I lived, a man beat his wife to death. It took him two years to do it. Two years of listening to her scream as he slapped her with his hands and hit her with his fists. I used to try to bury my face in the pillow and wish he would go away, or she would leave him or that the screaming would stop. Then one night it did. He'd killed her."

"Haley, I—"

"I'm not finished. I've worked until my back was nearly broken in two. Until my hands were bleeding from the lye in the soap I used to scrub floors. I've gone without food for as long as three days because I didn't have any money. I've come out of my building in the morning after a bad winter storm and seen people frozen to death in the street."

She had to pause to catch her breath. Ugly memories filled her head, things she'd tried hard to forget. "I'm not saying it isn't hard here, Jesse. I'm sure it is. Just as hard as everywhere else. Montana is very beautiful and I suppose it's deadly, too. You can think what you like, but don't you dare tell me that as a woman, I'm not strong enough to survive. I know men who couldn't survive in the city. People either have the strength to fight and keep going or they don't. It's not the place."

"I'm sorry you had to go through all that," Jesse said. "I'm sorry there wasn't someone around to protect you."

She shrugged, indicating it didn't really matter to her, but of course it did. She'd hated being alone. That was why her dream about a loving husband and family was so important to her.

"I never thought of life in the city as being hard," he continued and leaned against the barn wall. "Maybe you're right. Maybe the will to survive is in a person. Claire wasn't like you."

Haley wasn't sure what he meant, but when he paused, she didn't speak. Something inside whispered she might not like what he had to say about his late wife, but her desire to hear him talk about her was stronger than her fear of what he might say.

Jesse pulled off his hat and slapped it against his thigh. His hair was dark and too long, covering the collar of his shirt. As she thought of how soft his hair would be if she touched it, her fingers curled into her palms, anticipating the contact.

"Claire was from Georgia, a small town outside of Atlanta. The family had money and she'd never had to do much for herself. She was slender and pale. Very pretty."

"A lady," Haley said.

"A decoration," Jesse corrected. "She could have made someone a lovely wife, but our marriage was a mistake. She hated the ranch, the hard work. She had perfectly white hands without a single blemish. She was very proud of her hands."

Haley straightened her fingers and stared at her short nails, the red mark where a chicken had pecked her. There were bruises and scars. When she turned her hands over to look at the other side, she saw calluses and more scars. These were not the hands of a lady. She worked hard and expected that to continue.

"She sounds lovely," she said, hoping he couldn't tell

how inadequate she felt when compared with Claire. Jesse's
wife sounded like everything she'd ever wanted to be.

"Yes, she does. Claire always wore white, even in the
winter. Pretty white dresses with short sleeves and lots of
ruffles. She moved silently through the house, like a
ghost."

"Was she beautiful?"

He nodded.

Not like me, Haley thought sadly. Jesse had said that. So
he didn't think she was pretty. Funny how she'd never
much paid attention to her looks, but after Jesse had kissed
her, she'd hoped he would find her attractive. Obviously he
didn't.

"Haley, no." He crossed to her side and sat next to her,
then took her hands in his. "You're not to think ill of
yourself."

"Oh, I don't," she said lightly, wondering how he'd
known what she was thinking. "I'm sturdy and sensible.
Not like Claire, but I'm a good person and a hard worker."

His dark gaze searched hers. "You're so much more than
that."

She liked the feel of his fingers wrapped around hers.
She wanted to lean close and have him take her in his arms,
but she didn't have the courage to ask.

"Do you want to know how she died?" he asked.

As he spoke the question, she realized she didn't. Somehow she knew she wasn't going to like what he said. But
she didn't have a choice, so she nodded slowly.

"She started talking to herself," he said. "Just a sentence or two at first, then entire conversations. The winter
was especially hard and we were all trapped indoors. Claire
wore her summer dresses and refused to cover up with a
shawl. Her skin was always cold to the touch, but she didn't
seem to notice. Then one day, she opened the back door
and walked outside into the snow. She just kept walking. I
didn't notice she was gone for a couple of hours. By the
time I found her, she'd frozen to death. Right by the barn."

Haley heard the pain in his voice and ached for him. For both of them. She squeezed his fingers, knowing there were no words to ease his suffering.

Jesse squeezed back, then released her. "I knew right away the marriage wasn't going to work," he said. "I should have sent her back home. Instead, I tried to make her happy."

"It wasn't your fault," she told him.

"Then whose? Claire's? She came out west expecting to find a life like the one she'd left behind. Maybe she wasn't strong and wouldn't have been happy anywhere, I don't know. But I won't be responsible for the unhappiness and death of another woman, ever."

He stood and walked out of the barn. She saw him pause long enough to pick up her trunk, then carry it toward the house.

What strange forces had driven Jesse's wife to take her own life? Had she even known what she was doing? Haley felt sorry for them both, but believed Jesse was wrong to blame the land. People had different strengths. Claire couldn't survive in Montana, but Haley knew she could. If someone would give her the chance.

What was going to happen now? She wasn't sure she could bear to meet Stoner, but eventually she was going to have to. Jesse might threaten to keep her a prisoner forever, but he wasn't really going to do that. What would she do when she was free? Go to town? If she didn't marry Stoner, how would she survive? Could she find a job? Did she want to stay here?

The one thing she was sure of was that she wasn't going back to Chicago. She'd worked with a doctor for several years and she was a good nurse. Surely she could find work helping the sick. Maybe there was a doctor in town who could use her assistance.

She told herself she didn't have to decide today. The Baxters were kind people and wouldn't mind her staying for a little while. Until she figured out what she was going to do. Until she figured out what part Lucas Stoner played in the raids and why exactly her body tingled whenever she thought about Jesse Kincaid.

Chapter Fourteen

The gelding shifted uneasily as Jesse lowered the saddle onto the animal's back. Muscles rippled and the horse stomped its feet.

"Hell of a way to make a living," Jesse muttered, collecting the reins in his left hand, then preparing himself to spring into the saddle. In his case, he wasn't even making a living at breaking horses, he was paying Bart back for his help and hospitality.

His friend didn't expect reimbursement, but Jesse insisted. It was the least he could do. Two thousand longhorns were a lot of extra work for Bart and his men. While Jesse would give Bart a few bulls for the herd, he also liked keeping his hand in with the ranching work. It was spring, and spring meant rounding up the horses that had been let loose all winter. Someone had to break them, and he'd volunteered.

He spoke softly to the gelding. The animal's ears twitched, as if he were listening. Jesse hoped so. All he wanted was to remind him that he was a working animal and that being ridden wasn't so bad.

He put his foot in the stirrup and swung onto the horse's back. There was a moment of complete stillness, then the gelding lowered his head and started to buck.

Jesse hung on. He'd already tired out three horses that

morning, but he had a feeling this one was going to be tiring *him*. The horse spun and kicked out, trying to dislodge the intruder from his back. There were those who believed the best way to break an animal was to beat it nearly to death, but Jesse didn't use a whip at all. He preferred to let the horse get the bucking out of his system, then ride him around for an hour or so. If the procedure was repeated daily for a week, the animals were calm enough for ranch work. The cowboys expected a little feistiness from their mounts.

The gelding settled down. Jesse relaxed his grip, then realized a moment too late that he'd been tricked. One sharp, strong kick sent him sailing over the animal's head and onto the dirt. He landed on his back.

For a second, he couldn't catch his breath. Pain flared in his chest. Then he inhaled and sat up slowly. Nothing was broken or bruised…except maybe his pride. The gelding had trotted to the far side of the corral and watched him warily.

"You might have won this time, but I'll get you yet," Jesse told the animal.

"It's nice to know I'm not the only one who gets thrown off her horse."

He rose to his feet and turned toward the voice. Haley stood on the other side of the fence and smiled at him.

"It happens," he said as he walked toward her. He brushed off his clothes. "They've been out roaming free all winter," he said, pointing to the horses in the next corral. "They've forgotten what it's like to wear a saddle and be ridden and they're not much interested in remembering."

"Why not keep them in the stable during the winter? Then they wouldn't get so wild."

He took off his hat and slapped it against his thigh, then placed it back on his head. "That's a lot of feed, especially for animals that aren't earning their keep. If we let them loose, they take care of themselves. They're tough. Not much to look at, but strong with great endurance.''

"Sort of like me," Haley said.

He gazed at her, at the sun reflecting off her shining curls, at the bright green of her eyes and the way her mouth turned up in a tempting smile. "You're strong," he agreed, "but unlike those cow ponies, you're *definitely* worth looking at.''

The compliment made her blush. Jesse liked the flare of color on her cheeks and the way she ducked her head slightly, as if she wasn't used to being told she was pretty.

Like the cow ponies, she seemed suited for the land. He wouldn't have thought that was possible for any woman, but he'd been watching her these past few days. She fit in easily, taking to the hard work and doing more than her share. Christine was always singing her praises. Jesse knew the other woman was hoping to encourage a match.

"Now what happens?" Haley asked, pointing to the horse. "Did he win?"

"Nope. I get back on him again until he accepts that he's going to be ridden. It might take a while, but I'll turn him around.''

"And if he throws you again?"

"I'll keep getting back on."

She glanced at the horse and grinned. "I don't know, Jesse. He looks pretty stubborn to me."

"I can handle it."

"Pretty confident talk from a man who just got thrown."

He laughed and she joined in. The horse pricked up his ears as if he, too, wanted to share the joke.

Haley leaned against the fence railing separating them. "I'm going to make butter this afternoon. Christine's been showing me how to use the churn. Did you know they have their own icehouse? Bart already cut up blocks and they'll last most of the summer."

"You sound surprised. Didn't they have ice in Chicago?"

"Yes. Men brought it around in carts. No one I knew could ever afford it, though. Here you can have your own ice. You don't have to buy it. Or butter or milk or eggs. Christine keeps going on and on about how horrible it is that people have to pay for eggs." Haley grinned. "I'm trying to picture what my room would have been like if I'd kept a couple of chickens around. I don't think the landlord would have liked it."

"I don't think *you* would have liked it. Chickens can smell."

"Just about everything smells, but I still like this better than the city."

A single curl escaped her bun at the nape of her neck. He pulled off his right glove and tucked the strand of hair behind her ear. Even as he told himself to pull away, he found himself gently touching her cheek, then tracing the line of her jaw.

"You'd never go back, would you?" he asked.

"No. Not even if—" She bit her lower lip.

He dropped his hand to his side. Had she guessed the truth? "Not even if what?"

"Stoner," she said softly. "I've been here more than a week, Jesse. Except for when you went into town and got my trunk, there hasn't been any talk of the ransom or releasing me or anything."

Now it was his turn not to know what to say. How could he tell her the truth? He couldn't release her and he couldn't bear to disappoint her. He'd backed himself into a corner and he couldn't see a way out that didn't involve hurting Haley.

"These things take time," he said at last.

"Maybe." She stared at the ground for several seconds, then raised her gaze to his. "You are still talking to him, aren't you? Stoner, I mean. You really did speak with him when you were in town?"

"I swear I spoke to him, Haley." He wondered how

close he should come to the truth. "You know how I feel about him."

She nodded.

"I've come to—" He paused to pick his words carefully. "We disagree on your fiancé's fundamental nature."

"I don't think he's perfect anymore," Haley said quickly, interrupting him. "I have this image of him, and I want it to be who he is, but I'm not really sure what to expect."

Relief filled him. Maybe there was a way out of this. If she no longer thought Stoner was goodness personified, then he could hint that there were problems. Over time, she would figure out that her fiancé wasn't interested in her anymore.

"I know you want to be married," he said. "I understand about your dreams and why they're important to you. In the past couple of weeks I think we've become friends."

She nodded. The color had returned to her cheeks and he found himself wishing he knew what she was thinking. His mind filled with the memories of what it had been like to hold her in his arms. Of the taste and scent of her, of the sweet curve of her breast as he'd touched her.

Heat flared. He shifted so that his instant arousal was less noticeable. "I don't think Stoner is the kind of man who can make you happy."

"He and I don't really know each other," she admitted. "But he did send me a ticket and I did promise to marry him. That means something."

If it was just the price of the ticket, Jesse would be happy to reimburse Stoner. He'd hand him the cash right before they hanged the man. But he didn't say that to Haley. She was starting to question what she believed about her fiancé and he didn't want to appear too eager to have her abandon the man. Better for both of them if she let go of her fantasies on her own. That way the truth wouldn't be as painful for her.

But even if she was willing to hear what he had to say

about Stoner, what was he going to do about her reputation? That had been ruined beyond repair and there was little to do to fix it.

Except marry her.

He looked at Haley and found himself wishing it were possible. Haley had dreams of a loving husband and a family, but he wasn't willing to take a chance with another woman's life. Haley might be tough, but he couldn't be sure even she would survive. As for love—did it even exist? His father had loved his mother, but when she'd died, he'd taken up with Daisy. In his way, he'd loved Daisy, yet he hadn't been willing to marry her. He, Jesse, had never loved Claire, yet he'd married her and bedded her. And Claire—well, he wasn't sure what she'd felt about anything. Loving or not loving—was there a way to avoid the hurt?

"Nothing has to be decided right now," Jesse said. "You're happy on the ranch, aren't you?"

She nodded.

"I'll be going into town in a few days. Maybe we can get things settled then." It was a small lie, but it made Haley smile and for now that was enough.

A few days later Haley came into the kitchen with an apron full of eggs. She held them carefully as she stepped into the bright, sunny room. No doubt in time she would get tired of the routines of the ranch, but for now, she reveled in them. She liked doing things with her own hands, preparing a meal then serving it. Back in the city, she'd cooked some, but it hadn't been the same. She'd had to buy all the ingredients, not grow them. She liked being connected to the land.

She heard someone opening the kitchen door. She glanced up and saw a man's silhouette through the window. Instantly, her heart fluttered in her chest. Then the man entered and she saw it was Bart, not Jesse. Her pulse returned to normal and the fluttering faded from her stomach.

It wasn't that she didn't like her host, or enjoy his company. It was just that he wasn't Jesse. Her world had been reduced to two kinds of people—Jesse, or not Jesse. No other definition seemed to matter.

"Good morning," she said, moving to the counter and transferring the eggs to a basket Christine kept there.

Bart smiled at her; he poured himself a cup of coffee, then took a seat at the table. "My work brought me back close to the house, so I thought I'd grab a snack." He motioned to the biscuits he'd put on a plate, the bowl of butter and the crock containing jam Christine had put up the previous summer. "Are you gonna tell on me?"

His wife was always teasing her husband about his sweet tooth. Haley glanced over her shoulder toward the hallway. "Christine is lying down, so if you don't make much noise, she might not know you're here." She pointed to the plate of biscuits. "Of course she's going to notice that a few of those are missing."

Bart frowned. "I don't suppose you'd say you ate them?"

Haley laughed. "No, but I won't mention anything if she doesn't ask me directly."

"Fair enough." He motioned to the chair opposite his. "Why don't you keep me company while I eat these?" he said.

She poured herself coffee and sank down across from him. Bart broke the first biscuit in half, buttered it and finally topped it with a thick layer of jam. He took a big bite, then closed his eyes in obvious pleasure.

"I swear, my wife is the best cook in the country."

"Yes, she is," Haley agreed. She enjoyed spending time with the Baxters because they were so obviously in love with each other. She'd caught them exchanging glances and secret touches when they thought no one was looking.

Haley picked up her coffee cup and took a sip. That was what she wanted for herself. A man to love and respect, who cared for her in return. Now that dream was disappearing through her fingers. There were too many people talking as if Lucas Stoner were responsible for all the horrible things that had happened around Whitehorn. Even if he wasn't the leader of the renegades, he was obviously somehow involved. Where did that leave her?

"I want to ask you about Christine," Bart said, when he'd finished the first biscuit. "Jesse tells me that you've worked with a doctor for several years. Prescott says she's fine, if a little nervous what with this being her first child and all. What do you think?"

The love and concern in his voice made her chest tighten. She leaned toward him. "Your wife *is* fine," she said. "She's frightened by all the changes in her body and she's worried she's not going to be able to deal with the delivery. But Christine is strong and content. Those are the two most important concerns for a woman in her condition."

Bart nodded. "She says you've been talking to her about things." He waved. "About the baby coming and all. That makes her feel better. I want you to know we both appreciate you taking the time."

"I'm happy I can help. I like Christine very much." She wanted to say something about hoping she and the other woman could be friends, but that seemed a little presumptuous. She was still, after all, Jesse's prisoner and Stoner's mail-order bride.

"We've been talking about sending her away," Bart said. "What with everything going on around here, we'd both feel safer if she was with friends. It's about a half day's journey. Would that hurt her?"

"No. Just drive slowly and stop to let her walk around when she feels like it. She's having a baby, Bart, not fighting a wasting disease."

"I know." He picked up a second biscuit. "But I worry. She's my wife."

And I love her. He didn't say the words aloud, but Haley heard them anyway. Heard them and was glad for the woman who had been so kind to her. Heard them and hoped that one day a man would say them to her.

"Have you made any plans for yourself?" Bart asked. "I don't guess you'll want to spend a lot of time in town now."

His question confused her. Plans? "Nothing's been settled," she said carefully. She was going to have to figure out something. She couldn't stay with the Baxters forever.

"But not in town," Bart said.

Why not in town? Then she realized he probably didn't think she knew about the ransom. "Jesse told me about the ransom," she said. "That he's been raising it and Stoner needs more time. I haven't decided what I'm going to do about that. I did agree to marry him, but we *are* strangers. I think it depends on several things."

"What ransom?" Bart asked.

Haley blinked. "Jesse asked Mr. Stoner for money to get me back. I suppose Jesse needs it because of his ranch being destroyed and all."

"Jesse's got plenty of cash," Bart assured her. "If he runs short, he has several thousand head of cattle he can sell. Jesse didn't want money, he wanted information. Now that Stoner's decided—"

He stopped talking suddenly and pressed his mouth into a straight line. A knot formed in Haley's stomach, and with it a growing sense of dread. Something was very wrong.

She'd known all along, she realized. From the first time Jesse had told her he'd decided to hold out for money, she'd sensed he wasn't telling her the truth. But she hadn't wanted to ask, hadn't wanted to know. Now she didn't have a choice.

"Now that Stoner's decided what?"

Bart shifted in his seat. "It's not really my place to say. You should talk to Jesse."

"Jesse's not here right now. He's out with the herd and won't be back until later. Tell me, Bart. What has Stoner decided?"

Bart swore under his breath. "I'm sorry, Haley. Jesse never asked for a ransom. He didn't want you to know the real reason he wasn't turning you over to Stoner."

She swallowed hard and clutched her hands together to still their sudden shaking. As much as she didn't want to hear what he was about to tell her, she had to stay and listen.

"What's the real reason?"

Bart's eyes darkened with compassion. "Stoner decided he didn't want you anymore. You'd been out in the forest too long and he said he wasn't interested in damaged goods."

The room spun once, then settled back into place. Haley had never been the fainting kind and she wasn't about to start now. Stoner didn't want her. Hadn't wanted her for a long time.

"I see," she said, although she didn't. "Thank you for telling me."

"You all right?"

She nodded. "I'm fine. I wish Jesse had told me before, but I know why he didn't. He didn't want to hurt my feelings. How very kind of him."

Her body felt numb. She was surprised her lips moved enough for her to speak. She forced herself to her feet. "If you'll excuse me, I'd like to spend some time alone in my room."

Bart stood up and shifted uneasily. "I'm real sorry, Haley, but it's for the best. Stoner is a bastard and you would have regretted marrying him."

"I'm sure you're right. Thank you."

She didn't remember leaving the room or climbing the stairs, but she must have because she found herself sitting on her bed and pressing her hand to her mouth to hold in the sobs.

What had happened? What had gone wrong? One minute she was wondering what she was going to do about her commitment to marry Lucas Stoner, the next she'd found

out that he didn't want her, hadn't wanted her for days.
Weeks. Jesse had known all this time and he'd never said
anything.

She squeezed her eyes tightly shut and bit back a moan.
She recalled all the times they'd talked about her dreams
for the future. Had he been laughing at her, or worse, pity-
ing her?

Half-remembered bits of conversations drifted back to
her. Jesse asking if she would ever return to Chicago. No
doubt he was worried he would be responsible for her forever. How he must regret having kidnapped her. All he'd
wanted was information. Instead he'd been stuck with his
enemy's mail-order bride.

He'd tried so hard to be kind. She realized that now.
He'd wanted her to learn the truth about Stoner on her own.
He'd wanted her to want to break it off with him before he
had to tell her there was no engagement.

Stoner didn't want damaged goods. Did that mean her
reputation was truly destroyed? She shivered as she thought
of the nights she and Jesse had spent together in the forest.
Did everyone in town know about that? Was she ruined?
She wanted to cry out that nothing had happened, that she
was still innocent, but what was the point? She knew all it
took was a few whispered words. It wasn't what the woman
had done that mattered—it was what people thought she'd
done.

She opened her eyes, stood up and crossed to the window. Now what? Where would she go? What would she
do? Stoner wasn't going to show up to claim her and even
if he did, she wasn't willing to go with him. Not until she
was sure he was a decent man.

She nearly laughed aloud. Decent? Hardly. Jesse had
been right. About everything. Anger began to replace hurt.

How dare Stoner abandon her? He'd promised to marry
her, but instead, when he'd found out about the kidnapping,
he'd left her to her fate. What if the man taking her hadn't

been Jesse? What if he'd done horrible things to her? She could have been killed, or beaten, or worse.

Anger flared in her. Anger for the injustice of the situation and for Stoner's reaction to it. Who did he think he was? He'd given his word and even though she didn't want to marry him, she wanted to see him stand by what he'd promised. She wanted to hear the words, or at the very least, an apology.

Anger grew into rage and it burned white-hot in her belly. She spun on her heel and spotted her shawl folded on top of the dresser. She marched to the door, grabbed the shawl and hurried downstairs.

Whitehorn couldn't be all that far. Jesse had made it there and back in less than a day. She could, too. She was going to confront Lucas Stoner and tell the man exactly what she thought of him.

Chapter Fifteen

By the time Haley reached the road at the end of the long drive, some of her anger had burned off, leaving behind grim determination. How dare Lucas Stoner turn his back on her? While she wouldn't marry him now if he were the last man alive, she was going to find him and tell him exactly what she thought of him.

But first she had to find Whitehorn. In her agitation, she'd simply walked out of the house and down the drive. Now that she was staring at the road, she didn't know how far she had to go or even which way to turn. Maybe she should go back and get a horse. At least then she wouldn't have to walk all the way. But if she went back, someone was likely to see her and she didn't think the Baxters or Jesse would allow her to take a mount so she could ride to town and confront her soon-to-be-former fiancé.

Before she could decide what to do, she heard the sound of hoofbeats. She turned to see a wagon rounding the bend in the road. An older man sat holding the reins as an equally elderly horse pulled the small wagon. When the man saw her, he smiled and raised his battered hat.

"Ma'am," he said politely, then glanced around. "Were you headin' to town?"

She studied him and decided he looked harmless enough. Thin except for a large belly, clean shaven with ruddy skin and smallish facial features. "Yes. I'm..." She thought quickly, then came up with what she hoped was a believable story. "I'm visiting with the Baxters. I'm a distant cousin of Christine's. I thought I would do some shopping today, but I didn't want to bother anyone. Is Whitehorn very far?"

"About three miles," the man said, pointing down the road. "It's a walk for a lady like you. Ma'am, I'd be proud to give you a ride. My name's Albert Cooper. I have a ranch 'bout ten miles back." He jerked his thumb over his shoulder.

Haley had heard the Baxters mention Albert Cooper, whom they'd described as a good neighbor, so she didn't feel wary about accepting the ride.

"Thank you, Mr. Cooper. I'd be delighted to accept a ride to town." The faster she could get there, the faster she could have everything settled with Stoner.

When she was settled in the wagon, he clucked to the horse and it started forward at a slow walk. Haley wasn't sure she would get to town any quicker than if she'd been on her own two feet, but at least she wouldn't be tired.

"How long are you visiting?" Albert asked.

"I'm not sure. A few more weeks."

He nodded. "Summer's real nice out here. We have our hot days, but it usually cools down at night. You're from the east?"

She nodded.

"My wife was from Pennsylvania," he told her. "She died a few years back."

"I'm sorry to hear that."

Albert exhaled a deep breath. "Yup. I still miss her. I won't be sorry when my time comes. She said she'd be waitin' on me, and I expect she'll be there."

He continued to talk about his wife and his ranch. He had about five hundred head of cattle, which, when compared to either Jesse's or Bart's herds, wasn't much at all. She told him a little about her life in Chicago, being careful not to mention the name of the city. She wasn't sure everyone knew about Stoner's mail-order bride, but she suspected they might. It was the kind of gossip that would travel quickly. So far Albert didn't seem to suspect her identity and Haley thought the less clues she gave him, the better.

After a few minutes, the conversation slowed. As they got closer to Whitehorn, she felt increasingly nervous. Maybe it would help if she practiced what she was going to say to Stoner when she saw him. Her mind went blank. What did one say to a man one had agreed to marry without ever meeting? She knew one thing—she'd better keep a hold on her temper or she was going to end up screaming at him. Every time she thought of how he'd turned his back on his promise and abandoned her, she wished she was a man so she could take him out back and teach him some manners.

How could she ever have thought he was decent and kind? Jesse, who had kidnapped her, was ten times the man Stoner was. Jesse had acted like a gentleman from the beginning. Even now, when it would be easy to tell her the truth and get rid of her, he lived a lie so she could hang on to her dreams.

Her reputation was ruined. How could it not be? She'd never given it a moment's thought when she was out in the forest with Jesse, but now it made perfect sense. She'd been a fool not to realize what people would think. She pressed her hands to her suddenly heated cheeks. Telling herself it didn't matter that a group of strangers chose to think the worst of her wasn't helping her embarrassment. At least Jesse knew the truth. Except the truth was they'd kissed and she'd let him touch her breasts and, if he'd tried anything more, she would have let him do that, too. Because she'd felt things in his arms she'd never felt before. Because being with him had felt so very right. Did that mean she was what the people in town thought? Because she'd enjoyed rather than protested?

Too many thoughts tumbled around in her head, about Stoner, about Jesse, about what she was supposed to do with herself. She would have to get a job, but where? Who would hire her in Whitehorn? Did she even want to live there? Did she have a choice? She couldn't stay with the Baxters forever.

She dropped her hands to her lap and squeezed her fingers together. She wouldn't think about any of that right now. All that was important was her upcoming meeting with Stoner.

By the time they reached town, she wasn't any closer to figuring out exactly what she wanted to tell the man. Every time she tried to come up with a few sentences, she got angry and had to hold in the urge to yell at him. Maybe that was what she would end up doing. It was no more than the man deserved.

She studied the neat row of buildings that lined the main street. Whitehorn was small, but larger than many towns she'd passed through on her way west. There were several saloons, two banks, the stage office, a mercantile and, right at the beginning of the street, the land office.

Haley turned away as they drove by it. She was afraid if she looked in the big glass windows, she would be spotted. Which was ridiculous because Stoner didn't know what she looked like. She'd sent him a general description that could have easily fit a hundred other women.

"You said you were doing some shopping," Albert said. "How 'bout if I drop you off in front of the general store? Would that be suitable, ma'am?"

"Yes. Thank you." When he pulled the horse to a halt, she thanked him again, gave him a big smile, then climbed down. Albert tipped his hat and called out a goodbye.

Haley waited until he'd rounded the corner before she glanced around. It was midafternoon and there weren't many people on the street. Two women gave her curious looks as they walked on the opposite boardwalk, but other than that, no one seemed to notice her. She made a show of studying the display in the store windows, as if contemplating a purchase, then she headed back the way she'd come, toward the land office.

By the time she reached the building she'd worked herself into a fine rage. She could feel the blood rushing through her body. Her fingers curled tightly into her hands and she allowed herself a brief fantasy in which she slapped Stoner hard across the face, turned on her heel and stalked out of the office. Of course in the fantasy, he rushed after her, apologizing, offering a plausible explanation for everything that had happened and begged her to reconsider breaking off their engagement.

"Then he'll hand you a gold nugget the size of a carriage wheel and you'll be rich, too," she muttered. The ridiculousness of it all made her smile slightly.

When she reached the land office, her smile faded. She squared her shoulders and opened the door. "Good after..."

Her voice trailed off as she realized there was no one in the office. She crossed the few feet to the chest-high counter. "Hello?" she called.

No reply.

A large desk sat on the other side of the counter. Papers were scattered all over the surface, as if the owner had been called away unexpectedly. Against the wall were large drawers for files. Probably all the records for the land deals in the area. She eyed them and wondered if there was anything in there about the railroad.

A quick glance over her shoulder showed her that there wasn't anyone on the street nearby. How long did she have until Stoner returned? Enough time to go through a few files?

She wasted valuable seconds trying to decide, then determined it was just too risky. But there was nothing to be lost by casually strolling toward his desk and looking at what he'd left out.

She pushed open the half door that separated the counters

and moved quickly into the land office itself. There were stacks of papers on the floor and more in wooden crates around the edges of the room. Stoner wasn't very tidy about his record keeping.

She moved to the desk and picked up the document on top. It was a letter addressed to someone in Washington and listed government land in the area. She frowned and put it down. She was looking for something different. Something...

She shuffled through several piles, scanning names and the first couple of lines of the letters to try to quickly figure out the contents. Minutes ticked past. She kept glancing over her shoulder, but so far, there wasn't anyone on the boardwalks or in the street. She would read just a few more letters, she told herself. Then she would retreat to the safety of the other side of the counter.

She'd about given up hope when she found a letter from a man in Boston. A Mr. John Cahill. In the letter, Mr. Cahill confirmed Stoner's promise that the land necessary for the railroad would soon be in his possession. There were only five more tracts to go. Mr. Cahill expressed his pleasure that he and his investors would soon be free to begin construction.

"That's it," Haley breathed in triumph. The proof they needed. Instead of confronting Stoner, she would simply take the letter and return to the ranch. Once he saw it, Jesse would—

A hand closed over her mouth. Instinctively Haley screamed, but it was too late for that. Even as she tried to pull away, she found herself hauled backward. The letter fluttered to the desk and was lost in the confusion of papers there. She lunged for it, but her attacker didn't release her. Panicked, she tried to spin around to defend herself.

"Stay still," a voice commanded. "If you don't do exactly what I say, you're going to die."

The gelding put his head down and started to buck. Jesse was prepared and hung on. After a couple of minutes, the horse snorted and settled into a bone-jarring trot. Jesse took the animal around the corral a couple of times, then dismounted.

"You'll never be a pleasure horse," he told the animal, "but you're broke enough for herding cattle."

The horse snorted again as if telling Jesse how disgusted he was with the assessment.

"It's just a few months," Jesse reminded him. "Then Bart'll let you free for the winter. It beats pulling a stage cross-country or carting folks around in the city. You remember that."

The horse was not impressed. Jesse took off the saddle and bridle, then opened the gate so the horse could walk into the main holding pasture. As he went to get the next gelding, he saw Bart approaching the corral. The set of his friend's shoulders told him something was wrong. He met him at the fence.

"What's happened?" he asked.

Bart shook his head. "I don't have an excuse, except I wasn't really thinking."

Jesse's chest tightened. "Has Stoner been here? Did he see Haley?"

"No. I'm sure Stoner's in town where he belongs, but this *is* about Haley. I stopped by the house to get some coffee and biscuits. Christine had gone to lie down so Haley and I got to talking. I didn't mean to say anything. It just slipped out."

Jesse didn't bother asking what. He simply waited.

Bart stared at the ground, then raised his gaze. "Hell, Jesse. I told her the truth. That there wasn't a ransom, never had been. That Stoner didn't want her because she'd been out too long with you and that he'd called her damaged goods."

Jesse's chest tightened. He'd known Haley was going to have to learn the truth, but he'd wanted to find a way to tell her that wouldn't hurt so much. He'd never wanted her to learn it like this, just blurted out unexpectedly.

"I'm real sorry," Bart said.

Jesse knew he couldn't blame his friend. "If there's any fault, it's mine. I should have told her the truth a long time ago."

"Easy to say now," Bart told him. "When I first figured out you were lying to her, I thought you'd gone soft or something. But now I've met Haley, I like her, too, Jesse. She's a sweet lady. You were trying to do the right thing."

His friend's words were well meant, but they didn't help. "How'd she take it?"

"Really well. She was a little quiet, but she didn't cry or anything. She went up to her room."

Quiet? Not the Haley he knew. She'd yelled at him plenty of times, especially when he'd left her tied up at their camp. She had a temper and backbone. She wouldn't take this kind of information quietly.

"I have to find her," he said. "Try to explain." Even though he knew there wasn't a good explanation. Not one that would make sense to her. She was going to be furious and he couldn't say as he would blame her.

"Want me to come with you?" Bart asked.

Jesse shook his head. "No. I'm the one who lied in the first place. This is my responsibility. I'll talk to her."

He set the saddle and bridle on the ground, then climbed through the railing. How was he going to explain this so Haley would understand? What was she thinking right now? He imagined her curled up in pain, devastated by the truth, and by the death of her dream. As he neared the house, he broke into a run.

"Don't make a sound," the attacker said. "Do you understand?"

Stunned, unable to believe what she was hearing, Haley nodded. The hand over her mouth fell away, as did the grip on her arm. Haley sucked in a breath, then turned slowly.

Instead of a tall man fitting Jesse's description of Lucas Stoner, Haley found herself staring at a woman who was only a few years older than herself. The pretty redhead had wide blue eyes and a mouth that turned up at the corners.

But the woman wasn't smiling now. Instead, she looked grim and frightened. "You must be Stoner's mysterious mail-order bride," she said.

"Yes," Haley said. "Who are you?"

"Daisy Newcastle. I'm a friend of Jesse's. Don't tell me he's in town. He risked too much the last time he was here."

"He's not," Haley said quickly, trying to figure out who the woman was. She remembered Jesse mentioning something about a friend—a woman—who had helped him get back his mother's cameo from a saloon girl.

"Then what are you doing here?" Daisy asked.

Now that she'd been caught, Haley realized how foolish her plan was. "I came to talk to Mr. Stoner."

"About what?" Daisy asked, then shook her head. "It doesn't matter. We've got to get out of here. Stoner is furious about something, and trust me, you don't want to be here when he gets back. When he gets angry the safest thing is to run for cover."

"But there's a letter on his desk," Haley said and turned toward the stacks of papers. "It's about the railroad coming here. Stoner *is* involved. I have to get that and take it to Jesse."

"We don't have time," Daisy said, but she, too, began picking up papers and glancing at them. "Who was it from?"

"A Mr. Cahill in Boston. It was—"

Something *thunked* against the rear of the building.

"Stoner's back," Daisy said. "We've got to get out of here."

"But we haven't found the letter."

Daisy grabbed her arm. Her blue eyes darkened with

fear. "Don't you understand? If Stoner finds us here, we're dead. We can come back for the letter later. Come on!''

She pulled Haley toward the front of the land office. Haley glanced frantically at the desk, then she heard the back door opening and her heart fluttered against her ribs.

"They're coming inside," she whispered, trying not to panic. The front door was too far away. They'd never make it outside without being seen.

Daisy glanced around, then raced through the swinging half doors and pulled Haley along with her. "We'll hide here," she said. "Squat down behind the counter."

"If they come out here, they'll see us."

"You think I don't know that?" Daisy said quietly, her voice laced with fear and tension. "We don't have another choice." She crouched and tugged Haley down next to her.

Haley found herself trying to balance on trembling legs. Her whole body shook and she was afraid her teeth would start chattering. Something horrible was about to happen. She could taste it in the air.

There were the sounds of male voices, then footsteps.

"Whatever happens," Daisy whispered, her voice so low Haley could barely hear her, "whatever you see, whatever Stoner does, you can't make a sound. Do you understand?"

Haley didn't trust herself to answer. She nodded, then bit down on her lower lip and began to pray.

"You're putting me in a difficult situation," a man said. Haley knew with a certainty she couldn't explain that the man speaking was Lucas Stoner.

Beside her, Daisy clutched her arm. Haley didn't know if the gesture was to offer support or to warn her not to speak. She didn't bother telling the other woman she had no intention of making any noise at all. She just wanted to get out of this situation alive.

"Mr. Stoner, I never meant no trouble."

Haley stiffened. The speaker sounded familiar. Yet that was impossible. She didn't know anyone in town. Except...

The unmistakable thud of flesh pounding flesh broke

through her thoughts. She recognized the dull, nearly muffled blows, the gasps as the injured man struggled for
breath, the involuntary cries of pain. Recognized him and
silently winced. And then she knew who the second speaker
had been. Albert Cooper. The rancher who had given her
a ride into town.

"Mr. Stoner, please," Albert said, his words muffled.
"I've done like you said. I've done everything."

"Except give up your ranch."

"It's all I have."

"I see."

A shiver shot up Haley's spine. Every part of her body
screamed at her to run. She didn't know how long she could
manage to stay crouched here behind the counter. Yet she
knew if she tried to flee, she would be caught.

Fear tasted bitter on her tongue. Her breathing came in
shallow bursts that sounded so very loud in the room. In
an effort to ease the screaming pain in her cramped thighs,
she shifted slightly. A glimmer of movement caught her
attention. She realized that if she leaned forward she could
see through the narrow slit by the hinges on the swinging
doors. She closed her left eye and squinted, bringing the
scene behind the counter into focus.

Then she wished she hadn't. Stoner's attack on Albert
had started long before the rancher had entered the land
office. If Haley hadn't recognized his voice, she would
never have been able to place him. His entire face was
swollen and bloody, both eyes puffy and closed. Two front
teeth were missing.

One large man held Albert's hands behind his back while
another methodically hit his belly and chest. The rancher
moaned with each blow.

Haley's stomach rose toward her throat. She swallowed
to keep her breakfast down, then pressed a hand to her
mouth to hold back a scream. How could this be happening?

She glanced to the right and saw the man she knew to

be Lucas Stoner. He was as tall as the other two, broad, but instead of a work shirt and worn wool trousers, he was dressed in an expensive-looking suit. Perhaps some would call him handsome, but she shuddered at the sight of him. Then he turned and she saw the scar running down the side of his face.

Haley wanted to scream. She wanted to run. She wanted to beg Stoner to stop what he was doing. Instead, she huddled behind the counter and prayed that it would end soon.

A particularly hard blow sent Albert to his knees. "You promised me, Mr. Stoner. You said I could keep the ranch. I've done everything you said. Everything." He spit blood onto the floor.

"I've changed my mind. I want the ranch. You can keep the cattle, I just want the land."

"Where am I supposed to put the cattle?"

"That's not my problem, is it?"

Albert shook his head. "All right. I'll do it."

Stoner smiled. "I knew you would. Unfortunately, you took a little too long to decide." He made a quick dismissive gesture with his hand.

Behind her, Daisy pulled on Haley's arm, as if urging her to look away. Haley ignored her. The man who had been holding Albert's arms released them and grabbed his hair, tilting his head back. There was a flash of something shiny, a scream that was silenced nearly as quickly as it had begun, then blood. Blood spraying everywhere.

Haley could feel the terror building and with it the need to both cry out and vomit. She gagged and held in her fear. The blood kept coming, even after the man released Albert and let the dead man's body slump to the floor.

Dear God, Stoner had ordered Albert's death. He'd had his throat cut not five feet from where Haley was hiding.

She *hadn't* really seen a man die—murdered. Albert had agreed to let Stoner have his land, but Stoner had still killed him. Oh, he hadn't wielded the knife, but that didn't matter.

Stoner was the murderer. Jesse had been right about every-thing.

"What a mess," the man with his back to her said. "Guess you want us to clean this up, right, Lucas?"

"Of course. Get rid of the body first. Take it far away. I don't think anyone saw Albert drive into town so there shouldn't be any questions. His children have moved away and his wife is long dead. Actually, considering everything, this has turned out well." He glanced at the blood on the floor. "Except for this stain. Well, it couldn't be helped."

He stepped over the body and headed for the back door. "Get going."

The two men bent over, picked up the body and carried it outside. Haley watched them go. She couldn't believe what she'd just seen. Any minute now she would wake up and find out it was just a very vivid dream.

Daisy tugged on her arm. "Come on," she said, getting to her feet. "We have to get out of here before Stoner comes back."

Haley struggled to stand. Her legs were cramped and stiff. She followed the other woman to the door, then out onto the boardwalk.

"Start walking," Daisy said, taking her arm and urging her forward. "Put your hand at your side and try not to look so shocked. Pretend it never happened."

Haley hadn't realized she was still covering her mouth. She straightened her arm and forced a smile. "I'm fine," she said. "Really, just fine."

"No, you're not, but you're going to have to be. At least for a while. You've got to get out of town before Stoner finds out you were here."

Haley stared at the other woman. "What are you talking about? We just saw a man murdered. We have to go to the sheriff and tell him."

Daisy's expression was weary. "By the time Lindsay decides to investigate, the land office will be clean again.

They'll never find the body. It will be our word against Stoner's.''

"But there are two of us. We *saw* him. Besides, Albert will be missing."

"Lindsay is paid by Stoner. Don't you understand? There's nothing we can do. If you tell the sheriff, Stoner will kill you. Is that what you want?"

Haley couldn't believe what was happening. Nothing made sense. The world had become an unfamiliar and dangerous place. Had she really just seen a man murdered?

"I don't understand," she said, clutching her hands together. "This didn't happen. It didn't."

Daisy grabbed her shoulders. "It did and if you don't get out of here, you're going to end up as dead as Albert Cooper." The other woman shook her. "Get back to the ranch as fast as you can. Run all the way and don't look back. Do you understand me? Run!"

Haley's eyes filled with tears. She was alone and afraid and nothing made sense. "I can't."

Daisy released her. "Then you're going to die."

As simple as that. Haley stared at her, then turned and started to run.

Chapter Sixteen

Jesse reined in his horse and stared at the house in frustration. Now what? He couldn't find Haley anywhere. He'd searched the entire north and west side of the ranch. Bart had taken the south and east, while Christine looked through the house and the nearby buildings. He was avoiding the inevitable because he didn't want it to be true. Haley had gone to town. She'd decided to find out for herself.

His gut clenched as if he'd been punched and he swore loudly. Even though he wanted to blame Bart, he knew it was his fault. He'd been the one lying to Haley. He'd been playing a dangerous game by withholding the truth. Instead of telling Haley in his own way, he'd risked her finding out from someone else…and she had.

He didn't want to think about what would happen if she made it to town. What if she found Stoner? What would he do to her? Jesse wasn't worried about the man physically hurting Haley, but he knew Stoner could be a mean son of a bitch. He wouldn't give a damn about a young woman's sensibilities, or her tender dreams and feelings. Haley would be devastated and he had no one to blame but himself.

He urged his horse forward and headed for the house. Christine stepped out onto the porch and waited for him.

"Anything?" she asked when he was close enough to hear her.

He shook his head. "She went into town to see for herself," he said.

"I'm not surprised, Jesse. You know what she thought of Stoner. I had the feeling that over the past couple of days she'd started to change her mind about him, but that's not going to be enough. This has to have really upset her."

"I know. I should have told her the truth when Stoner first changed his mind. It would have hurt her at the time, but at least she wouldn't have had a chance to build up even more daydreams."

Christine nodded. "What are you going to do?"

"Head into town. Maybe she *didn't* make it. It's a long walk." He didn't want to think about the fact that she could have gotten a ride with someone, which would mean she'd spent most of the day in town. Whitehorn wasn't that big. It would be easy for her to find Stoner.

Christine glanced at the sky. "It's getting dark, Jesse. What if she didn't get to Whitehorn? What if she's lost?"

"We'll worry about that if I don't find her. When Bart comes in, tell him to stay put at the house. If she's in town, I'll bring her back. If not, I'll come here and we can both head out together."

"All right. Good luck."

"Thanks."

He tugged on the reins, urging his horse to turn around. At the slight touch from his heels, the animal broke into a trot, then a canter. Soon they were moving quickly down the dirt road toward Whitehorn.

As he rode, Jesse tried to figure out a plan. He would need help locating Haley. If Stoner had her, then the sheriff wouldn't do anything to get her away from him. He wasn't sure he wanted Lindsay to know Haley was in town anyway. If Stoner didn't know about Haley's trip, he sure didn't want the man finding out. Daisy, he thought, then shied away from seeing her. But she was his only hope.

Even if it wasn't safe for her to look for Haley, she would have suggestions about who else could help him.

He rounded the last bend in the road to town. The sun had already started sinking in the western sky. Even as his gaze registered something on the side of the road, he pulled in the reins. The horse stopped abruptly. Jesse was already out of the saddle. He hit the ground hard and broke into a run.

The dark gray dress was familiar, as were the light brown curls. Haley sat on the side of the road, her legs pulled up to her chest, her forehead resting on her knees. His relief was as sweet as honey. He hadn't known how heavy the fear had been until it dropped away. His shoulders straightened and his body relaxed. Thank the Lord he'd found her.

While meeting Stoner in town was the greatest danger, there had been others. Wild animals, drifters. She could have gotten lost or injured. But she looked fine. His heart thudded painfully in his chest. Unfamiliar emotions filled him. He wondered if he cared for her more than he'd realized. That wouldn't be so bad. Caring was allowed. It was the loving he had to stay away from. It was the loving that caused the pain.

A couple of stones crunched under his boots. When she heard footsteps, she looked up.

Stunned, Jesse stumbled to a stop. Her eyes were red, her face tearstained, and there was a haunted expression on her face. As if she'd seen the devil himself and thought that he still might be chasing after her soul.

"Haley?" He spoke her name softly. "Are you all right? What happened?"

She didn't answer. Instead she stared at him, almost as if she didn't know who he was.

"Haley?"

He crossed to her in three long strides and crouched next to her. She blinked several times. He had the oddest sensation she'd just realized he was there.

"Jesse? I think I've been lost. Did you find me?"

He nodded. "I'm right here." He touched her chin, turning her face toward him, checking for injuries. Except for the tracks from her tears, there weren't any bruises. "Are you hurt? What happened?"

He put his hands on her shoulders, then moved them down her arms. She sat passively, submitting to his examination without comment. When he was sure she was physically fine, he sat back on his heels and stared at her. "Haley, where were you? I've been looking all over for you."

"I've been here."

She wasn't making any sense. "Right here on the side of the road?"

"No. I've been walking." She looked at him. Something dark filled her eyes.

"Bart told me about your talk. I'm sorry. I should have explained everything to you before."

"I know." She shrugged. "I guess there's a lot I don't understand. I—" She bit her lower lip and her eyes filled with tears.

"Haley, please don't cry." Jesse bent over and gathered her close. She sank into his embrace, leaning her head against his shoulder. Sobs racked her body and she cried as if she'd been wounded down to her soul. Jesse supposed she had been. He ignored the disappointment that told him how much he'd wanted her to be over her infatuation with Stoner.

He rocked her gently, murmuring soothingly as he would to an injured horse. His father had always told him horses and women weren't that different.

"Did you go to town?" Jesse asked, needing to know if she'd actually seen her fiancé.

Haley didn't answer for a long time. At last the tears slowed and she wiped her face. But instead of looking at him, she pressed her face into his chest. He didn't mind. Her reluctance to talk gave him an excuse to rub her back and gently stroke her hair. The long curls had escaped their confines and he twisted them around his fingers.

"When Bart told me about Stoner, I thought I would go to him and find out if he'd really abandoned me. So I started walking." As she spoke, she grabbed a handful of his shirt and held on tight. "I walked for what felt like hours, and then I got turned around. I didn't know which way to go, so I stopped walking and waited for someone to find me."

Jesse continued to hold and rock her. Something about her story didn't sound right, but this wasn't the time to press her for details. He was just glad to have her back and safe. He told himself he should let her go, but he didn't want to. If he had his way, he would hold her like this always. This was where she belonged; where they *both* belonged.

But the shadows were getting longer and the sun was going to disappear soon. "We have to get back to the ranch before dark," he told her.

She sniffed, then stood up. Keeping her face averted, she wiped away the last of the tears. "I'm sorry," she said.

"You have nothing to apologize for."

"I've been nothing but a bother since you kidnapped me."

He stroked her cheek, brushing the back of his fingers against her soft skin. "That's the point, Haley. I kidnapped *you*. You didn't ask me to take you away. I'm the one who is sorry—for everything. I've really messed up your life."

She raised her head then, and looked at him. "No, Jesse, you didn't…I think you might have saved my life."

He didn't like the sound of that. "What do you mean?"

She turned away and headed for the horse. "Just that I wouldn't want to be with anyone who would change his mind about getting married. Lucas Stoner isn't the man I thought."

He accepted her explanation because they didn't have

time to stand here and argue, but he promised himself he
was going to pursue this later.

Christine came out of the guest room. "Haley's fine,"
she said. "A little tired from all the walking, but the brandy
is making her drowsy, so she should sleep."

Jesse shifted from foot to foot. "Can I go see her?"

"Sure. But don't be surprised if she dozes off on you."

He didn't care if she fell asleep in the middle of a sentence. He just wanted to make sure she was all right.

As Christine made her way to the kitchen, Jesse pushed
open the door and stepped inside. Haley reclined on several
pillows, her long curly hair secured in a neat braid that lay
over one shoulder. Her eyes were closed and he took the
opportunity to study her face. There were no obvious signs
that anything bad had happened to her, yet he couldn't
shake the feeling that something was wrong.

As he neared the bed, he saw her fingers stirring restlessly, clutching then releasing the sheet and blankets. Her
long white nightgown reminded him of Claire's fondness
for impractical white dresses, yet there was nothing similar
about the women. Haley was determined, vibrant, exciting
and, most important, alive. Claire had hidden from life in
many ways, ultimately choosing to run away rather than
face all the possibilities. Haley had left everything she'd
ever known on the simple word of a stranger.

He sat on the edge of the bed and took her right hand in
his. She stirred and opened her eyes. "Jesse?"

"I'm right here."

Her eyelids were heavy and she was obviously close to
sleep. Despite her ordeal, she'd never looked more beautiful. He wanted to gather her close and hold her in his
arms. If he were honest with himself he would also admit
that he would like to kiss her and lie next to her on this
bed, touching her the way a man touches his wife.

She tried to smile, but her mouth didn't cooperate. It
trembled and he thought she might be close to tears.

"What is it?" he asked, his voice low and concerned. "Are you afraid?"

She nodded. "I'm sorry."

"Don't be sorry. I'll stay right here and keep you safe. It's all right to sleep, Haley. I'll be beside you."

Then she did manage a faint smile and her eyes slowly closed. She exhaled, her breathing deepening. Jesse stayed, as he'd promised, holding her hand, wishing for more. And all the while telling himself that wanting to give himself a second chance to care for someone wasn't the same as loving her.

Haley paused in the hallway. A good night's rest had helped her feel better physically, but she was still shaken by all she'd seen the previous day. Despite her fears, she hadn't dreamed at all, and every time she'd opened her eyes, she'd seen Jesse sitting in the chair at the side of her bed. A couple of times she'd urged him to go sleep in his own room, but he'd refused. His presence had made her feel safe and comforted. Now it was daylight and he'd left her for a few hours. She told herself she was going to be fine, but she wasn't sure she could trust those words to be true.

Some part of her barely believed what had happened. She'd been too stunned to tell anyone what she'd seen...even Jesse. Nothing in her life had prepared her to witness a brutal and senseless murder. She'd seen people die before, had seen violence, although not often. But this had been too horrible to imagine. How could people do that to each other?

Her stomach grumbled, reminding her she hadn't eaten since breakfast the previous day. Although she recoiled from the thought of food, she knew she had to eat to keep up her strength.

As she walked to the kitchen, she heard the rattle of pots. Christine was already up and working. Haley hurried toward the sound, knowing that being with someone would help her feel better. She drew in a deep breath, forced a smile, then stepped into the kitchen.

"Good morning," she said. "I think I overslept."

Christine looked up from the pot she was stirring and smiled back. "I'm glad you did. You had a long and difficult day yesterday. All that walking after you got lost. You must be exhausted." She pointed to the table. "Have a seat. There's coffee and biscuits, of course. Why don't I make you some eggs? It won't take a minute."

The other woman's kindness made her want to cry. Everyone was being so nice to her. Jesse, Christine, even Bart. She knew he hadn't meant to tell her the truth about Stoner. Everyone had conspired to allow her to have her dream. But all their efforts didn't change the truth about the man she'd nearly married.

"Just biscuits are fine," Haley said, knowing even if she could eat the eggs, she wouldn't be able to keep them down.

"Are you sure?"

"Yes." She crossed to the cupboard and got down a cup. "Go on with your cooking. I can pour the coffee myself."

She filled her cup, then topped off Christine's. After collecting a plate and a couple of biscuits, she walked to the table and sat. Christine chatted about the ranch and how she was waiting to hear back from some friends who lived a half day's ride away. They were the ones she was considering visiting until she had the baby.

"I think that's a good idea," Haley said, trying not to remember what she'd seen yesterday, even as unwelcome images drifted through her mind.

"Really?" Christine sounded surprised. "I thought you said I was fine."

"You are," Haley assured her. "But with everything that's happening with the ranches and the attacks, you and Bart would both rest easier if you were somewhere safe. He wouldn't be distracted by you, and together he and Jesse could work to end the trouble."

Originally she hadn't had an opinion one way or the other about Christine's going to stay with friends for the last few weeks of her pregnancy, but all that had changed. She'd seen what Stoner was capable of and she didn't want him around anyone she cared about.

Christine set her spoon on the counter and took the chair across from Haley's. Her hazel eyes were wide and troubled. "What's wrong?"

"I—" Haley shrugged. "Nothing really. I just think it would be better if you weren't here."

"Are you all right?"

No, Haley thought. She would never be all right again. Except maybe in Jesse's arms. When he'd found her yesterday, and held her, she'd felt safe and comforted. As if his presence had the power to make the evil go away.

Haley drew in a deep breath. "I was in town yesterday."

Christine looked startled. "I didn't know. I thought you'd gotten lost on the road, but I didn't know you'd been to Whitehorn."

"I haven't told Jesse yet."

"Why not?"

Haley stared at the table. "I couldn't. It was too horrible." She glanced up. "I'm going to tell him. I need to, I think. But that's not important. What matters now is that I understand about Lucas Stoner."

Christine leaned back in her chair. "Understand what?" she asked cautiously.

Haley didn't know whether to laugh hysterically or break down and sob. After everything that had happened with the ranches and Jesse's father and who knows how many other deaths, Christine was trying to protect her feelings.

"He's not a good man," Haley said, not willing to discuss what she'd seen with anyone but Jesse. "He'll do anything to get what he wants. I know you three were telling the truth when you said he's behind the raids. I'm sorry I didn't believe you."

Christine leaned forward and squeezed her hand. "Oh,

Haley, how could you? The man wanted to marry you. Of course you would want to believe the best of him.'' She frowned. ''Did you talk to him? Did he know you were in town?''

''No, he never saw me, but I saw him. After that, I didn't want to speak with him.''

''I wish you hadn't had to find out the truth,'' Christine said. ''I wish your idea of him could have been true.''

''The picture in my mind was someone I just made up so that I wouldn't have to be frightened about marrying a stranger. I'm grateful that Jesse kidnapped me—otherwise I'd be married to Lucas Stoner right now.''

Both women were silent at the thought. Haley shuddered to think about having blindly gone into marriage with a man like him. Who knows what would have happened to her, what he could have done behind the closed doors of their house?

She finished her coffee and rose to her feet. ''Do you know where Jesse is? I need to thank him for finding me.''

''He's in Bart's office in the back of the barn going over some figures.'' Christine smiled. ''He said he spent most of the night sitting in a chair beside your bed, so he's a little tired.''

''I know.'' Just one more debt she owed Jesse. How was she ever going to repay him?

Haley found Jesse where Christine had said he would be—in a small office at the back of the barn. The room held a desk and two chairs, plus a couple of drawers for files. There was a window that looked out onto the corrals. Sunlight streamed through the sparkling glass, illuminating the thick ledgers open in front of Jesse.

He didn't hear her come in. She paused in the doorway and looked at him, at the man who had come to rescue her. After all the trouble she'd been to him, she would have thought he would be grateful to have her gone. He could have just let her go and not bothered to come looking for her. After all, she was of no use to him now. But he hadn't. He'd known what was waiting for her in town and he'd wanted to protect her from that.

As she watched a lock of hair fall across his forehead, she thought about how handsome he was. How gentle. How kind. He'd been good to her, even when it had been inconvenient. He made her feel safe. He made her want things she didn't understand.

In a few short weeks, her entire life had changed. She was still reeling from all that had happened. She'd come west to marry one man, yet now found herself with feelings for another. Feelings she couldn't name; feelings she'd never experienced before. All she knew was that her world was a better place with Jesse in it.

She didn't think she'd made any noise, yet he suddenly looked up, as if he'd heard something. When he caught sight of her, he smiled. The slow grin made the corners of his eyes crinkle as it exposed a flash of white teeth. Pleasure flooded her and she found herself smiling in return.

"You're awake," he said and motioned for her to take the chair opposite the desk. "How do you feel?"

"Better." She perched on the edge of the seat and rested her laced fingers in her lap. "Thank you for staying with me last night. I feel badly that you slept in the chair. It would have been all right if you'd gone back to the bunkhouse."

He shrugged. "I didn't want to leave you alone. You were pretty upset."

"I know."

Jesse set down his pencil and leaned forward. "Haley, what happened yesterday? You didn't spend the day lost, did you?"

She wondered how he'd guessed. Instead of asking, she shook her head. "A rancher came by and gave me a ride into town."

He stiffened visibly. "Who?"

"Albert Cooper. I remembered Christine and Bart mentioning that he was a good neighbor, so I thought it was all right to ride with him.''

Jesse relaxed. ''Albert is a good man. I know you were safe with him. So what else happened to upset you? Did you see Stoner?''

She'd thought she could talk about this, but she'd been wrong. Even as she tried to keep control, her body started trembling and tears filled her eyes. She pressed her hand to her mouth to hold in a sob. ''Oh, Jesse.''

He was at her side in an instant. Somehow she was standing, then sitting again, but instead of the chair, she found herself resting on his lap. His strong arms encircled her, pulling her tight against him. He touched her cheek, urging her to place her head on his shoulder.

''Everything is fine,'' he murmured. ''You're safe and you're right here. Tell me what happened when you got to town. We can fix this, Haley, but only if you let me help.''

He couldn't fix it, but he didn't know that yet. She appreciated that he wanted to try.

''I wish I'd never answered the ad,'' she said, clutching his shirt and burying her face in the crook of his neck. He was warm and smelled of soap and a masculine essence that reminded her of their kisses in the cave. The memory was a good one, warming her from the inside and making her less afraid. ''Except then I wouldn't have come here, and I like Montana, and the ranches. Despite everything, I'm glad you kidnapped me.''

''I am, too.''

Something soft brushed against her hair. Her heart thudded in her chest. Had Jesse kissed her? She closed her eyes and willed it to be true. She wanted him to kiss her. She wanted him to want to be with her and—

''Tell me what happened,'' he said, interrupting her thoughts.

She drew in a deep breath. Maybe the telling would ease some of her pain and fear. If nothing else, she had to explain about the letter she'd read. It proved that Stoner was responsible for the destruction to the ranches, and that he had set up Jesse's father.

"I was so angry after I talked to Bart," she began. Her voice was slightly muffled against Jesse's neck, but she figured he could still hear her. "Not at him or at you, but at Stoner. He'd been the one looking for a mail-order bride. The least he could have done was come get me when I was kidnapped." She raised her head. "I'm really glad you did that, Jesse. If you hadn't—" She shivered.

"I know." He rubbed the back of his hand against her cheek. "You're safe now. You aren't married to him, and no matter what, I'm not going to let him have you."

"Thank you." She sniffed, then continued. "I decided that I wanted to confront Stoner and tell him what I thought of him. I hadn't figured out exactly what I was going to say, but I planned to light into him good."

"I'll bet you did. Stoner wouldn't have known what happened. So you walked to the road and Albert gave you a ride into town."

She nodded. "He was very nice." She made the mistake of closing her eyes. Instantly she saw the blood flowing from the slit in the rancher's neck. Her stomach rose and she had to swallow several times to keep down her coffee.

"I found the land office," she said, forcing herself to go on. "There wasn't anyone there, so I decided to wait. There were a bunch of papers on his desk." She raised her gaze to meet Jesse's. "I saw a letter. From a man in Boston. A Mr. Cahill. He was writing Stoner about the railroad coming through. It's just like we thought, Jesse. It's going to run north and south from Texas to Montana. Stoner promised to have the tracts of land ready for them. He's one of the investors, too. It's all in the letter."

Jesse's expression hardened. "I knew it. The bastard." He drew his eyebrows together. "I'll see him hang for this."

She hated to tell him the rest of it. "I don't have the letter," she said softly. "I'm sorry."

"Don't worry about it. Now that we have the name of someone in Boston, we can investigate from there, too. We'll catch him. Tell me what happened next."

She told him about someone coming up behind her and catching her, then how she and Daisy had tried to escape, but it had been too late. Haltingly, she relived those moments when the two women had been trapped behind the counter while Stoner's men had beaten Albert. As she described seeing the man's throat slit, Jesse cursed Stoner, then drew her close again and began to rock.

"Hush," he murmured. "It's over now. There's nothing you could have done. If Stoner knew you'd seen what happened, you'd be dead now, too."

The tears began to flow, leaking out of her tightly closed eyes and dripping onto his shirt. "That's what Daisy said," she told him. "She pulled me out of there and told me to run back to the ranch. She wouldn't let me go to the sheriff." She raised her head and looked at Jesse. "Is he really one of Stoner's men?"

Jesse hesitated. "Lindsay is in Stoner's pay and he's not a strong-willed man. There are times he does what's right, but there aren't many of those. Daisy was smart to get you out of town. I wouldn't trust Lindsay with this kind of information. Two women would be easy for Stoner to get rid of."

"Oh, J-Jesse."

"Hush, love. I know this is hard." He cupped her face and used his thumbs to wipe away her tears. "I promise that when we get Stoner for the other things he's done, he'll pay for Albert's murder, too. He'll be stopped."

"I believe you." She had to.

"Good. Now I want you to try and put this out of your mind. It's going to be difficult, but you have to try."

She nodded. "I know that, I'm just not sure I can." She squeezed his shoulders. "You are so kind to me. I don't know how to thank you."

Something mysterious flitted across his face. If she'd had

to name the emotion, she would have said hunger, but that didn't make sense. Gradually she became aware that she was still sitting on Jesse's lap and that he was holding her face. The room was suddenly spinning and she found herself swaying toward him. A wanting filled her. A wanting that could only be satisfied by...

He kissed her. As his firm lips brushed against hers, she knew that was what she'd been waiting for all this time. That was what she needed. The power and affection in his touch gave her strength. The shared heat warmed her and chased away the dark places in her soul.

He moved his mouth back and forth against hers. She remembered their last kiss, the hot sparking that had singed her skin and made her body ache. She remembered the sensation of his tongue brushing against hers. She raised her arms and placed her hands on his shoulders, then opened her mouth.

As if he'd been eagerly awaiting an invitation, he swept into her. His tongue traced the tender skin on the inside of her lower lip, then moved in deeper. They danced around each other, tongues moving, reaching, stroking. Need filled her. Unfamiliar wantings that made her strain and wish he would touch her...everywhere. Her body trembled as it had for more than a day, but this trembling was different. It left her weak, yet filled her with contentment. Whatever she wanted, whatever she needed, she would find it in Jesse's arms. Here she could be whole. Safe, happy. She shied away from the last word lingering in her mind. Love. To find love in his arms would be a gift from the Lord above.

But for now it was enough to have him kissing her, holding her close and murmuring her name. And when he finally pulled back, she found herself wishing they could kiss forever. Perhaps if they kissed long enough, she could ease the strange longing that filled her body and made her heart ache for something she couldn't quite explain.

Chapter Seventeen

It was after nine when Daisy heard a knock on her front door. Her heart rose in her throat and she had to bite back an involuntary cry. No! Not tonight. She couldn't bear to see Stoner tonight, to have him touch her and take her. It had only been a couple of days since he'd murdered Albert. She'd yet to sleep more than an hour or so at a time. She was too tired, too frightened, too enraged to play the eager-to-please mistress.

The knock came again. Daisy wished she could pretend not to be at home, but Stoner wouldn't give up. He would pound on her door until she finally answered. Until he got what he wanted. That was what she resented the most. That no one ever had the power or courage to tell the man no. No one, including her.

She set down the book she'd been reading and walked to the parlor. After smoothing her hair and brushing her hands down the front of her skirt, she pulled open the door.

But instead of Stoner's handsome albeit scarred face she saw Leland Prescott standing on her front porch. The soft light of the moon illuminated his gold-blond hair. Shadows prevented her from seeing much of his face, so she couldn't tell what he was thinking. She glanced left and right, trying to see if any of her neighbors were watching.

"No one has seen me," Leland said, "but that's going

to change if you keep me standing out here much longer.
May I come in?''

Without thinking, she stepped back. He brushed past her.
She realized that his horse wasn't hitched in front. He followed her gaze and guessed what she was thinking. ''I put
him in the barn. There's no need for anyone to know I'm
here.''

Daisy nodded, closed the door, then led the way into the
parlor. Stoner had never seen any reason to take the same
precautions. If anything, he seemed to take pleasure in leaving his rig in front of her house. She wasn't sure if he was
simply thoughtless, if he wanted to claim her in such a
manner that no other man would look at her, or if he was
deliberately cruel. Whatever his intentions, she had been
shut out by the women and no man had ever come calling.
Except for tonight.

As they walked into the parlor, Daisy paused to light
several lamps. When the room was well lit, she motioned
to the large sofa opposite the drapery-covered window. As
Leland took a seat, she found herself fighting a sad smile.
Whatever had brought him to her house at this late hour,
Daisy knew the good doctor wasn't calling on her. So what
did he want?

She sat on the opposite end of the sofa, as far from him
as possible. Politeness dictated that she offer the man re-
freshment, but she couldn't seem to utter the words. Her
tongue had thickened in her mouth, making speech impossible. Fortunately, Leland took matters into his own hands.

''I'm sure you're wondering why I'm here,'' he said,
angling so he faced her.

She nodded.

His hazel eyes brightened with what she would have,
under different circumstances, called affection. Perhaps
even desire. But that couldn't be true.

He moved down the sofa toward her, stopping when their
knees touched. ''Daisy, my regard for you grows every day.

You're a beautiful, intelligent woman and I want you in my life."

She felt her mouth drop open. She couldn't have been more surprised if he'd slapped her or taken off his clothes to sing and dance naked. "Dr. Prescott," she began.

"Leland, please."

She shook her head. "*Dr. Prescott,* you are mistaken about my character."

"No. I've been mistaken in the past, but I'm not this time. Not about you."

He took her hands in his. She told herself to pull back, that it was wrong to let him touch her, but she found she couldn't. It felt too nice to have long, strong fingers stroking her own. He was gentle and she needed gentleness in her life right now. There had been so little these past few years.

Still, she had no right to lead him on. Perhaps he hadn't heard the rumors, the whispers. Perhaps he didn't know what she did in this house.

Carefully, because the withdrawing was painful to her, she pulled her hands free and clasped them together on her lap. "Dr. Prescott—"

"I know what you're doing," he said, interrupting her. "I know that you're helping Jesse Kincaid prove that Stoner killed his father and is behind all the raids in the area. I've never liked Stoner. I think the man's a complete bastard." He paused and shrugged. "Excuse my language, Daisy, but I feel strongly about this."

She nearly laughed aloud. Excuse his language? He was talking to her as if she were a lady. "You don't understand."

"Yes, I do. You're strong and brave, and I admire you tremendously."

The sincerity in his eyes was nearly her undoing. How was she supposed to bear this? She would rather endure one of Stoner's painful visits than have to listen to a wonderful man tempt her with what she could never have.

"I am neither strong nor brave," she said firmly, forcing herself to meet his gaze. "It's true I'm trying to help Jesse, but do you know why?" She went on without giving him a chance to answer. "I'm helping him because I was in love with his father. Michael Kincaid meant the world to me and I would do anything to restore his good name."

"We've discussed this," Leland told her. "I know you had feelings for Michael, but he's gone. It's been more than half a year."

Why was he making this so difficult? Why didn't he understand? "I didn't just have *feelings*," she insisted. "I was his lover. I went to his bed knowing that he would never marry me. I meant what I said, Leland. I will do anything to avenge him. That's exactly what I am doing. I'm selling myself for justice. You must know that Stoner is here at all hours. Don't you hear the whispers?"

Her eyes began to burn and she had to blink back the tears. "They don't even bother to whisper anymore. They say the word aloud and I'm not sure that I blame them. I'm Stoner's whore. What could you possibly want with me?"

Leland drew in a deep breath. She braced herself for the insults, or the silence when he left. If he hadn't known before, she'd made the truth as plain as possible. Few men would understand and certainly none could ever forgive. She wasn't sure she would ever forgive herself.

He leaned close and recaptured her hands in his. "I am not one of them. I don't care about the whispers or the shouts. Let them say what they will. You are the one I care about."

She stared at him. "How can you say that?"

"Because it's true." He brought her hands to his mouth and kissed her knuckles. "Don't you understand? I love you. When this is over I want to court you openly, then I'm going to convince you to marry me."

If she hadn't been sitting, her knees would have given out and she would have fallen to the floor. "But I've bedded other men. Not just my husband. Michael, and now Stoner.''

He raised his eyebrows. ''Shall I confess my sins? There was a lady or two before my late wife and there have been several since. I'm not a saint, but I try to be a good man. I was true to my wife and I will be true to you. All I ask is that you think about this.'' He squeezed her fingers. ''Think about us. About how I want to hold you close and be with you.''

He released her hands and touched her red hair. ''I want to watch the silver blend with the fire. I want to watch tiny lines form here—'' he touched the corners of her eyes ''—and here.'' He touched her mouth. ''I want you, Daisy Newcastle, and I'll wait to have you until this business with Stoner is finished. But no longer than that.''

She didn't know what to say. This couldn't be happening to her. ''I don't understand.''

''You don't have to understand as long as you believe.'' He leaned close and pressed his mouth to hers.

She was too shocked to protest, then she found she didn't want to resist. Stoner's kisses made her want to retch, while Michael's had been romantic and stirring. She could barely remember what her late husband's kisses were like. But with Leland she felt an explosion of passion she'd never experienced before. It was as if her body became caught up in a whirlwind of fire and need. In seconds her limbs were heavy and that secret woman's place damp.

Strong arms came around her. She ran her hands up and down his back, straining to get closer, to experience all he had to offer her. His tongue invaded and she nearly wept with relief. How she wanted him, wanted to be with him.

As the kiss went on, she found herself drowning in him, surging toward him, whimpering, whispering his name. He whispered back. Half phrases, single words, of love, of promise, of forever. At last he pulled back slightly.

''It seems I have your attention at last,'' he said, a rueful smile tugging at his lips. "That's very good, because you certainly have mine."

He took her hand and placed it on his hardness. There was no fear as she explored him, none of the revulsion she felt with Stoner. Only desire and regret that they couldn't be together tonight.

"I want you, Daisy. I want you and I love you. Do you think you can believe me now?"

She nodded.

He brushed his thumb across her damp lips. "Do you think you could come to care for me a little."

That was so easy. "I already do."

"So I will wait until this business with Stoner is finished." He held up a hand to stop her from interrupting. "Don't worry. I'm not going to make it a habit of visiting you. I won't do anything to risk your reputation further or make trouble for you. But I'll be watching. If you ever need me, just let me know. When the time is up and Stoner is caught, you must promise to come to me. Will you promise?"

"Yes, Leland. I'll come to you." She gazed at his handsome face and allowed herself to believe it might all be possible. That after all these years of uncertainty and unhappiness she'd finally found someone who could care about her. "But if it takes too long and you've already given your heart to someone else, I'll understand."

He rose to his feet and walked to the door. "Would you? I won't understand if you give your heart away, so you must promise not to. As for me giving mine away to someone else—that's impossible. You already have it in your possession."

She followed him to the door. He gave her one last parting kiss, then disappeared into the night. She closed the door behind him and leaned against it. For the first time in a long time she allowed herself to hope there might be a happy ending to all that had happened. For the first time in a long time, she allowed herself to pray. For Leland to wait, for Stoner to come to justice and for herself to stay alive long enough to experience the happiness waiting just out of reach.

Jesse looked around the dining room table. Bart and Christine listened intently as he finished telling them what Haley had seen in town. Their faces mirrored his own horror and concern. Albert's death was a senseless tragedy. The situation could have been so much worse if Daisy and Haley had been caught. Thank God Daisy had seen Haley and protected her.

"The question is what do we do now," Jesse said. "We have the information from the letter, but not the actual document."

"Does that matter?" Bart asked.

"The letter would help," Jesse answered. "I thought we could wire a detective in Boston and start the investigation from there. Thanks to Haley, we have the name of the man Stoner's dealing with. There are probably a dozen letters in the office and all proclaim his guilt. We're going to have to make do."

Bart nodded. "I have a few friends in the city. I could wire them first and get the name of someone reputable. Once they start to find out some real information, we'll be able to get the federal marshals involved. That takes care of any problem we could have with Lindsay."

Christine grimaced. "I can't believe the sheriff isn't going to help at all."

"He's been bought and paid for," Jesse reminded her.

They continued to discuss what actions they would take. Jesse glanced at Haley, who sat quietly in her chair. "How are you doing?" he asked.

She gave him a faint smile. "Fine. Just listening. I wish I could have taken the letter with me. For all we know, Stoner has already destroyed it."

He covered her hand with his. "It doesn't matter if he does. We're going to get him, Haley, and it's all because of you. You've already done more than enough. Don't worry about the letter.''

She nodded, but he could see she didn't believe him. He didn't know how to tell her he didn't give a damn about the letter or anything else she might have found in Stoner's office. Even a signed confession wouldn't be enough for her to have risked her life the way she had.

''Once the wires are sent, we're going to have to figure out a way to keep the other ranches safe,'' Jesse said.

''We have a general idea of where the railroad line is going to be,'' Bart added. ''There are only five or six ranches left in the way. If we warn the people there, we might be able to save some lives.'' Bart looked at his wife. ''You're going to have to leave, Christine.''

''Why?'' she asked. ''We're not in the way. They're not going to attack us.''

''It doesn't matter. I can't help Jesse with this problem if I'm worried about you and the baby.''

She thought for a minute then nodded her agreement. ''I'll go if it will make it easier for you.''

''It will. I figure we can arrange everything in two days. Can you be ready by then?''

''Of course,'' Christine told him.

Jesse looked at Haley. ''I want you to go with her.''

Haley's green eyes widened in surprise. ''Why? There's no danger to me here.''

''I—'' He clamped his mouth shut. He didn't have the right to use Bart's argument, that he wouldn't be able to think straight with her around. Haley was neither his wife nor his intended. He had no claim on her.

''I'll be gone a lot,'' he said. ''You'll be lonely.''

''Nonsense.'' She raised her chin stubbornly. ''I'm not running away from this, Jesse, and you can't make me. With Christine gone, someone has to take care of you and Bart. I can do that. I'm not helpless.''

I'm not Claire.

She didn't say the words aloud, but he heard them all

the same. She wasn't Claire and he was grateful for that fact. Haley was many things his late wife had never been, including a partner. He wished his life were different, that he hadn't learned the price a woman paid if she stayed on the land. He wished he was strong enough, or maybe it was foolish enough, to believe it was all right to give in to his feelings for her. That he hadn't seen firsthand the proof that love caused pain. Maybe when this was over, if she wanted to stay in the area and if she thought there might be a chance for them, they could talk. Perhaps there was a way to have what he was beginning to realize he'd always wanted.

"I'm staying," Haley said.

"Fine," he agreed, and found he was looking forward to spending more time with her.

"You know Stoner's cousins are loyal, but they're not stupid," Bart said.

"Meaning?" he asked.

"If we catch them in the act and threaten them with murder charges, I'd bet they'd be willing to turn in Stoner. Let the man in charge take the worst of the punishment."

"It's a good idea. All we have to do is figure out which ranch they're going to hit next and be there first."

Bart frowned. "One out of six odds. I don't like that."

Jesse agreed. "If we see the smoke from their fires, we know we're too late. If only we could find out where they're going next."

Christine folded the last of the sheets and glanced toward the window. "It's like being a child again and waiting for Christmas. I feel as if the time is never going to come."

Haley followed her gaze. Streaks of rain dripped down the glass. Ever since Bart had decided to take Christine to stay with friends, the weather had conspired against them. It had been raining steadily. The brief spells of sunshine hadn't been enough to dry out the roads yet.

Christine glanced at her and smiled. "I want you to know

that I do appreciate your company, it's just that I'm anxious
to be off.''

"I understand," Haley assured her. "Once you're settled, Bart and Jesse can concentrate on catching Stoner.
Everyone wants that finished so life in Whitehorn can get
back to what it was.''

Christine patted the side of the bed. Haley finished fold-
ing the nightgowns her friend would be taking with her and
settled next to her on the mattress.

"I've been worried about you," Christine said, her face
soft with concern. "You saw something no one should ever
see. If you want to talk about anything, I'm happy to listen.''

Impulsively, Haley squeezed the other woman's hand
and Christine squeezed back. "I know you're concerned
and I'm glad that you care, but I think I'm fine.'' She
thought about the dreams that sometimes came at night. "It
will take me a while to forget, or at least not remember as
much. I'm not worried that Stoner is going to find out what
I know, or that he'll come after me. I just want to help
everyone so that he can be caught and tried. I just wish—"
she sighed "—I wish I'd managed to bring the letter.''

"That doesn't matter," Christine said. "Won't you
change your mind about coming with me? You'd be more
than welcome and I think you'll like my friends.''

"I'd rather stay here," Haley said. "Bart and Jesse are
going to need someone to take care of them.'' She glanced
at the clock on the wall. "Speaking of that, I'd better get
started on dinner.''

"I'll help.''

Haley shook her head. "You look tired. Just lie down
for a while. Once the rain stops and the roads clear, you're
going to have a long journey. You need your rest.''

The other woman smiled. "I'm glad you're here, Haley.''

"Thank you. I am, too.''

She left the room, carefully closing the door behind her.

Once in the hall, she hurried toward the kitchen to begin fixing the noon meal.

In the past couple of days she'd taken over more and more of the daily chores in the house, freeing up Christine to pack and to relax. The other woman was healthy and strong, but she was only a few weeks from the birth of her first child. Haley knew she was having trouble getting comfortable enough to sleep. Besides, Haley liked working around the house. She'd never had a home of her own, and while this one wasn't hers, sometimes she let herself pretend that it was. That she had found what she'd been looking for here in Montana, that all her dreams had come true.

As she slid the pan of bread dough into the oven and closed the door, she admitted to herself that her daydreams weren't just about having a home. There was always a man involved, a husband who loved and cared for her. That wanting hadn't gone away, although it had changed. Now, instead of picturing a stranger whose face was always changing, she imagined one man—Jesse.

When it was time for meals, she watched for him from the kitchen window. When she had chores outside, she made excuses to visit with him if he was close to the ranch house. At night, when Christine and Bart retired to their bedroom, she sat up with Jesse and they talked. The more she got to know him, the more she liked and admired him.

On those nights when they sat up, she wondered what he was thinking. Was he remembering their kisses? They were often on her mind, and she wished there was a way to ask him to kiss her again. She didn't know anything about men, but she was reasonably sure that he'd enjoyed touching her in that way.

Sometimes, when the memories of Albert's murder threatened to keep her up all night, she pushed those pictures aside and thought about Jesse's kisses. They soothed her, although sometimes her body got hot and tingling from the thinking. She wondered how she could have gone so long without knowing how it could be between a woman and a man. What if Jesse hadn't kidnapped her? What if she'd married Stoner?

She opened a can of tomatoes and poured them into the pot on the stove. How horrible to have to kiss someone like him. She didn't think she could do it now. Of course, before Jesse she wouldn't have had anything with which to compare Stoner's kisses. She wouldn't have known what she was missing.

Although she was sorry about the raids and the destruction, she wasn't sorry she was able to spend time with Jesse. She thought about him and wanted to be with him. She picked up a spoon and paused. Was this love? This wanting and needing to be with someone? Had she grown to care about him the way wives cared about their husbands? She wasn't sure and there wasn't anyone to ask.

Did it matter? What if she had fallen in love with Jesse? He'd made it clear he wasn't interested in taking another wife. Even if he was, would he believe her affections were sincere or would he think she was just looking for another husband? After all, she'd made the long journey west just to get married. He wouldn't think that her feelings were about him specifically.

She heard familiar footsteps on the porch and her heart leapt in her chest. A smile tugged at her mouth and, despite the rain, the day seemed brighter. Jesse had come home.

Chapter Eighteen

Haley watched the two men dismount from their horses and start for the house. "They don't look happy," she said.

Christine crossed the kitchen floor and joined her. "I don't suppose I can blame them. I had a feeling they wouldn't make it on time."

Earlier that morning a cowboy had come in from the range and told Bart about seeing three men dressed up as Indians riding toward the old Smith place. Bart and Jesse had gone after them, hoping to stop the raid.

The men came in through the back door. Jesse pulled off his hat. "We managed to chase off Stoner's cousins before they burned down the main house, but it doesn't matter. Jonathan Smith is dead and his widow is already packing up to head east. She says she doesn't care what happens to the ranch. Coming out here was all her husband's idea, and she has three small children to worry about. Her family is in Maryland. She's going back as soon as they wire enough money for the train fare." He sighed. "Dammit, Bart, we need to get there before they start the shooting, not after."

"I know." The other man looked equally grim. "There's too much killing, Christine. It isn't right."

His wife walked over and wrapped her arms around him. Her extended belly made the action awkward and uncomfortable, yet Haley found herself envying them. She wanted to be able to go to Jesse and hold him. She wanted the rights and privileges that went with being someone important in Jesse's life.

The envy burned through her, making her turn away so no one could see what she was thinking.

Jesse placed his hat on a peg by the door and ran his fingers through his long, shaggy hair. "The good news is the roads are drying up. You and Bart can leave in the morning."

"Are you ready?" Bart asked his wife.

"I have been for several days," Christine told him. "Haley, if you can take care of things in here for a minute, I would like to check the trunks. They can be loaded this afternoon, so we don't have to worry about them in the morning."

"Go ahead," Haley said. She hoped that Bart would go with Christine, leaving her alone with Jesse. She liked when the two of them had a chance to talk. But Bart settled into a chair at the kitchen table and Jesse muttered something about seeing to things in the barn, then left.

She looked out the window, following his progress until he disappeared from view. When she returned her attention to her host, she found him watching her.

"Jesse is taking this more to heart," he said. "Everyone who is murdered reminds him of his father's death. He blames himself for not being here to stop it."

"There was no way for him to know what was going to happen when he left for Texas."

"You and I know that, but I'm not sure Jesse believes it. After his mother died, he and his dad only had each other."

"If Jesse had been here, he could have been killed, too." She didn't even want to think about that.

"We're all frustrated by the situation," Bart told her. "I want to get Christine as far away from this as possible. Jesse wants to make it right." He leaned forward and rested his forearms on the table in front of him. "Are you going to be all right here?"

There was something about the way he asked the question that made her uncomfortable. "Why wouldn't I be fine?"

He shifted in his chair. "Well, we are leaving you and Jesse alone for a few days. I'm just concerned about..." His voice trailed off.

It took her a couple of moments to figure out he was embarrassed. Then she realized what he was trying to say.

"From what I understand, my reputation is already in tatters," she said. She crossed to the table and took a seat opposite her host. "If you're trying to ask if I'll be afraid to be alone with Jesse, the answer is no. You're forgetting that he and I were in the forest for a week by ourselves. I trust him to be a gentleman and to keep me safe."

Bart leaned back in his chair and stared at her. "I'm glad you've noticed."

Now it was her turn to shift in her seat. "Why wouldn't I notice?"

"You were convinced Stoner was the man you wanted to marry."

"Not anymore." She thought about all she'd seen while she was in town. "Believe me, I don't ever want to have anything to do with that man. I made up a picture in my mind, based on a letter and a few girlish dreams. That's all it was."

If only it would be as easy to get over Jesse. But she had a feeling that she was going to be thinking about him for a long time. When she finally figured out where she wanted to go, she would be leaving a piece of herself behind, with him. Unfortunately, he wasn't ever going to know.

"Claire has been dead for a long time," Bart said. "Jesse wasn't happy in his marriage. She wasn't the right woman for him, or for the ranch. He never cared about her."

"He's told me a little about what happened with her."

"Really? I didn't think Jesse liked to talk about that time." Bart raised his eyebrows. "Isn't that interesting?"

Haley hoped that the heat she felt on her cheeks came from the stove and not from a blush. "I don't know that it's interesting. We've talked about a lot of things."

"Then you know that Jesse believes ranch life is hard on women? He's not convinced a woman can survive and be a strong, happy partner."

She nodded.

"That's not the real reason he doesn't want to get married again."

If Bart had wanted her full attention, he'd found a way to get it. "What do you mean?"

"Jesse doesn't want to care about anyone. He watched his mother suffer on the ranch. She didn't much care for the life, but she endured it because she loved her husband. After she died, Michael took up with a woman in town. Daisy. She's the one—"

"The woman who rescued me," Haley interrupted. "She knew Jesse's father?"

"They kept company for a couple of years. Everyone knew they were in love, but Michael wouldn't marry her. He had some notion that he'd made Jesse's mother miserable by bringing her to the ranch, so he owed it to her to be loyal to her memory by not taking another wife. Jesse saw both Michael and Daisy hurt by this decision. The folks he cared about most have been hurt by love. He doesn't want that for himself, or for someone he cares about."

While Haley appreciated the information, she wasn't sure what she should do with it. "I don't know why you're telling me this."

"I think Jesse deserves more than a life spent alone," Bart said. "But someone is going to have to convince him of that."

Haley thought about what he'd told her. Obviously Bart thought she should be the one to show Jesse that caring about someone didn't have to hurt. If only that were possible; if only she *could* be the one. But she knew something Bart didn't. All the time she and Jesse had spent in the forest, she'd talked endlessly about wanting to be married to Stoner. If she hinted that her feelings had changed, Jesse wouldn't think she was doing anything other than trying to make sure she found her dream of a husband. There was no way to prove to him she'd come to care about him for himself.

She looked at Bart, then rose from the table. "I'm sorry," she said. "I wish I could be that person, but I'm not."

"I thought you had feelings for him."

"I do, but he'll never believe that."

Bart and Christine left the next morning. At noon Haley prepared a meal for Jesse, but as she put the thick steaks into the pan, she was surprised to find herself oddly nervous. It couldn't be because they were alone. They'd been alone many times before.

But not like this, a small voice in her head whispered. They were alone in a house, which was different from being alone in the wilderness after he'd kidnapped her. For one thing, they were friends now. For another, her feelings about him had changed.

She crossed to the window and looked out at the ranch. At the barn, the cattle grazing in the distance, the horses in the corral. Above, the sky was bright blue. Just below the sill, she could see the garden she and Christine had started. Soon vegetables would sprout, then grow. In the late summer, they would need to put up enough to last through the winter. She would like to do that, to know that she was feeding her family through her hard work.

She could be very happy here—with Jesse. She was no longer content with the thought of marriage to a faceless stranger. It wasn't the union she coveted. She didn't want just to be married; she wanted to be married to Jesse. She wanted him to look at her the way Bart looked at Christine.

She wanted to know that they were going to share a bed together every night, that they would stand by each other through the good times and the bad. She wanted, like Christine, to grow large and round with his child inside of her.

She inhaled the scent of cooking meat and hurried back to the stove. By the time Jesse had come in from washing up, she'd served the meat and was placing a bowl of beans on the table.

She glanced up at him and smiled. "I don't see any dirt on your jeans. You must be nearly finished breaking the horses."

He glanced down at himself and grinned. "Yup, not one threw me today. They're about fit to ride. I'll let the cowboys know tonight. They can pick out their strings so they're ready when we start roundup in a couple of weeks."

She poured him coffee, then settled across the table from him. "Didn't you tell me the roundup starts at one end of Whitehorn and works to the other?"

He grabbed a couple of hot biscuits and put them on his plate. "That's right. Everyone helps, so it goes faster. Bart and I were talking about that this morning before they left. We're going to tell the cowboys to get the word out. With that many men going back and forth between ranches, we'll have a chance to catch Stoner's cousins in the act. If enough people see them raiding a ranch, there's nothing Stoner can do to hide what's been going on."

"What about the detective in Boston?"

Jesse shrugged. "I still hope he'll come through, but we can't wait on that. We have to be willing to take care of this ourselves."

"Do you think the sheriff will help?"

"I don't know. Lindsay seems to be sitting on the fence about this. He's working for Stoner, but he didn't arrest me when I was in town a while back. His men never caught up with us while we were in the forest and I can't believe they were that bad at tracking. Maybe Lindsay will join us.

If there are enough people to stand with him. We'll have to see.''

Or if Lindsay had seen the letter, she thought. It all came back to that.

"It seems as if everything is happening at once," she said.

"I've been putting pieces together for months now." He grinned at her. "It all started to come together when I kidnapped you."

"I'm glad."

He sobered. "Are you still mad about that, Haley? With all you've been through, I know you don't still want to marry Stoner, but I know those first few days on the trail were hard on you."

"I'm not mad at all," she assured him. "I know you were desperate. I'm just glad it worked out the way it did."

"I know you like Montana and that you don't want to go back to Chicago," he said. "Maybe Whitehorn would be a good place for you to settle."

His words made her fingers tremble. She set her fork down so she wouldn't drop it on the table. What was he saying? "I do like the West and what I saw of Whitehorn seemed very nice. It's a pretty little town."

"If you'd like to stay, I want to help with that. It's my fault you're not married. I thought when this is over, I could rent a house for you. You're pretty and smart, and a real fine cook." He motioned to his plate. "Any man would be honored to have you as a wife."

Any man but me.

The disappointment was a sharp pain that cut through her like a knife. He wanted to set her up so someone else could marry her. Bart was wrong; Jesse didn't care about her at all. He was being kind because he felt responsible for her. He'd been the one to keep her from marrying Stoner and even though Stoner wasn't someone she wanted, he represented her goal. A husband.

Haley knew she had no one to blame but herself. When

she thought about all the conversations they'd had while on the trail, she wanted to throw something. There she'd been, going on and on about what a wonderful man Lucas Stoner was. She'd made it clear that he was her ideal and that her only goal in life was to be married. She'd been so caught up with the image in her mind, that she'd missed the goodness of the man in front of her.

Jesse wasn't perfect—she knew that. But he was perfect for her. He was everything she wanted. And now there was no way to convince him that she cared about him because of who he was. He would think she saw him as a means to an end.

"You aren't responsible for me," she told him. "If I stay in Whitehorn for a while I'll be getting a job. I'm a good nurse. Christine has been telling me about Dr. Prescott in town. Maybe he would like to hire me."

Jesse frowned. "I don't like the idea of you working."

"I don't like the idea of you supporting me."

"Why not?"

"There's no reason for you to. I'm strong and healthy. I've been working since I was twelve. Why wouldn't I take a job now?"

"It doesn't seem right."

"It's all I know." The last thing she wanted was for Jesse to feel responsible for her, as if she were an old maiden aunt thrust upon him.

"Let's talk about this later," she said. "After everything is settled."

He frowned as if he wasn't going to let her change the subject, but then he mentioned that there were several more calves this year. The mild winter had helped increase breeding stock.

When Jesse had left, Haley cleaned the kitchen. She worked slowly, trying to shake the feeling of sadness that threatened to spoil her day. She was, she realized, tired of waiting for everything to happen to her. For the first time in her life, she'd acted. Coming out west had been something she'd wanted to do to change her life. She'd liked taking charge of her future, even if things hadn't turned out as she'd hoped. Yet here she was…waiting again.

"I want to *do* something," she said aloud. Anything would be better than just waiting. If only there was something she could do to help.

She thought about her time in town, about what Stoner had done to Albert and she had to swallow her fear. If she closed her eyes, it was too easy to think she was back in the office, crouched behind the counter, hiding. Praying that she wouldn't be discovered. Hoping that—

She put the dishes into the soapy water, then slowly dried her hands on a towel. She hadn't been caught that day. Daisy had saved her. Which meant Stoner didn't know she'd been to town. How could he know? He didn't even know what she looked like. He didn't know she'd been in his office or that she'd seen the letter from Mr. Cahill. All he knew was that Jesse had kidnapped her.

Her breath caught in her throat. If she went to him now, what would he do? Would he really tell her to her face that he wasn't interested in her as his bride? What if she told him she'd been kept locked up and had just managed to escape? What if she pretended that she was still very much in love with him and was assuming they were still getting married? If she pretended to hate Jesse, Stoner would have no reason to believe anything had happened between them. He was the one who had started the rumors about her reputation, but he knew Jesse well enough to know he would never take advantage of a woman.

The plan was so simple, it could work. If she was able to make Stoner believe she didn't know anything about him, he might give her a chance. That was all she needed. If the man trusted her, even a little, she would be able to go to his office and find the letter she'd read before. She might even be able to find others. They had to be there. With enough evidence, the sheriff would have to do something. Especially if she and Daisy came forward about Albert's murder. Then she could get a job in Whitehorn and Jesse wouldn't have to worry about her anymore. Maybe through her actions she could prove herself to be strong and resourceful enough to impress Jesse.

She leaned against the counter and thought her plan through. The worst that would happen was Stoner would refuse to have anything to do with her. She felt safe about the murder because he didn't know she'd been a witness.

No, she told herself. Stoner rejecting her wasn't the worst. His believing her was. If he truly thought she cared and he was willing to give her another chance, he could want to marry her. Then what would she do? She couldn't refuse without making him suspicious.

Which meant she might have to go through with the ceremony—and the night after.

Her stomach churned at the thought. She couldn't do that. The thought of kissing Stoner was hideous enough without actually imagining joining with him in that intimate way. Despite being a virgin, she knew exactly what went on between a man and his wife. Women occasionally talked about the marriage bed and working with Dr. Redding hadn't left much room for modesty.

Did she have a choice? Was there another way? Was she willing to wait until the men figured out another plan? She shook her head. She knew the letter existed. She'd read it. Finding it was the best thing she could do. If that meant enduring Stoner, then she would. Maybe she could find it and run away before anything happened between her and Stoner. She wanted the man stopped. Not just for Albert, but for Jesse's father and everyone else he'd murdered.

That decided, Haley started making plans. She would head to town in the morning. If she came up with a good story, Stoner would believe her. There was no reason for him to think she was lying, so why wouldn't he trust her? She wished she could go now and get it over with, but there was one thing she had to take care of here first.

She walked to the window and stared out at the range. Once her plan was set in motion, there was no telling what might happen. Circumstances might force her to marry Stoner and even to let him into her bed. That she could not endure. Her body—herself—they were a gift. Women were supposed to give themselves to their husbands, but then women were supposed to marry for love. She might not get that choice. If she escaped Stoner, then what? Her dreams were gone, her future uncertain, save for one piece of information. She loved Jesse and she wanted him to be the one. She trusted him and sensed that he would recognize the gift as something of value. Stoner never would. If she was with Jesse first, she would at least have the memories of their time together to sustain her.

She sighed. Was it wrong to want to be with Jesse? She loved him. Didn't that matter more than convention? Was it right to give herself to a murderer? But there was no other way. She *had* to help stop Stoner. The only problem would be convincing Jesse to be with her. After all, he was an honorable man.

Chapter Nineteen

Jesse washed up in the bunkhouse before heading over to the main house for supper. He took extra care cleaning and thought briefly about shaving again. He grimaced at his reflection in the cracked mirror above the outdoor sink. Why on earth would he want to shave again? He was just going over to the house to eat, the same way he did every night. Nothing was different. Except that Bart and Christine were gone and he and Haley were going to be alone.

"We spent a week alone," he muttered aloud, reminding himself of their time in the forest. "This isn't any different."

Yet it felt different, but he couldn't say why. Maybe it was because he knew Haley better. Before she'd been a means to an end, but now she was someone he cared about. Or maybe it was because being alone in the wilderness was one thing, but being alone in a house was another. Or maybe he'd just been on his own too long and he was seeing trouble where it didn't exist.

He grabbed the towel beside the sink and dried his face. He would walk over, eat dinner with her, then go upstairs and sleep in Bart and Christine's room. He paused. Was that it? That he planned to spend the night under the same roof? He didn't have a choice. Bart had taken him aside and asked him to sleep in their house while he was gone, but Jesse had been prepared to do it without urging. He'd always been concerned about Haley's welfare, but ever since she'd gone into town and witnessed Albert's murder, he'd been especially aware of her vulnerability.

It was nearly sundown as he crossed the path leading from the barn to the house. At the back door he paused long enough to smooth down his hair, then he pulled open the door and stepped inside.

Delicious smells assaulted him. Steaks, biscuits, pie. His mouth watered. If his nose was telling the truth, Haley had fixed all his favorites.

"Right on time," Haley said as he walked into the kitchen. She was bent over the stove, pulling out a pan of biscuits. They were fluffy and golden brown.

He grabbed a cloth from the counter and took the hot pan from her. After setting it on the counter, he glanced around. "Anything I can do to help?"

"Everything is ready." She straightened and smiled.

It was as if someone had punched him low in the belly. He nearly staggered from the impact of seeing her.

Something was different. Several somethings. She had on the dress she'd been wearing the day he'd kidnapped her. The garment had obviously been washed and pressed. Green wool, the exact color of her pretty eyes, hugged her chest and waist, emphasizing dips and curves. She'd caught up her hair in a lace snood. Curls danced along her forehead and around her ears. She was flushed from cooking, her cheeks pink, her mouth a few tempting shades darker.

"You're beautiful," he said without thinking.

Her blush deepened. "Thank you." She smoothed her hands over her skirt and pointed to the dining room. "I thought it would be pleasant to eat in there."

Jesse swallowed hard. No doubt Haley thought she was being nice, preparing a special meal and taking pains with her appearance. He supposed he should appreciate the effort. But what she didn't know, and what he could never tell her, was that her efforts were having a very different effect on him. He didn't just want to thank her. He wanted to pull her close and kiss her. He wanted to feel her body next to his as he ran his hands over her curves. He wanted to undo all the tiny buttons in the back of her dress, lower it and taste her naked skin. He wanted to be on her, in her, hard and hot, needing her.

Hell, who was he trying to kid? He was already hard and hot, and he *desperately* needed her.

"The dining room *will* be nice," he said, pleased his voice sounded normal. He swore to himself he wouldn't even hint what he was thinking. For one thing, Haley deserved better from him. She trusted him and he would rather die gut-shot than destroy her trust. For another thing, she was a virgin. He couldn't take what rightly belonged to her husband. Not unless he was willing to marry her himself.

As she led the way into the dining room and served up supper, he played with the idea of marriage. He still believed that the land was hard on women, but he was willing to admit some females seemed to thrive on the challenge. He suspected Haley was one of those kind. He could use a wife. The nights were long, especially in the winter, and he got mighty tired of his own company. But—always but. But he was afraid. He was ashamed to admit it, but there it was. Fear. It had been easy to marry Claire because he'd known right from the start he could never love her. But Haley was different. From what he'd seen, love hurt as much as it helped, sometimes more. He wasn't ready to take that kind of a chance. Better to be alone.

Haley had seated him at the head of the table. She sat on his right. He had the oddest feeling that he was living a moment that could be replayed over and over for the rest of his life. If he was willing to take the chance. She smiled at him. He found himself wanting her with a fierceness that was unfamiliar. As if he would stop breathing, stop living if he didn't have her.

Her smile faded. "Jesse, what's wrong? You look angry about something."

He forced the unsettling thoughts away and lightly touched the back of her hand. "I'm fine. Just thinking about what we're going to do when Bart gets back. But let's not talk about that tonight."

"All right." She passed him the bowl of butter. "Christine says the first berries will be out inside a month. She told me you know some of the best spots to go picking."

He nodded. "There's a little valley due east of here."

They spoke of inconsequential things through supper. Jesse kept having to remind himself to eat. It wasn't that the food wasn't excellent, but the hunger burning in him couldn't be satisfied by biscuits or steak, or even pie. He was mesmerized by Haley. By her quick wit, the graceful movements of her work-roughened hands, by the laughter in her eyes and the way she wrinkled her nose when he teased her.

When they'd finished and she suggested they move to the parlor, he told himself he was making a mistake by agreeing. Sitting next to her on the sofa would be nothing but trouble. Especially when she gazed up at him, all trusting like. As if she believed in him—which she probably did—and didn't have any idea what he was thinking—which she probably didn't.

"I've made up Bart and Christine's bed with fresh sheets," she said, her skin luminous in the light from the lamps.

He stared at her. "What did you say?"

"The sheets on the Baxters' bed are clean. Christine said you'd be sleeping here while they were gone so I changed the linens."

The reminder of where he would be sleeping only added to his discomfort. "You're right," he said. "I'd forgotten."

She was so sweet smelling, and so close. Without thinking, he angled toward her on the sofa. Then she was looking up at him, her green eyes dark with an emotion he could have sworn was desire. Not the white-hot heat searing him, but a wanting, all the same. Somehow his hand came to rest on her shoulder and he was leaning toward her. Somehow his lips brushed against hers and the need flared hotter in his belly.

If she'd stiffened, or pulled back or in any way told him she didn't want him to kiss her, it would have been so much easier to resist. But instead, she placed one hand against his chest, her fingers curling toward him, catching the fabric of his shirt, her smallest finger lightly grazing his left nipple and making him stiffen even more.

She responded to his kiss by pressing her mouth against his. When he began to move back and forth, she opened for him. The invitation was irresistible. He swept inside. She tasted sweet from both the pie and the essence that was hers alone. Damp heat welcomed him. Her tongue brushed against his in a shy greeting. They circled each other, touching, stroking. It was as perfect, as arousing, as he remembered. He had no right to be doing this.

He pulled back and rested his forehead against hers. "Haley, I'm sorry."

"Don't." She pressed a fingertip to his mouth. "Please don't apologize. I love how I feel when you kiss me. I get all tingly inside and my skin feels too tight for my body. I want—" She laughed, the sound soft and embarrassed. "I'm not sure what I want. But I do know that I feel good near you."

He doubted she meant the words as an invitation, but he heard the welcoming all the same. She wanted him. In her innocence, she didn't realize that fact, but he knew. Dear God, how was he going to find the strength to resist her now? He should stand up and walk away, at least to the Baxters' bedroom, where he would be tormented by visions of what they could have done, but relatively safe from Haley's heady presence.

"Jesse." She breathed his name, then touched her lips to his cheek.

It was a soft, innocent caress. He told himself he shouldn't even notice. But her mouth was damp from their kisses and the faint whisper of contact jolted him like a lightning bolt.

He cupped her face. "Haley, I don't want to hurt you. We have to stop. If we don't, I won't be able to control myself. You don't want what would happen next."

Her steady gaze met his. "I'm inexperienced, but I'm not ignorant. I worked with a doctor for several years, Jesse. I know what happens between a man and a woman."

Haley hoped Jesse couldn't feel her trembling or guess how terrified she was. What if he refused her bold invitation? She believed that he wanted her. The heat in his expression, the way he kissed her and held her, all indicated that he felt the same drugging desire she did. She wanted him desperately. Not just because she didn't want to go to Stoner a virgin, but also because she loved Jesse. She craved to join with him the way wives did with their husbands. She wanted to be able to remember this night for the rest of her life.

"Knowing what happens and doing it are very different," he said, his voice strained. "You don't know what you're saying."

He was going to be a gentleman. She could feel it. Frantically she tried to think of a way to keep him with her. In the end, there was nothing but the truth. Because Jesse was a certain way, she loved him. It was wrong of her to tempt him into betraying himself for her own selfish gain.

"I do know what I'm saying, but that doesn't matter," she told him. She squeezed his hands, released them, then slid back on the sofa. "You're a good man. Decent and kind. I thought—" She shrugged and turned away. Disappointment filled her, tightening her throat and making her eyes burn with unshed tears. She couldn't force him. She told herself it didn't matter, but she knew she lied.

"Haley? What's going on? I don't understand."

She made herself smile brightly as she rose to her feet. "It's getting late, Jesse. Why don't you go on upstairs?"

He stood and frowned. "It's too early for bed. Haley, there's something you're not telling me."

There were many things she hadn't shared, but he wasn't going to hear any of them now. She'd tried and failed. She would go to Lucas Stoner untouched and pray that he wouldn't want to bed her. Even if he did, as long as she was able to get the information from him, it would be worth it. She would sacrifice anything for Jesse.

A single tear escaped. She turned her head so he wouldn't see, but she wasn't quick enough. He swept it away with his thumb. Dark eyes flashed with questions. "How have I hurt you?"

She had no more strength for pretense. She crossed to the fireplace and picked up a small framed portrait resting there. "What they say about me in Whitehorn is true. I'm a fallen woman."

"No." He came up behind her and placed his hands on her shoulders. "You're innocent."

"Yes, but I don't want to be."

She whispered the words, then waited for him to recoil in shock. She braced herself for the accusations, the disgust, for the sound of his footsteps as he left the room. She'd confessed her deepest, darkest secret; he knew the worst about her.

He was silent for a long time. The strong hands resting on her shoulders were the only proof that he was still in the room. She set the portrait back on the ledge, then let her arms hang at her sides.

"You didn't want me to stop," he said.

She shook her head. Her eyelids fluttered closed as she waited for the condemnation. At least he hadn't asked her why. She wouldn't have been able to lie and she refused to tell the truth. That was something, she supposed. She could keep her reasons to herself.

He spun her so suddenly, she stumbled and fell against

him. Jesse didn't seem to notice. He grabbed her and pulled her hard to his chest, then wrapped his arms around her and pressed his mouth to hers. There was no gentle brushing this time. No soft exploration, no tentative touching. Instead he opened his mouth wide and plunged inside her.

She could feel the rapid pounding of his heart. Instantly, hers picked up the cadence until they echoed each other in speed and intensity. She clutched at him, wanting to be closer, wanting him kissing her more and deeper. She rose on her toes to meet him, then follow him back to his mouth where she tasted his flavor. She found herself weak with a longing she couldn't explain.

His hands moved up and down her back, from shoulders to hips, rubbing, drawing her against him, making her wish there weren't so many layers of clothing between them. She would like to feel his hands on her body.

Her bold thoughts made her blush, but she didn't pull away or try to ignore them. Instead she thought about being with Jesse, about how she needed him, trusted him, loved him. About how long she had loved him.

"Haley," he murmured, as if her name were a prayer.

He moved to her hair and began to pull the pins free. The snood loosened, then fell to the floor. Long curls tumbled down her back. "You are so beautiful," he told her, then returned his lips to hers and swept inside of her.

There were too many sensations to feel, too many new experiences for her to focus on any one. Tremors rippled through her, making it necessary to cling to him or collapse to the floor. His body was hot and hard against hers, a plane of male muscle and sleek strength. As he arched toward her, she thought she might have felt something else, something that would prove how much he wanted her, but the layers of her petticoats and skirt prevented her from being sure.

She had so many questions. While she thought she understood what was going to happen, she couldn't picture it in her mind. Between her legs she felt a dampness that was both unfamiliar and exciting. Her limbs were heavy, her breasts swollen. It was as if her body knew to prepare for this time with him, as if a part of her had always been waiting for Jesse.

He buried his fingers in her loose curls and she followed his actions, cupping his head and feeling the cool, silky strands of hair slipping against her skin. When he squeezed the back of her neck, she did the same to him, applying pressure where he did, liking the way he stiffened slightly, as if her touch had some small power over him.

When his hands swept lower, down her back to the curve of her hip, then around to her derriere, she boldly followed along, faltering only at the last minute, not sure she was allowed to touch him there.

He felt long and sinewy. Strong and different from her own body. Muscled ribs led to a narrow waist and hips. Her hands rested there as he squeezed the fullness of her behind. Through the layers of fabric, she felt his individual fingers. Fire shot through her as the trembling increased. She wanted him to continue touching her there, and maybe have him touch in a few other places. She wanted... She wasn't sure what, but *something*.

Finally, hoping that the feel of her hands on him was half as nice as the feel of his hands on her, she moved her arms. Her palms slid against the rough fabric of his trousers. Hard, flat hip gave way to lean flank. She gently cupped the high, round curve and he surged against her.

This time she was sure. This time she felt a firm ridge pressing against her belly. Relief filled her. Relief and more of that liquid heat that made her entire body feel so relaxed and tense at the same time.

His tongue continued to sweep around hers. Without thinking, she closed her lips slightly and sucked. Jesse went completely still. Before she could figure out if she'd done something wrong, he cupped her face in his hands and held her head. He must like that, she thought, and tried it again.

This time he groaned low in his throat. Still learning, she

circled his tongue with hers, moving quickly, then withdrew. He followed her, angling his head, driving in deeper, making her want to moan too.

She raised her hands to his back and squeezed him. Was it supposed to be like this, she wondered? Pleasing and being pleased? Caring for each other, learning different ways to touch and feel? She couldn't believe that anyone, anywhere, had ever experienced something like this. Surely they were discovering something new and wonderful. Something meant just for them.

Before she could decide whether or not she wanted to ask that particular question, he broke their kiss and bent over her. After sweeping her up in his arms, he placed her gently on the sofa and knelt beside her on the floor.

The lamplight bathed them in a warm glow, allowing her to see his handsome features. Fire burned hot and bright in his dark eyes. Something almost stern pulled his lips into a straight line. She touched the corner of his mouth.

"You're not smiling," she whispered.

"You haven't said anything funny."

That made her smile. "Aren't you happy?"

"Very. But it's not the kind of happy that makes a man smile. Not yet anyway."

She thought about that and remembered Dr. Redding describing how men's bodies changed, pressuring them until they found release.

"So you'll smile after you've spilled your seed in me?"

Jesse's eyes widened. "What did you say?"

"I understand this," she told him. "Dr. Redding explained it all to me when I was working for him. You'll be inside me and you'll spill your seed. I guess you're feeling a powerful pressure. Does it hurt?"

"I'm not sure I approve of this conversation you had with Dr. Redding. There are some things a man shouldn't discuss with a lady."

"I was his nurse. People came to me with questions. I couldn't help them if I didn't know anything."

The corners of his mouth tilted up slightly. "So you've discussed seed spilling with others?"

She frowned, trying to remember. "I don't think so. After he gave me the information, no one seemed to have any questions. Which was probably for the best. After all, some of the things he told me didn't make sense."

"Like what?"

She felt her cheeks getting hot. It was one thing to discuss this with Dr. Redding, who was older and very kindly. It was another to tell Jesse what she'd been taught. "Um, well, that the pressure builds inside the man until he spills his seed. He also told me that if a man is with a woman he cares about, he'll make her feel the same pressure. But women don't have seeds that spill. So how can it be the same? I don't think I want anything spilling from my body."

Jesse leaned close and kissed her mouth lightly, then traced a damp line down her jaw to the ticklish spot below her ear. "I bet I can change your mind."

Before she could ask anything like how, or why would she want him to, she felt his fingers whispering across the front of her dress. The button at the base of her throat became unfastened, as did the next and the next. Even though she was lying on her back on the sofa, the tremors still swept through her. She raised her hands as if she might help him, then realized she didn't know what he was going to do. She felt both hot and cold, afraid and bold, torn between telling him she wanted him to stop and knowing she would die if she didn't learn about this great mystery.

When all the buttons had been unfastened, he pulled open the bodice of her dress, laying her chemise bare to his gaze. He had touched her breast once before, in the cave. She felt the sensitive mound pucker in anticipation of that happening again.

He didn't disappoint her. His large hand closed over her curve, sealing it in a cocoon of pressure and delightful caresses. Fingers swept over and around. She arched toward him, wanting more although she wasn't sure how that was possible. When his thumb brushed across her nipple, she felt the contact clear down to the soles of her feet. She clutched at the sofa and had to hold in a small cry of pleasure.

He repeated the touch again and again, stroking, teasing, circling, as if his life depended on his learning all about her breasts. A faint coolness made her realize he'd opened her chemise and was now looking at her bare skin. She wanted to cover herself. She wanted to have him touch her again. Need won out over modesty as she tucked her hands under her full skirts, pressing her fingertips under her hips.

He stared at her for a long time, then touched one finger to her bottom lip. "You are so perfect," he murmured as he moved that finger down her throat, across her chest, then between her breasts. "So lovely."

The single finger made the return trip as slowly, then took a turn at her collarbone and circled around the base of her breasts. Delicious flames licked at her. Her toes curled, as did her fingers. More heat and dampness surged between her legs.

He moved slowly, deliberately, circling a little higher each time. She sensed that her nipples were the ultimate goal. Even though he'd already touched them, she felt desperate to have him do that again. She wanted to tell him to stop what he was doing because it was frustrating her and yet the journey left her breathless in such a way that she never wanted it to stop.

At last, when she was sure she was going to go mad, he reached the crest of her right breast. But he didn't touch her taut peak. Instead he kept her waiting until each breath was agony and her heart pounded as if it was about to leap out of her chest.

Then he did the most amazing thing. He leaned close and kissed the tip of her breast. The warm moistness of his lips was an incredibly gentle pressure. She wanted to raise herself up closer and sink down into the sofa, all at the same time. With his hand, he reached for her other nipple. His mouth and fingers worked in tandem. Soft cries forced themselves past the tightness in her throat.

Somehow she'd freed her hands and she buried them in his hair, as much to feel him as to keep him in place.

"Jesse," she cried, her voice not sounding at all like it should. Dr. Redding had mentioned this type of touching, she thought, but he hadn't been at all clear on what it would feel like. It was better than kissing, which she wouldn't have thought could be true.

His hand left her chest and moved lower. She felt him reaching for the fastening of her petticoats. Without being asked, she turned toward him so he could work more easily. The action caused him to raise his head and he looked at her.

Part of her couldn't believe she lay in his arms, half-naked, her breasts still damp from his kisses. Yet there was nothing she wanted to change. Jesse was the man she loved and this was where she belonged.

"Sweet Haley," he murmured, pressing his lips to her forehead, her cheeks and finally to her mouth. She kissed him back, opening to admit him, needing the feel of his body against hers.

He broke away long enough to pull down her petticoats. At his urging, she shrugged out of her dress, then her camisole, until she wore only pantaloons and stockings. She wasn't sure what had happened to her shoes.

As he gazed at her, she became aware of his hand resting on her belly. His fingers were close to the point of her heat and that place where she felt an odd aching. She knew that was where a man spilled his seed by placing his... She frowned. Dr. Redding hadn't been as clear during that portion of his explanation.

"You look serious," Jesse said. "What are you thinking?"

"I'm not sure what happens next," she told him. "I mean where exactly does the seed go?"

"I could show you, if you'd like."

She nodded, more comfortable with the idea of a demonstration than the actual seed spilling itself. Despite how much she cared about Jesse and how desperately she wanted him to be her first, she was willing to admit to a few nerves. But a medical explanation was familiar.

Still, she wasn't prepared for him to slide his hand between her legs and probe into her most feminine place. Embarrassment flared, but stronger was the unexpected thrill of pleasure.

"In here," he said, dipping one finger deep inside of her.

She jumped as her body tightened around him. He moved in and out, creating friction and tension. Her legs fell apart. She tried to close them, but couldn't seem to summon the will.

"So wet," he told her and kissed her softly. "Wet and ready for me."

He was so close, all she could see was his face. Dark eyes welcomed her and she found herself wanting to fall into him and never even try to find her way out.

His finger moved back and forth, stopping occasionally to circle around the sensitive opening. "Do you like that?" he asked.

Her eyelids were heavy and she was having trouble meeting his gaze. "It's lovely."

"Tell me if you like this better."

He moved out of her and she nearly whispered a protest. His finger began to move a little higher until it touched something small. Something that made her jump in pure delight. Her eyes popped open, her knees came up toward her chest and she half rose on the sofa.

"Jesse?"

He rubbed that spot with a circling motion. "What?"

She'd never felt anything like this before. It was like melting into the sun, or all the happiness of her life crammed into a physical touch, or something so perfect, so wonderful, she wasn't sure she could ever describe it.

"Jesse, I—"

He smiled at her. "I know, Haley. Don't be frightened. It's supposed to feel good."

"Is this the pressure Dr. Redding was talking about?"

"Yes. Just relax. Close your eyes and let me please you."

She couldn't possibly relax, not when every part of her focused on what he was doing there. But she could close her eyes. In the darkness the pleasure intensified. So much so, she got scared and opened her eyes.

"Jesse?" She clutched at his arm.

He shifted positions so he could cradle her against his chest while he continued to touch her there. "Hush, Haley. I'm going to be right here until you understand everything."

"You promise you won't go away?"

He smiled at her then, a beautiful smile that made her want to weep. "I promise."

Chapter Twenty

Jesse kept his word. Even as Haley clung to him and the world began to spin, he stayed with her, holding her close, touching her in that magic way that left her breathless and straining. She felt something was just out of reach. Something as pure as water, or even light. Her body tensed and released. She caught her breath, then let it go. Perspiration coated her limbs, her legs trembled, mouth parted as she gasped out his name. And still she searched for an unknown destiny.

At his urging, she moved until she was sitting upright on the sofa. He pulled off her pantaloons and stockings, leaving her naked before him. Yet the hunger inside her made her not care. It was as if all of life had been reduced to a single question and only Jesse had the answer.

He drew her down until her rear rested on the edge of the seat, then he knelt before her. She wasn't sure what he was going to do so she was unprepared for him to kneel between her thighs and press a kiss to her most secret place.

The thought of protesting never entered her mind. When his tongue swept over her, the tension returned tenfold, bringing with it a white-hot burning light that filled her. He stroked her half a dozen more times until she found herself hovering on the edge of a great discovery. Her body trembled, her breathing stopped, the light filled her. He licked her again and she began to fall.

It was the most perfect, incredible, undescribable feeling of her life. She clutched at his shoulders because she needed him to find her way back to the familiar. The light surrounded her, supported her, but when she surfaced, she found instead of light, she was cradled in Jesse's arms. The passion still filled his face, but a faintly self-satisfied smile tugged at his lips.

"That's what Dr. Redding was talking about," he said.

She took a shaky breath and leaned her head against his chest. "No, it wasn't. He never once made it sound like it was so...wonderful."

He hugged her tightly against him. "I'm glad you think that."

Her body returned to normal. Her breathing slowed, the heat faded, the tension eased. Only the feeling of well-being remained. But they weren't, she knew, quite finished. There was still the matter of Jesse and his seed.

She raised her head and looked at him. "Jesse?"

He shook his head. "You're a virgin. You should stay that way."

"I don't want to." He couldn't stop now. Having experienced part of the magic in his arms, she had to know everything. "Jesse, this is important to me." She held her breath and prayed he wouldn't ask why.

Her prayers were answered. His muscles tightened as if he waged a silent battle inside himself. Then he groaned softly, gathered her up against his chest and rose to his feet. He carried her effortlessly through the house to the bed she'd slept in since her arrival. Once there, he placed her on the feather mattress and lit the lantern on the dresser.

By the faint glow of the flame, he undressed. She watched the unveiling of his tanned skin, the ripple of muscle, the play of light and shadow. When he reached for the buttons at his trousers and hesitated, she raised her eyebrows.

"I'm a nurse," she reminded him. "I've seen naked men before."

"Have you now?" His voice was low and teasing. "Aroused men?"

She thought of the one she'd stumbled upon. "Yes."

Now it was his turn to raise his eyebrows. She folded her arms over her chest and dropped her chin. "It was an accident at a boardinghouse. I thought I was walking into an empty room and I wasn't."

"Got an eyeful, did you?"

"Let's just say we hadn't been properly introduced."

The whisper of cloth caught her attention. She glanced up in time to see Jesse stepping out of his trousers and drawers. That most male part of him thrust toward her, a hungry predator ready to devour. Yet she found she wasn't afraid. Not of Jesse. He was all she wanted, in every way. He'd already shown her sensations she'd never dreamed existed. She trusted him to teach her the rest.

So when he approached the bed, she held open her arms. He reclined next to her, his long body pressing against hers. The hair on his chest and legs tickled and excited. He gathered her close and she went willingly, opening her mouth for his kisses, arching into his touch. He began the now-familiar journey, tracing the curves of her breasts before turning his attention to her sensitized nipples.

She hadn't thought she could feel the tension again, but it returned quickly. Her body began to tremble. When he moved his hands lower and gently toyed with her center, she let her legs fall open. Slick fingers moved in and out of her, making her hips surge against him. She felt the dull pressure building as the promise of release returned.

Jesse broke their kiss and knelt between her thighs. He parted her damp flesh and thrust forward slowly, his maleness filling her. Haley wasn't sure she liked the pressure. Knowing what was going to happen and having it happen were very different. Her body stretched, but she was afraid and she squirmed. He stopped moving, then thrust forward quickly.

Sharp pain radiated up her belly. She caught her breath at the unexpected burn, then scolded herself. It was, she knew, the proof of her virginity.

Jesse bent down and kissed her mouth. "I'm sorry," he said. "I should have warned you."

"It's fine." She shifted, trying to find a comfortable position.

"Do you want me to stop?"

So there was more. She shook her head. She would see this through to the end.

But instead of moving in deeper, he reached a hand between them and rubbed against that tiny pleasure spot. Her body eased into the exquisite flickers that rippled through her. She relaxed onto the mattress and closed her eyes.

In the back of her mind she became aware that he was moving in and out of her, slowly, so slowly it was difficult for her to judge his progress. That provided a delightful counterpoint to the steady circling of his fingers. She found herself pulling her knees up and back toward her chest and pressing down, as if to take more of him. He obliged her by going deeper and moving a little faster.

The tension increased. Her hips arched as her fingers grasped for the bedcovers. She couldn't think of anything but the need he'd created. Then, without warning, his hand was gone. She opened her eyes and saw he'd braced himself above her. He began to move in and out more quickly, going inside so far that she wondered if he would get lost.

At first she wanted him to touch that one special spot again. But in a few minutes, her body became caught up in the rhythm he created and she found she could think of nothing else. This tension was different, but just as awe inspiring. She wanted more, needed more. Needed him.

She opened her eyes and gazed at him. "Jesse."

"I'm right here," he told her. "I can feel you tensing, Haley. It feels so good to be inside you. So very good."

She saw him close his eyes and she closed hers, too. She remembered the light, the sensation of falling and being caught, and then it was upon her. As her body cascaded into pleasure she felt him move even deeper. Then he stiffened and called out her name. She knew he was experiencing what she had—was. Together they were bound in the light. His seed spilled into her and she knew that she would always belong to him.

Jesse woke before dawn. He could see the first hint of light at the edges of the drapes over the windows. Careful not to disturb Haley, he slid out of the bed and crossed to the window. The morning air was cold, making him fold his arms over his bare chest. He parted the drapes slightly and stared out into the gray darkness.

Now what? A simple question with no simple answers. Last night had changed everything. They'd joined together twice more. Although he'd wanted to hold back so she wouldn't be sore in the morning, he found he couldn't resist her sweetness. Once he'd tasted her, felt the hot slickness of her body, he couldn't turn his back on her. The last time, she'd been the one to wake him, reaching for him in the darkness.

He knew the pleasure of being with a woman. Yet that pleasure was meaningless when compared to the unique passion that was Haley. It was as if they were made to be together. In her body, in her arms and in her eyes he found a place to belong. If he were a different kind of man, he might call it love. Might. But he knew better. He knew the price of love—the pain that followed as surely as the seasons came one after the other.

And yet, he couldn't forget what had happened. He couldn't walk away. For one thing, when they'd finally crawled under the blankets, the lamplight had fallen across the coverlet. He'd seen the bloody stain—proof of what he'd stolen from her. He'd done the wrong thing for the wrong reason. He hadn't been able to resist her because she was everything he'd ever wanted. If he were to describe the perfect woman for him, she would be Haley.

Now what? He'd done nothing but hurt her from the moment he'd first kidnapped her. She hadn't asked to be made part of his crusade for justice. She hadn't asked to have her dreams destroyed or her life turned upside-down. She hadn't asked to have her virginity spoiled.

When a voice in his head whispered that she *had* asked for just that, he dismissed it. She'd felt the fire between them and had wanted to explore it. She was the innocent, asking, but not knowing what that asking would lead to. He was the experienced one. He knew and he should have been able to resist.

He hadn't resisted then, so he had to do the right thing now. He would honor her and then he would send her away. Because the alternative was loving her and he knew the price of that.

Behind him came a faint sound. He turned and saw her stirring on the bed. He would do it now, before she had time to regret what had happened between them.

Jesse stood silhouetted by the window. As Haley opened her eyes and stared at him she had the thought that this was how she would like to begin each day. In the same room after having shared the same bed. She wanted to learn everything about him. His moods, his body, what he thought, what he liked, his dreams. All of him. She wanted to know him as well as she knew herself. She wanted to have children with him, grow old with him. She wanted so much. But mostly, she wanted him to love her.

As he moved toward the bed, she saw the outline of his body, the ropes of muscles, the hair on his chest, the broad, comforting shape of him. Last night he'd touched her and held her and taken her to places she hadn't known existed. But he'd never said a word about loving her. No matter how his body tightened in passion, no matter how many times he hoarsely called out her name, he'd never once said those words.

She told herself it shouldn't hurt. Better that he not love her. If he did, she wouldn't be able to leave him and she must leave to find out what she could from Stoner. If Jesse loved her, she would confess her plans and he wouldn't let her go. If necessary he would lock her in her room.

A part of her wanted that declaration, that proof of his love. But most of her knew better. He hadn't said the words because he didn't feel them. It was so strange. She'd grown up in a world without love and it was all she wanted. He'd grown up with a family who cared about him and each other, yet he was afraid to love. How had life taught them each such different lessons? How was she going to find the strength to leave him?

He sat on the edge of the bed and smiled at her. "How do you feel?"

She knew what he meant. Despite the blush she felt climbing her cheeks, she met his gaze. "Fine. A little sore, but very happy."

"I'm glad."

He took her hands in his. The sheet slipped down to her waist, but she didn't think to cover herself. He'd taken her in the lantern light—he knew every inch of her. He'd seen her and touched her and tasted her. Save the secret of what she planned to do with Stoner, she had nothing to hide.

"Haley, I have great respect for you. I think you're a lovely young woman. Last night—" He paused.

She hoped he wasn't going to speak of regrets. She would hate to think he would want to take back what they'd done. No matter what might happen in town or later in her life, she would always remember last night. She would hold the memories close to her, treasuring them for the precious things they were.

"I'm not sorry," she said quickly. "I don't want you to be, either. I knew what I was doing. I wanted us to be together."

His dark eyes met hers. As she gazed at him, she felt her heart skip a beat. He was so handsome. And wonderful. And special, and everything she'd ever longed for.

"I'd like you to do me the honor of becoming my wife," he said.

The words were as bubbly as a glass of champagne she'd had once. Light and sweet, like swallowing a cloud. She squeezed his fingers tightly between hers, unable to contain the happiness welling inside of her.

He wanted to marry her. Her! After all they'd been through, after all that had happened he'd finally realized that—

The thought ended abruptly as she recognized an ugly truth. "You don't love me," she said, not asking a question. "It's because of last night."

He exhaled sharply. "Love is difficult," he admitted. "I've seen how it can wound. My father was devastated by my mother's death. Then he found a little happiness with Daisy, but he wouldn't marry her. He suffered and made her suffer, all in the name of love. I never loved Claire. Perhaps if I had, she wouldn't have taken her own life. Love is complicated and I believe it does more harm than good. It's better this way, Haley. I care about you and I respect you."

These were not the words she longed to hear. "But without loving me, you would still take me as your wife?"

"I would give you my name. After that, you would be free to do what you liked with your life. In time, if you found someone you wanted to be with, we could divorce. That sort of thing is much easier out west."

The pain was much sharper than the mere tearing of her virginal body. It cut deep, but the blood wouldn't appear on the coverlet. It would stain her from the inside, blackening her heart, leaving her soul shattered and empty. Worse than not loving her, he didn't even want her to be around him.

She wasn't sure she could survive this. For the first time

in her life, she wished she could cry easily. Perhaps that would help. Something had to. Was it possible to feel this horror and still survive?

"Haley?"

He wanted an answer. She nearly laughed. Of course. An answer. If only she could think of something clever to say. A polite refusal that wouldn't offend or let him know how he'd destroyed her.

In the end she could think of nothing. And when she felt the edges of her control beginning to fray, she leaned forward and buried her face in his shoulder. There against the warmth of him, she inhaled his scent and knew that she would die a slow death because of him. Like Claire, she would walk into the snow and fade away. Only her end wouldn't happen in winter. It would be slower. Bit by bit, over her lifetime, she would freeze inside until eventually everything she was disappeared.

He kissed the top of her head. "You won't regret this," he said.

At first she didn't understand, then she nearly laughed. Nearly.

Jesse didn't know she was trying to hide her feelings from him. He took her embrace as agreement to his plan. He thought she'd said yes. She started to correct him, then realized it was better this way. Let him think what he liked—she would be gone before nightfall.

Chapter Twenty-One

Haley shifted in the saddle, stroked the brown gelding's neck and wondered if taking one of the Baxters' horses made her a horse thief. If she survived this ordeal, she would explain the situation to Bart. Surely he would understand. She needed to get to town and she couldn't take the chance of Jesse returning early and noticing she was gone. If that happened and she was on foot, Jesse would have a chance to catch her. With a little luck, he wouldn't go back to the house until sundown. She should have already found Stoner by then.

She rounded a curve in the road and could see the first buildings of Whitehorn. Her body tightened and her stomach rolled uncomfortably. It was just fear, she told herself. She'd been afraid before and she'd survived. She would survive this, too. So much was at stake. All of Jesse's hopes for the future, the lives of innocent people, and justice. Stoner had been doing as he wanted for too long. He murdered when it was convenient and someone had to stop him. She knew his secrets and she had a perfect excuse to go looking for him. While Jesse wouldn't approve of her plan, she knew he didn't have a better one.

All of this, all the sacrifice, was in the name of love. It was the right thing to do. If nothing else, she could cling to that thought. And the memories from last night. They would be enough to last her a lifetime.

As she rode into town, she deliberately gathered her courage like a cloak. She straightened in the saddle and thought about what she was going to say when she first saw Stoner.

The land office was near the eastern edge of town and was one of the first buildings she recognized. She reined in her mount, then slid from the saddle. A dark silhouette was barely visible through the sparkling window. He was there. This was her chance.

She drew in a deep breath, squared her shoulders, then walked purposefully to the door and flung it open.

Lucas Stoner looked up, obviously startled by the intrusion. There was no change in his neutral expression, no hint of recognition. Then Haley remembered that while she'd had a chance to observe Stoner, he had never seen *her*.

She clutched her hands to her chest. "Lucas?" she cried, her voice thick with genuine emotion.

"I'm Lucas Stoner," he replied, sounding somewhat cautious.

"At last." She thought about Jesse and the fact that she might never see him again. She thought about Albert Cooper's senseless murder, and the death of the two children on the ranch she and Jesse had found. When combined with her lack of sleep and her fear, it was enough to start the tears. They flowed down her cheeks. She was careful not to brush them away. She *wanted* Lucas Stoner to think she was overcome by emotion.

"I thought we'd n-never meet. Never be together. I thought—" She broke off and flung herself at him.

It was the hardest thing she'd ever done. As she flew across the room, her stomach rose in her throat. She had to swallow to keep from throwing up. When she reached him, she wrapped her arms around his tall, lean broad body and clung to him as if she would never let go.

She hated this man for what he was, yet when he placed one hand on her shoulder and the other under her chin, she allowed him to raise her face so he could stare into her face.

Up close, he was handsome, in a sinister way. The scar didn't bother her as much as the deadly coldness in his eyes. How could she ever have idolized this man? She'd been a fool. Thank God Jesse had kidnapped her or she might be married to this murderer.

"You must be Haley Winthrop, my missing mail-order bride."

She sniffed, then nodded. "Oh, Lucas, it's been so horrible. For both of us, I know. You've been worried and I've been frantic about you."

Speculation hardened his features. He was dark, like Jesse, but there the similarity ended. Stoner was several inches taller. Expensive clothing emphasized his size and strength. A well-dressed murderer and thief, she thought, knowing if he suspected her at all, he would kill her with as little regard as he'd shown when he killed Albert.

"Have you really been thinking about me?"

The tears had slowed. She brushed her cheeks with her hand. "Constantly. I was devastated when I was kidnapped. All I could think of was that I'd come so far and gotten so very close to you. Having that dream ripped away was terribly cruel." Her speech had just the right ring of sincerity. Probably because at one time it had been true.

Still keeping his hand on her chin, he turned her head to the left and then to the right, as if examining her. No doubt he was. Would she pass the test?

"You're prettier than I'd thought," he said.

She ducked her head, pretending to be embarrassed by the compliment. "You're too kind."

She could practically hear what he was thinking. He was tempted to believe her. Tempted, but not convinced. Stoner hadn't achieved all he had by being a fool.

He took her arm and led her to a chair beside his desk.

She sank into it while surreptitiously glancing around for
the letter she'd read when she'd last been in his office.
There were neat stacks of papers on his desk, but nothing
lying around. She was going to have to plan to come back
at a time when she could go through his things.

"So," he said, settling on the desk and crossing his arms
over his chest. "Tell me what happened?"

This was it—the moment where she made him believe
her or not. Everything hung on his decision, including her
life.

She drew in a deep breath. "I hate to even think of it,"
she murmured, trying to recapture her fear when Jesse had
first kidnapped her. "The stage collapsed, then this man
with a gun came and got me. He dragged me away." She
looked Stoner in the eye. "I didn't want to go with him. I
fought him until he was forced to throw me over his shoulder and carry me."

That much was true. As much as possible, stay with the
truth, she told herself. She spoke of the first night in camp,
of her terror and her attempted escape. She told him about
being tied up while Jesse had left to meet someone, and
detailed her second bid for freedom.

Stoner raised dark eyebrows. "You were determined,
weren't you?"

"Of course. Lucas, all I've wanted since I received your
letter was to come to Whitehorn and marry you. I couldn't
believe someone wanted to keep us apart." She folded her
hands in her lap. "I suspect I was a difficult prisoner."

His gaze narrowed. "What do you think of him?"

"Kincaid?" She gave a shrug. "He didn't hurt me, he
wasn't cruel, but I'll never forgive him for taking me away
like that. Every night I told him that he was nothing but a
criminal, that he wasn't half the man you were."

This time her embarrassment was genuine. She *had* said
those things to Jesse. Now that she knew the truth, she was
amazed he hadn't just left her out to die. How could she
have been so foolish?

Stoner chuckled. "I'll bet he enjoyed that."

She forced her mouth to curve up slightly. "Not really."

"How did you escape the ranch?"

That was more difficult. She'd thought up a story on her way into town. "They kept me locked up in a back bedroom. There was a woman and a strange man. I guess he's her husband."

She paused. As expected, Stoner nodded. "The Baxters. You were at their ranch."

So he'd known and he hadn't bothered coming after her. Well, she might not want him for herself, but she was going to do her best to see that he suffered for his bad manners along with everything else.

"A couple of days ago, they left the ranch. I'd been working to get the window open. Someone had nailed it shut. When I realized I was alone this morning, I broke the glass and climbed out. Then I took one of their horses and here I am."

She waited, trying to make her expression expectant. For all the world, she was an adoring bride, waiting for her soon-to-be husband to accept her. Her mouth was dry and her stomach continued to rise into her throat. Did he believe her? Was he willing to take a chance?

The silence stretched out for so long, she thought she was going to scream. At last he leaned forward and pinched her cheek. "Well, my dear, you must be exhausted from your ordeal. Why don't I take you to the hotel? You can rest this afternoon, and tonight, if I may, I would like to escort you to supper."

She wanted to collapse with relief. He accepted the story. Instead of sighing with relief, she allowed herself a small smile. "You are too kind. I can't tell you how happy I am at this moment. I can't imagine being happier."

"Ah, a challenge. I shall gladly take this one on." He stood up and offered his arm.

Haley rose and placed her hand in the crook of his elbow. He led her out of the land office. The early afternoon was bright and warm. Dozens of people walked along the board-walk. Haley felt their attention on her. She wanted to shrink back, to disentangle herself and run the other way. She wanted to scream out that she was only pretending, that she really hated Lucas Stoner and knew him to be related to the devil.

Instead she gazed lovingly at the tall stranger next to her. When he held open the hotel door for her, she smiled her thanks. In the name of justice she would do whatever she had to—including taking Lucas Stoner to her bed.

"I'm coming," Daisy called as someone continued pounding on her front door. She was in the middle of baking bread. Flour covered the front of her apron and coated her hands and arms up to her elbows.

As she crossed the parlor, she glanced at the grandfather clock against the wall. It was a little after two in the afternoon. Who would be visiting her now?

Even as she told herself it didn't matter, she felt her heart beat a little faster as she wondered if it could be Leland. She hadn't seen him since he'd visited her and declared himself. She knew it was for the best. If Stoner found out about the good doctor, he would have the man killed. For now it was enough to have that precious secret and hold it close. When everything threatened to overwhelm her, she remembered Leland's words and promise. The strength of his feelings allowed her to survive.

She pulled open the front door and gasped in surprise. Stoner stood on her small front porch. He usually didn't worry much about who saw him visiting, but he rarely came in the middle of the day and almost never without warning.

"Lucas," she said, holding the door open wide. "What an unexpected treat." She gave him her usual false smile. "I wasn't expecting you until this evening."

He stepped into the parlor and kissed her cheek. "That's why I came by. I can only stay a minute, but I wanted you to know that I'm going to have to change our plans."

''All right.'' With a little luck, he might cancel them altogether. That would suit her fine. She hated being around him, having him talking to her and touching her.

He took one of her hands in his and began to stroke her skin. His dark fingers brushed away the flour. ''Daisy dear, I'm afraid I have some bad news.''

She stiffened. ''What's wrong?''

''My mail-order bride has come to town looking for me.''

Daisy didn't have to pretend to be shocked. Haley was in town? She'd gone to Stoner? Had she lost her mind? ''I don't understand.''

''It seems that I might have misjudged her. Apparently she didn't succumb to the questionable Kincaid charms after all. The sweet thing tried to escape from him several times and finally succeeded today. She seems quite devoted.'' He gave her a quick smile of apology. ''I know this is upsetting to you.''

''It is.'' She could barely stay standing. What was Haley thinking, coming back to Whitehorn after what had happened during her last visit? Didn't the girl realize the danger she was in? Hadn't she learned her lesson? When Daisy thought about how they both could have been caught in the land office, she wanted to swoon. Only pure luck and nothing else had saved them.

He led her to the sofa and pulled her down next to him. ''I must pursue this,'' he said. ''She's presentable and, as an orphan, all I want in a wife. So I'll be dining with her tonight. That's why I can't see you until later.''

She was still trying to figure out Haley's plan when Stoner's words sank in. ''Later?'' she questioned.

''Of course.'' He leaned close and kissed her. ''I'll leave her at the hotel and come by to see you. Would you like that?'' He took her involuntary shiver for passion, dropped her hand and squeezed her breast. ''Ah, Daisy,'' he whispered. ''You are an amazing woman.''

Amazing in her ability to fool him, she thought grimly,

knowing she would have to endure his hateful rutting that night. Was Haley really the bigger fool? Daisy wasn't so sure anymore.

Stoner rose to his feet. "I must get back to the office. I'll see you later."

"Yes." She stood on tiptoes and kissed him warmly. "Please come see me."

He laughed. "You have no need to be jealous, but I do enjoy it." Then he was gone.

Daisy stood with her back pressed against the closed door. What was going on? What was Haley's plan? Surely the girl had one. She couldn't have just come to town without a specific reason.

"Oh, no." Daisy remembered the letter Haley had found and read. No doubt she wanted to get it as proof of Stoner's wrongdoing. "She's going to get herself killed."

Haley was a fool if she thought she could go up against Stoner and survive. Daisy tried to figure out what she should do. What had Jesse been thinking, letting Haley come to town? Then Daisy realized he probably didn't know what was going on. He wouldn't have let Haley visit Whitehorn at all, let alone come by herself.

Walking to the kitchen, she untied her apron and wiped her hands. She unrolled her sleeves and buttoned the cuffs, then collected her reticule. She was going to have to get word to Jesse. He was the only one who could rescue Haley. But she couldn't go to the ranch herself—she couldn't afford to be spotted at the Baxter place. There was only one person she would trust with this errand.

Fifteen minutes later, she walked into Leland Prescott's office. He was sitting behind his desk. When he glanced up and saw her, his face brightened and love filled his eyes. She felt herself wanting to respond in kind, but she didn't dare. Not here where anyone could see them and report back to Stoner.

"I need your help," she said quickly. When he made a move to stand, she motioned for him to stay seated. "Don't get up. If someone walks by and sees me here, I want everything to look normal.''

''I've missed you.''

She clutched her reticule and twisted the cords between her fingers. ''I've missed you, too. More than I want to tell you.''

''I'm glad. I meant what I said, Daisy. When this is over, I want to marry you.''

She still wasn't sure about that. After all she'd done, she wasn't sure she deserved so much happiness. But that discussion would have to wait.

''Haley Winthrop is here.'' At his look of confusion she added, ''Stoner's mail-order bride. She's come to town and is with Stoner now.''

''Is that who she was?'' Leland said. ''Earlier, I saw him walk by with a young woman. I didn't think anything about it.''

''Where did they go?''

''The hotel.''

''At least she's not being kept hidden,'' Daisy said. ''That will make it easier.'' She took a step toward his desk, then stopped herself. ''Leland, I need you to ride out to the Baxter ranch and tell Jesse that Haley is in town. I don't know why she's here, but I suspect she has some kind of plan. She's being foolish and is putting everyone at risk, including herself. Jesse must come and get her.''

''I'll go right away.'' His gaze never left her. ''Tell me you want me as much as I want you.''

She bit her lower lip, then smiled. ''Of course I do, Leland. You are the most wonderful man I've ever met.''

She left his office and paused on the boardwalk. Now what? She could return home, but she knew she wouldn't be able to think of anything but Haley. Perhaps she could go see the girl and convince her to head back to the ranch.

Daisy walked to the hotel. As she entered the three-story building, she saw a familiar large shape lurking in the lobby. Before she could retreat, he turned and saw her. Orin Stoner, one of Lucas's cousins, crossed the wood floor.

"What are you doin' here?" he asked. He was a faded version of Lucas. Tall and dark, but without the handsome features or any of the intelligence. But he was mean like a wild dog, and he preferred hitting to talking.

She swore silently. Orin would tell Stoner that she'd been by. It had been foolish to come, but she was trapped now.

Daisy deliberately slumped her shoulders and turned down her mouth. "Lucas told me she's here. That woman from Chicago. The one he's going to m-marry." She thought the crack in her voice was a nice touch and hoped Orin would appreciate it.

She took a step closer to Orin and tried to ignore the rank odor of his unwashed body. "I want to see her. I want to know if she's prettier than me. I want to know—" She turned away as if overcome by tears.

"I can't let you go up there," Orin said. "Lucas told me no one is allowed in her room. Now you git on home, Miz Newcastle."

She retreated because there wasn't another choice. She nodded as if defeated and left the hotel. Once outside, she glanced up at the windows and hoped Haley knew what she was doing. If not, Lucas Stoner's mail-order bride was going to find herself very dead.

Jesse walked out of the stable and came to a stop. The house was completely dark. He took a deep breath and realized he didn't smell smoke from the stove. It was as if everyone had disappeared...including Haley. Something cold and hard took up residence in his gut.

He hurried toward the back porch, wondering if something had happened to her during the day. Had she fallen or taken a walk and gotten lost or—

The sound of a galloping horse caught his attention. With a certainty he couldn't explain, he knew the approaching rider had something to do with Haley. He changed directions and headed down the path leading up from the main road.

The man was nearly upon him before Jesse recognized Leland Prescott, the doctor from town. The knot in his gut tightened a couple of notches.

"What's happened?" he demanded as soon as the man was in shouting distance.

Prescott reined in his horse and dismounted. "Daisy sent me," he said. "Your friend, Haley Winthrop, rode into town sometime today. She's staying at the hotel and she's with Stoner."

Jesse stared at him, sure he couldn't have heard right. Why would Haley have left the ranch for Whitehorn? "There has to be a mistake."

"No mistake. Stoner told Daisy himself and she came to tell me. She asked me to let you know. Said you have to get Haley away from Stoner before she gets herself killed."

Jesse was already heading for the barn. "Wait for me and I'll ride back with you." He entered the large building and ran for the stalls. "What the hell was she thinking?" he asked aloud as he grabbed gear and selected a mount. "She knew better."

His body grew cold at the thought of Haley trapped with Stoner. If the man found out what she knew, he wouldn't hesitate to kill her. He'd probably take pleasure in the act—especially if he learned that Jesse had feelings for her.

"How could she run off like that?" he asked the gelding as he saddled him. The horse merely flicked its ears. The only person who had the answer was Haley herself. Pray God she survived long enough for him to rescue her and her to explain.

Haley slipped into the land office. She couldn't shake the feeling that someone was watching her, but every time she turned around, she couldn't spot a familiar face.

"It's just nerves," she whispered to herself as she

crossed the wooden floor and stepped through the swinging half-doors.

She'd left the hotel a half hour before Stoner was supposed to arrive to escort her to supper. She hoped he would be at home getting ready for their meal and she could use the time to search his office. Later, when he couldn't find her, she would pretend to have misunderstood their meeting place. It wasn't much of a plan, but it was the best she could come up with under the circumstances. If only her heart would stop beating so loudly. She could barely hear herself think.

She approached the desk and studied the papers stacked there. Which one contained the letter? She knew she didn't have much time. It was getting dark outside and that made it difficult to see. She reached for the first pile and picked up a handful of sheets from the top.

Working quickly, she scanned the first few lines, then moved on to the next paper. Nothing looked familiar, and so far all the letters were about land office business. If only she'd thought to take the letter with her the first time she'd been here. She'd had it in her hands, too. It was frustrating to think that she'd been so close only to—

Behind her, something clicked. The sharp sound made her jump and she spun toward the noise. Lucas Stoner stood inside the land office, his scarred face unreadable.

"My cousin told me you'd left the hotel," he said, his voice all the more deadly for being so reasonable. "I thought you might have been confused about where we were meeting, so I decided I'd join you here. Unfortunately, I thought you would be waiting like a well-behaved bride, not shuffling through my letters."

Haley didn't know what to say. The fear was instant and it froze her in place. She felt the papers in her hand flutter to the ground, but she didn't remember releasing them. She told herself to run, but she couldn't move, not even when Stoner approached her.

Without warning, he slapped her hard across the face.

The impact made her ears ring. She cried out and tried to step back, but he already had a hold of one arm. His strength bit into her. She wasn't going anywhere.

Dark eyes burned with cold hatred. ''You'll pay for this, you little slut.''

Haley's throat was too dry for her to swallow. Her cheek was on fire and her arm felt as if he were trying to squeeze it in two. She knew she was going to do more than pay for getting caught. She was going to die.

Chapter Twenty-Two

It was dark by the time Jesse and Leland left the hotel. There was no sign of Haley anywhere in the building and although she'd been in her room at one time, she wasn't there now. Their next stop was the land office. Jesse cursed when they stopped in front of the building and he saw it was dark. Even though he knew Stoner was gone, he dismounted and stalked to the front door. Once there, he rattled the knob and pounded on the wood, calling for the other man to come out and face him. There was no reply.

"We should go talk to Daisy," Jesse said. "She might know where Stoner is."

"I don't want her involved in this," Leland told him. "She's in enough danger."

Jesse glared at the other man as he swung up into the saddle. "Right now Daisy is safe. She also has you to take care of her. Haley is with Stoner and she's on her own. I don't give a damn about anything but getting her back."

Leland met his angry gaze, then nodded. "You're right. Let's go see Daisy."

They rode in silence. Jesse tried to quiet the frantic voice in his head, the one that said it was already too late. He refused to believe that. Stoner had no reason to kill Haley. Jesse didn't know what she was doing in town, but he suspected she thought she was trying to help. No doubt she'd

planned to pretend to be Stoner's happy mail-order bride.
If she could gain his confidence, she would think she could
get information from him. She was fine, he told himself.
Unless she got caught.

He didn't want to think about that. Couldn't think about
her being with that bastard. Why had she left without telling
him? He hunched forward in the saddle. He knew the answer to that. Because he would have tried to stop her.
Which made sense when she was running off to do a fool
thing like this.

His gut felt as if he'd swallowed a boulder and his chest
ached from the band tightening around his ribs. While in
his head he could follow her thinking and almost understand her decision to act, his heart didn't agree at all. How
could she have gone to Stoner after they'd spent the night
in each other's arms?

He pushed the thought away because it hurt too much to
dwell on it. As they neared Daisy's house, he found himself
going over all the possible places Stoner could have taken
her. He didn't know of that many. They'd never found
where Stoner's cousins were hiding. If Haley was there—

He forced himself to let the pain go, at least for now. He
had to concentrate on finding Haley.

Daisy met them on the front porch. Her normally pretty
face was pulled tight. Fine lines radiated out from her eyes
and her mouth was pinched. "Did you get her?" she asked.
"She's at the hotel."

"No, she's not," Jesse said as he tied his horse to the
split log fence in front of her house. "We were there. Her
room is empty and the clerk isn't sure when she left."

Daisy tugged her shawl more tightly around her. "Did
you see Orin there? Stoner's cousin was guarding the lobby
when I tried to see her this afternoon."

"I didn't see him," Jesse said and glanced at Leland.
The doctor shook his head.

"They're not at the restaurant," Daisy said. "I went
around there about an hour ago."

"We were at the land office," Jesse told her, the coldness inside of him growing. Stoner had Haley and something had gone wrong. He could feel it. "It's dark and
empty."

"I don't know where they could be," Daisy said, her
voice trembling. "I never did find out where the cousins
were hiding. I would guess he's taken her there. Or to another hideout."

Jesse told himself to stay calm. They needed a plan. He
pointed at Leland. "Bart Baxter should be coming through
town anytime now. Go wait by the main road. When you
see him, stop him and tell him what's happened. I'll meet
up with you shortly."

"What are you going to do?" Leland asked.

"See if Sheriff Lindsay is willing to do the right thing."

He mounted his horse and kicked the animal into a fast
trot. When he reached the sheriff's office, he jumped down
and hurried into the building.

Lindsay was sitting at his desk, but there was something
odd about his posture. Jesse realized the man was dead
drunk and sleeping in his chair.

He swore loudly, then stalked forward and grabbed the
man by his jacket front. "Wake up, you good-for-nothing
bastard."

Lindsay raised his head. His eyes were bloodshot, his
breath thick with alcohol. "'m awake," he muttered.
"Whatcha want?"

"Stoner has Haley—the mail-order bride. He's taken her
somewhere and I have to find her before he kills her."

That got Lindsay's attention. Jesse watched as the other
man tried to straighten. But when he released Lindsay, the
sheriff collapsed on the desk.

"Find hideout," Lindsay said, his voice barely audible.

"Do you know where it is?"

The only answer was a gentle snore. Jesse kicked the
desk in frustration, then stalked out into the night.

* * *

Haley tried to make herself as small as possible. She curled up in a corner of the partially burned kitchen and shivered in the cold night air. They were talking about her. She couldn't hear everything, but enough of what they said drifted to her for her to figure out the rest.

When she drew her knees closer to her chest, the chain around her ankle clinked. She froze, waiting to see if they'd noticed. The conversation in the next room continued uninterrupted and she allowed herself to breathe again.

They were on a ranch somewhere near Whitehorn. After Stoner had taken her out of the land office, he'd tied and blindfolded her, then thrown her into the back of a wagon. She wasn't sure how far they'd traveled, but it hadn't seemed to take too long to reach their destination. Once they'd arrived, he'd taken off the blindfold. In the twilight, she'd seen a beautiful valley with trees and cattle. It was the kind of place she'd dreamed about back when she was in Chicago. Before she could pause to appreciate the beauty, Stoner had pushed her inside the partially burned house.

Haley drew in shallow breaths as she struggled to hear what the men where saying. There were four of them altogether. Stoner and his three cousins. The cousins had wanted to kill her right off, but instead Stoner had chained her to the stove in what had once been a very large and bright kitchen. She huddled there now, awaiting their decision.

The occasional word and phrase drifted to her. She thought they might be arguing about whether or not it was too risky to kill her outright. She sent up a quick prayer that they would keep her alive long enough for her to escape.

At last she heard footsteps in the hallway. She pushed herself into a sitting position and swore that she wasn't going to let Stoner know that she was terrified. She would act strong because she *was* strong. She'd survived much in

her life and she would survive this. After all, she had a
reason to keep living. She loved Jesse.

Stoner strolled into the kitchen. He carried a lantern in
one hand and set it on the counter. The left side of the
room was untouched by fire. The stove, one counter, a table
and six chairs had survived. Then the room ended abruptly,
as if the fire ravishing the house had been extinguished
without warning. Haley wondered if a rainstorm had put
out the fire and saved the rest of the structure.

"Well, Miss Winthrop, you'll be pleased to know that
I'm not going to let my cousins kill you this evening."

She met his gaze unflinchingly, but that was all she could
manage. There was no way she would be able to speak. It
wasn't just the fear that kept her quiet. Stoner's slap had
made her head ache and her face swell. Her lips felt twice
their normal size.

He squatted down in front of her and stroked her un-
bruised cheek. "I'm sorry it turned out this way. You were
exactly what I wanted in a bride. However, I do value loy-
alty above all else, and in that you've already failed me."

She glared at him. "You're not going to get away with
this," she told him, anger overcoming fear, pain and common sense.

"I already have, Haley. That's what makes this so interesting. It seems Jesse Kincaid has arrived in town and is
quite frantic about getting you back." He smiled cruelly.
"I have you in my possession, which means I now control
him. But I don't need to control him anymore. My plans
are set."

She shook her head, then when the pain exploded again,
she forced herself to sit very still. "We know about the
railroad and the man in Boston," she said. "Jesse's going
to stop you."

Stoner stared at her for a long moment, as if weighing
her words. Then he rose to his feet. "I would like to allow
my cousins to kill you tonight. I prefer simple solutions to
difficult problems. However, too many people saw us to-

gether and I don't want to answer any questions about you. Not now. So I'm going to ask you to be patient for a few days."

He nudged the chain with the toe of his boot. "It doesn't appear that you're going anywhere, which is good for me. I don't think I can trust you anymore, my darling bride. In a few days, I'll spread word that you left because you couldn't face living in a place where your reputation was ruined. Then I'll let the boys do as they will." He smiled faintly. "Don't worry. They like to make death quick. It's a point of honor with them."

"Honor? Men who shoot women and children in the back?"

"I'm not going to discuss philosophy with you. Try not to draw attention to yourself, Haley dear. The boys have been very busy these past few months. I don't imagine they've had much time to get into town and men have needs. Or are you still a silly virgin?"

She raised her chin and stared at him.

He laughed. "It doesn't matter. You'll be dead shortly. Goodbye."

And then he was gone.

Haley shifted until she was pressed more firmly into a corner of the kitchen. She shivered in the cold. One of the cousins walked into the room and tossed her a couple of blankets. He left without saying a word.

As she wrapped herself in the thick wool, she realized the man had left the kitchen door open and she could hear much of what they were saying to each other. They were discussing the next raid.

"Lucas said we hit that ranch," one of them said.

"But it don't make sense," another commented. "It's not gonna be where the railroad's going."

"Don't matter," the first one replied. "Lucas said we do it, so we do it. Wait three days, then go to the Baxter ranch. And don't leave anyone alive to talk."

* * *

Two days later Jesse was ready to rip the town apart with his bare hands. He and Bart had been through every square inch of Whitehorn but it hadn't helped. Haley had disappeared and no one knew where to find her.

"No one but Stoner," Jesse muttered to himself.

Bart glanced at him sharply, but didn't say anything.

Jesse knew he sounded like a madman with his ravings about Stoner, but he couldn't bear the thought of Haley in his clutches. The only thing that kept him from giving in to complete despair was that Stoner had been very visible in town these past couple of days, so he wasn't with her. Of course she could be with his cousins, which might be worse. Those amoral creatures were like feral dogs, snarling and willing to turn on anyone.

The knot in his gut had become a permanent companion, as had the fear. He didn't want to admit how worried he was, or how the idea that he was already too late haunted him like a waking nightmare. But it was impossible to hide his feelings from Bart.

"She has to be somewhere," he said.

"She is. We just have to figure out where." His friend's voice was calm, a marked contrast to his own.

Jesse took a step toward his horse tied to the railing in front of the hotel. Then he paused. In the distance, he saw a tall man walking toward Millie's Restaurant. He recognized the long stride, the familiar bearing, the expensive clothes. He and Haley had spent two days in hell because of this man. That was about to change.

He started down the boardwalk. Bart hurried after him. "Dammit, Jesse, what do you think you're doing?"

"I'm going to ask Mr. Stoner a few questions."

"That won't do any good."

"Maybe not, but I'll feel better for the asking." His footsteps rang out loudly on the wooden sidewalk.

When Stoner reached the door of the restaurant, he glanced up and saw Jesse approaching. Instead of going inside, the man paused expectantly. He raised one dark eye-brow.

"Evening, Kincaid," he said when Jesse was in earshot.

Jesse told himself to stay calm. A fight wouldn't accomplish anything. But the well-meant advice didn't sink down to the rage building inside of him. He could feel himself filling with a pressure that was about to explode. He was vaguely aware of Bart standing beside him, and of other people stopping to watch. Someone sharply called his name. He thought it might have been Lindsay but he wasn't paying attention.

"Where is she?" he asked. "Where's Haley?"

Stoner adjusted the cuff of his coat, then flicked off a speck of lint. "I'm sure I don't know. Haley who?"

"Don't give me that. She came to town to see you two days ago and no one has seen her since. Where are you keeping her?"

Dark eyes widened slightly in surprise. "What exactly are you accusing me of, Kincaid? If I remember correctly, you're the one who kidnaps innocent women. Miss Winthrop was here. Briefly. And then she left. She said something about returning to Chicago, but she wasn't specific about where she was going, so I can't pass that information along to you. Although even if I had it, I wouldn't tell you. Obviously the young lady had grown tired of your company. Otherwise why would she have left the ranch?"

Jesse held on to the thin coil of self-control. He knew exactly why Haley had left the ranch. She'd been trying to help, hoping that by getting close to Stoner, she could find the information they needed to prove he was guilty of stealing land and murdering innocents.

Stoner's mouth turned up in a cruel smile. "It seems the lady has taste after all. I'm only sorry I didn't get the chance to discover all her secrets. Assuming you'd left any to be discovered?"

The insult to Haley's honor was more than he could stand. Perhaps fueled by the guilty knowledge that he,

Jesse, hadn't left her any secrets, he launched himself at Stoner.

"You bastard," he growled as he landed several body blows in quick succession. "Where is she? Where are you hiding her?"

Stoner tried to get off a shot of his own, but Jesse was like a madman. Rage gave him speed and drove him in harder. He felt the big man stumble back.

Then hands grabbed at him. He fought them, but there were too many. Voices intruded into the red fog that filled his mind. He twisted against his captors, trying to break free, to escape to continue his attack on Stoner, but they held on firmly. At last Jesse realized Lindsay was talking to him. Several deputies had him restrained. His only consolation was the sight of Stoner wiping blood from the corner of his mouth.

"Kincaid, you can't do this," Lindsay was saying. "We all know you're worried about Miss Winthrop. My men are going to join in the search."

"That's not necessary," Stoner said, his cold gaze freezing to ice.

Lindsay ignored him. "You listening to me, Kincaid? We'll get a lot more done if we work together."

"Since when have you cared about anything but the man who hired you?" Jesse jerked free and glared at Stoner. "We're not finished."

"Oh, but we are," Stoner told him. "You'll regret this, Kincaid. I promise you that."

The knot in Jesse's belly doubled in size. Would Haley be the one paying for his impulsive action? Dear God, anything but that. He couldn't stand to think of her suffering for him. It was too cruel.

He took a step toward Stoner. Bart and Lindsay moved in to stop him.

"This isn't the time," Bart said. "You know that. Later, Jesse."

Lindsay nodded. "Listen to your friend."

They were right. It wasn't even dark yet. There were too many people around. What was the point of trying to do this now? There would be a better time and place. He would find Haley and he would bring Stoner down. Or he would die in the attempt.

He turned away. As he did he realized that for the first time since he'd returned from the cattle drive, he was staring at a sober sheriff. Lindsay still looked as if he was one step from the grave, but he wasn't shaking and he didn't smell like the inside of a whiskey bottle. Maybe they would be able to count on the man after all.

Jesse started down the boardwalk. Bart fell into step beside him. "Now what?" his friend asked.

"I don't know. Just keep walking, I guess."

So they did. They walked to the end of town and started back. By then the sun had nearly set. Jesse saw the land office across the street. He glanced left and right, but no one was around. An idea formed. He tried to dismiss it, then figured what the hell?

He crossed to the front door, bent his arm and used his elbow to break the glass in the door.

"Dammit, Jesse," Bart said, hurrying to his side. "Now what are you doing?"

"What we should have done as soon as we realized there was information in this office." He reached through the window and turned the lock, opening the door. Then he stepped inside.

The room was dark. It took him a couple of minutes to find a lamp and light it. By the soft glow, he saw stacks of letters on Stoner's desk. There were boxes of them around the office as well as a big file full of them against the back wall.

He waved to the drawers. "Why don't you start there?"

"What are we looking for?" Bart asked.

"Anything to do with the land deals. Anything that points to Stoner as the one behind the raids. Maybe that letter Haley read."

They worked for an hour. Jesse found a couple of letters to investors back east. Bart found the one Haley had read, along with some deeds. When they thought they had enough, they walked out into the night.

"Stoner's going to know it was us," Bart said.

"Yeah. He'll come after us. That will give me an excuse to kill him."

"If he's dead, he can't tell us where Haley is."

Jesse nodded slowly. His friend had a point. He had to get Haley back. Had to. There were so many things he had to tell her. That he was sorry about all that had happened to her in her life. That he wanted to hold her and comfort her, that he wanted to be with her. Half-formed words hovered in his mind. He wasn't sure what all he would tell her, except that he understood she had a dream for her life. He was just a man with a burned-out ranch and a few thousand head of cattle. There was nothing romantic about his world, but he'd never cared about anyone the way he cared about her and if she was willing to take him on, he wanted her with him. No matter what.

He closed his eyes. They weren't pretty words, but they came from the heart. She would want to hear about loving and he wasn't sure he was ever going to be able to do that, but caring was something. And he did care. He would promise her that it would be enough. He would spend the rest of his life showing her. But first he had to find her. If she was still alive.

Haley strained to listen to the sound of their voices. She could hear the low rumble, but not individual words. Frustration filled her, frustration fueled by exhaustion and hunger. In the past three days she'd had little more than water from a bucket they filled each morning and a couple of bowls of badly burned stew. Perhaps Stoner's plan was to simply starve her to death.

She rolled onto her knees and crawled toward the closed door that led to the rest of the house. Once there, she

pressed her ear against the wood and tried to listen. Today
was the day. Today Stoner's three cousins would attack the
Baxter ranch and kill everyone there.

A sob rose up in her throat, but she choked it back. She'd
whispered prayers for Jesse's safety until her throat was
raw. She was chained and there was nothing else she could
do. Still, she strained to hear what the cousins were saying.
She caught the odd word about the value of stealing a few
of Baxter's horses. He was supposed to have some of the
best horseflesh in the area. Then the sound of chairs being
pushed back sent her scurrying to her corner. When the
cousins walked into the burned-out kitchen, she was cow-
ering, her dirty blankets pulled up around her, her head
down.

They ignored her. Their inattention was so constant, she
thought they might actually forget she was around until one
of them happened to spot her. Fortunately that didn't happen this morning. They headed for the barn where they
saddled their horses, then rode off to start their deadly day.

When they were gone, Haley rose unshakily to her feet
and stared after them. She couldn't let this happen. Somehow she had to stop them. Bad enough that those three men
would destroy the beautiful house, but they were also planning to kill Bart and Jesse. Thank God Christine was safely
away.

Tears welled up in her eyes. It wasn't fair. Dear God,
there had to be a way. She didn't care if *she* died, but not
Bart and certainly not Jesse. She couldn't stand knowing
she'd had some small part in their murders.

The tears flowed faster, until she couldn't see. She
crouched, rocking back and forth, letting her pain pour forth
in an anguished melody of sobs. She clutched her arms to
her chest to ward off the chill. In a few hours the sun would
warm her, but for now, she was as cold as she'd been in
the night.

In the middle of her pain, she had a thought that a fire
would be nice. She pushed the image away, knowing it

would do no good to dwell on what she couldn't have. Besides, she had to think of a plan. Even if Jesse didn't want her in his life, she still loved him. She would always love him. If Stoner hadn't caught her in his office, he might not have decided to go after Bart and Jesse. This was all her fault, so she had to find a way to make it right.

She rose to her feet and started pacing. The chain didn't allow her to walk very far. On one of her passes, it caught on a pile of logs stacked by the battered old stove. The great hulking piece of iron might have worked at one time, but it was rusted through and had cracked down the middle.

Wood skittered across the floor, nearly making her stumble. She kicked at a log, then stopped and stared at the wood. The idea formed slowly. She could build a fire. Not for warmth, but to make smoke. When Jesse and Bart were watching for the raids, they looked for smoke in the sky, a sign that the ranch being attacked was on fire.

She lunged at the stove, pulling open small storage drawers until she found a tin of matches. She shoved them into her skirt pocket, then gathered all the wood she could reach and piled it in the center of the kitchen, as far from her corner as the chain allowed. There was plenty of garbage and debris around to use for kindling and in a matter of moments, she had the wood blazing.

After that, it was a simple matter to toss the rest of her morning coffee onto the fire, sending up plumes of smoke. There were damp rags, too. She watched the gray-white clouds drift up to the heavens. If anyone was looking in this direction, he would be able to see that something was burning. If Jesse or Bart were searching the area, they would come to try and stop a raid. Then she could tell them about the Baxter ranch being in danger.

The flames reached higher and the heat drove her back. She eyed her pile of wood and knew it wouldn't last long. There were a couple of broken chairs by the door to the dining room. She collected them. She threw cupfuls of water from the bucket and steam rose to the sky.

A faceful of smoke made her cough. She tried to get out of the way, only to realize a breeze had come up, blowing the smoke back toward her. She retreated to her corner and covered her mouth with a corner of one of her blankets. It didn't help much. Her eyes burned, as did her lungs. The air seemed hotter here. She squinted against the smoke and realized the fire had burned through the wooden floor. Some of the planks were smoldering. She stared in horror as fire moved toward the dining room. The house was on fire and she was trapped.

"No!" she cried, dropping the blanket and tugging on her chain. While the stove was rusting, it was still large and heavy. The end of her chain had been secured against one of the monstrosity's legs. She pulled with all her strength, but it didn't budge. More and more smoke filled the sky. She coughed so hard, she began to retch. The heat grew more intense. Sparks flew toward her, landing on her dress, her face and her hands. Haley began to scream.

Chapter Twenty-Three

"I'm going to kill him," Jesse announced, touching the gun he'd strapped to his hip. It had been three days and there was still no trace of Haley anywhere. He hadn't slept, hadn't been able to eat and at this point, he would sell his soul to the devil just to know that she was safe.

"Stoner can't talk if he's dead," Bart told him again.

"Stoner won't talk anyway." Jesse glared at his friend. "Tell me you'd feel any differently if Stoner had Christine instead of Haley."

Bart raised his eyebrows in response. Jesse knew what he was thinking. When had his feelings changed? A couple of weeks ago, he, Jesse, had been intrigued by Haley's spirit and intelligence. He'd admired her beauty and enjoyed her company. A few days ago he'd realized that she was very special to him—someone he could care about. But the past twenty-four hours had changed everything. If she died, he didn't see the point in living. All his dreams for the ranch and the cattle were meaningless without her. He didn't give a damn about justice or revenge. All he wanted was Haley back where she belonged...with him.

Was that love? He sure as hell wasn't fond of the word, but he couldn't think of another way to describe his feelings. He needed her the way he needed air to breathe. If that meant facing down a few demons from his past and risking everything he was and everything he had, so be it. Anything was better than being without her.

"Maybe we could just torture him," Jesse muttered.

"That I'm in favor of," Bart said, then shrugged when Jesse shot him a startled glance. "Why not? The man's a murderer. It's no more than he deserves." He stepped into the stirrup and swung up into the saddle. Jesse followed suit. "We don't have another plan."

Bart was right. They'd run out of options. Jesse grimaced. "We'll take him from the office. I doubt anyone will stop us."

"The cousins might, if they're in town." Bart pulled his hat low over his forehead. "Don't tell Christine about this, though. I don't think she'd approve."

Jesse nodded. He wasn't too proud either, but he didn't have a choice. They couldn't let Haley be killed.

He turned his horse toward town and urged it into a fast trot. Thirty minutes later, they crested a rise. A wisp of a fragrance caught his attention. He turned toward the smell and inhaled. "Is that smoke?" he asked.

Bart reined in his gelding. "Could be. Where's it coming from?"

Jesse stood on his stirrups and looked around. There was a faint dark plume in the distance. He glanced at the sun and quickly calculated the position of the smoke, then frowned. "That doesn't make sense," he muttered. "If I didn't know better, I'd say it was coming from my ranch."

"Can't be. No one's there."

Jesse nodded slowly. "Stoner's men already burned most of the house down. All that's left is the front half. Some of the kitchen and…"

His voice trailed off. The knot in his gut tightened, but this time with a certainty he could neither explain nor deny. "That's where they're hiding," he said.

"What are you talking about?"

"Stoner's cousins. They've been hiding out at my ranch,

the bastards.'' He kicked his horse sharply. The animal bolted into a canter, then a gallop. Bart was close behind.

"Jesse, that's crazy. Why would they hide out there?"

His friend's voice came to him in bursts on the wind. Jesse bent low over the saddle and urged his mount faster. "Because no one would think to look for them there. Not even me. They've been close. It's the perfect location."

"If you're right, why is it on fire?"

"Because Haley is there and she's trying to signal us."

Bart didn't respond. Jesse was glad. He couldn't have explained how or why he was so sure, but he would have bet his life on the fact. He was betting hers. A gnawing sense of worry grew as they approached the smoke rapidly filling the sky. There was too much smoke. He swore under his breath. Had something gone wrong?

They rode across the open grazing land, through the shallow valley and at last burst through the grove of trees by the partially burned house. Flames licked out of the ceiling and the remaining walls were near collapsing. Jesse urged his horse as close as he dared.

"Haley!" he screamed. "Haley, are you in there?"

"I'll go check the barn," Bart said, heading toward that structure.

Jesse rode around to the back of the house, to what had once been the kitchen. The fire had obviously started there. He could see the scorched marks in the floor and the ash trail left by the flames. He was about to turn away when a flutter of movement caught his attention.

He was off the horse in a heartbeat and racing toward her. Charred lace stuck out from beside the stove. Jesse caught his breath and braced himself for the worst. His stomach rose in his throat and his heart froze in his chest.

"Dear God, no. She can't be dead. She can't!"

He ran to her side and fell to his knees. She was turned away from him. Gently, he gathered her in his arms. Her face was covered with ash, but she wasn't burned. She also was unconscious.

"Haley? Can you hear me? Haley, please." His voice was thick with emotion. He coughed as smoke filled his lungs and stung his eyes. He felt as if he weren't really here, as if he were watching this from a long way away. As if it weren't real. It couldn't be real. She couldn't be gone. Not now. Not when he'd just figured out how much he loved and needed her.

He had to get her outside, to fresh air. He started to lift her in his arms, then saw the chain that had kept her trapped in the inferno.

He crushed her to his chest, willing her to live. Her skin was still warm, but he didn't see her chest moving and he didn't have the courage to place his ear to her breastbone and listen for her heartbeat. If she was gone, he didn't want to know.

"Haley, you can't die. You can't. I love you. I need you to be with me. Nothing else matters. Not Stoner or the ranch. Just you. Please. Please God, don't take her from me now."

He heard footsteps. "How is she?" Bart asked.

"I don't know." He showed Bart the chain. "There's an ax in the barn. Get that so we can free her. I've got to get her to Doc Prescott."

"It might already be too late," Bart said softly.

"Just get it!" Jesse yelled.

His eyes burned and his throat tightened. He prayed and rocked her, trying to pass on his strength. He stroked her beautiful hair. "Sweet Haley. Don't leave me. I swear, I'll make all your dreams come true, if you'll just give me the chance. We can have those children you wanted, and roots right here on the ranch. We'll build a new home. It will have two stories and a beautiful staircase. You can plant vegetables, then Christine will help you put them up in the fall. Haley, please."

She lay as still as death. Defeated, Jesse closed his eyes. He'd been too late. He'd found love only to have it ripped

from him. Nothing mattered. He would just stay here with
her in his arms until he could join her in death.

"I've always wanted a piano."

Jesse stiffened. He hadn't recognized the froggy voice
and he was afraid to look. Maybe it was just a dream.

"I want to learn how to play." Something soft and
lovely stroked his cheek. "Jesse, what's wrong? Your face
is all scrunched up."

He opened his eyes. Haley stared up at him and smiled.
"Don't be sad," she told him. "I'm fine. I thought the fire
was going to get me, but at the last minute, the breeze
shifted and it turned away."

She coughed. He helped her into a sitting position until
the spasm passed. "We have to get you to the doctor," he
said.

She shook her head. "I'm fine. You've got to get to the
Baxter ranch." She clutched at him. "Oh, Jesse, I was so
scared. That's where they're going. They're going to burn
the house and kill everyone. I was afraid you and Bart
would be there and it would be my fault that you were
dead."

"Hush." He pulled her close and wrapped his arms
around her. "We're fine."

"You have to hurry."

Bart came around the corner. He carried a heavy ax. "I
think this one should—" He stared at Haley, then broke
into a grin. "Hey, you're all right."

She nodded. "Bart, you have to hurry. They're going to
your ranch."

Jesse held out his hand. "I'm going to get Haley to Prescott. You go on ahead to the ranch. I'll bring Lindsay with
me."

Bart was already running to his horse. "Don't worry
about me," he called over his shoulder. "This time we're
going to surprise them!"

Haley coughed. "You should go with him."

"No. He'll be able to hold them off until I get there. I

want Dr. Prescott to look at you. You might feel fine, but you're pale and weak.''

He had a thousand questions, but knew this wasn't the time. After chopping through the chain, he carried her to his horse, then climbed on behind her. She leaned back against him and he wrapped his arms around her.

''I knew you'd come find me,'' she said. ''That's why I started the fire. I knew you'd figure out what it meant.''

''That was dangerous, Haley. You could have been killed.''

She nodded. ''When the fire came at me, I thought I was going to die. The thing that I hated the most was that I wouldn't get to see you again.''

''Haley.'' He kissed the top of her head. She smelled of smoke. He shuddered when he thought about how close he'd come to losing her. ''Don't do anything like that again.''

''All right,'' she said meekly.

''I mean it. You shouldn't have gone into town on your own. Did you really think you could get proof from Stoner without getting caught?''

''I suppose. I'm not sure I'd thought everything through. I just wanted to help.''

''Next time, talk to me. I was frantic with worry. I thought I'd lost you forever.''

She looked up at him. ''Would that have mattered so very much?''

Her wide green eyes drew him in. He could get lost in their clear depths, but he couldn't think of anywhere else he would rather be. ''Yes, it would matter. I love you, Haley. This is a damn poor time to be making that kind of declaration, but it's true. I don't want to lose you.''

Tears filled her eyes.

''Ah, Haley, don't cry.''

''I'm not,'' she said, then sniffed. ''I love you, too, Jesse. I have for a long time.''

Her words eased the last of the knot in his gut. He

squeezed her tighter. Enough had been said for now. They rode the rest of the way in silence.

Once in town, Jesse left Haley with Prescott, who promised she would be fine. His next stop was the sheriff's office. Jesse stormed inside, stalked to the desk and grabbed Lindsay by his shirtfront.

"I don't give a good goddamn about what Stoner's paying you. He kidnapped Haley and held her at my ranch. His three cousins are at the Baxter ranch right this minute, prepared to burn the place to the ground and kill anyone who gets in their way. I want the law on my side but if necessary I'll do without. What I want to know is are you coming with me or am I doing this alone?"

Lindsay's pale eyes were still bloodshot, but for the second day in a row, the man wasn't drunk. He shook himself free of Jesse's hold and squared his shoulders. "I'll round up my three deputies. We're with you."

Jesse stared in amazement. "You're going against Stoner?"

Lindsay nodded. His too-long blond hair fell onto his forehead and he brushed it away. "I got a telegram this morning. It seems the investigator you hired back east found enough to get the federal marshals interested. One of them is heading out here to arrest Stoner and take him back for trial. They want me to cooperate by keeping track of Stoner's whereabouts."

Jesse let the information sink in, then he grinned. "Then let's go."

On the way to the Baxter ranch, he told Lindsay and the deputies where he'd found Haley that morning. He also informed Lindsay about the papers he'd taken from Stoner's office. The sheriff nodded. "I knew about that."

Jesse was surprised. "Someone see me breaking in?"

"Yeah." Lindsay's gaze was level. "Me."

"Well, I'll be." Jesse didn't know what to make of Lindsay. Maybe the man wasn't a spineless drunk after all.

When they turned onto the narrow trail that led to the ranch, Jesse began to scan the sky. "I don't see smoke. Looks like we're in time."

They broke into the clearing. Henry and Orin stood in front of the house. Each held a lit torch. Lindsay pulled his gun. "Hold it right there, boys. Your raiding days are over."

The brothers glanced at each other, but didn't put down the torches. "You can't tell us what to do," Orin said. "Stoner gives the orders. You forget you work for him?"

Lindsay pulled back the trigger and his deputies moved close to the brothers. "I recently remembered that I'm the sheriff in these parts, so I'm only going to ask you boys one more time. Then I'm going to shoot you. Put down the torches, nice and easy like."

Jesse dismounted. "I'll go find Bart." He headed around the house and called out his friend's name. There wasn't any answer.

A telltale wisp of smoke warned him of the danger. He turned in a circle, looking for the source. Orin and Henry were up front with the sheriff, which still left George loose.

"Where's the fire?" he muttered. He circled to the rear of the house, but couldn't see anything. Behind him, a horse whinnied in panic. "The barn!"

He headed for that building. Smoke drifted out the back. "Lindsay," he yelled. "The barn's on fire. Help me with the horses."

He pulled open the huge double doors and ducked inside. There wasn't much smoke yet, so they had time. The deputies joined him. They opened stalls and dragged out panicked horses. Jesse led two to freedom, then went back for more. As he worked, he kept having the feeling that he was missing something. Then he realized what it was.

He hadn't seen Bart.

His friend should have been here long before Jesse and Lindsay. So where was he?

Jesse searched the empty stalls. The smoke was thicker

now, and he could feel the heat of the flames. In desperation, he ran to the tack room.

Once inside, he glanced around and didn't see anything. He was about to leave, when he heard a faint groan.

"Bart?"

No answer. But he stepped back into the dim room anyway. There were saddles and bridles, brushes and some old barrels stacked in a corner. A shadow beside them stirred slightly.

"Bart!" Jesse coughed as the smoke filled the room. He crouched down and saw his friend was stirring slightly. He'd been hit on the head. A large bruise formed at his left temple, darkening visibly and making his eye swell shut.

"You're going to feel pretty bad come morning," Jesse said as he pulled Bart into a sitting position. With a little more maneuvering, he got his friend over his shoulder and started out.

The fire had spread. Flames licked at the ceiling, fed by the hay stored above. The beams creaked as he hurried beneath them. He couldn't see anything, nor could he breathe. He was moving on instinct, heading for what he hoped was the door.

A wall of flames stopped him. The heat drove him back two steps. His chest was so tight, he thought it might explode. There was fire behind him, moving closer. He had nowhere to go.

"Jesse! Over here!"

Lindsay's voice drew him. He turned toward the sound. There was no way out except through the fire. He sucked in one last deep breath, then jumped.

Flames licked at him. When he was free of the barn, he dropped Bart to the ground and rolled them both in the dirt. There were small burns on his arms and hands, but nothing that wouldn't heal in a few days. He stared up at Lindsay.

"Thanks. I couldn't see the door."

The sheriff nodded. "My pleasure. Check on your friend. My men and I will take the Stoner boys into town and lock them up. The federal marshal might be interested in arresting them, as well."

Bart groaned, then stirred and sat up. "What happened?" He opened his eyes and saw his barn. "Lord have mercy."

"He did," Jesse told him. "There's not much wind and the barn is the only building that's going to burn. It could have been a lot worse."

Bart looked at him and nodded slowly. He touched the darkening bruise on the side of his head and nodded. "Thanks for coming after me, Jesse. One of those bastards jumped me. I never saw him coming."

"I'm glad I went looking for you. I sure wouldn't have wanted to explain to Christine what happened to you."

The deputies came around the side of the house. The three cousins had been handcuffed and then tied together. They stumbled against one another.

"Quit pushin' me," Orin growled. George shoved him hard and all three sprawled onto the ground.

Lindsay grinned. "Guess I shouldn't lock them up in the same cell. Like as not, they'll kill one another. Of course that would save the marshal some trouble."

"Isn't this nice."

The low voice sent a cold chill down Jesse's spine. He spun toward the sound, then rose to his feet. His heart stopped. He felt a single beat, then nothing at all. But he didn't give a damn. Nothing mattered because Lucas Stoner stood in the clearing. Behind him was his horse. In front of him stood Haley. She shook slightly, but otherwise didn't move. Stoner held a gun to her head.

Her once green dress was streaked with dirt and smoke. The cuffs were gray, the collar half-torn off. The fear in her eyes told him she hadn't come easily or quietly and as he stared at the bruise on her face, Jesse vowed Stoner would pay for it with his life.

Stoner ignored everyone but Jesse. "I want those papers," he said. "The ones you stole from me."

Jesse dropped his hand to his gun.

"Don't do it," Stoner warned. "I'll kill her. You know that wouldn't bother me, Kincaid. Give me the papers and I'll give you the girl."

Jesse frowned. What was so important about a few letters and some land deeds? The confusion cleared. The land deeds. He needed them to prove that he owned the land so he could sell it to the railroad. But before Jesse could offer them in exchange for Haley, Lindsay stepped between the two men.

"That's enough, Stoner," he said. "Let her go."

Stoner waved the gun. "Get out of the way, Lindsay. Go get drunk. It's all you're good for anyway."

Lindsay didn't move. "I've had a wire from back east. A federal marshal is coming to arrest you. Seems your friends in Boston didn't tell you everything. For example, they were buying land with stolen money. You should be more careful who you do business with."

Stoner's gaze hardened. "You're lying."

"Nope. Can't say that I'm sorry. Whitehorn will be glad to see the last of you."

Stoner shook with fury. "Get the hell out of my way, you worm. Kincaid, I want those papers."

Jesse pulled his gun free, but he couldn't get off a clean shot. Lindsay and Haley were both in the way.

"Don't do it," Stoner ordered. "I'll kill her, I swear I will."

Lindsay also pulled his gun. "Then you'll have to shoot me first, because I'm not going—"

Stoner fired without warning. Lindsay stopped talking, but stayed on his feet. Then he fell to his knees and onto his chest.

Haley screamed. She twisted, trying to get away. Stoner grabbed for her hair. She ducked to escape him. In that second, Stoner was exposed. Jesse took aim and fired.

Like Lindsay, Stoner was slow to fall. A circle of red appeared on his shirt, the blood spot growing wider and more uneven. His eyes rolled upward and he collapsed onto his back. Haley sank to the ground and began to sob.

"What were you thinking of?" Daisy asked as she finished wrapping Leland's upper arm. "Stoner was armed."

The handsome doctor shrugged. "I couldn't let him just take Haley. I had to try and fight him."

"You got shot for all your pains."

Leland glanced at the bandage. "It's just a flesh wound. In a few days, I'll be fine."

Daisy leaned toward him and brushed his hair off his forehead. When they'd brought Bart and Haley back to town, no one had been able to find Leland. She'd been the one to locate him in the back room of his office. The pool of blood under him had made her sick to her stomach. For a heartbeat, she'd thought he was dead.

"Besides," Leland said, offering her a grin. "With all the attention you're giving me, I'd say it was worth it."

He wrapped his good arm around her waist and pulled her close. She went willingly. With Stoner dead, the nightmare was over.

She placed her hands on his shoulders and dropped her head so she could kiss him. The tender sensation of his mouth against hers made her want to weep with pleasure. At last, she'd found a place to belong.

"You're mine," he said between kisses. "All mine. I'm going to marry you and bed you every night for the rest of our lives."

She pulled back a little and stared at him. "Leland, I have to tell you something."

She watched carefully, looking for a hint of impatience, or some tension that would show he was withdrawing from her. Instead, his face stayed open, his eyes warm and loving. "What is it, Daisy? You can tell me anything."

"I have nightmares sometimes. About Stoner, or Michael's death. I wake up screaming."

"I see." He stroked her cheek. "They'll go away in

time. And until they do, I'll hold you in the dark until you feel safe again.''

She flung herself at him. "I do love you, Leland. I'm not sure what I've done to deserve you, but I love you.''

"I'm the one who's undeserving, Daisy. You are the miracle. Now that you're mine, I'm never going to let you go.''

As he kissed her, he reached for the buttons at her throat. She blushed. "Leland, you were just shot. Are you sure you can..." Her voice trailed off.

He smiled. "While the injury to my arm might influence the way in which we do this, the most important parts of me are completely healthy. And very hungry for you, Daisy. I've been waiting for you for a long time."

She touched his cheek, then his mouth, then she pushed his hand away and unfastened the buttons herself. "Then let's not keep either of us waiting a moment longer."

Haley fidgeted with the hem of the coverlet. She'd been stuck in bed for nearly three days and she was tired of it. At first she'd been eager to sleep and eat, but now she wanted to move around some. But Jesse wouldn't let her. He was a most stubborn nurse. He was also acting like a distant stranger. That troubled her deeply. Had she just imagined his declaration of love? Hadn't he meant it, or had the words been forced from him and now he was wishing he could take them back?

Her bedroom door opened and Jesse walked in. He was carrying a tray with her dinner. She looked at the stew and biscuits without much interest. What did food matter, or her life even, if she'd lost Jesse?

"How are you feeling?" he asked.

"Better. I'd like to get up."

"In the morning," he promised. He set the tray on the small table next to her. "I made the biscuits. They're edible, but just barely."

She forced herself to smile at his humor, even though

her heart was breaking. But she couldn't bring herself to glance at the tray. She didn't want food, she wanted her Jesse back. She wanted to hear those words again, she wanted to know that he cared about her as much as she cared about him.

He settled next to her on the mattress. "You don't seem very hungry."

"I'm not." She stared at her hands, lacing her fingers together, then pulling them apart. Maybe she should just leave. If Jesse hadn't meant what he said, she didn't want to be around him. It would be easier to forget him if she went somewhere else. Not Chicago. She never wanted to go back there. Maybe Texas. She'd heard lots of things about that part of the country.

"You could at least look at your supper."

"I don't want anything."

"Haley, please look."

She drew in a deep breath and turned her attention to the tray. There was a bowl filled with stew, a cup of coffee and a small covered dish. "What's that?" she asked, pointing.

"Why don't you find out for yourself?"

There was something odd about his voice. She glanced at him, but his dark eyes were unreadable.

She reached to the table and picked up the cover. There, on a bed of snowy white cotton, sat the cameo that had belonged to his mother. The pale pink carving seemed alive in the glow of the lantern light.

"It's to help you find roots," Jesse said, picking it up and fastening it to her dressing gown. "That's what you've always wanted, isn't it? A family to belong to. Mine is gone and it wasn't much to start with, but you're welcome to my memories. And to my mother's cameo." He touched it gently. "In time, you can pass it on to our oldest daughter. Maybe when she gets married. Or you can keep it. It's yours. I mean, I want you to have it." He shifted as if he was nervous, then cleared his throat.

Haley stared at him. "Jesse?"

She didn't dare believe, yet what else could she do? He'd given her the cameo, the one that his father had given his mother. She touched it, feeling the perfect lines of the carving, the warmth of the gold.

"Oh, Jesse, it's so beautiful."

His smile was lopsided. "So are you, Haley." He cupped her cheek. "I meant what I said before. I love you. I thought I couldn't, or that it wouldn't matter, but it does. More than anything. I don't want to be alone anymore. I want to be with you. Please say you'll stay here in Whitehorn with me."

She reached for his hands. "Of course I'll stay. I love you, too. I have for a long time. I was afraid you wouldn't believe me, that you would think I just wanted to get married to anyone who would have me."

"I would never think that of you." He sucked in a breath. "So you'll marry me?"

She laughed. "I'm certainly not going to agree to be your mistress, Mr. Kincaid."

Jesse Kincaid actually blushed. His cheek darkened with color. "I would never suggest that."

"I know. I was teasing."

He briefly pressed his mouth to hers. "Bart has gone to get Christine. They should be back in two days. I thought it would be nice if they stood up with us in church."

His tongue was performing its usual magic, which made it hard to think...let alone talk. "I'd like that."

"Good." He slipped his hands free of hers and drew her close. "I should probably leave you to get your rest."

She touched his face, then rested her fingertips on his shoulders. "I'm feeling very rested right now. I don't think I could sleep for days."

"Really?"

Her eyes fluttered closed as he kissed her again. It was a while before he spoke again.

"But I shouldn't stay tonight," he said, even as he reached for the bow at the neck of her robe.

"Why not? The bed's big enough." Haley shifted to make room. "And we are going to be married in a couple of days."

He stretched out next to her and gazed into her eyes. "Thank you, Haley. For coming into my life and allowing me to believe in love."

"I'm going to be with you always," she promised.

"I know." He traced her mouth. "I'm going to make all your dreams come true."

She snuggled close, enjoying the scent of him, his warmth, the sound of his heart beating in his chest. "I know."

"For always," he said, then pressed his lips to hers.

"For always," she repeated, her words getting lost in the passion. Then speaking didn't seem so very important anymore as they showed each other exactly how much they loved each other.

Between them, they had created a miracle…the kind of love destined to last a lifetime. And a legacy of love that would be passed down for generations.

Epilogue

Five years later

Haley stirred on the bed. Christina looked up from her sewing project and smiled. "How are you feeling?"

"Tired, but happy. This is baby number three for me, so I'm getting used to giving birth by now."

Christine touched her own swollen belly. "I know what you mean. In another month, I'll have this one, and then between us we'll have six children."

Haley glanced around the beautiful, large, bright bedroom. It was here, each night, she and Jesse lay together under the quilt she'd made that first winter. They each talked about their days, they held each other close and whispered words of love, then, more often than not, they used their bodies to reaffirm their feelings.

Three babies in five years. There were some who would say that was too many, but she'd never been happier. Pregnancy and birth were easy for her. Sometimes she felt as if she were the most blessed woman alive.

There was a faint knock at the door. "Come in," Christine called.

Jesse stuck his head around the door and grinned. "Oh,

good, you're awake. There's someone who wants to see you."

Haley barely had time to sit up before four-year-old Matthew barreled into the room. "Mama, you had another boy," he crowed with pleasure as he moved close for a hug. Jesse followed, looking equally pleased.

"Yes, I did," she said, hoping the next time she would have a little girl. Christine had one of each. Jesse had promised they would keep trying until she had a daughter, but Haley knew they would keep trying no matter what. They loved their children.

Her husband moved to her side, picked up Matthew, then settled on the bed. Christine rose. "I'll go start supper," she said and then left them alone.

"Where's Christopher?" Haley asked, then glanced at the clock on the dresser by the door. "Sleeping?"

Jesse nodded. Their two-year-old still needed naps in the afternoon. "I'll bring him in as soon as he's up."

He kept one arm around his oldest and leaned close enough to stroke her face. "The baby is perfect. Thank you."

She cupped her hand over his. "Thank *you*. I couldn't do this by myself."

"Three sons," Jesse said. "More than enough to work the ranch. People in town say between us and the Baxters, we're creating a dynasty."

Haley laughed. "And that's before they found out about the rest of your family."

Jesse nodded. "I had no idea. Cousins. Aunts, uncles."

"If I didn't adore them all, I would be jealous," she teased. Not that she really could be jealous of Jesse or the place he'd found with his new family.

Two uncles he'd never met had moved to Whitehorn a couple of years ago. Where Jesse had once been alone in the world except for her and their children, now he had cousins only a few years older, their spouses and their children, all sharing his name.

Both Haley and Jesse had helped them find land. The

community of Whitehorn had raised both houses and barns. Jesse had provided ranching expertise. The "new" Kincaid had offered hearty stock in exchange, allowing all the Kincaid herds to improve.

Haley thought about the loud family dinners every other Sunday, weather permitting, and how looking down the long table at all the family members let her know that she at last belonged. Those lonely Chicago days were behind her. And when she dreamed about that time in her life, she awoke with a spirit of gladness, knowing she would never be alone again.

"Speaking of my relatives," Jesse said. "I'm taking young Caleb with me on my next buying trip."

"I'm glad." The boy was only ten, but he showed all the signs of being a fine rancher. "You could use the company."

Matthew squirmed to be released. Jesse set him on the ground, then lightly brushed her cheek with a kiss. "I'd rather have you with me," he murmured into her ear.

Warmth filled her heart. She thought about the happiness she and Jesse shared. She and her husband worked hard, as did all the ranching families they knew. Life in Montana wasn't easy, but she'd never minded. There were so many rewards. Not just the success of the ranch, but watching their children grow. Seeing the ever-expanding Kincaid family put down roots in a land as big as the Montana sky. They had a future here.

She settled into Jesse's embrace. "The people in town are right. We *are* creating a dynasty."

And that was just as it should be.

IS PROUD TO PRESENT
bestselling authors

Susan Mallery
&
Maureen Child

in

SHOTGUN GROOMS

Two brand-new Western historical stories that
feature the MacIntyre brothers, who are forced
into marriage, only to discover everlasting
love with two sassy and sensual women!

SHOTGUN GROOMS

AVAILABLE IN STORES SEPTEMBER 2001!

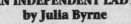

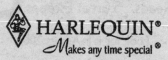

In August look for

AN IDEAL MARRIAGE?

by *New York Times* **bestselling author**

DEBBIE MACOMBER

A special 3-in-1 collector's edition containing
three full-length novels from America's favorite
storyteller, Debbie Macomber—each ending
with a delightful walk down the aisle.

Father's Day
First Comes Marriage
Here Comes Trouble

Evoking all the emotion and warmth
that you've come to expect from
Debbie, AN IDEAL MARRIAGE?
will definitely satisfy!

Double your pleasure—
with this collection containing two full-length

Harlequin Romance®

novels

New York Times bestselling author

DEBBIE MACOMBER

delivers

RAINY DAY KISSES

While Susannah Simmons struggles up the corporate
ladder, her neighbor Nate Townsend stays home baking
cookies and flying kites. She resents the way he questions
her values—and the way he messes up her five-year plan
when she falls in love with him!

PLUS

THE BRIDE PRICE

a brand-new novel by reader favorite

DAY LECLAIRE

On sale July 2001

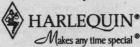

HARLEQUIN®

Makes any time special ®

Visit us at www.eHarlequin.com

PHROM

MONTANA MAVERICKS

THE GUNSLINGER'S BRIDE

by *USA Today* bestselling author

CHERYL ST.JOHN

Discover the origins of Montana's
most popular family in the
MONTANA MAVERICKS
HISTORICAL SERIES

Outlaw Brock Kincaid returns home to make peace
with his brothers and finds love in the arms of an
old flame with a secret.

MONTANA MAVERICKS

RETURN TO WHITEHORN—
WHERE LEGENDS ARE BEGUN AND LOVE LASTS
FOREVER BENEATH THE BIG SKY...

HARLEQUIN®
Makes any time special ®